Charles Evans was born in St Asaph, North Wales in 1959 before moving to Stockport in Cheshire at the age of seven where he lived until joining the Royal Navy in 1976. During the next 10½ years he served on several warships and shore establishments before finally ending his military service in 1986 as a Petty Officer Caterer. He saw active service during the Falklands War in 1982 on the Type 22 Frigate HMS Brilliant where his primary role during action stations was as a Medic covering the bridge, upper deck and operations room and was ashore during the latter stages of the operation to take back South Georgia supporting ground forces. He is a holder of the South Atlantic Medal with Rosette.

After working in operations and supply chain management within the pharmaceutical industry for many years he took a short career break and travelled extensively to locations within the UK, the Falkland Islands and to other locations across the world to research the key elements of the story. *Falklands Revenge* is his debut novel.

He now lives in Gloucestershire with his wife Jackie and is a member of the Royal British Legion, South Atlantic Medal Association and is an active supporter of military charities to which donations will be made by the author from the proceeds of this book.

For:

Jackie, whose support, encouragement and love is unwavering

And:

For all who serve and have served their country

Charles Evans

FALKLANDS REVENGE

AUSTIN MACAULEY
PUBLISHERS LTD.

A CIP catalogue record for this title is available from the British Library.

ISBN 978 1 78455 389 0

www.austinmacauley.com

First Published (2014)
Austin Macauley Publishers Ltd.
25 Canada Square
Canary Wharf
London
E14 5LB

Printed and bound in Great Britain

Harry Glass, serving Royal Marine Sergeant in the SBS, had fought for the lives of his comrades, and for his own life during the Falklands War.

Now fit again after recovering from his wounds, it was time for revenge. More Argentines had to die for what they did.

Falklands Revenge – Glossary

Bergen – Small Army rucksack
Bino's – Binoculars
Bootneck – Royal Marine Commando
Casevaced – Extraction of the wounded
CIA – Central Intelligence Agency – USA
CO – Commanding Officer
Day sack – Small rucksack
DPM Jacket – Disruptive Pattern Material Jacket
DMS Boots – Directly Moulded Sole Boots
ERV – Emergency rendezvous point
ETA – Estimated Time of Arrival
Facón Argentine – dagger
FBI – Federal Bureau of Investigation – USA
Gaucho – Resident of the South American Pampas
Gemini – Small inflatable boat
GPMG/Gimpy – General Purpose Machine Gun
HF – High Frequency
Intel – Intelligence
Ju Ju Bag – Slang for a type of jock-strap
Jungleys – Army Sea King Helicopter
LUP – Lay-up point
Main Drag – Central corridor on a warship
Mess/Mess deck – Rest area on board warships for ratings
Malvinas – Argentine name for the Falkland Islands
Matelots – Royal Navy – Junior ratings
Minging – Smelly/dishevelled
MP – Military Police
NBCD – Nuclear, Biological & Chemical Defense
NCO – Non-Commissioned Officer
Numpty – Idiot
NVG's – Night vision goggles
OP – Observation post
Para – Member of the Parachute Regiment
PO – Petty Officer – Royal Navy
POW – Prisoner of war
QARNNS – Queen Alexandra's Royal Naval Nursing Service
QT – On the quiet
Raider/RIB – Rigid inflatable boat
Recon/Recce – Reconnaissance
Red and Green Life Machine – Field hospital in Ajax Bay – Falkland Islands
RNH – Royal Naval Hospital
Rounds – Bullets

RTA – Road Traffic Accident
Ruperts – Military slang for commissioned officers
RV – Rendezvous point
SAS – Special Air Service
SBS – Special Boat Squadron
Scran – Food
SEALs – Sea, Air and Land Teams – US Navy
Shell dressing – Padded first aid dressing
SLR – Self Loading Rifle
SOP – Standard Operating Procedure
State 1 Condition Zulu – Warship at Action Stations – All hatches closed
Stoker – Marine Engineer – Royal Navy
Tabbed – Walked
Villas – Argentina slums
Wardroom – Commissioned Officers' rest area
XO – Executive Officer on warships – Royal Navy
Yomping – Royal Marine slang for long hikes across open ground.

Part One

The Conflict

1

Somewhere on the Falkland Islands

June 1982

I can hear something. I hear a loud clattering noise. I hear people talking. Where the fuck am I?

I am lying on something cold, hard – and it is wet. Wet with what, I do not know right now. There are dull lights overhead penetrating my eyelids and there is the deep humming sound of a generator that is running flat out somewhere close by.

Are those people shadows near me? Can I smell sheep shit? Fuck – why can't I open my eyes?

Someone has just said my name. I am sure of it. Am I sure of it? I don't know.

Someone just said my name again. Someone close by.

'Ken, Sergeant Glass is next, he is over there on the steel table. His first name is Harry and he is in pretty bad shape so let's get him ready for theatre at the rush.' That conversation was about me – it was definitely about me.

Am I dreaming? Am I dead? If only I could open my eyes. I smell blood, fresh blood on me. There is lots of fresh blood on me and I can feel it leaking from my body. I know I can. Maybe I can? The searing pain in my head is back with a vengeance and there is something in my arm; I can feel it, I know I can feel it.

Maybe I am not dead yet.

I try to move my head but can only manage an inch or so and only as far as the crusty bloodied and soiled collar of my shirt. I still can't open my eyes. Then the pain in my head has gone and it's getting quieter. I must be dying now. A cool breeze crawls over my body and rolls up over my head like a sea fog. I am then engulfed in darkness and then nothing, just silence.

Now I know I am going to die.

In the darkness and the quiet, my brain is still working though. It's working overtime, telling me things, showing me things. I feel my battered and broken body twitching on the cold hard surface of the table. I think it's twitching, although I can't be sure. I'm trying to stop more bullets hitting me, trying to stop the pain, trying to help my mates, trying to get the fuck out of there, but I can't move a muscle and I still can't open my eyes.

I feel the first bullet tearing a hole through my body, left side, the force of the impact dumping me onto the sodden ground in a big shitty heap, the searing pain ripping down my left leg making me curse my fucking head off.

I can't feel anything now.

I can see Tom, I can hear him shouting at us to move our fucking arses and get to cover as the ground around us begins to boil and burst as incoming rounds spit up and shower us with great clumps of sodden earth and rock fragments.

John is hit, his left arm cleanly taken off at the elbow by a high calibre round, a split second later he gets another through his guts. He's totally fucked, but not dead. Yet.

I'm up on my feet again. I'm hit again. Hit in the right leg now. Fuck that hurts. I'm down again in another shitty heap.

I haul myself up and get to John. We stumble and drag each other a short distance to a small 10ft x 10ft hollow in the ground surrounded by sparse rocks and tussock grass. It's no more than 4 or 5 feet at its deepest but our heads are below ground level and it's the best and only cover we have for now.

I frantically try to get a tourniquet around John's stump to stem the flow of blood before I can start to plug the holes in me. I'm not even close to getting the tourniquet on John's arm properly or the other dressing in place when I feel something sharp pierce my right cheek. I don't even have time to check it out before I feel the hot spray of blood on my face followed immediately by a splattering of bits of brain, bone and flesh. I was pretty sure that's what it was.

The top of Jimmy's head, what was left of it, was just a big ugly exit hole where the high calibre bullet had passed through it from back to front. He had stayed above ground for a while longer laying down covering fire for us as we all had scrambled into the hollow. He was dead before his body hit the ground beside me.

I try to lift my hands to touch my face, to wipe the bits away, but I can't. Did this really happen? Am I dreaming this? I just don't know.

I feel my body twitching again, or I think I do, as my brain continues to play me this horror movie, sometimes it's even in slow motion. I want to open my eyes, scream, do something, but I can't.

I look into Jimmy's lifeless eyes and I know there is nothing more anyone can do for him. I turn and take a few seconds through all the noise and the flying shit to check if there are any signs of life in John. His eyes are firmly closed. My instincts tell me it's probably forever.

Larger clumps of dirt and rock are showering down on us now as the impact of the incoming rounds are intensified the closer the Argies get to us. The noise of the gunfire seemed to be in the hundreds of decibels now.

Bob was kneeling on my right at the edge of the hollow when he took a hit in his right shoulder. I wasn't fast enough to catch him or break his fall and as he hit the deck heavily he cried out in pain. Bob managed through sheer anger, adrenaline and whatever else to get himself up into a sitting position within moments, but as I reached him he took another round close to the entry point of the first, but lower in his chest this time and absolutely more deadly. He landed flat on his back in the dirt on the other side of John. I could see he was still alive, but he was in big trouble and he wouldn't be contributing much else to this little jolly, I was sure of that.

I kill the Argie solider that appeared at the edge of the hollow a moment later with a double tap.

The noise of gunfire increased a few more decibels, if that was possible, coupled with the dull sound of rounds thumping into the ground above us and only inches from our heads. I knew if they burst through the sodden peaty ground and into the hollow they would still kill us.

I'm shouting at Tom and tugging on his combat trousers with my bloody hands. 'Tom, we are fucked. John and Bob are down and Jimmy's dead.'

Tom continued to scream obscenities into the gloom of the night, his weapon spitting out bullets and tracer rounds as many per second as it could manage. His face contorted with anger and rage as he took the fight singlehandedly to the enemy. Then he was out, the weapon stopped firing, magazine empty. Argentine tracer lines pierced the air above us providing sparks of light so we could see each other clearer in the gloom. We slid a little further down into the hollow and waited for the gunfire to cease. We didn't need to say anything to each other as we both knew we would all be dead very soon if we didn't stop the shooting and do the right thing for our fallen comrades, whether they were alive or dead.

It took nearly a minute for the firing to stop and then an eerie silence descended over the sparse semi-moonlit moorland that has been our temporary home for the last few days and nights. Tom grabbed hold of my jacket and dragged me to my feet with one hand whilst raising the other in surrender. As I got to my feet I slowly began to raise my right hand to match Tom's left but before it was fully up in the air I'm tumbling backwards again.

The bullet creased the left side of my head taking a lump of hair and skin from my scalp with it. I'm sure it's taken a little bit of skull bone with it, as well. Tom is falling with me. I didn't feel it, but I heard the loud crack of bone hitting rock as my head impacted with the ground. Then nothing. I don't know for how long.

My eyes open again and I can see Tom back on his feet screaming into the blackness of the night.

'We fucking surrender you bastards, stop firing, I have wounded men here. We fucking surrender.'

Moments later I see the fuzzy outline of soldiers, I count 10 or more. They appeared directly above us. All with their weapons trained on Tom as he's the only one still standing, and making a noise. None of the soldiers speak, they just stand in silence looking down at the bloody scene below them. Tom is screaming at them to get a medic into the hollow to help us. Nobody moves. It's another minute before I see them slowly part down the middle and back away from the edge of the hollow.

The atmosphere changed instantly from something shit scary to something even more sinister as two faces I instantly recognise appear above me. It was them, the two nasty fuckers we had seen at Rincon Grande kicking the shit out of their own men. One was the short heavily built 'Bully Boy' officer, the other a big Sergeant with a very visible scar that ran backwards a couple of inches towards his neck from just below the right corner of his mouth. The other deep and ugly scar above his right eye finished the mean-looking bastard off.

Tom took a step forward obviously to say something to the officer. Next thing I see is Tom taking two heavy kicks, one in the ribs and then one to the face that knock him back down into the hollow. I black out again for a second or two, but then angry noises penetrate my brain and I force my eyes open again to see Tom out of the hollow with his hands around the throat of the officer who had kicked him.

The big NCO was having none of it though and leaped in to defend the officer. The force of his first punch to his guts knocked the wind out of Tom and the second one to his jaw catapulted him backwards into the hollow where he landed on Jimmy's lifeless body. The language above us now is Argentinean and it is loud and the people are very animated. I narrow my eyes in the gloomy light to better focus on the scene directly above me.

Tom had got himself up on one knee and was looking up at a young Argentine lieutenant who had also appeared above us. We had seen him at Rincon Grande with the other two. He was getting a tyrannical bollocking from the senior officer who was screaming at him just two inches from his face. As the young officer raised his hand to wipe away something from his right cheek he suddenly took a vicious blow from the butt of the officer's browning pistol. He went down briefly but as he tried to get up he got another one across the face dumping him back down onto the sodden ground.

The big NCO also now got in on the act and viciously kicked the young lieutenant twice whilst he was on the deck. The final kick to his head almost brought him tumbling into the hollow and on top of Tom. I'm drifting in and out of consciousness, but I see the young officer's limp body being hauled up and dropped onto a soldier's shoulder before disappearing from sight. The officer, big NCO and three others are the only ones left at the edge of the hollow now and are all focusing on Tom who is standing fully upright again.

The sound of the first shot snaps me back into the land of the living just in time to see the exit hole in the back of Tom's combat jacket from a second. It was much louder than the first and most likely from a rifle rather than a pistol.

Tom is now falling towards me, his body spinning from the force of the bullets before crashing down on top of me, knocking out any remaining wind left in me. The impact from Tom's lifeless head busted my nose good and proper, fresh blood was smeared across my face before his right shoulder finally came to rest on my forehead.

I'm going to kill you, you mother fuckers, I try to scream at them but no words or noise come from my mouth. I am pinned down, can't see and right now, most importantly, I can't breathe. I am fucked.

Tom's body jerks violently on top on me as the third bullet penetrated his back. I heard, and felt, the bullet break his spine. Tom's body slid a little further forward and off most of my face allowing me to suck in a huge breath and open my left eye as much as I can.

I hear more shots fired and see muzzle flashes, at least seven or eight of them. Moments later I smell the cordite and although I cannot see who or what the rounds were targeting, I can guess. They were making sure we are all dead.

The officer comes into view, his handgun aimed directly at what I thought was my head, but then Tom's body jerks violently on top of me again as the pistol round enters his back. I see him, I see the officer, arm straight out with his handgun aimed directly at Tom. Then he did something I didn't anticipate. He smiled a huge smile, blew the smoke away from the end of the gun and then re-holstered it.

Not even the pain or the rage inside me can save me from the darkness now as I feel myself slipping away again. Maybe for good this time.

The last thing I know I can hear, getting fainter and fainter, is laughing.

2

Off the Falkland Islands – 2 weeks earlier

27 May 1982

SAS Sergeant Tom Dye finished the mission briefing at 0050 and then turned to Bob.

'Bob get off and sort out the boat. It needs to be in the water in 10.'

'OK.' Bob responded and picked up his kit and was out of the room in less than 30 seconds.

When he had gone, I concentrated on finishing off another check of my own gear before walking over to Jimmy where I started to pull and tug at the various straps and belts on his kit.

'Fuck all needs to fall off or make noise.' Tom was talking to John as he pulled the strap on his map pocket down tight.

'You're good John.' He said. 'Thanks' was the short reply from John.

'Come on Harry, let's go.' Tom said as he tapped me on the shoulder on his way to the dining hall door. I fell in behind him as we made our way down the main drag of the ship, up the stairs, through the open hatch and then out onto the upper deck. Bob was already on the water in one of our rigid raiders and had skilfully put it right next to the steps that had been lowered down the side of this new type 22 Frigate, HMS Brilliant. It was exactly 0110.

It was a quiet, still night, for a change and the seas were calm for the South Atlantic at this time of year. Thankfully the raider was only rising and falling a couple of feet on each swell tonight. The fine rain was still there though, but we would all be getting wet sometime tonight so there was no point in whingeing about it. I stepped in first, ditching my kit in front of the console where Bob was tickling the throttle controls to keep us in close to the steps. Tom and Jimmy stepped onboard without incident, but as John stepped in the raider it rose in the swell and his left boot just clipped something on the side. He fell forward banging his knee on the centre console. crashing onto the kit lying in front of it.

'Bollocks,' he cursed. 'Can't you lot stow your bloody kit any better and can't you keep this bloody boat stable for a minute while we get on?' John was rubbing his knee vigorously and looking straight at Bob before carrying on his tirade. 'It might stop us poor squaddies getting fucked up before we have to go and kill people.' The reaction was collective and swift from Jimmy standing in the front of the raider and Tom. 'You big fucking pussy.'

'I'll have a special word in Major Colwill's ear when we get back and ask him to sort out these Royal Marines for you.' Tom, like the rest of us, was grinning like a Cheshire cat as he spoke.

John looked up from his lying position in the bottom of the raider and saw us all grinning. He then saw the funny side himself and smiled, but was still muttering under his breath as we got ready to move away. It was good for all of us to crack a smile, it definitely helped to release some of the tensions.

Bob gunned the powerful 140hp outboard motor to get us away from the side of the ship and then towards our destination, the Teal Inlet Settlement on the East Falklands shoreline. As we got closer to land, everyone has eyes on the shoreline and the surrounding hills. We were searching for lights, or any people movements, which in this drizzle would be much more difficult to see than the lights.

Bob was looking ahead to pick up Sea Lion point on the starboard side. This was our first marker where we would turn to port and then run straight in past Braze del Mar and 'Big Shag'. After clearing 'Big Shag' we needed to turn hard to starboard on a bearing of 205° making sure Centre Island stayed on our port side. We would have to stay close to the shoreline at this point then take a new bearing of 220° and head straight down the inlet. The Rincon Grande settlement would be on our port side for only a minute or two then it was straight across Port Salvador Water to the Teal Inlet settlement a couple of miles away. We all knew the route just in case Bob didn't make it back, god forbid. Jeannie and the kids would kill me.

I had taken my place at the front of the raider leaning on the starboard side. Tom was on the port side opposite me. Behind Tom, John was cradling his favoured 7.62mm GPMG, 'gimpy', machine gun to his huge chest. The spare one we had brought with us was wrapped up by his feet next to the rest of the kit he had fallen onto earlier. John was looking relaxed, but his eyes were alight and scanning the shoreline that was fast becoming clearer with each bounce of the raider on the freezing South Atlantic sea. Behind me, Jimmy had been very quiet on the journey so far, but I knew he was fully focused and concentrating on the mission ahead and what we were about to do. My own focus was firmly on getting the job done and then, most importantly, getting back off the Island alive.

The plan was for Bob to get us in there quickly, but also quietly. He was then going to secure and camouflage the raider once we found the best spot to hide it. We brought everything we needed to camouflage it and using a combination of our own netting plus seaweed and any other bits of beach debris, he would get this done quickly and with no fuss. Bob was then going to track us from a distance and be our eyes and ears behind for a while. He had brought along his trusty sniper rifle so he could deal with individual targets confidently and completely if we were compromised.

It had been a bit unusual to take five on a job like this, but because the ships had to get in and then back out to sea quickly for their other jobs in the task force, there wouldn't be enough time to get the raider back to Brilliant without leaving it exposed. Tom had also agreed with Major Colwill that giving Bob some 'on the ground' experience would not be a bad thing and his shooting abilities would definitely come in handy if we got into a fire fight.

The wind and rain were blowing up a bit now as we progressed steadily across Salvador Water. Rain started to run down all our faces, but not hard enough to impair the vision we needed right then. Even with my hood up the water still managed to trickle down my neck sending a cool shiver down my back, but maybe it was also because we were very exposed in this stretch of water and not travelling very fast to keep the noise down. I could see Teal Inlet ahead of us now. There were some outside lights burning that helped us all to see the open rolling hillside that led up to the red, green and blue corrugated topped buildings sparsely scattered over half a square mile or so. The brightest light on top of the largest building would lead us straight in. We knew there was a lot of open ground here from the mission briefings and photographs we had seen, that was except for a few trees acting as windbreaks in front of the buildings closest to the water.

The bow of the raider bumped almost silently onto the narrow shingle beach. We landed exactly where we should have in a sheltered alcove just under a mile north of the main settlement. John and Bob dragged the raider inshore a couple of yards whilst I took up point. Bob quickly got the kit out that he needed to camouflage it, whilst the rest of us headed off in a south easterly direction towards the planned observation points.

The steep incline that led up from the beach was easy compared to some of the training stuff we had all done at Lympstone, Hereford and the tough Arctic training in Norway. Once in the open field we were moving quickly, at a crouch, through the thick tussock grass that covers large swathes of the islands and does everything to sap every bit of strength out of you. At the same time, all of us trying our best to dodge the peat bogs and the rats we knew were here somewhere. The bogs were something to avoid at all costs, but the last thing any of us needed was to land on a big hairy nasty rat if we had to go to ground.

Tom had the lead now, the rest of us spread out to the right and left of him. We tracked in about three-quarters of a mile with no dramas. I thought I caught a fleeting glimpse of Bob about 500 yards behind us, but I couldn't be sure. He was very good at this shit, I knew it. He would make the call when best to approach using the signal we had agreed in Brilliant's dining hall earlier.

All seemed to be going OK and I was happy. Bob was still covering our arses for a minute but would be joining up with us soon. There were no signs of any men or military equipment on this side of the settlement yet and it was very quiet except for the sound of our boots squelching on the soft ground and the wind and drizzle that was continuing to swirl around us. The drizzle had increased a bit but was still not causing us any issues right now and thankfully was still lighter than when we were out on open water.

I laid up a couple of hundred yards from the main building, Tom and John on my right, Jimmy on my left. Tom indicated that we needed to move up now and get behind a thick hedgerow another hundred yards in front of us.

That was when I saw them.

A couple of Puma helicopters tucked up away from the main force of the wind behind the large sheep shearing shed we had seen on the recon photos. A green military refuelling truck was 50 feet away behind a smaller corrugated shed. Everything was tied down and very quiet. It was a cold and miserable night so no one at the settlement seemed to be outside, not a bad thing for us, and the lights we had seen from the water were definitely in our favour. They were pointing away from us towards the opposite side of the settlement keeping the side of the building we were close to in almost total darkness. Good cover if we need it, I thought.

'Harry, Jimmy, you take the shed on the left. John, you and me that one,' Tom whispered and used his hand to indicate the buildings he meant. Tom then used his hand again to signal Bob to stay put and cover our arses. He got the message 100 yards back down the field where he was tucked in behind a large manure heap next to the boundary fence.

It was only 50 yards to the two animal sheds sitting at the high point above the settlement, but they were across more open ground so we would have to be quick. Jimmy was off first moving fast at the crouch, I'm behind him. Tom was already moving and in front of John heading away from us up the hill.

The quiet of the night was gone in a heartbeat as all hell broke loose after the first five seconds on the move. Rapid gunfire and red tracer lines were coming straight at us from the two buildings we were heading for. I was flat on the deck in a millisecond. Tracer lines flashed by directly over our heads and then rounds began hitting the ground all around us spitting up lumps of sodden peat and grass into our faces. We needed to get the hell out of here and pretty sharpish.

I look up to see if I could see Tom. No chance, too many rounds were coming at us. I stuck my head back down into the sodden ground for a second to think. Manky smelly fluid seeped into my mouth. It tasted like shit. I had to move now or die. I knew grenades would be useless, the distance to the Argies' position was too great.

Where in the hell had they come from? Why hadn't we seen them? How had they seen us? All questions in my head for later.

I got eyes on Tom who signalled me and Jimmy to take specific targets. We didn't need telling twice. We let rip at the same time as Tom and John, hundreds of 7.62mm rounds ripping through metal corrugated sheets and splintering the wooden frames within the buildings. I thought I heard a couple of screams, but couldn't be sure because of the ear shattering noise from my SLR, M16's and the GPMG that John had set up on the ground 10 yards on my right.

After our barrage of fire on the building, the bullets that had been raining down on us stopped. They must have taken a few hits, maybe we had wounded or killed their commander. This was our moment to get the fuck out of here and away from our current position. Jimmy was the first to start moving back the way we came, on our bellies at first then up, running in a crouched position. No additional lights had come on so it was still pitch dark when sporadic enemy fire started up again, but still aimed at the original contact position. They couldn't have night sights and that's a bit of luck, I thought briefly.

I was wrong though, as the next second, the ground in front of me started to explode from multiple rounds penetrating it. I was now running as fast as I could behind Jimmy, darting left and then right, so whoever was firing at us couldn't zero in on me. We all covered the next 700 yards of open ground running at full pelt directly towards the landing point.

I was surprised how fast such a big man as John could move, he was keeping pace with young Jimmy who was doing a good impression of Alan Wells, the current 100 metres Olympic champion, to get further out of the range of fire.

A minute later, I slid in beside Bob at the edge of the ridge that led down to the alcove, and the camouflaged raider. His eyes straining and searching the ground we had just come over to see if any of our pursuers were getting close.

We quickly regrouped around Bob and all knew there was some serious firepower not very far away. We could also be very sure they would be on the radio calling for reinforcements now. They would be after us in minutes so Tom had to call it. It was down to the raider or change direction, put some distance between us and then go to ground. I was sure I knew which option he was going to take, we only had one choice really, this was a total screw up and we needed to get the fuck out of here.

At least we did know they had a couple of choppers and some troops on the ground here so we had something to feedback to the Ruperts.

Tom called it, 'Back to the boat now.'

There was no discussion, this situation was not winnable and we all needed to come back and fight another day.

Bob was already legging it to uncover the raider and get it ready for the off as Tom shifted us back into a better position at the top of the incline. It was only a short run back down the hill now and across the shingle beach to Bob.

John set up the GPMG to cover our retreat in what could have been a purpose-built foxhole, but was, in fact, just a man-sized hole on the downside of the ridge. It did have a couple of rocks on the edge of it though giving him good firm ground to rest the gun on. He also had a good clear view across the field that we had just run down.

Once John was ready he gave us the OK signal to move. I had just started down the hill after Tom and Jimmy when a hail of bullets came straight at us from the field. Luckily, my head was just below the ridge so their rounds hit dirt and fresh air. I was halfway across the beach now running towards Bob who was next to the raider and down on one knee. His sniper rifle tight into his shoulder and up in the air ready to return fire the second he saw anyone, other than John, coming over the ridge behind us.

Tom started shouting at Bob as he ran. 'We will cover John; just get the fucking boat ready to go.'

I saw John start to move away from the top of the ridge. He made it to the bottom of the slope and was still running when I saw the first human shapes appear above him. Tom was now kneeling next to me on the beach firing up at anything that was moving behind John while Jimmy helped Bob push the raider back into the water.

Bob leapt onboard, had the outboard down and flashed up in seconds. But the Argentine rounds had already started to rain down on us from the ridge, rough sand spurting up all around us and shingle pinging off in all directions. Bob was keeping the raider's engine idling in forward gear just enough to keep the bow bumping lightly against the shore. I look back briefly to see how far I needed to run and saw Bob now braced behind the steering console, feet firmly planted on the deck, sniper's rifle tight into his shoulder. He was firing individual rounds at specific targets amongst the chasing Argentine troops who were now trying to move down the slope towards us.

Bob downed at least two before John spun around and laid down a fierce volley of fire into the chasing pack with his GPMG. They hit the deck instantly. Everyone was in the raider now except John. Jimmy had the other GPMG going and that coupled with the accuracy of Bob's shots had the Argies' heads well and truly down. John was now able to move his massive frame across the final few yards of the beach and into the raider. Bob didn't need any orders and as soon as John's arse was inboard he gunned the powerful outboard motor in reverse and we were away from the shore and into the middle of the estuary in seconds.

The Argies hadn't been in any great hurry to continue down the slope and onto the beach after the last volley of fire and as we sped away there were only a couple of wild shots fired in our general direction. Bob had us well out of range and out of sight by the time they would have all eventually got down onto the beach.

The RV point with HMS Brilliant was a couple of miles off the coast, but not this early. Bob got through to the ship as soon as we cleared the inlet, telling them we were on our way back and needed a pick up. We didn't need to hang about now or be stealthy and expected to cover the miles back to the RV with Brilliant in just over 30 minutes. Bob only slowed down to quieten the engine noise when we had to hug the shoreline to get past the Rincon Grande settlement where there could be more Argentine troops.

Brilliant's Captain, John Cornwall, had done us proud and turned the frigate around as soon as they had received Bob's message. Tom got back on the radio again as soon as we were out in the open sea.

'She will be at the RV in seven minutes,' he shouted over the sound of the powerful outboard at full throttle.

The sea was a lot rougher now and the bitterly cold spray was driving into our faces pricking us like thousands of little needles. Twice Bob had to throttle back to stop us ploughing into increasingly bigger waves as none of us needed to end up in the drink now. That would just top the night right off I thought to myself.

Back on board and before getting into clean and dry kit, Tom went off to debrief the mission to all and sundry as usual. In the end we thought it must have been bad Intel and just bad luck that we had run into something a bit more than a few helicopter mechanics and a couple of conscripts, with one or more of them, unfortunately for us, being awake.

3

8 weeks earlier
HMS Brilliant at sea steaming away from
Gibraltar

28 March 1982

I knew I was sitting there with a big grin on my face, but I couldn't help it. The Senior Rates mess on board this new Type 22 Frigate was comfortable and spacious, well spacious for a frigate anyway. It was clean, well lit and had 'appropriate' modern multi-coloured prints on the walls that I actually thought some demented kid had knocked up in his dad's garage. Sadly, no tits, bare arses or anything even slightly suggestive were allowed on the walls these days. They were the rules for all senior rates messes in today's modern Royal Navy.

I was not the only one to dislike these prints, because during the first hour in my new mess, three of the younger Petty Officers commented loudly that they thought they were just 'brightly coloured crap.'

'Hey Harry, congrats on the stripe, let me get you a beer.' Taff Jones had always been a friendly guy, always a smile on his face, unlike many PO stokers, who were usually a bunch of miserable bastards.

'Cheers Taff, I'll have a lager.' I said as I glanced down at my right arm again still admiring the three stripes proudly sitting there.

It had been a great moment for me as I had sewn on my new stripes last night after being rated up by Major Paul Colwill, the senior Royal Marines Officer on board. John Cornwall, HMS Brilliant's Captain, was also standing alongside him to play his part in the formal proceedings.

'Sergeant' Harry Glass, Royal Marines, Special Boat Squadron. It had a good ring to it and I didn't mind admitting that I was feeling very pleased with myself, 28 years old and a full Sergeant already. Another major bonus for me was now sharing a cabin with only six men rather than a mess deck with 30 plus in it. I knew the best thing would be not having to listen to the snoring and farting of at least 20 of my former Mess mates, especially my best mate Bob May who was probably the worst of them all. He had almost choked when he had to call me Sarge this morning.

It has been a very good day so far.

It had also been good to have a tube of lager with Bob last night, just him and me on the quarterdeck chewing the fat for a couple of hours. We had come through a lot in the past few years and been in a few scrapes together, mainly in Northern Ireland, but also in a few other obscure places around the world. He was someone I trusted with my life.

We had both been drafted onto HMS Brilliant in January, brought on especially for the Springtrain Naval exercises in the Mediterranean. Our orders had been simple, train up members of the permanent Royal Marine detachment on board, and a couple of selected Royal Navy seamen, to handle the 17ft rigid raiders that we use in the SBS. We would also do some work with the ship's own rigid inflatable boat or RIB as it's known by the matelots. So far, I was pleased that the training had gone well and a couple of the Navy boys in particular had really got to grips with these small fast boats, especially in choppy seas.

The core-training objective had been to teach the guys how to approach ships at sea in both daylight and darkness. We had also done a couple of beach landings, getting the boats in close and dumping the bootnecks out of them. I had to be honest with myself because it had been more of a jolly these past few weeks rather than work and I had my third stripe and more pay now to boot. Life was good. The weather had also been very good so the tan had been building nicely, my girlfriend Kathy would never believe I had been working really hard all this time, as I had told her. The runs ashore had not been bad either. Gibraltar had been the last stop and I had taken third place in the Rock Race.

'Not bad for an old git,' had been Bob's little quip, who had taken second, the spawny git.

Unfortunately, some of the dumb arse matelots from the assembled ships wanted to fight each other again and had then sucked in some of the current pongo battalion based on the Rock. I was glad I had been at the Captain's table for my promotion in the morning, because when he got the news that members of his crew had been arrested by the MP's and were going to be brought back to the ship later that afternoon, he was as pissed off as I've ever seen a skipper.

Later that day when he received the order via a signal from Flag Officer Gibraltar, 'as soon as all members of your crew are back on board, you are to depart Gibraltar,' he had apparently blown a massive fuse. An earlier call from the Admiral said the 2nd Light Infantry Battalion Commanding Officer was a deeply unhappy man.

We sailed at 1700hrs.

That was my night's piss up gone, screwed up by the fighting boys on board. When will they learn, I've thought to myself many times in the past few hours, although I did hear that some of the boys accounted for themselves very well against the Army lads, so it wasn't all bad news.

More of my new Mess mates had been arriving steadily throughout the evening, which I hadn't taken much notice of as I had been mulling over the events of the past few days and chin wagging with Taff some more about the hideous choice of prints on the walls, and Kathy. The tradition of buying new Mess mates a drink on their first night had not been lost on me so I had amassed a good few that were now sitting in front of me waiting to be consumed.

A few hours later, I leave the Senior Rates Mess with a bit of a speed wobble that had nothing at all to do with being back at sea. I think I am going to enjoy being a Sergeant.

4

2 April 1982 – At sea heading South 2000hrs

'Why the fuck would anyone want to invade Scotland? Especially Argentina?' This was the question being asked to anyone who would answer.

'Fucking Outer Hebrides, why would you want to go there, it's windy, pisses down with rain most days and is full of Jock twats and their sheep,' Taff was wittering on in the corner of the mess.

'They have not invaded Scotland you dumb arse, the Falkland Islands are in the South Atlantic about 7000 miles from where we are now.' A burly PO stoker I hadn't met properly yet was busy enjoying ripping Taff a new one so I decided to try and deflect some of the attention away from him.

'Argentina has been disputing the sovereignty of the Malvinas, as they call them, for years.' I said out loud.

'How the fuck do you know that then, smart arse?' The burly PO stoker had turned on me now. I didn't bite, I just held up the hastily printed ship's newsletter that I had razzed from the Chief Writer's office on my way down to the Mess.

I read from the top of the first page, 'apparently around 0430 Falkland Islands time this morning, about 150 Argentine Special Forces or *'Buzo Tactico,'* as they are called, landed just outside Port Stanley, the Capital of the Falkland Islands, and after a few hours of fierce fighting the current small Royal Marine detachment based there had to surrender.'

'I bet it was one hell of a bun fight in the House of Commons today,' A voice from the corner commented.

'You could bet your arse on that one, Maggie won't be happy,' Taff was grinning as he answered.

'The Falkland Islands.' I carry on reading, 'Are made up of two islands with about 200 small islets and all together would be slightly smaller than Wales but the population is only around 1800 people so there is lots of room for them!'

I paused to wait for a reaction. There wasn't one, so I read on.

'Most live in either Port Stanley or Goose Green, the rest of the islanders live in isolated sheep stations scattered all over the Islands.'

'You Welsh boys will be all right then if you get ashore.' The burly PO stoker's comment was directed at Taff.

'Boyo don't knock it until you've tried it,' came the curt response through his gritted teeth. Taff was still grinning though. Just.

I continue reading out loud. 'The wind always blows hard and the seas around there at this time of year are usually very rough.'

'Excellent news, just what we need.' An older Petty Officer just coming into the Mess said very sarcastically.

I had seen him on the flight deck earlier getting ready to receive stores and ammo from one of the ships that was going home. He was probably just knackered and grumpy, I assumed.

'Is there anymore Harry?' Taff asked.

'Yeah, it says the Islands were first sighted in 1592 by John Davis on the good ship *Desire*. The Islands' existence was then confirmed a couple of years later by Sir Richard Hawkins, but it wasn't until 1690 that they were landed on and named the Falklands by Captain Strong of the *Welfare*. They were actually named after the 3rd Viscount Falkland who later was the First lord of the Admiralty.'

No one said anything so I read on.

'Settlers from France, Spain, Britain and Argentina have occupied it, but it wasn't until 1833 that a Captain of the naval sloop *Clio* claimed the Islands for Britain. Argentine peaceful protests have been continuing ever since for nearly 150 years, until now of course, when they have resorted to force.' I stopped reading and then added:

'I suppose it's now our job now to go and kick them out!' That bit wasn't written down.

Over the next few days, the war machine began to move through the gears. There was a definite change in atmosphere on board, everyone felt it, especially after the news that Argentine Naval forces had also taken South Georgia on the 3rd April by forcing the 22 Marines based at Grytviken to surrender. It had also been reported that some Argentine Marines were amongst the group of scrap metal merchants who had raised the Argentine flag on South Georgia on the 19th March that actually kicked the whole thing off.

Major Colwill issued new orders for me and the rest of the Marines. I needed to check and double check systems, procedures and all our equipment, plus all the fast boats on board. The Marine contingent had to make sure all their personal weapons were sighted and true and in perfect working order. When we had done that job we were to help out with sighting the ship's own small arms weapons. The damage control exercises, being closed up at action stations and defence watches would surely be coming very soon. They did.

We passed through the equator yesterday; it had been my first time on a ship, but the traditional crossing the line ceremony had been cancelled.

'You were lucky Harry.' Taff ribbed me again as we stood in the sunshine on the flight deck.

'We will make sure we get you on the way back though,' he promised me.

I knew I had got away with eating the vile chilli concoction that Billy, one of the chefs, had been looking forward to knocking up and feeding to us. Next, it would have been some other disgusting flavoured and coloured slop being slapped over you before being dunked in cold seawater by the 'bears'.

I felt sure we would be coming back up again soon so the usual ceremony to pay homage to King Neptune would definitely go ahead for me and the other poor unfortunates who had not been subjected to it yet. I secretly wanted to go through it, as it would be a terrible thing to miss out on such a great naval tradition as that.

There were lots of buzzes flying around the ship now. Are we going to continue south or are we turning back?

'We arrive at Ascension Islands tomorrow, maybe we will get some news then and hopefully a letter from Jeannie and the kids.' Bob said with anticipation in his voice.

I could tell he was really missing his family now.

'I should have been at home now tormenting the hell out of Tom, Lucy and Joe,' he said as we dismantled the faulty outboard off one of the rigid raiders.

It was the right time to have a break and I'm back down in the Mess having a cuppa listening to the one main topic of conversation buzzing around the ship, well two now.

'Christ it's hot in here, we don't want to be hanging around here too long,' moaned Smudge, the burly PO stoker, for the second time today. I'd found out his name now and he was really beginning to get on my tits with his moaning and his bullying of Taff and some of the younger guys. Try it on with me you fucker I'd thought to myself on a few occasions during the past couple of days. Not that he would though as I know he had read my face on a previous occasion when he was getting stuck into someone else. I decide it's time to leave and get on with the repairs to the faulty outboard that Bob and I needed to get fixed today.

Brilliant had been filled up with just about everything we could possibly need and we were now leaving Clarence Bay and the capital of Ascension, Georgetown, behind us in our wake.

'That was a wild three days.' I said to Bob as we hung around together on the flight deck. It was good to be having a bit of down time with him as it had been non-stop since Gibraltar and no one's feet had been touching the ground. We were standing there quietly just appreciating the glorious sunshine and the calm deep blue colour of the sea, watching, only a short distance away, the four ships that had fallen in astern of Brilliant.

The Arrow, Sheffield, Coventry and Glasgow were all keeping up the steady 22 knots the ships' Captains had been ordered to make. We may have to throttle this back a bit when we get to the rough seas of the South Atlantic, but not just yet.

I finished briefing the boys on the rules of engagement at 1600hrs and was now ready to hand over to Joe 'Buster' Brown. He was the Brilliant's PO Medic and was going to talk about what to look for on the dog tags we now all had and where to find the medical information and the reasons for having it. We were also going to get a lesson on how to use the morphine ampoules every man in the task force had been issued.

'Sergeant Glass, report to the wardroom,' boomed out over the ship's tannoy system.

What next, I thought, as I made my way up the forward ladder to the wardroom door.

'Sergeant Glass,' Major Colwill handed me a signal. 'We need to get our Marines fully ready for engagement.' He had a strained look on his face.

'And we need to strengthen the upper deck small arms defensive positions, so get to that with Corporal May ASAP Sergeant.'

I felt my skin and fingers start to tingle and the hairs on my neck stand up as if I were watching a scary movie. This was no movie though.

'Yes sir.' I responded and then I paused for a second.

'It's really going to happen then? We are going to have to kick them off the Falklands?'

'Looks like it Sergeant, let's get your men to work.'

I hadn't walked two paces when the wardroom door closed again and the Major was heading back to the meeting with the group of ship's senior officers that I had caught a glimpse of over his shoulder.

The next few days, we had brackets welded to the upper deck rails to hold small arms and GPMG's and I had all the Marines and selected matelots blasting plastic drums to pieces off the stern with everything we had in the armoury, including bazookas! I did note that some of the matelots were better shots than the Marines, much to their disgust, and mine.

No one was ready for a real fire fight though. Yet.

5

25 April 1982

Grytviken – South Georgia

This is it, I am ready. I can't be any more ready. I can feel the adrenalin pumping through my veins at one hell of a rate as the Lynx Helicopter puts air between Brilliant's deck and its wheels.

As soon as we are clear the pilot makes a sharp left turn and heads straight towards the Grytviken settlement just over a mile away. Bob and I are hanging on the outside of the chopper, standing on the foot rails that had been welded below the open doors on both sides. Bill and Pete from Brilliant's Royal Marine detachment are doing the same on the other side. Six more marines are crammed inside the Lynx cabin.

The deafening noise from the rotors just a couple of feet from my head was not the worst part of the ride by far. The vibration almost shook our hands off the rail above the door and I make a mental note to talk to the pilot about it when we get back. It's a murky, cold drizzly morning with a stiff westerly wind that is blowing the chopper around a bit as we head inland, and which is also adding to the challenge of hanging on.

Thankfully, it was nothing compared to the previous few days when severe gales had blown continuously causing complete whiteouts right across South Georgia.

I see the drop off point ahead. We had been in the air for less than a minute. Everyone is tense but switched on and ready as we all do one last check that the safety is off on our individual weapons. The pilot put down exactly on the marker just to the right of a large green wooden building that looks like the main accommodation block.

I step off the Lynx sharpish freeing space for the rest of the team to pile out. I was expecting to receive incoming fire at any second as the guys fanned out to the left and right of me. But there was none. I move quickly towards the green building with Bob and the team close behind me, thinking any second someone is bound to take a pop at us.

We reach the bottom of the stairs leading up to the block and tuck ourselves in close to the wooden frame either side of them. I'm about to head up the stairs and the door above us opens.

'Tommy Gun.' was shouted from the door.

It was the safe word for all British units on this operation.

A soldier in full combat kit and blackened face steps out of the door in front of us. He looked like one of the SAS boys, but not one that had been on the Brilliant. He was probably from HMS Antrim's contingent, I thought.

'All sorted Sarge.' he called out. 'We are just mopping up a few stragglers over that hill behind you and we're done.'

I paused for just a second.

'Bollocks.' I thought to myself. 'You heard him boys but keep your wits about you.' I said as we turned to walk back towards the landing area.

The first sight of our enemy is seeing a group of them exiting a rusty old shack and being hustled down to a holding area next to the flagpole on the beach. As we get closer they are all standing with their arms raised, any weapons are piled on the ground 20 feet away from them being guarded by a bloke you really wouldn't want to be fucking around with. They all look shit scared and pretty miserable.

SAS and SBS guys appear from every corner of the old whaling station. They are shouting and screaming at the Argies in their charge, intimidating them and making sure they are doing what they have been told to do. None of them have weapons now and their hands were definitely as high up in the air as they can get them. It only takes a second to see there was going to be no more resistance from this lot.

An SAS Captain, who I didn't know, called over to me.

'Sergeant, you and your men round up all the prisoners and get them in one place. By this flagpole will do fine.'

His order was clear and by the time we had got the last few stragglers buttoned up with the rest of the prisoners the Argentine flag was on the deck next to me and the Union Jack was up and proudly flying from the mast again.

A minute later Brilliant's Lynx reappeared and I watch as the ship's Doc, PO Medic, Captain's steward and Billy the killick chef exit it and then leg it past me towards the accommodation building, all wearing their very visible Red Cross vests.

They came out of the building after about 20 minutes. One of the SAS boys told me a couple of minutes earlier that there was an Argie inside from the submarine that had been crippled that morning. Most of his leg had been blown off so he was not in good shape. He also told me that the assault group's medic had been injured and been casevaced out of there already and that's why Brilliant's medical party had to come in.

As the medical party filed back past me I asked,

'All sorted doc?'

I got the thumbs up and then they moved amongst the sullen bunch of prisoners and started to check them out. None of them objected as they were still very wary of the hyped up SAS, SBS and Royal Marines that were wandering around. They knew they were absolutely ready to kill somebody, if they wanted to fuck about.

6

At sea heading west towards the Falkland Islands

'It doesn't seem like only two days ago we were rounding up those prisoners on the beach.' Bob said as we headed off for breakfast.

I agreed, because all sense of time had disappeared due to the constant battle we had been fighting against the foul weather and heavy seas since leaving Grytviken. It had worn everyone down, but now everyone was feeling the increased tension as we closed in on the Falkland Islands themselves. We all knew that we would have to deal with much larger forces that were dug in and waiting for us on the Falklands rather than just the few Marines that had been left to defend South Georgia.

'The sea is rough today.' I commented to a couple of seasoned matelots over breakfast.

They just shrugged and said nothing as the 'Brilliant' bounced and crashed through another massive wave, everyone then bracing themselves waiting for the huge wall of water to smash down onto the upper deck causing the whole ship to shudder under its weight. Travelling at speed through these seas makes anyone of a nervous disposition want to keep checking out the ship's bulkheads. Taff told me he always did, probably because he was below the waterline for most of his day. I know I saw some of the older senior rates twitching nervously and probably not just because of being in these rough seas.

The ship was now full of SAS kit and its owners, for the passage to the RV point with the Carriers and remainder of the task force a couple of hundred miles away from the Falkland Islands. Their kit had been squeezed into every nook and cranny to keep it away from the main drag that ran the full length of the ship. There had been way too many problems and far too much hassle when stuff had been dumped there after storing up in Ascension.

The XO had also gone arse over tit after tripping up on something during his rounds. His sense of humour failure was of biblical proportions and miraculously everything had then been cleared away by the time the next morning watch had appeared. No one was going to let the same mistake happen again. We had been warned.

Some of the SAS boys didn't like the rough seas very much either and had been chucking up frequently, much to the delight of their unaffected mates. It had been too good an opportunity to miss and a great excuse for them just to take the piss mercilessly.

They had some serious moments too and there had been time for the SAS boys to tell us what had gone on at South Georgia before we got there. The weather had certainly taken its toll on the men, equipment and machines. Aborted missions, helicopter crashes, freezing feet and hands, the whole thing sounded like a nightmare, but it was all in a day's work and everyone was happy with the end result.

The Union Jack was flying again over a little bit of Sovereign British Territory but now it was time to finish the job on the big bit.

7

Five miles off the Falkland Islands

29 May 1982

The combined power of the four Rolls Royce Olympus and Tyne gas turbine engines was at full tilt. The deck beneath my feet vibrated like hell telling me we are on our way back inshore again and it would soon be time to get the rest of my gear on and ready for a fast run in onboard the rigid raider. We would be only a couple of miles as the crow flies from our previous landing a couple of nights ago at Teal Inlet, but this time we would be further north close to the Rincon Grande Settlement on East Falklands.

Current intel is the Argies are fully entrenched at this settlement as they have been since day one. Just like at Teal Inlet. The job is to assess the strength of their positions and then work our way further down to Horseshoe Bay to do the same, weather permitting. This will provide critical intel for the top brass to plan the main assault groups' routes to Stanley from current locations near to San Carlos. A couple of nights out and we should be done, back on board by Friday for hot showers and some good hot scran.

The rest of the ship's company had all disappeared after finishing their evening meal. I am sitting in the main dining hall mentally sorting out what I needed to do next. My gear is on the deck around me and a fresh cup of tea on the table.

A couple of minutes later and I am ready. All I have to do now is my final weapons checks before strapping it all on.

A dull thump on the blue lino flooring draws my attention, and everyone else's, as the grenade rolled slowly towards the corner of the dining hall.

Nobody moved.

I lift my head, after checking the safety was on on the Browning pistol I am holding, and take a few moments to look around the dining hall at the three rough looking SAS soldiers and my mate Bob. I then cast my eyes on the lump of high explosive gently rocking back and forward only several feet from me.

The pin is still in. I feel my body relax fully and carry on sorting out all the ammo at my feet, that was coming with me tonight. Someone will pick the fucker up in a minute, I thought.

I couldn't help thinking about the previous mission and what a gang fuck it was. New intel earlier today said we had apparently run into a few boys from an Argentine 601 Special Forces unit. They had arrived at Teal only an hour before we did and the worst thing was they had only been in transit and were just about to fuck off when they pinged us.

This mission was a whole new ball game though as we would be on the ground for at least a couple nights, and maybe more. I had been lucky so far and except for the other night had been dishing out the pain for the Argies rather than receiving it.

The easiest day had been the main landings in San Carlos Bay on the 21st May. It had been a quiet affair for me really as I had been tasked alongside the Paras to take a small team of Marines inland from the beachhead to set up defensive positions at a key point on one of the hills above the bay. With the beachhead secured, I watched from above, as a couple of thousand men and hundreds of tons of equipment had poured ashore all day. It had been a good start for the task force and me.

The following days though had shown us that some of the Argentine military were no mugs, but were, in fact, highly trained and motivated people trying their best to kill us now. The courage of the Argentine pilots' attacking our ships in San Carlos Bay was the stuff of legends already. One time I saw right into the cockpit of a low flying Mirage as it screamed over our position on the hill. I'm sure he was smiling as he went past, but whatever, he was a brave and skilful man that's for sure. He didn't waver from his course one degree even though we were pumping thousands of rounds into the sky at his aircraft. I did wonder if he got back to Argentina or not as he was definitely trailing smoke as he briefly disappeared over the far hillside before we watched him bank away and back out to sea.

Now is not the time for daydreaming though and it's time to check out how the rest of this missions team assembled in Brilliant's junior rates dining hall are doing.

It is the same team as for the Teal job. The mission commander is again Sergeant Tom Dye of the SAS, a small powerfully built man who was a veteran of covert operations all over the world. He had been on the ground in this conflict several times already. The first time was on the Fortuna Glacier screw-up in South Georgia where he had crashed twice in two separate helicopters, on the same day.

We had joked earlier that was fucking unlucky by anyone's standards.

I had first seen Tom on the beach at Grytviken. He had been in the main assault group with the other SAS soldiers, SBS and Royal Marines. He told me of his unceremonious arrival in the South Atlantic after being lifted out of Belfast to get involved in this 'little skirmish' as I had heard one of the SAS boys call it. All my dealings with Tom had been very positive up to now, but I had seen on a couple of occasions, when things were just not right, a look in his menacing blue eyes that told me he was not a man to fuck around with.

Tom calmly stood up and walked over to the corner to retrieve the grenade. On his way back to his seat, he placed it back into the open hand of John Williams.

'Twat.' was all he said.

'Thanks Sarge,' was the almost contrite reply.

As well as the obvious tension, there was also an atmosphere of sadness, for all of us, but especially the three SAS men in the room. They had all lost mates the other night when the helicopter carrying them had ditched in the freezing South Atlantic sea killing 21 of these elite troops. It was a small comfort to know that it was Brilliant that had picked up the survivors, including as I had found out earlier, Tom's brother Bill.

Our objectives for this new mission were to recon the positions of the Argentine troops further down the coast of East Falklands. We were after the usual intelligence: numbers and type of troops, whether they were conscripts or regulars, the amounts and type of weapons they had plus locations of dug-in positions, and the state of their morale, if we could get good eyes and ears on them.

Previous intelligence suggested that there were well trained and heavily armed Argentine Marines and Special Forces right in the path of what could be a potential route into Port Stanley and our job is to find out if this is still current.

Jimmy Blake was a tough, unforgiving soldier by all accounts. He was only a couple of feet from me sorting out his kit. Jimmy was a tall skinny bloke with thin bony hands who right now looked more like a young pop star than a soldier with his long floppy blond hair.

He was another SAS man plucked from god knows where in Northern Ireland to be here but was taking some stick about his poncy looks from the last SAS member of the team. John Williams was a veteran Corporal and was another one who had been plucked from somewhere in Northern Ireland at the same time. He was enjoying giving Jimmy shit because he just had his haircut by the barber on board, although you wouldn't have known it as it was still half way down his ears and well over the collar.

It was a pretty impressive cut seeing that Steve, one of the leading stewards and ship's barber in his spare time, was definitely not used to having a huge, and I mean huge, pony tailed, rough arsed SAS bloke growling at him.

'Give me a haircut and don't cut it too fucking short,'

John had apparently been very precise when indicating exactly how he wanted it cut and how long it was to be left. He certainly wasn't expecting a nip with the scissors on his right ear though.

I had got to know Steve the barber well over the past few months. He had given me a number two all over with his trusty Wahl clippers a couple of times. He told me after the event that he was crapping himself when cutting John's hair. His said his hands were shaking so much it was a wonder he didn't cut his whole fucking ear off especially as the ship had been pitching and rolling like a bugger in the South Atlantic swells that night.

John had apparently been very quiet during the rest of the haircut whilst frequently dabbing away at the blood that had dribbled continuously onto the back of his neck. It wasn't exactly what you would call a regulation cut, in fact, far from it, but there was a very good reason for it. John had told me that after this 'little job', if they needed to go back into Northern Ireland in a hurry, 'the last thing I need to look like is a fucking squaddie.'

John's dulcet tones filled the room again. 'Fucking nancy boy, what's with the blond locks then Jimmy boy? I suppose you think you are a bit of an undercover shagger don't you. You knob head.'

'Fuck off you big ugly mother. You are only giving me shit because you haven't had a shag in years, and not likely to either.' Was the swift and curt response from Jimmy.

'Fuck off Corporal, you cocky little bastard,' was John's reply as he leaned over and gave Jimmy a slap on the back of the head that would have downed most men, if he really meant it.

I thought to myself at that moment that I am a pretty big man at 6' 2" and 230lbs but John had a few inches and few pounds of extra muscle on me.

John was 6' 7" and 280lbs of hardened muscle. His giant hands were covered in tough, weathered skin, from his six years with the SAS on covert and overt operations around the world. He had also done three years 'probation' in the Paras before that, as he had called it. It wasn't hard to see that he had been in a few scraps over the years and for his sins had collected an angry looking scar than ran down the whole left side of his face from just below his ear down all the way to the front of his chin. Courtesy of a now dead Chinaman apparently.

Bob and I had quietly joked earlier that most of the scar wasn't visible from his right side profile because of the huge bulbous nose that was attached to his hardened chiselled face. Not that anyone would have mentioned this to him, especially if they had a desire to continue breathing.

I had learned a few other things about John in the past few days. He told me he loved engineering and just making things. But playing rugby was his real passion, as it is mine. When I asked him where he liked to play, 'anywhere in the pack except in the front row, that's just for nutters,' he had scoffed.

I felt very comfortable in John's company and even after just these few days of knowing him I was glad he was with us on this mission. A definite asset in the team and this was going to be the third time I had been alongside him on the ground.

He had been on the first helicopter during the main assault on Grytviken in South Georgia, along with Tom. It hadn't been much of a fight for me, in fact, not one at all, but I knew he had been in the thick of it. He was the man who dragged the only 'casualty' on our side out of the line of fire. The guy had only sprained his ankle, but the piss taking the Royal Marine medic had endured from everyone on the journey back to the carrier group was incessant, especially as the Navy had to send in the Brilliant's medical team to sort out the injured Argie.

The final member of the team is my best mate Corporal Bob May. He is a brilliant coxswain and could handle expertly the squadron's rigid raiders, Navy RIB's, Geminis or any other boat for that matter. He had been picked for this job specifically by the boss, Mayor Bill Colwill, a very decent Rupert, who had made all the right calls to date when he knew his men's lives could be in jeopardy.

Bob was there, apart from his boat skills, because he was a tough fighter, an excellent navigator and was a brilliant shot. Major Colwill knew he would also gain some valuable experience working in a combat situation with Tom and the rest of us. I often joked with him that he must have some weird birth defect that meant he could see in the dark or it was because of all those carrots he was constantly munching. What I did know was that he could find his way by sea to the most obscure places with unnerving accuracy, especially during the night.

His excellent 20-20 vision and calmness also were the reason for the accuracy of his shooting. No one was better right now in the Royal Marines with the regulation SLR. Bob had won the Marine shooting championship using the rifle for the past two years.

Taking the title from me, the little shit.

He was even better with his personalised sniper rifle, but his very irritating boast that he could shoot the middle out of a gnat's fart, always wound me up. Still it was really good to know he wouldn't be far away from me during the next few days.

It had been quiet now for a few minutes as we all completed our final preparations in the dining hall but then the noise started to pick up. Bob was getting into the banter now with Jimmy and John. It was his way, and theirs, of just trying to relax a bit before we kick off. We all have our own way of dealing with things before any mission, these guys were just taking the piss and having a laugh to release the tension. Tom and I were different though. I could see him on the other side of the hall just quietly checking his gear again, ensuring nothing was hanging down or could snag and make unnecessary noise when we were on the ground.

Bob and I were kitted out with standard issue, heavy combat trousers, DPM jackets and windproof anoraks. Plus the usual personal undergarments that were well worn and had been tested in the field on many an occasion. Mums, wives and girlfriends were usually responsible for the procurement of these and were inevitably spot on with their choices. The only piece of kit we had been allowed to sort out ourselves, and not just for this situation, was a decent pair of civvy hiking or all terrain waterproof boots. They were always the first item in the kit bag before deploying anywhere.

The standard issue DMS boots were, as everyone agreed, cheap, uncomfortable, leaked and overall were completely fucking useless. My boots had come from a good old Millets shop in Gloucester a couple of years ago and had looked after my feet very well for all that time. They were exactly what I needed on the wet, peaty and boggy ground I had already experienced and what we would be yomping over later this night.

Tom, John and Jimmy's SAS kit was a mixture of the best stuff from anywhere in the world they could get it. Whenever they saw a great piece of kit, whether it was on a US Marine, Navy Seal, Russian Special Forces or any dead guy that had got in their way, they would have it. They looked like a rag tag bunch with their longer hair and non-uniform kit, but the one thing I knew was these were some of the best soldiers anywhere in the world. I was very happy to be with them and to learn from them over the next few nights.

'Hey guys knock it off, get your shit together and make sure everything is tight, we're off in 20.'

Tom didn't need to shout, his voice carried quietly across the hall. A voice of calm authority but with an undertone of control and menace for those who didn't want to listen.

8

I'm ready to go. The rest of the guys don't need anything done for a minute, so in my quiet corner of the dining hall, I give myself these last few moments before the off to think about my friends, family and especially Kathy.

She is the one for me, there is no doubt in my mind anymore. I love her more than anything in this world. I think I really knew it as soon as I met her that day at university in Manchester, but here I am 8000 miles away and can't tell her to her face. When this lot is finished I absolutely will though.

Right, OK, it's time to snap out of that wishy washy shit and get psyched up and the adrenaline flowing. I will need all of my senses running at peak performance very soon. For the other night's mission I used an incident involving my Mum, Gerri, and that twat of an ex-stepfather. Reliving that would do the job for me again, I'm sure of it.

I close my eyes and let my mind drift back to a few years earlier.

Gerri had married my real dad Ron very quickly and it had been great at first. Sadly it had not lasted any real distance due to Ron's military activities and the long silent separations as a result of those. They had met at the 1952 Olympics when they were both competing, but he was already in the US Navy so the impending separations shouldn't have been a surprise. After the wedding in 1953 Gerri moved over to the US almost immediately but then missed England and the rest of her family very much.

This was made worse when Ron passed the gruelling physical and mental requirements, to become a US Navy SEAL in 1954. She had seen very little of him during the first year of the course but when he moved onto the advanced training sections, she saw even less of him. She hated being alone and was always pissed off with him for not being around and then I came into the world.

After two years she decided enough was enough and in 1956 came back to Nigglesworth in Gloucestershire with two year-old me tagging along. The divorce had not been difficult or contested in any way, because both knew it was not going work for many reasons. But through it all they had not fallen out of love, it was just never going to work because of his job.

Something I was worried about myself with respect to Kathy and the similarities of my job. Something for me to pay attention to in the future, I absolutely knew that.

Things were not all bad for me as a kid though. I actually had a great childhood with two loving parents. The only thing was they were sometimes up to 6000 miles apart, depending on where Ron was serving, not that he could tell us most of the time anyway. The happiest times I can remember were when we were all together sharing Christmas or some other 'special' occasion.

There was always laughter and fun and secretly many times as a kid I wished they could have got it back together. But it was never to be. Ron never stayed in a hotel though when he was over. He always stayed with us and as I had found out later in life, in Gerri's room.

These 'occasions' carried on for a number of years but were declining as Ron got more senior and more entrenched in his work. Gerri then met a complete wanker and against all my, and everyone else's protestations, she married him.

I was 11 years old.

The second husband, Nick, actually lasted less time than Ron, due to the violence that erupted once the drink got into him. I had a bad gut feeling about the situation for quite a while before I actually witnessed anything myself. Three years had gone by and I could still barely bring myself to speak to the twat. I know it was tearing Gerri apart and for a while Gerri and I became almost strangers. My hormones were doing back flips and at home I just became a snotty, smelly, miserable, angry little shit.

We were just not communicating about anything and even when I heard the raised voices and arguments in the rooms below me I didn't care for a while.

Something I still feel guilty about now.

But all of a sudden I grew up and I started to notice the tears most days and then the bruises. Gerri told me it was nothing, just that she had argued with Nick and the bruise was from falling over or some other bullshit like that.

Finally, the day came when there could be no hiding the truth. I came back from rugby training early for some reason. I was then a big 14 year-old lad, almost 15, but could have been taken for a 17 or 18 year-old easily. None of my peers messed with me, not that I was an aggressive kid or anything. In fact, I think I was the opposite. Gerri had always taught me to use my size and strength for good things, even though at times that had been very difficult, I knew she was right.

The walk home from the bus stop had been short and uneventful as usual but even in the semi darkness of this early winter evening I was still aware of the stunning and calming traditional country scene that unfolded before me.

Cotswold stone cottages and other old houses were set back into the hillside of the opposite valley. They were still partially hidden in places by various mature trees with good leaf coverage still on them. Stone walls, some of them crumbling a bit in places, stretched for miles on both sides of the valley, many of them now all engrained with the greying effect of decades of weather.

I sauntered around the corner past the Jovial Foresters, the only local pub still open, then past the recently closed Old Star pub and swung left up the lane. As I approached our house I could see movements through the net curtains, the figures clearly highlighted by the light inside the front room. I saw a hand being pulled back and the clear shape of a fist being formed, it was then thrust forward viciously hitting the person that was obviously Gerri, squarely in the chest.

In the quiet of Brilliant's dining hall, I can feel my temperature rising, the veins in my neck are swollen and pumping with blood and my fists are clenched tight.

It's working.

The force of the blow catapulted Gerri across the room, taking with her the contents of the small phone table that was situated in the front of the downstairs window. The contents had smashed into various pieces when they hit the ground as I discovered moments later. I remembered freezing for just a second or two and staring at the scene unfolding before me. I saw what was obviously a man moving towards a hidden figure beneath the windowsill.

A red mist descended and I ran as fast as I could towards the house, my feet thumping the ground, the sports bag discarded by the side of the road, training shoes, boots and shorts all spilling onto the ground. This was of no concern to me though as I easily vaulted the three foot front gate and rushed up to the side door. I knew it would be open. My face was flushed purple and my eyes filled with rage and contempt for the man inside the house. I was going to tear him to fucking pieces.

I rushed through the kitchen not caring about the noise my shoes made or the pinging sounds of Gerri's highly prized, but now knocked off, brightly coloured metal fridge magnets as they hit the red terracotta tiled floor. I moved swiftly towards the front room where the sound of Gerri crying filled my ears. I then hear Nick's menacing voice telling her to get up and shut the fuck up. I was through the door in a heartbeat and it was clear that what I had seen through the curtains was not the first blow. Pieces of furniture were turned over in other corners of the front room and many ornaments and other prized possessions were smashed and scattered across the floor.

In a second, I closed the distance between him and me and I hit the fucker hard, as hard as I possibly could, using every ounce of strength and power I could muster. It was a good hit straight into his right cheekbone that smashed him into the wall just to the left of the window frame.

The surprise and force of the punch, and then a full body tackle, had him on the deck. The wind was knocked out of him for just the few seconds I needed. Even though he was a fully grown man, he wasn't as fit, strong or as angry as me right then, which put him at a great disadvantage.

I was back on my feet in half a second and took a step backwards to give myself some space. He tried to get to his feet but the next blow from me was a swinging right hand that connected squarely on his left cheek, knocking him straight back down to the floor.

I grabbed him by the hair and dragged him into a space where I could jump onto his chest and sit astride him. I then went to work on his face with my fists. I got at least 20 good hard punches in before Gerri could break my focus and almost uncontrollable rage by grabbing my shoulders and screaming at me not to kill him. It had been enough to slow the force of my punches on the now semi-conscious dickhead below me.

I did manage to have one last go at him as she was leading me away. I broke free of her grasp for just long enough to get two full on boots in, one to the balls and the other straight into the miserable bastard's guts.

The police and ambulance had arrived together and once Gerri had been checked over, after refusing to go to hospital, the ambulance crew had taken the dickhead away. The police took our statements and after Gerri had refused again to go to hospital they left us in the devastation of the bloodstained and smashed up front room.

It was another hour before we had sorted the house and it was properly quiet again. I cradled my badly beaten mother in my arms for a long time. She had sobbed quietly whilst I gently rocked her back and forth. It wasn't until the early hours of the following morning that we had curled up in our own beds.

I didn't sleep much, if at all. My mind was still racing as all I wanted to do was inflict more damage to that bastard. Sergeant Porter of Stroud Police came back the next day and said that, after discussions in the hospital, no charges were going to be pressed by the dickhead. I did laugh. Gerri had already told them that she wouldn't be pressing any either as all she wanted was him out of her life.

This was definitely going to happen now, no more second chances. We didn't need to see a counsellor either, we would sort this out ourselves. Once all the necessary paperwork had been completed, Sergeant Porter asked me to walk with him to his car. When we stopped I remember well the last thing he said to me

'Nice one son, that fucker deserved it from what I hear; you just look after your mum now.'

We only saw the twat once more after that when he came back to the house with the police in tow to pick up some of his stuff. Gerri cried and it made me mad as hell again. The baseball bat was never far away from my hand. I only needed a small reason to pick it up and use it.

Sadly he never gave me the opportunity.

9

Falkland Islands – 29 May 1982

I am abruptly brought back to the present day. It takes a few moments to relax my fists and take a deep calming breath. I look at the dining hall clock and it tells me it's 2031hrs. The ship's tannoy system is blasting out 'hands to action stations, hands to action stations, assume NBCD state one condition Zulu.'

I poke my head out of the dining room door and see matelots emerging from their mess decks, cabins and workplaces in their blue No 8's working kit, anti-flash gear on their heads and arms, their gas masks strapped to their sides or slung over the shoulders. Each one of them has a specific job to do and their own action station to get to, all at a quick, but controlled pace.

The last men through the deck hatches and corridor bulkhead doors closed them and then clamped them down tight. Within two minutes the ship was fully closed up ready for enemy action or in this case to take me, Tom and the rest of the team to the drop-off point off the coast of East Falkland.

I am ready to go now.

The clock in the dining hall clicked over to 2134hrs.

'I hear the Paras have taken Goose Green and gave the Argies a real good kicking on the way but they have got fucking hundreds of prisoners to look after now though. Christ knows what they are going to do with them all, I wouldn't want to be stuck as a nursemaid for that lot, that's for sure. I also heard we didn't take too many casualties either. Fucking great guys those Paras.' John spouted to the rest of us.

'Well, you would say that wouldn't you.' Jimmy piped up. 'Which regiment did you come from originally? Um let me see, wasn't the Paras was it?'

We're all smiling now.

'Fuck off you little shit,' was the curt response from John, but with a wry smile slowly curling across his lips.

'OK guys let's go over the plan one more time,' Tom said as he spread the map over a couple of the dining room tables.

We huddled up and Tom identified the landing point first, read out the coordinates of the first LUP and the RV point at the main objective. The farmhouse at Rincon Grande. The return RV and time and the ERV if everything went tits up were confirmed.

'Bob you got the landing site and RV's sorted?' Tom asked.

'Yep and I've prepped the boat already and put some extra juice on board just in case.' Bob replied.

'Good, thanks,' said Tom.

Tom looked at me and was waiting for my update.

'Tom, the extra rounds and 'spare' gimpy plus Bob's sniper rifle are in the raider. I've also stowed the extra grenades, map and compass we agreed should be in there.'

'OK Harry,' Tom said.

John didn't need to say anything. He was ready and had almost double the amount of ammo that most men would usually carry. He would be strapping it onto himself in one way or another once we got ashore.

We were going in pretty light, other than John's ammo, with only a couple of days' rations and a camouflaged space blanket for the freezing nights on the ground. Field glasses, night vision glasses, notepaper and pencils for the intel and an HF radio.

We only really had two choices on how we would get our intel back from this job. It would either have to be short HF transmissions or through our extraction and reporting back on board verbally. Unfortunately, the satcoms gear had not caught up with us and the High Frequency radios had been a bit unreliable to date so we were all expecting to be writing stuff down and communicating the intel verbally when we got back.

'If we get split up and any of us miss both the RV's I suppose we just stay low until our guys arrive?' Jimmy asked.

'Yes, and with the pace they are going that won't be long, but you just better not get lost. It's our job to get this intel back to HQ as soon as we have enough so they can either sort out a battalion strike at Rincon Grande or leave it alone. Our guys will be past this point further south soon enough and the Argies will have nowhere to go anyway even if we don't hit them head on.' Tom replied.

We went through all the details one final time. It was a simple operation really we just didn't need to get pinged by any more Argies this time. We would get to the landing point and move inland heading for the northern end of the Rincon Grande settlement. Once there we would gather all the intel we needed and then tab the couple of miles to see if we could get eyes on Horseshoe Bay. The main house in particular is where earlier intel had indicated that there was possibly a significant number of Argies camping out there.

The one big problem we anticipated was going to be cover. In this region of the Falklands the ground is very open except for one area on the south side of Salvador Hill. That has a rocky enclave and will be our best option for cover at night. Getting to that enclave was the objective for tonight. It would be perfect for the OP's at Rincon, but the tab to do them at Horseshoe would be a challenge on all that flat open ground, but that is what we were there for and would have to deal with it.

A head came round the dining hall door.

'It is 2312hrs. Captain said 10 minutes to drop off point.' A fresh faced leading seaman said quietly.

I noticed he had hair much longer than you would usually get away with and was similar to John's new stylish cut.

Tom nodded to the seaman to say this was understood. The door closed quietly as if it had just closed on a funeral parlour door. I hoped it wasn't an omen.

It was time to go. Bob got sorted first and left quickly after I finished a buddy check on him. He was in good shape, his face was properly blackened with camouflage grease and all his kit was in the right place with no loose ends hanging down.

The ship's coxswain had said he would personally make sure that the raider would get into the water safely, but Bob wanted to be there just to make sure. I had no beef with that and neither did Tom. The last thing we needed was an upturned boat especially with all our kit already pre-loaded into it.

The rest of us finished gearing up and completed our buddy checks quietly with no fuss. The route to the upper deck and the lowered steps to the raider was a right turn out of the dining hall and then right again into the main passageway that was now lit only by the soft red lighting that all warships burned at night. This reduced the risk of detection from white light streaming out of upper deck doors and hatches when they are opened. White light could easily be seen from a sharp-eyed lookout on the headland if we were in close enough, or from another ship, or even worse a submarine.

'HMS Brilliant' was fully secured at action stations and closed up to NBCD state 1 condition Zulu. All doors and hatches were shut tight with the ship company closed up at their specific action stations with full anti-flash gear on and respirators hanging close to their bodies ready to put on if needed. Although it was very unlikely that there would be an attack using gas of any sort the respirators would be needed to get out safely from a smoke-filled area if the ship was hit and on fire. We know they worked and had saved the lives of sailors on HMS Sheffield very recently.

Brilliant's Captain had given the order to have each door and hatch on our route to the upper deck manned by a crew member. They would open and close them for us as we headed to the upper deck making our passage a lot easier with all the weapons and kit we were carrying.

I caught the eyes of a couple of the guys manning the doors as we moved through the main drag. It was written on their faces; I wonder if we shall ever see these guys again?

It was a bit unnerving and just as I was about to have a gloomy thought I was distracted by the young long-haired matelot who had put his head around the door earlier.

'Good luck Sarge. See you again shortly.' He said with a smile as I walked by.

'Thanks, I'll be seeing you.' I replied.

Tom was already talking to Major Colwill and Captain Cornwall as I move through the last door into the helicopter hanger. The hanger door was half up, which was easily enough height for us to get under and out onto the flight deck. It was then only a short distance to walk to the starboard stairs once they had been lowered. Inside the hanger was a good muster point right now as it was out of the freezing cold wind that was ripping down both sides of Brilliant as she steamed at 25 knots to the drop-off point.

Bill Colwill, Tom, and John Cornwall started to make their way over to us now all three of us had appeared at the back of the hangar. All the remaining ship's crew left through the hangar door we had just come through as they had been told to disappear during our final briefing. The last crew member to go through was securing the last of the clips on the closed door as the Captain spoke.

'The sea should be calm for your run in,' he shouted over the wind noise resonating around the inside of the hangar. 'But, be aware we are expecting the weather to deteriorate significantly around 0300 so you will have to let us know if you have to change your plans tonight. We will be back here at 0300 the day after tomorrow unless I hear different.' The Captain looked down at his watch.

'We will be stopped in two minutes gentlemen. Good luck.'

'Thank you sir.' Bill Colwill said and saluted as the Captain turned and walked away.

Bill then turned to speak to us directly.

'We didn't have it our own way on the last mission so let's keep our eyes and ears open this time. We need to know the strength of the Argentine forces and what they are up to so get the intel and get the hell out of there.' He paused for a moment before continuing. 'Most importantly though, I want you all back alive, OK?'

'Yes sir,' was our unified response.

He then turned directly to Tom, 'Good luck Sergeant.'

Tom saluted and turned away.

'Come on you lot let's go.' We quickly fell in behind him and exited the hanger.

Brilliant was almost stopped, but there was still a fierce biting wind whistling down the starboard walkway. I hear the crane motor whirring away before I see it gently lift our fully prepped rigid raider just high enough to clear the side rails. Bob was there alongside the chief coxswain making sure all was well and before Brilliant had come to a complete stop the raider was over the side and level with the bottom of the side rails. Two burly seamen held on to it to make sure it didn't swing or crash into the ship's side unnecessarily.

Bob hopped onboard and quickly stowed the gear that he had carried up from the dining hall also making sure John could have no more accidents this time. The drop-off point was only a mile offshore so Bob had to be quick getting the boat in the water, engine running and in position ready for the rest of us to step onboard. We then had anything from forty-five minutes to an hour in the boat depending on what we found once we were inside the mouth of the estuary and nearer to the landing point.

The Captain now had Brilliant's port side turned leeward facing the direction of the wind. On the lee side of the ship there was now a much calmer area of sea that would help us get on board the raider quickly and safely. We all knew we didn't have much time here so had to move our arses.

Before the boat had hit the water Bob flashed up the 140hp outboard engine and had it burbling away quietly. Simultaneously the ship's ladder was lowered the last few feet into place just above the water. Tom went down the steps first, then I follow heading for the landing plate. Even in the pitch darkness I can see the shimmer of the freezing cold sea below and I know it would kill me in minutes if I fell in and couldn't get out of the water and into dry kit quickly. I also knew I would be all right here being right next to the ship, unlike those poor sods who had perished the other night.

Bob had the raider alongside now, Tom was in first, then an easy step in for me, John and then Jimmy followed. We took up the same positions in the boat as we were in for the failed mission the other night. All this had been sorted out during our planning phase and was based on our weights and the kit we were carrying.

The most important thing right now was to have a well-balanced boat so it could perform at its very best. Bob and I both knew it takes a lot to bugger these boats up, but if the weight distribution is wrong they can be a pig to handle, especially at high speed across open water. On the way back, we could ditch some kit if we needed to and make it a lot lighter and a bit faster, but on the way in we needed everything to land the other end.

'Bob, let's go,' was the short command from Tom.

Bob eased the motor up and we pulled away smoothly from the side of the ship. The Brilliant was underway seconds later turning slowly to port, the ladder we had just stepped off was already halfway up the side of the ship. A raise of the hand and a short wave from the chief coxswain would be the last human contact from the ship for a couple of days.

Moments later we all hear the Olympus and Tyne engines beginning to wind up and push the Type 22 frigate away from us. Thirty seconds later she would be at full power cutting through the water at 25 knots plus heading back out to the main task force for whatever job she was needed to do next.

We were now moving along at a good pace ourselves, across water that was still pretty calm, thankfully. This was the second time we had been lucky on this piece of water. I was silently praying that this good luck would continue once we reached the island this time.

Every so often we hit a bigger wave and seconds later we are all showered with freezing cold sea spray. Half an hour in and the fine rain that had been with us the other night also started again. I roll down my heavy black balaclava over my ears and pull my anorak hood as far over my head as I can. No point in getting cold or wet this early on. The pace was quick and steady now and Bob had the raider under complete control heading straight for the first waypoint.

The constant slapping of the waves against the underside of the raider and cold sea spray took me back briefly to the many nights training in the cold waters off Plymouth Sound. This wasn't training though and very soon we would be up close and personal to some Argentineans, who if they saw us, would only want to blow our fucking heads off. Better not give them that opportunity, I smiled to myself, and then I huddled down in the boat a bit further to try and stay warm and dry for just a little bit longer.

I spoke too soon and moments later the raider hits a big wave showering all of us with a big dump of freezing cold salty water.

'Fuck.' John said as he shook the remainder of water from the top of his hood and then asked.

'Bob how long to the landing point?'

Bob peered at the waterproofed map under red light and checked the bearing on his compass.

'About 25 minutes John, not too far to go now.'

We all huddled down again but with eyes firmly fixed on the approaching shoreline.

We had travelled another half a mile when I heard it. Everyone heard it. The thumping sound of helicopter rotor blades. In a split second, all our heads were up, looking skyward, weapons ready.

'It sounds like one of ours!' I shouted.

'It's also coming from seaward.' I shouted again as the noise from the rotor blades got louder and louder.

Whoever it was they were coming straight towards us.

Out of the rain and darkness and only for a second or two I saw it. We all saw it. It was a Sea King helicopter and one of the few green 'jungleys' down here that are specifically designed to move troops and kit around rather than the blue Mk5 Sea Kings the Navy used primarily for antisubmarine warfare.

'Probably D Squadron on their way to blow up a few more planes, if they can find any left.' John shouted and then smiled.

I was in no doubt he was referring to the very successful SAS raid on Pebble Island only a few days ago.

As the noise abated and the chopper carried on its path, I settle down again in my position and scan ahead. The intermittent low cloud had masked the tops of the highest points briefly but now I can see clearly some of key features of the craggy coastline ahead. There are no signs of life or lights of any kind.

Everyone in the boat was even more alert now, our eyes straining to see ahead and especially for any signs of the vast kelp beds that lay offshore at this point. I see something up ahead, a dark shape in the water.

'Bob, there's something big straight ahead. It could be seaweed.' I shout.

A very sharp and fast turn to starboard and we were away from it.

'If any of that gets near the prop we will be fucked, keep your eyes peeled guys.' said Bob.

It was another ten minutes before we had cleared Centre Island, leaving it to starboard. Immediately we cleared the southern point of the island, Bob turned the raider south east towards the shoreline. The mixture of light rain and sea spray is running down my face but thankfully not impairing my vision at all. I can see the various entry points to the numerous coves and the rocky beach areas ahead. Most of them we must avoid at all cost because of the known hazards lurking just below the surface of the water.

Bob throttled the engine right back so it was purring as quietly as we could have it whilst still driving us forward to our designated landing point. I feel my own tension building and the tension in the boat, but everyone is alert, sharp and weapons are up. I put my balaclava back into a 'skull cap' mode so it's just sitting on top of my head like a small black tea cosy. I don't need anything accidently blocking my vision at this point. Nobody is talking now. Everyone is scanning the shoreline and listening for any sound.

The water is flat calm as we make our final approach to the sheltered cove we had been aiming for. Tom indicated to Bob to cut the engine by doing the fingers across the throat sign. The engine ceases its work for now and me and Jimmy have paddles in the water before it's silent. We continue to drive the boat forward with slow, powerful strokes. All we can hear now is the light wind that is ruffling our jackets and hoods and the fine rain that's making a swishing sound across the flat water.

The hull of the boat slaps gently against the water making hardly any sound and only small ripples roll away from each side as we move it slowly forward. With every heartbeat, I can see the shore getting closer, and us closer to our enemy. Bob has another oar off the back of the raider acting as a rudder and is guiding us gently toward the spot in the cove that we all have our eyes firmly fixed on now.

10

The hairs on the back of my neck, as usual when I find myself in these situations, begin to bristle and stand up. Significant levels of adrenalin are pumping through my veins and every sensor is in overdrive. This is potentially the worst possible point of the mission because if we are spotted now, totally exposed in an open boat, engine off and moving slowly, it would be like a turkey shoot. Unintentionally I take an extra hard stroke with the paddle just to get us in there that little bit faster.

'Stand by 10 seconds.' Bob whispered from the back of the boat.

The next sound is a dull thud and then shingle scraping on the bottom of the raider. We were on the Falkland Islands again. I follow Tom as the others bail out the other side and onto the small shingle beach. We spread out about 10 feet apart in a semi-circle around the front of the raider and take a few seconds to listen and search the darkness for any signs of life. Animal or human.

I check my watch, it's 0038. We had made good time and no sounds heard and no movements seen. We were good.

'Get your life jackets off and let's get the boat covered. We need to be geared up and on top of that ridge by 0050. I want to be off this beach in 12 minutes.' Tom said as quietly as he could so we could all hear him.

The raider was covered in five and all of us were geared up in another five. Tom led the way, then John, Jimmy, me and finally Bob. I was feeling the cold now and it was still raining. I'm sure the others must be feeling it too, but we had all been out in much worse so this was no time to be bitching about it. It was time to crack on.

'Harry, let's go find us some Argies.' Bob whispered in my ear.

There is definite excitement in his voice, but I think he is being a bit too keen for this stuff and I make a mental note to have a serious word with him when we get back. We clear the shingle beach quickly then it's a fast tab to the top of the hill. A well-worn animal track from bottom to top made the transition much easier. A few feet from the brow of the hill, we hit the deck.

A quick check of the watch again, it's 0100.

Tom inched forward to get a closer look at the terrain. We all are still and quiet, our eyes fully acclimatised to the dark and fixed on Tom. It still amazed me on cold, wet and gloomy nights like this one what the human eyes can make out. No need for night vision goggles yet.

One of the main things I had learned about the Falkland Islands, apart from its abundance of penguins, penguin shite and sheep, was that a constant westerly wind blows in at about a steady 15 knots or so on most days. A lot of the time it can be a hell of a lot worse than that. Other key items from the briefings that we had all attended over the past few weeks were that over the thousands of years of the Falkland Islands' existence, glaciations, wind and water erosion had stripped back the majority of the hill summits so they are now just outcrops of grey rock.

Their looks are deceiving though as most of them contain many crevices and gorges in which you can easily do yourself some damage. The existence of caves as well on the mounts were a concern as we knew from other intel that the Argies had dug in well and were using these for cover, and to store weapons and ammunition. Something to be keenly aware of when we approach our first planned observation point.

We also knew that on the days, when it came, the bright sunlight would light up the greens and yellows of the scrub grass of the moorlands and if we were not in good cover or dug in at the OP when that happened, we could be seen from miles away, and we would be fucked. The only cover from trees on these islands would be from the carefully cultured ones outside Government House in Stanley, which were no use to us right now.

The wind was beginning to pick up now, I can feel it on my face.

'Thank fuck we got ashore before the sea kicked up.' I said to Bob, who was now kneeling next to me.

'Yeah, it wouldn't have been fun with the weather against us. Let's hope we get the same good conditions on the way back.' He replied.

'Let's move out,' Tom's words were whipped away in the strengthening wind but we all heard him.

He was up and moving quickly, the rest of us on his tail. We set off over the hill and down a short slope to an open field. We are a 100 yards into the field when we hear something. We all stop dead. I screw my eyes up and focus hard.

Directly in front of us are large clumps of thick tussock grass just rustlings in the wind. I then hear the distinctive sound of squelching boots, John's quiet cursing is completely audible to all of us. He is only 10 feet from me so I can clearly see his huge feet sinking into the peat bog we had all just walked into.

'Get back,' whispered Tom. 'Let's move south to see if we can get away from this. Harry you take point.'

There was no need to respond verbally to Tom, eye contact had been enough. John was busy getting himself out of the bog with a hand from Bob and Jimmy as I took a quick bearing and headed south.

'Christ, what a fucking shithole.' Was the last thing I heard John say.

He was not happy but hopefully his feet would still be dry. His immediate next job would be to quickly check his boots for any stone cuts that could potentially let in water. That would be the last thing he would want so early into the job.

Some of the peat bogs on the islands had already thrown up a new hazard that lay just under the surface. These were hidden, deep, sharp ridges of stone that would cut through boots, tendons and down to the bone in a flash. That was another good reason we all needed the best boots on our feet right now. I hoped John had been lucky this time.

I led the team south along what could barely be described as a path through the long grass and stones. All the time just trying to keep us on the dry stuff. The intel we received from people who knew the islands had told us that the first mile or so inland from the landing beach was going to be like this, so it was just a case of head down and plough on.

It was still pitch dark, but we kept moving at a good steady pace even though the wind and rain were both getting much stronger and heavier. I had already seen first-hand what the weather could do down here. Standing in bright winter sunlight I had watched huge black clouds roll in across the moorlands and then in just a few minutes, dump heavy driving rain and sleet on everything in their paths. At least right now it was only rain and not the needle stabbing sleet that would really sting our faces and slow us down.

It also wasn't as cold as it could have been, but even so I pull my balaclava fully down over my face and as I looked back at the rest of the guys I could see they have all done the same. Collars were up on their anoraks with weapons cradled across their chests ready for action.

We were moving easily because the small bergens on our backs were relatively light and only contained enough rations, extra ammo and a few other essentials we needed for the couple of nights on the ground that we had planned for this job. My bergen weighed only about 30lbs in total rather than the usual that was anything from 60-100lbs. I was very glad about that right at this moment.

We tabbed along for another 40 minutes in almost complete silence. It was much easier going now because we were in flat open terrain but with the disadvantage of being very exposed. We needed to be in some cover before daybreak. Twice Tom stopped us en route just for a moment to take a bearing and to check that we were all happy.

'Harry, on my reckoning we need to be moving back north east as soon as we find a clear path. What do you think?' Tom asked.

'I agree.' I said and moved out again south, on point.

We stay on a southerly course for another 10 minutes and then turn northeast. 35 minutes later I had my first view of our target OP. I was sure it was the one but sometimes comparing the aerial photos from ground level in the dark can be a bit hit and miss.

I wasn't wrong.

'This is it. This would do us fine. We can hole up here for the day and then recon both the Rincon Grande and Horseshoe Bay settlements tonight.' Tom whispered in my ear as I stopped to take a final bearing.

With only 300 yards to go and no enemy contact so far, we were in good shape. I got a tap on the shoulder from Tom who pointed at Jimmy and then indicated he wanted him to come forward.

'Jimmy go and see if there is anyone around. You see the point just below that ridge.' Tom pointed to a large cluster of craggy rocks. 'That's where we need to be but keep your eyes peeled for mines. The Argies may have purposely laid some on the track or just slung a few anti-personnel ones out of a chopper just to cover the approaches to any high ground.' Tom whispered.

'OK Sarge.' Jimmy said.

He moved away crouched low to the ground, but at a quick pace. He reached the rocks within a minute. We could all see him clearly from where we had fanned out around the stop point. It would be almost impossible for anyone to see him from down the hill now that he was in the cover of the rocks. But there was always a risk the Argies had put some men up there even though earlier intel had said that shouldn't be the case.

Jimmy moved over the rocks slowly and carefully, weapon up in front of him and then sweeping it left to right and directly into the dark crevasses between the rocks. It took a couple more minutes before his search of the area was complete. When he was happy he gave the signal for the rest of us to come up and as dawn was close to breaking there wasn't time to hang around.

'Defensive positions now.' Tom gave the order as soon as we reached Jimmy. 'I am going to check out what we have here. John, Harry, find our best way out.'

Tom moved to a position where he could lie on a flat area behind a small group of rocks. This position was as good as it got for being able to look down on the Rincon Grande settlement and provided good weather cover at the same time. The main building in the small settlement was roughly 800 yards away and we could see it clearly across the open flat ground that stretched between us.

It was 0300 when I look over and see Tom lying flat between two rocks with his binoculars up to his eyes scanning the area below. John and I start to crawl east and west respectively along the natural paths between the rocks looking for ways to get away from this position and in a hurry if we needed to.

Our defensive and observation positions underneath a small rocky overhang were good, but the bad bit was the forty foot drop directly on the other side that stretched to our left and right about seventy yards each way. We would confirm those distances later when we had some more light, but we would definitely be needing ropes to get down there quickly, and in one piece.

The route we had taken to come up the hill was from the south west and had little or no cover for a daylight bugout. At night though it was easy ground to move over quickly towards to the cove and our hidden raider.

I use the NVG's to scan the bleak and windy landscape and I could see we had probably travelled half a mile further south than we needed to in order to get away from the peat bogs. But it had also taken us further away from the settlement itself and reduced the possibility of detection so I was happy with the route we had taken and the end result.

11

A couple of minutes later I am back learning against the rock I had left earlier and then I see John appearing through a gap in the rocks on his hands and knees. He was beside me a few seconds later.

'Harry, I think we are pretty much fucked if we have to leg it down the east side of the hill from this position. It's completely open ground and we would be cut to fucking pieces in seconds if anyone saw us,' he said.

'John, we are in the same boat if we head south and down the hill towards the settlement, it's open ground all the way.' I pause for a second and then continue. 'So we know the southern and eastern routes are out, the northern route is too, except by ropes, which we don't have. It has to be the way we came in, but I think we can cut the corner off a bit and save us an extra half a mile or so tab.' I said and finished briefing John.

'OK, let's go tell him.' John said as he rolled onto his knees and started to crawl towards Tom's position.

On our way over to Tom, I can see that Bob and Jimmy had got themselves into good positions overlooking the flanks, which were out of the direct force of the both the wind and driving rain that was now steadily coming at us. It only took a few seconds to brief Tom and he agreed immediately with our conclusion.

Tom pointed his finger as he spoke.

'OK, John I want you on my right with the GPMG just over there by that clump of rocks. Harry you stay here with me and take five now.'

We would all be spending the day taking turns to recce the Rincon Grande settlement, taking notes of anything we thought important so a few minutes' shuteye now was an opportunity not to be missed.

I got my first clear view of the Rincon Grande settlement at 0823 when I swapped position with Tom. It was fully light now.

I level the binoculars at the main wooden farmhouse building that had greyed significantly over the years from the beatings it had taken from the vicious South Atlantic weather.

A short distance to the south of the farmhouse was a large outbuilding topped with the usual red corrugated metal sheets that were commonplace all over the islands. Both the two main buildings and a small grey corrugated shed about twenty feet from the main farmhouse were sitting on top of a small hillock in about a five acre field.

At the bottom of the field, I can see an inlet and sheltered cove that is partially hidden by a few trees. All the tops of the trees are bent over at a ninety degree angle from the brutal force of the South Atlantic winds. We would have to check what is down there later although right now there doesn't seem to be any activity anywhere in the area.

I can see more buildings less than a mile away to the east and well away from the exposed shoreline. There are two main buildings constructed of stone blocks, or something similar, but still with the same red corrugated tin roofs as the other farm buildings. One of the buildings, and its tin roof in particular, is obviously much older than the others. The roof is a deep rust colour after many years' exposure to Falkland Islands weather.

The main farmhouse though looks new in every sense of the word with its freshly painted white walls and newly laid gravel track that weaved its way from the main road and around the several smaller buildings within the walled enclosure.

It is also the centre of activity for the few soldiers and men in blue overalls, who I assume are air mechanics, who frequently enter and exit the main farmhouse and a smaller building close by. My assumption about the blue overall brigade is based on them all congregating around the two very old-looking American built UH1B Hueys. Go for it Sherlock, I say to myself and I'm smiling at my own joke.

We would collate all this intel later and Tom would put the message together for Jimmy to hopefully send out on a short burst on the HF radio. If it worked.

I finish my stint watching the farmhouse and have the number of men, types of equipment and the main activities documented. There wasn't much here just a couple of old choppers and an estimated 25 men to guard, service and fly them. It was my time to get some scran down my neck, take a piss and maybe a shit. I hadn't decided yet. Definitely a priority though is another quick kip whilst the others are on stag. But before any of that I needed to check my feet and change socks. The last thing we needed was someone with a foot problem slowing us down and mine so far had stood up to the test pretty well even though they had taken a good beating in the last month.

It's 1428 and I'm all sorted and in good shape. John tells me the day so far has also gone by without any dramas. The only concern is no one has seen any civilians and we would have expected to see them here.

'Harry, I don't think the civilians are locked up there.' Tom said as we studied the rough map of the Rincon Grande settlement cobbled together by islanders.

'I didn't see anyone other than Argies enter or leave any of the buildings.' I said to Tom.

John settled down next to us.

'Maybe they have been moved to Stanley, or somewhere else, to be used as shields.' He said thoughtfully.

We had received sketchy intel that some people were probably being moved from the outer settlements to Port Stanley for this reason. Not confirmed but a definite possibility.

'The cowardly bastards have probably got them strapped to the Argie guns that are on the streets of Stanley.' John sneered with some venom in his voice.

Our notes confirmed there were around 25 Argies whose sole job seemed to be looking after the Hueys although most of the day nothing much happened because of the weather. It had rained all day, not really heavily, but the wind had blown consistently hard so they had taken every opportunity to get back inside the warm and dry of the commandeered farmhouse. There was no way this lot would be going out on any foot patrols in this weather tonight, we agreed unanimously.

12

At 1533 it all changed when we observed a truck full of professional looking Argie combat troops arrive at the farmhouse. We deduced they were probably marines from their kit as they left the vehicle. The truck had trundled very slowly down the main rough gravel road trying to avoid the potholes and the sharp edges of rocks littering the side of it. Contact with these could shred or puncture a tyre in seconds.

Once the truck was safely onto the new gravel track it picked up speed and eventually came skidding to a halt in the farmyard. A man who was clearly a senior officer jumped out of the cab of the truck and was soon standing beside it bolt upright with his hands on his hips. Were these Buzo Tactico, the Argentine Special Forces we wanted to find I asked myself.

The man with his hands on his hips was a Colonel we thought, from the epaulets on his jacket, although his rank wasn't definite at this range, but a good shout I thought. He immediately started shouting something at the young Lieutenant we had spotted earlier. He and a few other men had legged it from the farmhouse as soon as the truck had been seen.

The Colonel was a short stocky man and was obviously very irate about something. After much waving of arms, shouting and what we could only assume was a great deal of cursing and swearing, the little shit gave the young Lieutenant a hard slap on his right cheek. The force of the blow caused the young guy to go down on one knee. Just for a moment. He quickly brought himself back up to attention, saluted the senior officer, turned and ran quickly back into the farmhouse.

'Fucking little shit,' John muttered under his breath.

He was watching the unfolding scene too and obviously had the same thoughts as me. Tom fixed his binoculars on the huge NCO that walked up to Colonel 'Bully Boy' at the same time as I did. Both of us saw the crooked wry smile that had curled across his fat lips and the visible scar that ran backwards a couple of inches towards his neck from just below the right corner of his mouth. The Sergeant had another deep and ugly scar above his right eye that finished off his mean bastard looks. This guy was as big as John, maybe bigger, from this range it was hard to tell. That would be one hell of a scrap if those two got to it, I pondered for a moment.

'Shrapnel or knife wounds?'

Tom said looking at me as he knew I had also pinged this guy's face.

'Knife,' I said, 'too straight a line for shrapnel.'

Frenzied activity broke out all around the farmyard. The blue overalled men we had occasionally seen throughout the day casually ambling around the place were now running out of the farmhouse in all directions with the young Lieutenant standing by the door barking orders at them.

It would have been quite a comical sight in another situation as most of the men were in various states of partial dress as obviously the order had been to move their arses and move them fucking quickly. Benny Hill would have been proud of the scene.

Several ran towards one of the helicopters, others to a trolley with a bunch of equipment on it. Four men were now pushing a couple of 45 gallon drums of what had to be fuel towards the chopper and two further men behind them were carrying a manual fuelling pump. Most of these men became wet and would be freezing in seconds due to their state of dress, but I doubted the new arrivals and particularly the 'Bully Boy' Colonel would be worrying about that.

The Lieutenant ushered 'Bully Boy' towards the farmhouse, but interestingly his men had clearly split up into two distinctive groups. I counted 10 standing at the back of the truck getting lashed by the wind and rain, but the other three plus the Sergeant followed the officers inside the farmhouse.

I watched the group that was left by the truck closely and it was obvious there was some resentment and hostility towards those who had gone inside. I didn't need to hear words, the body language and gestures said it all.

13

A larger group of airmen and soldiers were now scurrying around one of the Hueys, obviously refuelling and checking the systems. One man was already in the pilot's seat, flicking switches and twiddling the dials. The co-pilot was also strapped in looking closely at the map spread out on his lap.

Tom nudged me and pointed his finger towards the other Huey. I could see the engine cover was off and three mechanics were frantically using wrenches and other tools to free something. Moments later one of the mechanic's hands was filled with something that looked like a pump.

I can't tell exactly what it was as I'm not too well up on the mechanics of choppers, but it was a fair guess. I watched as three other mechanics removed the same piece from the Huey that was obviously getting ready to fly. The exchange of parts happened quickly and within minutes they were fastening down the outer engine casing and signalling to the pilot to fire it up.

Immediately the signal had been given the rotors began to turn slowly, building up to full speed 20 seconds later. The thumbs up came from the pilot directed towards the senior NCO mechanic who had just closed up the casing. He was one of the few who had managed to get his kit on and I could clearly see his epaulettes denoting his rank of Sergeant.

He turned and ran towards the farmhouse and quickly disappeared inside. Within a minute the young lieutenant, Bully Boy, Sergeant Scarface and the three other soldiers moved quickly over the soggy ground to board the fully flashed up Huey. I saw the Colonel wave his hand towards the pilot and seconds later the Huey was in the air and moving away from the farmhouse and our position.

I doubted anyone in the Huey would bother to acknowledge the young Lieutenant, the NCO, or the men who were not given any chance to retreat from the Huey before lift-off and were now being severely buffeted by the downdraft from the rotors and being sprayed by the freezing muddy water that had pooled below it.

The helicopter moved off south west towards the waters of Port Salvador and the Teal Inlet settlement and was out of sight in less than a minute as it climbed into the mist. The fading twapp twapp twapp noise of the rotor blades disappeared shortly after our last sight of it.

The Argie Sergeant who had been left standing by the side of the truck raised his right arm, put his left hand flat over the top of his right bicep and extended his middle finger as far as he could. It was directed towards the departing Huey, which did raise a small smile from the three of us who were watching.

The journey for Bully Boy and his cronies to Teal Inlet would only take a couple of minutes by air if that was where they were going. It would have taken a good hour or more by truck using the dodgy roads and over the rough terrain. The only other way would have been by boat from Horseshoe Bay, our destination later tonight, but I was pretty sure the slap happy Argie Rupert wouldn't have gone for that option at all.

The young Lieutenant walked over towards the remainder of the men who had arrived earlier. Most of them were huddled inside the back of the truck now except for a couple standing next to the finger raising Sergeant. He brought himself to attention smartly and saluted as the two men came together. He stood easy shortly after this and we could he was listening to what the young officer was saying. None of it animated, no arms waving or slapping going on this time, just some clear orders being given.

There was a quick nod of the head by the Sergeant, followed by a salute. He then walked round to the back of the truck and spoke to his men huddled up against the increasingly inclement weather. I watched as they all exited the truck, the last one clipping down the end canvas flap to stop any more rain getting in and soaking the inside. By the time the last man had finished securing the truck, the Sergeant and Lieutenant had made it to the farmhouse door.

These men looked a demoralised bunch as they trudged towards the farmhouse, but all saluted the young officer as they entered the building. The young officer was the last man to go in. The soldiers and airmen under the Lieutenant's command soon followed the others into the building after squaring away all the kit they had used to sort out the Huey.

Lucky bastards, I thought to myself, I wouldn't have minded getting in there for a bit. It was getting a bit damp, to say the least, and fucking cold squatting down on these craggy sharp rocks. I couldn't think of too many worse places that I had been holed up in recent years so I would be glad to get moving later, just to get warmer.

It stayed quiet for the rest of the afternoon, all of us getting some more rest, food and doing all the other things we needed to.

'We will move around 2200, I want to get down to the bay, get the intel, and back here into some decent cover before dawn tomorrow, OK?'

'OK Tom,' I replied with nods of agreement coming from the others gathered close by.

Jimmy managed to get a quick burst off on the HF about the two Hueys, telling base one of them had gone and the other was unserviceable. The final burst sent details about the 25 soldiers and airmen we had been watching all day, and the new arrivals. Our full report would contain all the stuff on Bully Boy.

Darkness came and brought with it even more of a chill wind.

'Bob you have the coordinates, are you good to lead us down to the bay?' Tom asked.

'Yes Sarge.' Bob answered.

'John you're behind Bob, then you Jimmy, then me, Harry you are on rear guard.' Tom's instructions were clear and we all understood.

Our kit was stowed away in our hidden bergens. Any signs that we had been there were cleared away, even our shite was carefully wrapped up in cling film and then inside a tough sealable plastic bag. No one needed any of that leaking out onto the rest of your kit.

We moved off without another word. Bob headed off down the east side of the hill that had been our home for the past 19 hours. There were a couple of steep bits to negotiate and it was very slippery in places, especially on the flat wet rocks. We made it down to the flat ground though without any real dramas. I check my watch, it was 2230. Bob picked up the pace immediately. It was just over five miles to the objective so we had planned for a couple of hours of stealthy tabbing, keeping the occupied buildings on our right, whilst giving them a wide berth at the same time. Keeping our eyes and ears open in the gloom of the night was never so important as it was now.

Once at Horseshoe Bay the plan was to do a couple of hours recon to see if there was any Argie activity around there. If there was nothing going on we would backtrack to our rocky home and hole up there for one more day. Then we would exit the way we had come in and pray for calm weather so we could get back out to Brilliant on time.

Bob kept up a good pace and did a great job getting us within a mile of the objective in just over two hours. We initially headed off east keeping a good distance between us and the buildings at Rincon, then headed due south for just over half a mile. The tab wasn't too difficult because the ground was pretty flat in most places with only small undulations that did their bit to keep us out of direct view of anybody that could be awake and looking in this direction, which was unlikely.

The main problem right now is no cover at all, we are in the open so we need to get in and out again fast with the intel and then more importantly get back to our OP in the rocks and cover before sunrise. I check my watch again, it's 0048.

Tom raised his hand and stops us just as we were about to cross the main road that led back up to the Rincon Grande settlement.

'OK, not far now,' he said, 'you all know what to do so let's get in and out of there quickly and back to the OP before first light.'

A few quick nods and Tom was happy that we understood. He moved off in the lead now. Bob tucked in close behind him as they both moved quickly over the road and into another field of dense grasses on the other side. Bob's orders were to shadow Tom and not be out of his sight at any point in time.

As we close in on the bay we fan out, get low and then begin to crawl across the ground. It wasn't long before the wet and cold of the sodden peaty ground beneath me gets right into my bones. I see a small undulation in the ground immediately before the farm buildings, which would provide us with some minimal cover once we get there. Anything is better than nothing right now. The two main buildings have a few sturdy trees behind them that have purposely been put there to act as windbreaks. Better cover for later, if we need it.

I crawl along driving my sturdy boots into the squelching ground pushing it backwards and used my free arm on the big clumps of tussock grass to help me move forward. I can hear the rest of the guys close by all doing the same. I glance over to my right and can make out a couple of prone figures keeping their heads down and using the thick tussock grass as cover whenever they could. It has been pitch black all the way up to this point with low cloud cover cutting out the moonlight and the stars. On clear nights, they do seem to shine brighter here than in the UK but of course there are a lot less than the 25 million cars on the roads, which probably helps a bit. I mull over in a fraction of a second.

I hear it now and feel it. The wind is getting stronger building in its intensity, as it had been threatening to do ever since we left the OP. The cloud cover would be gone in minutes. Not a good scenario for us.

Within two minutes, we are bathed in bright moonlight that exposes the open rolling slopes and barren fields that we have been crawling over for the past 20 minutes. Everybody freezes, listens and looks around for each other. I see we are spread out over a fifty yard radius, all lying prone except for John who was leaning on one elbow on my right peering into the distance.

'This way,' John said pointing, 'there's a ditch 100 feet away just by the wire fence over there. Let's go.'

No one needed to be told twice and as soon as the others saw me and John move, they were with us. We covered the ground between us and the ditch quickly and quietly, everyone avoiding being tripped up by the thick lumps of tussock grass. A minute later and I am squatting down in the ditch John spotted with everyone else.

The ditch was about four feet deep and ran for about 50 feet before tapering back up to the level of the field we had just come across. It was definitely man made as some of the sides were very square. It looked like it had been dug some time ago because the grass and vegetation had grown back covering the inside so that it just blended back into the landscape.

We are only 500 yards from a large outbuilding that was less than 50 feet from the main farmhouse. Horseshoe Bay farm and all its outbuildings looked even more battered from the elements in real life. The old aerial photos we had been given must have been taken a fair few years ago.

Tom had the binos out scanning the area. So far there was no movement, no sounds or any signs of life, except for a few sheep sleeping in the field on this side of the main house. Where are the dogs? All these places have dogs for rounding up the sheep. As I look closer around the farm, as well as not seeing any dogs, I can't see any chickens, ducks, geese or any fowl. I can't hear them either, they can't all be sleeping. Maybe they are all inside their coops that I hadn't seen yet. No doubt we will find out in a minute. It is unerringly quiet though especially as there are about 15,000 extra 'visitors' on the islands right now and most of them are walking around with bad attitudes and big fuck off guns.

Where are the Goss family who should be living here? I ask myself. I hope they are fit, well and inside. 30 feet away there is one of those pig friendly domed shelters with an open end so that they can just come and go when they please. I was getting a good whiff of it now. A rustling sound close by startles me, my heart rate leaps up and adrenaline surges through my body, my weapon instantly pointing in the direction of the noise.

The flap was over as fast as it had started when a very healthy big fat sow stuck her head out of the shelter and looked straight at us. We didn't move and thankfully she wasn't that interested in the five heads peering over the ditch with blacked up faces and guns pointing at her. She gave us a short snort and backed into her cosy shelter. I take a long deep breath.

We then hear the thump of many pounds of plump pig flesh hitting the deck and after a few rustling noises she settled down again for more sleep. Not much was going to worry her tonight although I wondered if the Argies had already killed the rest of her mates for food and that this little lady was going to get it next. That would mean at some point someone would be coming back here, but not at this time of the morning, we could be fairly confident of that.

14

'This fucking light is killing us but I can see some cloud coming in from the west so we might get lucky. It looks like it's coming over from the Kings Ridge area so it won't be long.' Tom looked down again and pointed to an area on the map just south west of Salvador before carrying on. 'We need to move and get on with the job but I think we will give it another minute or two to see what that weather does.'

There was a collective nod, but it was a long three minutes until the cloud cover was over us again but not enough to completely block out all the moonlight. There was still enough light to see across the fields towards the buildings, which was not ideal for us, but we would have to make do. None of us had heard anything from the house or from anywhere else for that matter, apart from an occasional grunt from Gladys in her pig house.

'John, Jimmy, you go left and check out those silver corrugated sheds and the rusty building to the right of them,' Tom said as he pointed directly at them over the top of the ditch. 'Then move up to that other shed to check if anything is going on in there.' 'Harry, Bob, you are with me, we are going to check out that other building and the main farmhouse. RV in 20 minutes by that lone corrugated shed furthest to the right of the farmhouse.' Tom was pointing again so no one had any doubts.

The faint moonlight was still bathing the field so I can easily see a couple more pig shelters in front of us. The one Tom was pointing to was a good 400 yards from our current position and was on the east side of all the buildings. It was a much rustier and older version of the newer one that was housing Gladys. It would also be easy to get over the brow of the hill and out of sight quickly from there. Suddenly it went a lot darker. It was time to move.

John and Jimmy got to the first barn quickly. Tom, Bob and I are moving fast across open ground praying no one is going to get eyes on us. We keep a good distance from the farm building in front of us and get to another wire fence just by the main track leading down to the house. It's still very quiet. We then head straight towards the pig shelter close to the RV point. I got to the space behind the pig shelter first and was now only 30 feet from the side of the main farmhouse. Bob slid in quietly next to me seconds later.

Tom had gone straight to the back wall of the corrugated shed and was now crouching down next to it sheltering from the raw wind. He beckoned us over with his left hand, whilst clutching his M16 tightly with the other. It didn't take a few seconds to establish that the shed was empty. Good choice for the RV.

The three of us moved silently towards the main house, trying to avoid the various bits of debris that were scattered all around the side of the building. There were rotten and broken pallets, bits of old wood, fencing posts, birds' nests of wire, that would never be untangled in a million years, and bits of old Land Rovers. The absolute vehicle of choice on the islands. All were noise hazards and could have fucked us up if we got too close to them. We didn't.

I stop by the front porch and apart from the sound of the wind it was deathly quiet. No other sounds of any kind and no lights. Tom got to a window first and peered in through a crack in the blinds. I move to the next window along moments later and then have a perfect view of the devastation inside because the blinds and curtains had both been ripped down.

The place is in a hell of a mess, cabinet drawers are pulled out and the contents spilled everywhere. The settee is overturned and cushions are strewn across the floor, ornaments and glasses are smashed and the main mirror over the fireplace has two large cracks across the whole length of it.

Bob moved in next to Tom and through another gap in the blinds looked down what was the main hallway of the house. When I got there and looked for myself it was just a continuation of the wanton destruction I had seen in the lounge, walls had holes kicked in them, pictures and photo frames were smashed and coats and other bits of clothing were discarded on the floor.

'Why would they smash up the place like this? Where is the family? We need to get in there and take a closer look, I pretty sure no one's here.' Tom whispered.

Bob made it to the front door first. It was slightly ajar and had been kicked in judging by the broken lock and wood splinters on the right of the frame. Bob put his ear close to the door, out of the wind now, and listened for any movement.

Hearing nothing he slowly pushed the door open just wide enough to get through it. His weapon up and ready at his shoulder as he moved around the door and quickly over to the left side of the room towards the main hallway. I am right behind him, my weapon in the same place as his, my eyes moving steadily from left to right scanning every corner and every piece of upturned furniture, just in case someone had heard or seen us coming and were hiding ready to let rip into us.

Bob moved past the first downstairs rooms making his way to the end of the corridor ahead of me. I quietly open the door to the first room on my left. It was the only room with the door closed. I'm in scanning quickly for any signs of life, my SLR still up, tight into my shoulder and pointing directly in front of me.

Tom was close behind me, covering my back.

'Clear.' I whispered.

We back out and then do the same routine on the remaining three rooms. Nothing.

'Clear.'

It was Bob I heard as he came back into the hallway through the back door after clearing the garden.

'You need to come and see this.'

He said as he relaxed his weapon a little.

Tom and I follow Bob into the last room he had cleared before doing the garden. We walk into what I assume is the main bedroom. Painted on one of the walls in big red letters is unmistakably; 'HELP US.'

Someone had tried to deface the words and ripped off some of the wallpaper but had not been very thorough or successful. This room, as with all the others, had been ransacked and looted by the Argies, and quite recently by the look of it. The significant number of still damp muddy boot prints on the dirty cream coloured bedroom carpet told that story.

I heard a noise coming from the direction of the front door.

'Move.' I try to whisper but not very well.

Tom was out in the corridor first and I am right behind him. I drop to one knee aiming my SLR directly at the front door. Tom is next to me in the same position. Bob is standing directly behind us.

'Firefly.' 'Firefly.' Was the whispered call from the front door.

Everyone relaxed, it is the agreed friendly code word for this mission and it meant John and Jimmy were coming into the house. None of us wanted any blue on blues today as all of us knew about the friendly fire incidents that had happened shortly after the main landings. It had not been a surprise to anyone with the sheer volume of soldiers hitting the ground at the same time and the majority never being in this type of operational theatre before.

John spoke as he reached us.

'We saw you coming into the house from the barn. There's nobody around. The family have been taken away somewhere, and by force, from the look of this place.'

No one disagreed with him.

'OK, we need to get this intel back,' said Tom. 'There is no real concentration of troops here and most likely it is because they are not expecting us to come through this way. They are more likely to be concentrating their forces closer to Stanley now.'

Tom removed his small writing book and pencil from his jacket pocket as he finished talking ready to jot down some notes.

'It could be an option though if we could chopper in enough guys to this point, or even a bit further south at the Port Louis or Green Patch settlements. That's of course if it's the same scenario as this place and to be fair those 25 boys up the road and their one serviceable Huey are not going to cause us too much of a problem are they.' I surmised out loud.

'Time is getting on,' Tom said, 'give me a minute to get this intel down on paper and then we'll get the fuck out of here and back to the OP at Rincon Grande.'

Two minutes later and we had every detail down in the book ready for Jimmy to communicate over the HF radio later. Tom spoke directly to Bob.

'Get us back to the OP quickly Bob, I'm worried about the light.'

'OK boss,' Bob replied and headed for the front door.

I had to smile. Sometimes I didn't know what to do with him. 'OK boss,' what the fuck was that. He must think he is in an Al Capone gangster movie or something. God am I going to take the piss out of him later.

15

I am the last to exit the front door after John, Jimmy and Tom. It is 0320. I turn left and follow Bob across the yard to the RV point by the corrugated shed. We move straight away and keep low using whatever cover we can before we hit the open ground. Bob has already picked up the route and we are heading back the way we came in.

Thankfully the cloud cover is still with us and it actually seems to be getting darker. We tab along at a good pace confident there was no one behind us at Horseshoe Bay to compromise us. The chilling wind eased a bit, but the fine drizzle started again and was now driving straight into our faces.

We skirted around the couple of watery inlets and got to the brow of a hill half a mile away from Horseshoe in just under 15 minutes. Once over it we were out of sight of the farmhouse and barns and back to being completely exposed in the open fields.

We still had a couple of hours of darkness to get ourselves back to the OP and into the cover of the rocks. Jimmy could get a HF radio burst off as soon as we were back and then all of us could settle down to watch the boys fiddle with their other helicopter, or not as the case may be, especially if it was still raining.

Bob was doing a great job keeping us on route and getting us over the lumpy and sometimes very soggy ground. It was tough going though and we weren't moving as quickly as any of us would have liked. All of us are soaked to the skin and getting cold even with all the hard exercise from the tab.

An hour and twenty minutes later it's still pitch dark but my night vision is fully tuned in so I can see all the guys ahead of me spread out over 50 feet in a line. Bob stopped and signalled for us to look ahead using two fingers to his eyes and then to the target. Ahead I can make out a few faint lights coming from the farm buildings of Rincon Grande. We head off again keeping the lights at a thousand yards or so to the west of us as we tab steadily north towards the OP. It's not far now.

'Shit,' I said out loud.

Everyone stopped dead in their tracks. We all can hear it now. A chopper was definitely heading our way. We couldn't see it yet, but the noise was getting louder by the second as it closed in on our position. I pressed the button to illuminate the face of my watch. It was 0526.

What the fuck is it doing coming back at this hour. I angrily ask myself. It was only through frustration as I know that we are less than a mile from the relative safety of our OP hideaway in the rocks.

'Fuck it, get down, find some cover if you can,' Tom shouted.

We had already broken the line formation and were spreading out left and right before Tom had given the order.

I scan the surrounding area but cannot see anything that will give me decent cover. I hit the deck where I am. I have no other options. My heart is definitely trying to get the fuck out of my chest. I need to breathe slower. Calm down. I need to breathe.

'Fuck it clam down,' I say out loud.

The only thing I can do is tuck myself in hard against one the biggest lumps of tussock grass I can find. I'm lying on my back hoping my face is still as black as it was when we started tonight, my SLR is by my side, ready to go. I pile as much grass and clumps of earth as I managed to rip up in 20 seconds over my body. I think most of it is covered.

I instantly feel like I'm lying in a cold bath with my kit on as the sodden ground instantly soaks through everything I'm wearing trying to chill my body and bones even further. Not that any of this mattered now because if we are compromised it would be a turkey shoot in this open ground, and we would be the turkeys.

I am pretty sure it's a Huey because of the distinctive twaaping sound of the rotor blades. I always think of the 4077th M.A.S.H when I hear them. I would be smiling at the thought of Hawkeye getting up to no good if I wasn't shitting myself right now.

If it's the Huey from Rincon Grande I know I saw the men in blue overalls loading a hefty 7.6mm FN MAG Argentine-built machine gun onboard. I also clocked the gun mount for it just inside the right hand door.

It is another 30 seconds before I see the full silhouette of the chopper. It was a Huey. It was not flying particularly fast, but it was low. A hundred and fifty feet maybe. Surprisingly the men in blue had not disconnected the flashing red light on its underbelly, or the pilot had just fucked up and left it on, which enabled me to gauge its height. There were no lights on inside the Huey's cabin, just a low hue of green reflecting on the pilot's helmets from the dials on the main console.

It flew past me roughly 80 feet to my left. The downdraft from the blades blowing about the loose grass I had ripped up to cover me and spraying me with freezing smelly bog water at the same time. I could make out the shapes of men and their weapons inside. It looked pretty full in the back. I knew that five had gone out on it so I could assume that would probably be the minimum coming back.

I breathed a huge sigh of relief as I'm sure Tom and the rest of the guys would also be doing as I watched the Huey continue on its course towards Rincon Grande. I really thought we had got away with it, but my relief was short lived.

The Huey pulled up about 300 hundred yards past us and went into hover. My heart is banging against my chest again now as I watch it turn to face our position. I can see John on his belly staring directly at the Huey, his weapon locked and loaded and ready to blast the fuck out of that old chopper if it came any closer.

The sound from the rotor blades intensified as it very slowly began to move towards us. John hold your fire for a minute don't give us away just yet. I'm willing the words in my head to reach him. The Huey was only a 100 yards away now and heading straight for John's position. He had gone to ground 20 feet in front of me and about 60 feet on my left so would have been almost directly in its original flight path.

They must have seen him.

I check my weapon again. I am ready. So are Tom and Jimmy whom I can see roughly 30 feet in front of me. If the shit hits the fan we all knew what we had to do and that was to get as many rounds into that Huey as fast as we could. Bob was on his belly now tucked up behind a decent sized lump of tussock grass 20 feet in front of the others. He was using it to steady his left arm after wrapping the strap of his sniper rifle around it. The rifle barrel was pointing directly at the pilot's head.

No one moved a muscle even when the downdraft from the rotors started to blow away more of the sparse camouflage that we had all torn from the ground. The Huey's search light was blinding when it came on illuminating a vast area beneath it and even though it hadn't directly highlighted any of us I was sure it wasn't going to stay like that, especially for John and me.

Immediately the light began to sweep left and then right, the nose of the Huey following the sweep of light until it was head on to me. I would be in the light in a few seconds. I grip my SLR tighter ready to let rip.

The only bit of luck we had had so far was that the searchlight had come on behind where Tom, Jimmy and Bob were lying so if a fire fight started the Huey's passengers would be getting one hell of a wake-up call, which hopefully would put them off their aim long enough to give me and John the time to get into them with some rounds of our own, if we hadn't done so already.

The hairs on the back of my neck were bristling good and proper now. Every muscle was tense, adrenalin pumping through my veins, I'm scared but ready to go.

Suddenly we are pitched into darkness again. As quickly as the light had come on, it went off. I couldn't see anything for a moment as I had been temporarily blinded by the intensity of the Huey's searchlight even though it hadn't been directly in my face. The noise above me was deafening as the Huey hovered 80 feet directly above me. I couldn't tell if the side doors had opened or see if anyone was hanging out, but I had no doubts that Tom would make the right call if he saw anything threatening.

The silhouetted Huey turned away slowly heading south. 50 feet away the searchlight came back on again for a couple of seconds and then off again. Several seconds later it did the same again but this time it stayed on for a bit longer before shutting down. Fucking strange I thought. They had us bang to rights. Something was not right in that chopper.

The Huey moved further away from us and then started to sweep left and then right about 200 yards south east of our position. It then did a couple of passes up and down an imaginary 100 yard line, all the time moving further away from us. There was no point moving. There was no better cover to be had anywhere close by so we all stayed put and watched the Huey doing its stuff.

The searchlight began to flicker, then it was on, then off, then it flickered on again for a couple of seconds. Then it was off. I silently hoped it had given up the ghost completely.

The Huey was three hundred yards away when it went into a hover. In the early morning gloom, the silhouette of the Huey could be seen clearly as it hovered for about 20 seconds before finally banking away and heading towards the Rincon Grande settlement. It would only take them a minute, or two at most, and they would be on the ground.

My night sight was recovering as we all huddled together.

'I know I saw three heads in the cockpit of the Huey just before it turned away.' Tom said.

'And I saw a very animated arm in the middle pointing at the console and then poking one of the pilots repeatedly.' Jimmy finished off.

I would put money on that it was our friendly fucking Argie Colonel, I thought. We had been lucky but were not out of it yet.

'Let's move.' said Tom.

We didn't need telling twice, we were up and legging it full on with Tom in the lead. We needed to get as far away as possible from the point of contact as we could. If they had got wind of a contact they most likely didn't land because they wouldn't know the size or strength of the potential force below them. I also suspected Bully Boy would want to have the odds stacked in his favour and to be at the rear of any engagement with enemy forces. Standard SOP for any Bullies.

We keep low and move as fast as we can, tabbing hard through the drizzle and cold wind that hadn't let up since we left the farmhouse in Horseshoe Bay. I am sweating buckets, but I know it's not far to go now. Fifteen minutes later and totally knackered we carefully make our way up the east side of the hill that we had left several hours earlier.

We had added an extra mile or so on the tab to reach the foot of the hill. Tom had taken us much further east away from the settlement. This was completely the right thing to do, as common sense and good training dictates you would never take a direct route from the point of contact to the place you were originally heading for. The SOP would also say we shouldn't have gone back to the original OP. We had no choice though, there was nothing else around that would give us any cover for miles, except for these rocks. The Argies would have a field day if they caught us in open ground in daylight, we wouldn't stand a chance. No, we would take our chances here, at least from this position we could take a few of them out before they got to us.

16

The Rincon Grande settlement is lit up like a Christmas tree below us. Every light must have been burning and there is a ton of activity going on. I have got myself tucked back into a good position where I can focus my binoculars on the two helicopters that are now bathed in bright light. It has also finally stopped raining for a minute so I can ditch my hood whilst I have a good look. There are several air mechanics beavering around an uncovered Huey, one man is underneath obviously doing something to the searchlight, others were refuelling and pouring liquids into other orifices and containers on the old helicopter. Two men are cleaning the front cockpit windows and two others had taken off both doors to allow the gun mounts to be loaded up with two heavy calibre machine guns. Several more boxes of ammunition were being loaded as the pilots exited the house and started running back towards the Huey.

The Argie Colonel followed shortly after with his Sergeant walking closely on his right and the young Lieutenant on his left. The majority of the air mechanics had finished their jobs and were backing away by the time they got to the Huey, all except for the man underneath who was still trying to fix the searchlight. Another mechanic was inside the cockpit leaning in between the pilots' seats. I assumed he was there to flick the switches when asked to.

Standing in front of the Huey the pilot was not a happy man, his body language said it all. He could see his searchlight was still not working and Colonel bully boy and his nasty scar-faced Sergeant were now only 30 feet away. He began shouting something and gesticulating wildly at the man in the cockpit. When he obviously didn't get the right answer he physically manhandled the poor man out of the open door and threw him to the ground.

The airman didn't hang around and scurried away as fast as his feet would take him. The pilot was quickly in his seat flicking something up and down frantically in the cockpit, but it all felt a bit too late from my vantage point as our stocky little friend and his henchman arrived at the helicopter. Heated words were obviously exchanged with the man on the ground. A stubby finger thrust forward into the man's face. More words but the wrong answer must have been given because Bully Boy put two hefty kicks into the man's ribcage. Tom was silently watching everything beside me. Neither of us was in any doubt that Bully Boy had inflicted a lot of pain on the mechanic with his feet. The man's face was contorted with pain, but he immediately went back under the nose of the Huey and carried on working on the searchlight.

I didn't like this fucking man at all and I wasn't even on the end of his beatings. Unfortunately, or fortunately, the boot had the right effect from the Bully Boy's perspective because seconds later the search light came on.

'Bollocks that's not what we need.' I said to Tom next to me.

The pilot switched it on and off several times then left it on permanently whilst the mechanic secured the panel that had been removed to sort out the repair. The pilot fired up the engines and got the rotor blades turning whilst the Huey loaded up with six marines and scarface. The poor guy underneath was hardly out from under the thing when the Huey rose into the air and turned immediately south towards what was our position 30 minutes ago.

The searchlight was on permanently now.

The military truck that had been idling for a few minutes close by was fully loaded with the remainder of the marines and some of the original soldiers from the settlement. The Colonel and the young Lieutenant were in the front seats of the truck as it pulled away and headed off down the road in the same direction as the Huey.

Jimmy got the message away just before Tom called us together.

'We haven't got enough time to get back to the beach. It will be daylight shortly and if they find any sign where we went to ground, that Huey will be out all day sweeping the open plains. My decision is we stick it out here today as per the plan and then get back to the raider tonight as soon as it's dark. We'll take the shorter most direct route this time.'

It was the right call, we all knew there were big risks staying here, but Tom was right, we had no choice.

'If they come up here and it has to get noisy, we will just have to kill them all and get the fuck out of here, OK?'

No one needed to answer Tom we all knew what we had to do and as no more talking was required we all slipped away to take up our defensive positions.

17

Everyone was alert waiting to see if the Huey, or the truck, came our way. I couldn't see the Huey's searchlight because of the low cloud and fine rain that has descended on us during the past few minutes, or maybe, if we were lucky, the searchlight had failed again.

I wouldn't want to be in that mechanic's shoes if it had. Scarface and that other nasty fucker would definitely be giving him a good shoeing if it had.

The Huey came back into view; it was searching the ground in the slow sweeping movements as it had earlier. It looked like it was right on the spot where we had nearly been compromised but so far it wasn't venturing our way. Long may that continue.

Tom kept low as he made his way around the team quietly giving instructions. He got to me last.

'Harry, you take the first watch with Bob. I want all of us to get some rest if we can because we will need to move our arses tonight and we also need to be sharp. I don't want to be around here for a minute longer than we have to so we will be off as soon as it's dark.'

'Tom, no worries, I'm with you on that,' I replied.

'Thanks Harry, John will relieve you at 0900.'

Tom moved away to a position behind one of the few substantial rocks close to Bob. From there they had good views both up and down the East and West side of the hill. The South side of the hill looked directly down towards the farm house at Rincon Grande. I had that covered.

Tom decided we wouldn't put anyone on the cliff side as no one was going to get up there without a rope or without making a shed load of noise. Jimmy had also discovered a small cave on the cliff side that provided some decent shelter from the wind and rain. We would all be taking advantage of that at some point today so that side was covered as well.

The morning passed without incident. I had expected the Huey to come back at least once to re-fuel, but even that didn't happen. I talked to Bob about it and we both thought it had probably gone over to Stanley or one of the other big settlements to fuel up and maybe get some fresh pilots.

The Argie military truck reappeared at 1300. I heard it before I saw it pull into the farmyard. A very sorry looking bunch of soldiers and airmen slowly got out the back of it. Their body language said it all. They were cold, wet and totally fucked off. They had probably been shouted and screamed at by the Bully Boy for hours. He was nowhere to be seen.

The young lieutenant exited the truck's cab and then was obviously telling the men to get into the farmhouse, from his arm gesture. They shuffled along in twos and threes through the rain barely able to drag themselves to the farmhouse door. No one hurried as they couldn't get any wetter or colder.

Bully Boy didn't appear.

Everyone was awake now, switched on and watching the activities taking place in the farmyard. The young lieutenant was following the last of his men towards the farmhouse when he suddenly stopped. All of us are watching him intensely. He turned slowly and looked directly at our hill and the clump of rocks we were hiding in. It felt like he was looking directly at me.

In a split second, we all buried ourselves further into the ground, crevasses and holes that had been our homes for the past few hours. It was an instantaneous reaction honed from all the training and the crappy holes we had all been in on stags in Londonderry, Armagh and many other places in Northern Ireland.

One thing that my two tours of Northern Ireland had taught me was that if you think someone is going to get eyes on you, get your fucking head down quick and move as soon as you can. The alternative is to take the fucker down there and then if you can and then shift your arse. I raise my head slowly to peer through a tiny crack between two rocks.

'Is he still focused on our position, I can't see from here.' Tom directed his question to me.

Even without the binos I could see the young officer standing motionless, he was staring directly at our position.

'Yep, he's got eyes on us,' I said.

I look back through the gap again just in time to see the Lieutenant shrug his shoulders slightly, pull up his rain hood, and then start walking towards the soldier who was beckoning him from the doorway. He went inside without another look in our direction.

30 minutes passed with no further action. I'm watching the sentries who had been posted at the various points around the farmhouse. They were not moving very far from their posts now, if at all. It had started to rain heavily a short time ago and the wind blowing in from the North West had also picked up significantly, driving the rain through every gap in our clothes that it could find. Not that it made a difference because every bit of kit on me was saturated now anyway. The driving rain stung like an angry wasp though, if it hit you directly in the face. As I was finding out.

The Huey came back and landed at 1446, no scarface or the other marines, just the two pilots who got out and headed straight for the farmhouse. The weather is definitely getting worse but through the binos I can just make out a few blue overalled men scurrying around as they moved various bits of kit and barrels of fuel towards the helicopter. Twenty minutes later the short flurry of activity was over and the settlement was quiet again.

For the rest of the day it was just a case of keeping our heads down, having some scran when we could, getting water down our necks to keep hydrated and doing our other business. Jimmy came out the 'cave' with another delightful package for his bergen.

'Couldn't hold it any longer,' he said with a grin.

I gripped my nose tightly to ward off the non-existent smell. Sometimes it was days before anyone would need to take a crap in the field, mainly because the meals were small but high in calories, so not much volume actually goes in and therefore very little needs to be pushed out whilst on a job. We had been stuffing ourselves on Brilliant in the past few days so there were a few 'packets' in the bergens now.

I could tell from early on that the rain was not going to let up. And it didn't. I was cold, wet and just wanted to get the hell out of here now just like everyone else.

'Move in guys,' Tom called us together. It was 1830 and had been getting darker for a good hour or so.

'We are moving out in one hour at 1930. They will be feeding their faces at that time and then hopefully will be settling in for the night. It will be completely dark at 1930, although there is a good moon above these clouds so we may have a bit of light periodically.'

Tom's brief was over now, no one needed to say anything, a nod of the head had sufficed. I move back to my earlier position as everyone else did.

For the next hour, I didn't see anything that looked like new patrols heading out from the farmyard and most of the few sentries that had been posted had disappeared into warmer and drier places. One of the few sentries who was left was huddled under a cobbled together open sided tarpaulin canopy situated next to the two old Hueys. His temporary shelter would provide him with a little bit of cover when the rain was dropping vertically, but it wouldn't have done much for him when the wind changed and blew it in at the sides. As it was now.

If I could see his face under the hood of his great coat I know he would look a sorry state and would be as cold and wet as we all were right now. He wasn't looking too sharp or alert either and I seriously doubted he would be searching for anything except the door to the farmhouse when relieved, a hot drink, some food and his pit.

A nice thought and I'm sure that I am not the only one here on these rocks who would be thinking of getting back to Brilliant for some of the same.

Not long now before we move.

Shit, I'm cold.

18

Tom made his way down the rocks and stopped next to Jimmy.

'You're covering our arses Jimmy, so keep your eyes open for any movement from that farm until we are clear.' Tom said in a low voice, but I heard him. Just.

'OK Tom,' Jimmy replied.

'Let's go,' Tom whispered as he passed each of us taking up point straight away. We all inched forward towards the path that we had come up on the west side of the hill.

'Bob you are behind me for now, but when we are close enough I want you and Harry to go forward and get the raider ready.'

'OK.' We both answered in unison.

John fell in behind me as we headed down the hill, the pace quickening as we got nearer to the bottom. We were moving as fast as the conditions, and our night vision, would let us as we head straight to the point where the ground begins to slope down towards the water line and ultimately to the shingle landing point where we had hidden the raider.

It wasn't that far to the beach and I feel with every step we were moving further away from the Argies, and their threat. I am beginning to feel more confident with every passing minute that we will soon be on the water heading out towards Brilliant.

We tab hard for fifteen minutes. The rain is definitely abating and the wind has died down a bit. It wasn't his imagination either when Bob whispered in my ear that it was getting lighter. The moonlight was beginning to break through the clouds in places. Not a good thing for us right now.

'Keep your eyes peeled for the peat bogs. Don't forget we are cutting the corner from the original route in and John I don't want to lose you or your big feet in there.' Tom said just loud enough so we could all hear.

I didn't quite catch John's reply as it was in the form of a low grunt. I smiled.

We continue to tab hard towards a small clump of rocks we had identified and marked on the map on the way in. We were now heading due east so would keep these on our left to stay on the shorter route back to the beach. We had gone around them on our way in, keeping them again on our left and then had tracked further south trying to avoid the worst of the peat bogs before heading west towards the OP on the hill. Coming this way down had cut nearly a mile off the route back to the boat.

We knew there was a down side to this as we didn't know the ground we were travelling over, or the potential hazards facing us. It was even riskier as we were moving very fast, but it was a risk worth taking to get away from there after the Huey incident.

The breaking clouds and increasing moonlight helped us to see a bit clearer in the gloom of the night, but it also meant we could be seen easier if anyone was out here looking for us. We clear the clump of rocks by a couple of hundred yards and turned north toward the beach. All is going well I thought.

'Fuck!' I swear at no one in particular. I've taken a hit a couple of inches above my left hip an inch or so in, the bullet tearing a hole in my guts. I am spinning around from its force before I know anything else. I hit the deck and a searing pain shoots down my left leg and into my foot. I feel the warmth of my own blood leaking through my jacket from the open wound.

'Shit they found us. Hit the fucking deck.' Tom shouted.

'Fuck it we only have a mile to run.' Bob was cursing next to me whilst trying to rip open a couple of field bandages. Bullets were hitting the ground all around us now and screaming over our heads. Hundreds of red tracer lines were coming straight at us from at least three directions. Bob started to return fire from a prone position next to me, trying to shield me at the same time.

No time to fuck around with tying bandages now so I stuff the first one Bob had given me inside my shirt after quickly probing around the wound with my fingers. I knew I was lucky, the round had gone straight through and hopefully it had missed the major organs. I would find out if that was the case soon enough. I did have a decent sized hole in my left side, but there was no time to worry about that now.

A surge of adrenaline started to kick in so the pain abated slightly. We needed to find some cover and fast otherwise we were all dead. I was still on my back but missing my SLR. I knew it wouldn't be far away so I rolled over on my good side and it was there just within arm's reach.

Tom was shouting above the intensifying noise, 'Move, move, there's cover 30 yards over there.' His arm and finger pointing towards a small hollow edged by a small cluster of rocks and surrounded by thick clumps of tussock grass.

I grabbed my weapon as Bob hauled me upright by the collar of my sodden jacket.

'Move you big fucker,' Bob screamed in my ear.

I followed John, keeping low and firing off a few rounds towards the origins of the tracers in front of us. John was moving fast with the GPMG tucked into his side blasting away at the same point as me. Tom was just behind us now firing off rounds from his M16 towards the second of the three areas that we could see tracer fire coming from. Jimmy and Bob were behind Tom returning fire towards the last of the three positions that had opened up on us.

Suddenly the GPMG went quiet. My head was screaming with pain, not only from my own physical pain but from what I saw happen in front of me. John's left arm was taken clean off at the elbow, probably from a round of a 12.7mm machine gun. We knew they had some of those down here and they don't take any prisoners. The bottom half of his arm disappeared from sight instantly.

John roared like a wounded bull elephant and hit the ground with a sickening thud, the GPMG falling down beside him. A second smaller round had entered his gut three inches above his right hip before he had hit the ground. He didn't even acknowledge it as his right hand immediately felt for the ragged bloody stump that was now all what was left of his other arm. Fuck knows what goes through your head at that moment but whatever it was it wasn't going to stop him.

I'm still running when I take a second round in the top of my right leg that dumps me back on the deck again. Fuck that hurts as I grit my teeth hard, but I focus my attention on John who is only a couple of yards away from me.

It must have been pure adrenalin that made him sit up so quickly. His face was screwed up in a mask of pain and rage, but his eyes were still focusing hard at the ground and searching for his weapon. His massive right hand grabbed the pistol grip of the GPMG and hauled it up to his side with very little effort once he had found it. It still had a good 100 or more 7.62mm rounds dangling down on the left side.

The noise had been immense from the rifle fire but was now deafening as it was intermingled with the sound of heavy machine guns rounds that were coming at us from several places. It wasn't all one way through and we were laying down a shit load of fire as well that right now was probably keeping us alive.

I scrambled as best I could over to John and hauled him up.

'Come on you big fucker only a few feet to go.' I shouted.

I don't know if he heard me or not, but he moved and was up on his feet and still firing off rounds in a couple of seconds.

I knew I didn't have any time to think about the holes in my body right now because if I was going to save John's life I had to get a tourniquet above that stump to try and stem the free flowing blood spraying out the end of it. It would only take a few moments if I could stop him roaring and swearing at the Argies who were still saturating our position with what felt like thousands of rounds.

I knew I would have to sort myself out as well in a minute. The front of my right thigh was searing with intense pain and my own blood loss from both wounds would get critical very shortly and I would be out of it and no use to anyone.

I haul myself up and get to John. We stumble and drag each other a short distance to a 10ft x 10ft hollow in the ground that's surrounded by sparse rocks and tussock grass. It's no more than 4 or 5 feet at its deepest, but our heads are below ground level and it's the best and only cover we have for now.

'Where did those fuckers come from?' Tom was screaming as he slid into the hollow beside us, round after round continuing to spiral towards us pinging off the rocks and hitting the ground above our heads.

I am frantically trying to get a 'shell' dressing unwrapped so I could use it on John's stump and use the ties as an initial tourniquet, but the blood on my hands is making it difficult to open. I have another one ready to stuff inside his shirt once his arm is sorted. I am working as fast as I can, but I can see he was beginning to lose consciousness. I get the dressing in sort of the right place, but they will have to do for now. John's eyelids are struggling to stay above his eyes now as he fights with them to stay open. He has lost too much blood and needs to be in a hospital very soon or he is going to die. That is for certain.

The direction of the incoming fire had now changed as they were obviously trying to close in on us and cut off our intended route back down to the landing beach. Rounds from the heavy machine guns continued to hit the rocks inches above our heads, splitting them and spraying the sharp shards all over us. I managed to get a dressing on my leg and had stuffed one inside my shirt when a shard of flying rock pierced my right cheek tearing a small hole in it.

I ignored it as I had bigger worries than that right now.

I felt it before I saw anything. Blood, bits of brain and flesh splattered the side of my cut face and the side of my jacket. Out of the corner of my eye I see Jimmy falling forwards over the edge of the hollow and towards the ground. He was dead before his body hit it.

The force of the bullet had taken most of the top of his head clean off. Tom and Bob had also been on the receiving end of bits of brain and skull bone, plus a good splattering of Jimmy's blood.

Jimmy's body settled on his right side a few feet away, his eyes wide open in a ghostly stare looking straight at me, and John. Not that John would have noticed, his eyes were firmly closed now. Jimmy wouldn't have known what had hit him. Thankfully.

We were badly in the shit and we all knew it, the cover was sparse, to say the least, and rounds were still raining down on us from a number of positions. John was out of it, he was unconscious and dying, his weapon still gripped tightly in his right hand though. I doubted very much he would make it even if we could get him out of this hell hole right this second. I was not in that good shape either as the field dressings I had quickly shoved on my own wounds were not doing much as blood was oozing steadily from both of them.

In the next second, Bob was thrown backwards from the kneeling position he had taken up behind a measly rock. He had taken one in the right shoulder and it was quickly evident that it wasn't one of the big rounds that had removed John's arm so easily, but it was bad enough and powerful enough to leave a decent mug sized exit wound just below his right shoulder blade. I couldn't move fast enough to catch him or break his fall so he hit the ground hard and let out a sharp cry of pain, which was quickly followed by a loud grunting sound as he tried to right himself and get his weapon back in his hand. I reached him just as he had pushed himself into a sitting position on his good left arm.

A second bullet then smashed into his chest just below the other entry point making the hole that was already there, even bigger. I quickly got down beside him after he had hit the deck again to check if he was still alive. He wasn't dead yet, but he was pretty well fucked up and wouldn't be contributing much, if anything else, to this little jolly. I was sure of that.

I kill the Argie solider that appeared at the edge of the hollow a moment later with a double tap. His line of fire would have been directly on Bob and was the man who had most likely got the second round into him when he was sitting up. The Argie fell backwards and disappeared from view.

Tom was returning fire to all three enemy positions as I dragged myself up alongside him. Over the noise from Tom's weapon and the heavy incoming fire, I shouted at him so he could hear.

'Tom we are fucked. John and Bob are down and Jimmy's dead. I've taken two rounds and won't be fucking running anywhere for a while. Get yourself out of here if you can and hopefully the Argies will look after us three in the right way.'

'Harry there's no fucking way I'm leaving you all here to die,' was Tom's angry reply. I grabbed his jacket and over the noise shouted at him again.

'They have us in the bag. We're fucked and if you are not going, and we want John and Bob to live, the best thing is to give it up now and see if we can get some proper medical help in here. I can see no way out of this now mate. We will all be dead if we carry on.'

Tom ceased firing, only because he was out of ammo now. We slid a little further down into the hollow and stared at each other for a few moments trying to read each other's faces, trying to get the right decision made, trying to block out the noise of the fire fight that is horrendous, deafening and all around us. Tom made no effort to search for another clip of ammo for his weapon as we both now knew it was up for us and we needed to think about the others.

19

We tucked ourselves down as far into the hollow as we could and laid our weapons down beside us waiting for the gunfire to cease. It took another minute for it to stop completely and an eerie silence came over the sparse wet and windy moorland that had been our home for the past couple of days and nights.

I look over at Tom, his face is streaked with mud and the blood of his dead comrade and nothing could hide the pain he was feeling inside right now. As it was for me too. We looked at each other once more through the semi gloom of the moonlit night. We both knew this was it and with no other words Tom raised his left hand and started to stand up, his right hand grabbed a handful of material on my jacket and started to haul me up with him.

I had started to raise my right hand when the bullet creased the left side of my head taking a lump of hair and skin from my scalp with it. I'm sure it took a little bit of skull bone as well. The impact and shock causing me to spin violently around to my left and backwards towards the prone figure of John. I missed landing on him by about a foot, but my head hits one of the protruding rocks on the ground before I can cushion the fall with my arms.

The back of my head opened up like a bursting melon and the large deep gash instantly splatters the rocks and soaks the ground with more of my fresh blood. I heard my skull crack at the same time and then darkness began to engulf me as my head slid off the rock and onto softer ground. Tom had a good grip of my jacket so my sudden movement away from him meant he fell backwards with me. He landed on his back right beside me.

As soon as I can, I open my eyes a fraction, because that's all I can manage, I see Tom back on his feet screaming into the gloom of the night.

'We fucking surrender you bastards, stop firing. I have wounded men in here who need help. We fucking surrender.'

Moments later I see the fuzzy outline of soldiers, I count 10 or more. They appear directly above us. All with their weapons trained on Tom as he's the only one still standing and making a noise. None of the soldiers say anything, they just stand in silence looking down on the bloody scene below them. Tom is screaming at them to get a medic into the hollow to help us. Nobody moves and it's at least another minute before I see them slowly part down the middle and back away from the edge of the hollow.

Tom was looking down at the devastation around him. John has no left arm and a gut wound, but is still just about alive. I'm lying on my back seemingly unconscious, but I can still hear things and can see fuzzy human shapes standing above me. Bob has a big hole in his chest and was also just about hanging on in there. Jimmy was dead with no top to his head. His blood and brains slowly seeping onto the ground around him.

I was sure Tom would think he had failed us, but he hadn't. Nobody could have got us through this lot. We had been caught like rats in a trap.

I'm flat on my back and I can't move. Jimmy's and my own blood is covering the majority of my face and running into one of my eyes, blood is also leaking out of me at some rate now from the holes in my left side, right leg and the back of my head. Consciousness is something that I am definitely losing the fight with and I know I am more unconscious than conscious at this point.

I hear voices so force open my eyes as much as I can. I can focus more now and I see Tom with hands high in the air and he is shouting something but I can't make out what. Everything goes black again.

I don't know how long I was out, seconds, minutes, I have no idea. I hear something again and through the fog and pain that has invaded my brain and the blurred and bloody vision in my eyes I can make out a soldier standing with his back to us at the edge of the hollow. He is barking orders to unseen men so I assume he is an officer or NCO. Orders sound the same in any language and the soldiers slowly began to part.

That's when I saw them, it was a fuzzy picture, but unmistakably it was the short heavily built Colonel bully boy and the massive sergeant. The ugly deep scars on the right side of his face clearly visible as I strained to focus on him in the gloomy light.

They both moved closer to the edge of the hollow after roughly pushing aside some of the soldiers and were now standing only three or four feet away from Tom whose hands were still high in the air.

'So Mr. Special Fucking Forces man, you think you can spy on us and then escape from the glorious armed forces of Argentina,' I hear Colonel bully boy sneer at Tom in surprisingly good English.

Tom took a step forward but before he could say anything the Colonel swung his right boot which connected hard in Tom's ribcage. Tom didn't fall backwards but did double up in pain clutching his left side. I was sure the force of that kick must have broken something. The fucker then aimed his next kick directly into Tom's face, smashing his nose and probably breaking his left cheekbone as well. Blood sprayed from his nose and down the front of his jacket as he fell to his right and almost tumbled down again to where I was lying.

I black out again so I miss what happened immediately after that, but then angry noises penetrated my brain and I force my eyes open again to see scarface tugging at Tom's fingers, which are clamped firmly around the neck of bully boy.

'I'm going to fucking kill you, you bastard.' Tom was screaming at him. Bully boy was obviously not used to having anyone fighting back and from what I could make out from his face he looked like he was shitting himself. Then the big sergeant landed a hard solid punch in Tom's guts knocking the wind out of him and making him partially release his vice grip on bully boy's throat. The massive force of the second punch on Tom's jaw snapped his head to the side, his grip unwillingly released bully boy as he fell backwards and crashed into Jimmy's dead body.

My eyes close again. I still can't move, but my brain is sort of working, functioning, but my legs and arms won't budge. The dull sound of intense shouting makes me force my eyelids open again. It was the young Argentine Lieutenant we had also seen at Rincon Grande. He was having a very animated discussion with his superior officer. Scarface was standing very close on the right shoulder of bully boy looking menacingly towards the young man. Tom was back up on one knee looking up and watching the argument from close quarters, but he had a different expression on his face now.

The anger had subdued but had been replaced by a deeply worried look. Furrows lined his bloodied forehead and his eyes were screwed up focusing intently on the men above him. I couldn't quite get my head around what was going on, but we had surrendered and although I'm sure these boys wanted a bit of sport with us they would have to take us in for some medical help soon. They have to as they are bound by the Geneva Convention, just as we are.

I black out again for a few seconds only this time because the heated argument between the two officers was still continuing and escalating by the tone of it as my senses return. I feel a chill go through me as something dawns on me. I can't see the ring of soldiers that were there a few moments ago.

Where had they gone?

I focus on Tom again. He was scanning the edge of the hollow and then back again at the two officers who were now standing less than two feet apart from each other directly above him. Bully boy was poking and prodding the young Lieutenant in the chest and when he was not doing that he was flailing his arms about and gesticulating wildly just inches from the young officer's face. The young Lieutenant was standing his ground though and whatever bully boy was trying to do, he was having none of it.

The young officer then raised his hand to his right cheek to obviously wipe something off it and then it happened. It happened so quickly I almost missed it. The Colonel drew his 9mm browning automatic pistol and swiftly, but with tremendous force, brought the butt of the gun down onto the bridge of the young officer's nose.

The Lieutenant crumpled under the blow and went down onto his knees only to then get the butt of the gun again smashed into the left side of his face. Staying upright from a second blow of such force was not possible this time and he fell onto the sodden ground. Scarface got in on the act now and stepped in to deliver two heavy kicks, one into the ribs and the other directly at the head of the now prostrate man, almost sending him tumbling into the hollow.

I must have blacked out again for a few seconds. Someone is laughing loudly, then another joins in. I can't focus properly for a moment, but I can see the human shapes moving, like they were laughing. One big one and one shorter one. I'm certain it's bully boy and scarface.

Orders are barked by someone and seconds later two more human shapes appear. My focus returns briefly and I can make out two soldiers kneeling next to the badly injured and seemingly unconscious young Lieutenant. He is hauled up and placed gently over one of the soldiers' shoulders, and then he is gone.

It's quiet now, no more guns are firing, no one is talking and the wind and light rain that had been present when we had started our tab back to the raider had also abated. I hear Tom talking to someone, to bully boy, I assume. I force my eyes open just a little and try my best to focus on the Colonel's face. I didn't want to forget it.

For the first time tonight clear moonlight broke through the clouds casting some half decent light on the scene, which helped my eyes focus a lot better. I blink a few times and clear a bit more of the crap away and it is just enough in the new light to see bully boy looking very smug after just giving the young officer a good beating no doubt. Standing next to him, scarface had the very same expression on his face. I can see three more soldiers standing close to the sergeant and bully boy, their weapons all pointing directly at Tom. They are smiling, as well.

I strain to hear the muffled noises of a one on one conversation, but I can't make out the words. I'm getting weaker, I still can't move and I am only staying conscious for seconds at a time now.

Unconsciousness was about to take me again when I hear the first shot, followed immediately by a second much louder bang. I snap myself back into the world of the living and using all the strength I have left I get my eyes open, just enough, and in time, to see the exit hole in the back of Tom's combat jacket. Stuff was already spraying out the back of his head from the first round.

Tom is falling towards me, his body twisting from the force of the bullets before crashing down on top of me, forcing any remaining air out of me. The impact from Tom's lifeless and bloody head busted my nose good and proper. Fresh blood from my nose smearing across my face as his right shoulder finally came to rest on my forehead.

You mother fuckers, I'm going to kill you. I try to scream at them, but no words or sound come from my mouth. I am pinned down, I can't see and right now, and most importantly, I can't breathe. I am fucked.

Tom's body then jerked violently on top on me as the third bullet penetrated his back. I heard, and felt, the bullet break his spine. Tom's body slid a little further forward and off most of my face allowing me to suck in a huge breath and open my left eye as much as I could.

I hear more shots fired and see muzzle flashes, lots of them. I lose count. Moments later I smell the cordite and although I cannot see who or what the rounds were targeting, I can guess. They are making sure we are all dead.

Bully boy came into view, his Browning 9mm handgun aimed directly at my head. I knew I was going to die right then.

Tom's body jerked violently on top of me again as the pistol round entered his back. I had screwed my eyes tightly closed waiting for the inevitable as I knew I couldn't do fuck all about it, but now my eye was open as wide as I could get it and focused directly on the bully boy. I see him, his right arm straight out with his Browning aimed directly at Tom.

Then he did something I didn't anticipate. He smiled, brought the gun towards his mouth and then blew the smoke away from the end of the barrel. He then slowly slid the weapon into the brown leather holster strapped against his right hip. It was just like from a scene in a John Wayne Western movie. The bastard.

With every ounce of the diminishing strength I have left in me, I force myself to stay conscious and suck it all in. I had to remember as much of what I had seen and heard. I had to stay alive to tell the story. I had to tell the truth about what has happened here. I had to tell the whole world that bully boy and his cronies had murdered John, Bob and Tom, in cold blood.

Not even the pain or the rage inside me can save me from the darkness now as I can feel myself slipping away again. Maybe it's for good this time.

The last thing I hear, getting fainter and fainter, is laughing.

20

The crashing sound of an old rusty meat hook bouncing off the side of the metal table, which had been hastily brought into use as my stretcher and temporary bed, woke me instantly. I don't know where I am, how long I have been here, or how I had even got here. I am barely conscious, but the one thing I do know is I am in a completely shit state.

The commotion and noise following the crashing of things falling onto the floor quietens down a bit and I manage to lift my head, just a little. Medics were busying themselves with each of their casualties quickly and efficiently, there were Navy, Army, and Marines all working together in this ramshackle place that still had the smell of sheep shit from what must have been its previous inhabitants.

That's when I knew where I was.

I was in what was the old Refrigeration plant at Ajax Bay which had been turned into the main field hospital on East Falklands. We were right at the point where the main landing sites had been in San Carlos Bay. This had been Red Beach.

I slowly stretch my neck a bit more so I can look down at myself. I can see some work had already been done to stabilise me and clean the wounds to my side, leg and head. My wounds had been left open but packed with some light gauze, proflavine and then a loose field dressing resting over the top. There was also an IV pumping something into the veins of my left arm, it was probably a saline dextrose solution with maybe a little Diazepam thrown in for good measure.

I had definitely been given something good to ward off the pain from the injuries, but I understood more when I put my head back down and let it roll to my left. I was facing a metal tray that had been propped up at the side of the table I was lying on. I caught sight of the big red M on my forehead and everything was clear. Well as clear as it could be. I knew then that someone would have used the syrettes of morphine that had been secured around my neck alongside the plastic dog tags we had been issued on the way south. I also knew they would be giving me something through that tube in my arm as well.

The brain was working too hard now and the pain was again starting to reinvade the nerves and sensors in my body. A deep throbbing pain started to move from the base of my neck to the front of my head and a burning sensation began to smother my body as the effects of the morphine and whatever else started to fall away.

I couldn't help letting out a small moan or something akin to that as I moved my body into a different position. A Navy medic was quickly by my side after negotiating his way across the makeshift ward.

'Hi Sarge, I'm Ken. You've been shot up a bit mate and you are very lucky to have survived. We have got a few pints of O Neg into you and have patched you up a bit, so you are going to be OK. We're just waiting to get you away to the ship so you can be sorted out properly.'

Some incoherent rubbish came out of my throat followed by another moan as more pain attacked every nerve sensor it could.

'Hang on in there mate, I'll give you something more to knock that pain away, I'll just get the doc to have a quick look at you before I do,' Ken said as he eased me back fully onto my back.

Two guys are looking down at me now.

'Sergeant Glass, I'm Surgeon Lieutenant Bailey, I'm the one that patched you up. You were in quite a mess you know, but you're fit and strong and none of the major arteries were severed, thankfully. That is what kept you alive.'

It was all a load of mumbo jumbo to me at this point. Just give me the fucking shot, was all I could think of right now. My eyes were barely open, but I did make out the plunger of the syringe being depressed and the needle poking into the line leading down to my arm.

'Give it a minute Sergeant and you'll be out of pain and asleep. Rest well,' Surgeon what's his name was saying something but whatever it was I didn't care. The pain subsided almost immediately and I felt calmer as the darkness rushed in to take me swiftly to a much better place.

I wake up and find I'm still on my table, come bed, but somewhere a little brighter than before. There was the chatter of the medics that I had heard before but now the noise was intermingled with the sickening sound of several badly injured men. There was also the acrid smell of burned and charred flesh hanging in the musty air of this new room. I can hear the sound of a generator humming away at full tilt somewhere close by which is obviously why I can see the room I'm in and what's going on.

There were ten makeshift beds made up from anything that was flat and strong enough to hold a man on a stretcher, and some proper metal cradles holding actual stretchers that were just high enough to keep everyone off the deck. The place was warm and dry and I can see cork lining in the walls where the plastic covering had come away. This was why the room was holding in the heat from the shiny space heater blasting away in the corner.

I see Ken the medic heading my way.

'How you doing Sergeant? How's the pain?' he asked.

'Fine,' I replied.

I am not really fully with it just yet as I watch Ken fiddle about with the dressing and bandages seemingly covering my body. Throughout the process, he let out the occasional 'harrumph' and a few little nods of satisfaction.

'They will do nicely,' he said. 'We will be getting you out of here shortly onto the Uganda. They will be sorting you out a bit more once you are on board and then it will be home for you.'

'Thanks,' I said and then asked. 'What's your name mate?'

'It's Ken. Ken Parkin, Sergeant.' He replied.

'It's Harry, Ken. And thanks for everything.' I nodded my head a little when I finished speaking just to show my appreciation a bit more.

My head was clearing a bit now and before Ken could wander off I grab the arm of his green woolly pulley with my right hand.

He stopped and looked at me. He was startled a bit.

'What's up Harry?' he asked.

'How did I get here and was there anyone else brought in with me?' My hand gripping his sleeve as tight as I could just to let him know the importance and urgency of my question.

'I'm sorry Harry, you were barely alive and drifting in and out of consciousness when they brought you in. I was tasked to get you ready as fast as I could for the operating theatre and as soon as I was done I took you in straight away. We had minutes maybe seconds to save your life Harry so I didn't have time to look around for others. Leave it with me for a little while though and I will find out what I can for you, OK?'

'Thanks Ken,' I said wearily and slumped back onto my makeshift bed starting to feel the pain of my wounds again. I didn't care about that though, I just wanted to know what the hell had happened to the rest of the guys.

I wake up to a very different scene altogether from earlier. Something big has gone down. There are lots of bodies spread about the room, many with horrific injuries, limbs gone, big bullet-holes and swollen faces from the effects of something being smashed into them.

In the corner of the room only 15 feet from me I see several very scared looking young Argentine soldiers. Most of them also with swollen faces. Someone has been dishing out a beating I think to myself. They were under guard from a mean looking young Para, his SLR slowly panning from left to right, eyes firmly fixed on his prisoners.

The level of noise suddenly went up a few decibels as some badly wounded Argentine soldiers were carried in. Strong men were crying out in pain and agony, some calling for their mothers, wives, sisters, girlfriends, who knows. I could understand some of the words, but one thing I was sure of was the comfort they needed and cried out for was a long way from this hell hole.

The clatter of a tray and its contents of scalpels, tongs, tweezers and other implements falling to the ground close by distracted my attention away from the scene in front of me. I catch sight of Ken who was over in the corner of the room busy sorting out a leg wound on another young Para who I was sure was going to be OK from the expletives that were coming out of his mouth thick and fast and aimed directly at the Argentine prisoners.

On Ken's left I see the Lieutenant who had talked to me earlier, his hands busy trying to sort out a wound in the guts of an Argentine soldier. The soldier was being roughly held down by a couple of other medics to try and stop him thrashing around. Then in a moment it was over. I watched the soldier's legs suddenly relax. His left leg slipped off the table and then hung limply over the side. His upper body stopped its violent movements and although I could not hear the last expel of air from his lungs, I saw it happen. He would not be the only one to die today; I was certain of that from what I could see around me.

In the middle of all this shit all I want to know is how did I get here and where are Tom, Jimmy, Bob and John? I have been asking myself this question over and over again since I woke up. I knew in my heart they were all dead, but I also knew something was wrong with the way Tom had died. And the others too.

The noise and frantic activity continues around me for several hours. I occasionally lift my head and see bodies being moved in and out by soldiers that obviously had been brought in to help due to the amount of casualties. I only see one body fully covered, but I can't tell if he is ours or theirs. Maybe I would ask Ken later.

Ken had been over a few times to check everything was working with respect to the right levels of fluids and drugs going into me and the last time I saw him he was in a conflab with the Surgeon Lieutenant in the corner of the room. He then buggered off for a minute and when he returned he injected something into the IV tube without saying anything. I immediately knew that would be the last thing I would remember today.

21

I come to and the room is again quiet, well except for the low groaning noises from a couple of blokes on the makeshift beds at the far end of the room. From what I had seen of their wounds earlier I would be moaning too.

All the rest of the men had been cleared away and I assumed to the Uganda as Ken told me. I was still here though, which when I think about it may not be a bad thing because I must be doing OK.

A few minutes later and my head has cleared so I scan the room for any signs of Ken. He wasn't around, but there were two medics busying themselves with the other two guys and making sure they were OK. One of them made his way over to me a couple of minutes later. He was a young Royal Marine Corporal.

'You OK Sarge? Can I do anything for you?' He asked.

'Yeah, have you seen Ken Parkin? He's the medic that was looking after me earlier.' I asked.

'Yes I did. He was outside earlier talking to the Lieutenant and another officer who I think was SAS. There were a few other blokes with him and they had an Argie prisoner with them whose face was smashed up a bit. It looked bad, but nothing life threatening. I think Ken was asked to take a look at him quickly so I'm sure he will be back in a minute.' He said.

'Thanks,' I replied. 'Can you ask him to come and see me when you catch up with him?'

'No problem Sarge.' And with that he turned and walked out of the room.

About 20 minutes later Ken came through the door with someone.

I am shocked and confused at what I am looking at. I can't believe it. Tom is right next to Ken and walking towards my bed. Fuck no, it can't be possible I say to myself and screw my eyes together to be able to focus better when I open them again.

I'm positive I haven't imagined or dreamt Tom falling onto me, or the bullets smashing into his body. One of them snapping his spine as it did so. It was real, I know it was. I also know I am in a shit state and maybe the drugs are screwing with my brain, but I am struggling now to compute what I am seeing in front of me.

As they get closer to my bed even the voice is the same when I hear him talking to Ken. I squeeze my eyes together again and then open them a couple of times just trying to focus better. It was only when they were only a couple of feet away, I knew it was not Tom.

'Hi Harry, you OK? Pain level OK?' Without waiting for an answer, Ken went on. 'This is Captain Dye of the SAS and he wants to talk to you. He knows about your wounds and is mindful that he can't have too much time with you. Oh, and by the way, you are being moved to the Uganda on the first flight tomorrow morning. I'll be back in a minute or two.'

Ken nodded to the SAS Captain then turned and walked away, stopping briefly to check on another injured soldier.

'Sergeant Glass. Harry. My name is Bill Dye, you were with my brother Tom who was killed two days ago along with the rest of your recon team. You know that don't you?'

I couldn't speak for a moment because I now knew it was all true. There had been a big part of me that didn't want to believe it I suppose and I had been in denial up to now because of that. I couldn't help it as the tears began to well up in my eyes, but I needed to answer Bill's question. I take a breath and get a grip of myself.

'Yes I was with your brother Tom, sir. He was a great soldier and a very brave man.' I said fighting back real tears now.

'Thank you Sergeant, I appreciate that.' Bill responded with a pained and deeply sad expression clearly visible on his face. He obviously had loved his brother very much.

'Do you know how he was killed Sergeant?' Bill asked.

My head was clearer now and the brain had kicked into gear.

'Yes sir, I believe I do.' I said focusing on Bill's face.

'I am listening Sergeant,' Bill said.

'I believe he was murdered in cold blood by an Argentine Officer, his Sergeant and three others.' I said.

'The rest of the recon team, Corporal John Williams, Trooper Jimmy Blake and Corporal Bob May were all gunned down by superior Argentine forces in a real fight, but John and Bob were still alive when we surrendered. That was until, I believe, they were shot at point blank range by the same officer and the others that murdered your brother.' I paused for a moment to let this news sink in and so I could move slightly to take the pressure off my leg that was now throbbing like hell.

'Most of the other soldiers had been sent away so there must have only been three or four of the officer's men left. No one stood a chance. The murdering bastards. I believe I only survived because Tom fell on top of me after being killed.' I breathed hard as I finished the story.

The dimly lit musty smelling room in the old refrigeration plant was eerily quiet now. Captain Dye stared down at me intently with a deep frown across his forehead, I could feel instantly the dark rage that was brewing up behind his stone cold piercing blue eyes.

'Stay there Sergeant.' Bill barked loudly the order at me.

I was taken completely by surprise as I wasn't expecting that. Bill turned on his heels and headed towards the doorway and then just as quickly he stopped and turned back to face me again.

'Sergeant,' he paused, 'Harry, I didn't mean that. I apologise. You are not going anywhere are you, except home very soon I suspect. I'll be back in a minute I have someone here you need to meet.' Bill turned away and walked towards the door beckoning Ken to follow him.

I am alone with my thoughts now. Suddenly I feel my own emotions race to the surface and envelop me. My cheeks lift and forehead folds into several deep crevices as I clamp my teeth together. My face flushes red and I can feel the tears welling up in my eyes again.

I can't help myself now as the tears spill over the lids of my eyes leaving trails of water down my face. I hadn't known Tom, John or Jimmy for very long, but I had come to deeply respect them and their professionalism. They had been great soldiers, good men and most of all my comrades.

Bob was different though, he was my best mate and I had known his wife as long as he had. I was godfather to both his beautiful little girl Lucy and his first boy Tom. Tom was a mini-me of Bob and I loved him for that, but his youngest Joe was the coolest dude of them all and I was his uncle Harry who would never let anything bad happen to his dad. I promised him that and now I had failed him.

What the hell was I going to say to them?

I'm sobbing now with tears falling freely down my face. I don't have a sense of the time I'm in this state but then I catch some movement out of the corner of my eye and I'm aware of bodies standing in the doorway. They were all standing still, just waiting.

Ken got to me first as I tried to rub my face to get rid of the evidence with what was left of my blood stained and muddy shirt sleeve. Not much chance of that, but I tried.

'It's OK Harry, hang on in there, just give me a second and I'll sort this out,' Ken said as his hand dived into a box by the bed and pulled out an old but clean tea towel and a small bottle of water.

'Got some alternative supplies this morning courtesy of a few Royal Navy wardroom pantries. We have got to use anything we can get our hands on now since most of our fresh supplies went to the bottom on the container ship Atlantic Conveyor that the Argies got the other day with a couple of Exocets.'

Ken dampened the cloth and handed it to me so I could make a better job of my streaky face. A couple of seconds and I was done. Ken put the cloth down by the side of my makeshift bed and went off to look after someone else.

Bill moved slowly into the room and away from the door giving me sight of the four men behind him. One was an Argentine officer and there were three others. Two were men from Bill's SAS team I assumed as they both wore the odd pieces of kit from the various armies and Special Forces from around the world. Just as Tom, John and Jimmy had done. Their longer than regulation hair, distinctive combat knives, sidearms and civilian hiking boots were also a dead giveaway. The only regulation item amongst them was the US made M16 rifle, which everyone thought was the best combat rifle made right now.

The other man I recognise straight away. Sparky had transferred into the SBS from 40 Commando about a year or so ago and had become great mates with Bob. His death would hit him hard as well. I remember how they loved their rugby especially during the five nations when Sparky's red shirt would always be seen next to the white of Bob's. Those international days usually meant a huge piss up, if the girls let them out. I had been out with them a couple of times but on both occasions had to bail early. I just couldn't take that much beer in one day anymore. Sparky's face was not at all his usual jovial one. His eyes were narrow and cold and fixed firmly on the Argentine officer in front of him.

Bill was next to my bed now and standing directly in front of the young Argentine officer shielding him from my view. The tension in the room was electric and sinister. As soon as Bill moved left I immediately recognised the man even though the left side of his face was a swollen bloody mess. His left eye was completely closed and his nose was obviously badly broken in quite a few places. He stood there for a second staring at me intently through his remaining good right eye and then I saw the sudden recognition and realisation of who he was looking at. His facial expression changed and he started to take a step forward to say something, but before he could get anything but the word 'I' out of his mouth, Bill landed a solid left hook directly into the young officer's already battered face.

The punch split his left eyebrow instantly and as he went down he banged his head hard on the edge of the table I was lying on. One of the SAS soldiers stepped in and roughly manhandled the young officer back to his feet. Bill moved in very close and looked him squarely in the eyes before growling at him.

'You don't fucking speak or move unless I tell you to. Do you understand?'

The young Argentine Officer moved his head forward slightly to indicate he understood. Fresh blood dripping onto the floor as he did so. Bill then fixed his gaze on me.

'Do you know this man Harry?' Bill asked.

'Yes, yes. This is not the man who killed your brother, I'm absolutely one hundred percent sure of that.' I said frantically.

'Sergeant are you sure you know 'this' man.' Bill growled at me this time.

'Yes I do. This is not the man who killed your brother,' I repeated as forcibly as I could myself this time.

This man had taken enough from both sides and no more of his blood needed to be spilt today.

22

The young Argentine officer was struggling to keep upright and was obviously still concussed from all the blows he had received. He looked like he had just done a few rounds with Joe Frazier, or Ali had done a shuffle on his face.

Bill starting talking again.

'Sergeant,' he paused for a second. 'Harry. We captured this man and nine others half a mile from where we found you under the body of my brother. You were barely hanging onto your life. We had seen the fire fight from the distance as we headed towards your last known position. The rest of his lot were killed.' Bill said pointing at the Argentine officer. 'It was lambs to the slaughter, they had no fucking idea what they were doing. I actually think some of the poor sods were ordered to stand up so we could shoot them. Unfortunately whilst the turkey shoot was going on we know some escaped, probably the reason why we had such easy targets. Luckily for them we just didn't have the manpower to chase them down as we had to find you lot. I doubt now, from what we found later, we would have got them as the ones that legged it were well trained soldiers because they covered the ground very quickly and in the right way to throw off any pursuers. By the time these two' Bill pointed at two of the SAS men guarding the officer, 'had got eyes on them, they had got down to the Rincon Grande settlement and the Huey was already taking off. All the men left behind legged it in the only truck that was left as soon as the chopper had gone. They didn't even stay long enough to blow up the other Huey, which I'm sure someone is going to make good use of shortly.'

The Argentine officer opened his mouth to say something, but Bill raised his index finger and pointed at the man. He slowly moved the finger from side to side indicating that he was not to speak. Bill turned back to me and continued.

'Our medic gave you less than an hour to live unless we got you casevaced to this field hospital. You were very lucky that a Jungley was diverted to get you out of there, otherwise you would be dead as well now. When we found you we were suspicious straight away because of the amount of bullet wounds in the bodies. This officer told me that he is an honourable and professional soldier and that he did not kill my brother. He says they were trying to find and capture you after soldiers returning to Rincon in the Huey had spotted your team earlier the previous morning. They tracked you north and believed you were holed up in some rocks just north of the settlement as this was the only cover for miles. The senior officer decided that if you were in that position you had the advantage and could easily have taken out most of his soldiers in a fire fight. They found the raider that afternoon so planned the ambush based on the assumption that you would be making your way back to the beachhead that night, which of course you were.'

I broke eye contact with Bill and before he could continue I spoke directly to the young Argentine lieutenant.

'I saw you taking a beating at the edge of the hollow from the Colonel, or Bully Boy as we called him. You were trying to stop him doing what he did and you paid for it. Your face tells that story and that's why I am certain that you were carried away unconscious by two soldiers before he murdered Tom in cold blood. That bastard and his henchmen then finished off John and Bob for fun.'

Bill stared into the face of the Argentine officer, took a deep breath, and started talking again.

'Tom was shot four times, John, Jimmy and Bob had been shot indiscriminately several times each. They had taken rounds to the head, body, legs, arms, you fucking name it, they had holes in them everywhere. I could barely recognise John and Jimmy as most of their heads had been blown away. Bob I didn't know, but he was in the same shit state. Harry you were just fucking lucky Tom was on top of you and they probably assumed you were dead anyway.'

The pain etched across Bill's face was visible for everyone to see when he finished talking, but something in him changed as he realised that this young Argentine Officer had not murdered his brother but had, in fact, tried to stop the killings. He had endured a significant beating for his troubles from the as yet unnamed Argentine Colonel.

Bill was about to say something to the young Lieutenant, but I got there first.

'I know you did not have anything to do with the murder of my friends,' I said. 'But you need to start fucking talking to us and helping us. I saw the Colonel beat you more than once so I don't think you owe that man anything.'

I paused before asking the young officer.

'Who are you?'

'What is your name?'

'Help us and help yourself, please.'

He didn't speak straight away but then he looked directly at Bill and said slowly.

'I am very sorry about your brother, sir.'

He then turned and faced me.

'And your comrades Sergeant. I did try to stop him and his murdering compatriots, but you witnessed what he did to me. I'm sorry I failed you.'

The young officer's perfect Queen's English spoken with a public schoolboy posh accent took me a bit by surprise.

'I am Lieutenant Fernando Alberto Reynoso,' he said. 'I have been in the Army for three years and I am serving here on the Malvinas with my unit the 5th Marines, although the men at Rincon Grande were not from my regiment. I was only sent there to ensure security for the two helicopters was in place and operational. I learned English as a boy and spent several years in England at Eton College where I boarded for a number of years and then I went to Oxford to study law. This is where I developed the accent that has surprised you. It was my father's idea that I join the Army to get some 'leadership and life' experiences, but thankfully I now only have a few months left before I can return to civilian life and begin to practise law.'

Bill's hand shot up in the air.

'Lieutenant, I don't want your fucking life story. Just tell me the name of the man who murdered my brother and the other men.'

Reynoso looked down to the floor for a moment and then looked straight at Bill.

'His name is Colonel Octavio Pepe Muscardin and he is from a notorious family in Argentina who are known for their violence against my own people and who, I believe, are responsible for the deaths of many thousands in my country.'

Reynoso paused briefly and took a deep breath before continuing.

'Many members of this man's family hold powerful positions in the military and the secret police. They have operated outside the laws of my country for years. Sadly they have had the full support and backing of the military junta and anyone who speaks out against any of them, just disappears.'

Bill quizzed him again.

'Tell me Lieutenant, if you have gone against this man, at least twice now from what the Sergeant here says, won't you just disappear when you return to Argentina?'

'No sir I don't believe so as my Father is one of the largest landowners and horse breeders in Argentina. He also owns one of the country's top Polo teams so is connected to many powerful people and is respected by a large majority of non-corrupt government officials. He also has some good friends within the high command of the current military junta.' Reynoso took a deep breath and then wiped away a small trickle of blood from the corner of his mouth when he finished talking.

'What about your injuries and how will you tell people how you got them,' Bill asked.

'I was warned that if I speak up, Muscardin will come after me and my family and although I believe my father has enough power and influence to keep us safe for the time being, we will have to be very careful. There are many bad people in Argentina who would do anything for money or through fear of that particular family. I will watch my back and wait for the right time to deal with this man.' Reynoso replied.

Everyone was quiet and taking in what the young Lieutenant had told us, but there was more to this story I was sure.

'So when you said earlier you tried to stop him, what was going on?' I asked.

'Sergeant, he said that he was going to kill you all, take no prisoners, I believe he wanted to get some blood on his hands so he could brag about it back in Argentina. I can hear him now. I killed many SAS men in battle etcetera, etcetera. The truth was he wasn't even close to the action, he only appeared with his henchmen after you had surrendered. When he said what he was going to do, I told him he could not do it, and that under international law if he did, he would be tried for murder. It was then he hit me with his gun and the other one kicked me in the face and ribs.' Reynoso took a short breath and then carried on.

'I was very dazed from the blows to my head and it was when I was being carried away I heard the first shots. I couldn't get back to you because I could not stand without aid at that point and then I heard many more shots and I knew he had carried out what he said he would do. A short time later as I was being helped back to Rincon Grande the firing started again and the men around me just panicked. They just started running in all directions and even some straight towards your positions.'

Reynoso turned and looked at the two SAS men guarding him.

'I just couldn't stop them. They had no chance really as most of them were young, inexperienced conscripts and air mechanics. Most of them hadn't even fired a gun properly before being shipped to the Malvinas. I did not see Colonel Muscardin again, but I did hear the helicopter taking off soon after I had been captured. I only assumed it was him getting away. I am so very sorry I could not save your comrades.' Reynoso said finally with a genuine look of sadness and remorse on his battered face.

Bill took a few moments to look the young lieutenant up and down. He then put his hand on his shoulder. Reynoso flinched a little.

'I'm sorry we roughed you up earlier. I believed you had something to do with the execution of my brother and the other guys. It's clear to me now that you didn't,' Bill said.

Bill then turned his head to look at me and I gave him a firm nod indicating my agreement.

'My men will take you away now to be debriefed with the others. I hope that you will have the courage and strength to put down what you have just said in writing.'

'Treat him well.' Bill said to his men who acknowledged his instruction from behind Reynoso with a short nod.

Lieutenant Reynoso slowly raised his head and looked at Bill through his one open eye. He said nothing to him, but turned to me and said.

'Thank you Sergeant.'

He then turned and walked away holding his ribs with one arm across his chest and at the same time wiping away more blood from his face with his other hand. As he disappeared through the door I thought about his last words, 'Thank you Sergeant.'

I knew why he had said it, but he had just been honest, and so had I. He probably thought Bill would bury him in the same hole where he had found Tom if he hadn't got the truth. If it had been Muscardin standing there I honestly believed Bill would have done.

Bill was facing the door watching Reynoso and his men leave. He turned slowly and said.

'I don't know what we are going to do about this Harry, but we will have to do something. I seriously doubt we will get any joy from the Argies when this lot is finished and that won't be long now, I'm very confident about that.'

I looked at him not really thinking about the next move. I just needed Ken to give me some more juice for the pain in my side. It was really beginning to bite again now.

'I need to get back to my men Harry,' Bill looked thoughtful as he paused, 'I know you would have done everything to watch my brother's back, he told me you were a good bloke. We will talk again back in the UK but now you need to get yourself sorted.'

'OK.' I said and relaxed my head back onto the pillow hoping Ken would be coming back very soon.

'We have to do something about this,' Bill said again.

I could think of a lot of things I would like to do to the little bastard and scarface, but I needed to know the answer to one question that was in my head.

'Bill,' I said. 'Why were you at Rincon Grande? We were not briefed that there were other operations going on in that area.

'Harry,' Bill replied. 'We received intel that there was suddenly a lot of ground and air activity around Rincon Grande, Horseshoe Bay and the Teal Inlet settlements. The brass thought that you could be in trouble and from the signals you sent we knew there was not a big force in the area so I brought in 15 guys to make sure you all got out. I failed the others, but not you Harry.'

Bill was struggling to keep his emotions in check and I saw clearly tears welling up in his eyes.

'I'll be seeing you Harry,' he said before swiftly turning away and walking towards the door.

I knew then from the tone in his voice that I would be seeing him again, when and where I didn't know, but right now I really didn't care as the most important thing to me was where the hell was Ken with that pain relief?

23

Ken appeared shortly after Bill had left and filled me up with something that did just the job. The next thing I knew I was being carried out to a blue Navy Sea King for the short flight out to the Uganda. It was just after dawn and this was the first flight. Ken had been true to his word.

My stretcher was placed carefully on the ground for a moment whilst they were squaring away something in the chopper. Ken was soon by my side on his knees fussing about with something attached to the stretcher. This man had taken so much care of me over the past couple of days and I was so grateful. I knew his face would be one I would never forget. I raised my arm and our hands locked together.

'Good luck Harry you're going to be OK.' Ken was shouting over the noise of the Sea King.

'I know Ken. Thanks to you and everyone here. You look after yourself.' I shouted back at him.

Our hands released and Ken put his thumb up. Four soldiers lifted me again and seconds later I was through the open door of the helicopter. A minute later I am in the air leaving 'The Red and Green Life Machine' at Ajax Bay. It was a place that had certainly given me life. Without it, I and many others would be dead. The Sea King headed North over San Carlos water into clear blue skies for a change and then out into the open sea to the waiting hospital ship Uganda.

The helicopter ride was as smooth as it could be but on the occasions when it hit a lumpy bit of air and everything bounced, including me on the stretcher, I knew Ken's last shot of juice was definitely wearing off. My head hurt again and I could feel the stabbing pain in my right leg radiate all the way up the side of my body and then across to the hole in my left side.

To distract myself from the pain and generally feeling crap I raise myself up onto an elbow just to have a look where we are. All I can see is blue sky through the window in the Sea King door, which made me a little happier, as it meant at least the guys on the ground would have a decent day's weather for a change.

'You OK Sergeant?' the aircrewman asked.

'I'm OK,' I said. 'How long before we land?'

'Not long Sarge,' he replied. 'It's best if you stay flat though, let's get your head back down.'

And with that he carefully eased me back flat onto the stretcher.

'Thanks.' I muttered as another wave of stabbing pain shot down my side.

A couple of minutes later the pilot got us onto the deck with little more than a soft bump. Fortunately for me and everyone else on board, the sea was nice and calm. The Sea King's main door slid open and four pairs of strong hands gripped the stretcher and whisked me away quickly from the noise and downdraft of the rotors. I was being taken towards a door that was being held open by someone who was definitely not a man.

At least that radar was still working!

As I went through the door I could hear the Sea King's engines winding up for take-off. All the bits of kit and stores, that I had seen inside the helicopter, would have been removed swiftly from the cabin and secured away from the down draft of the rotors. The last things they would need are some FOD getting sucked up into the engines because someone hadn't done their job properly.

I was only sorry that I couldn't say thank you to the crew. I knew they had been flogging themselves and their machines every day since we got here. The air mechanics keeping them in the air must also be completely knackered by now as well.

After being carefully guided through more doors and passageways, I am finally put down on a table next to a theatre trolley in a brightly lit room. I can hear the low hum of air conditioning and the various motors that drive the workings of any ship and then I feel a soft small hand on top of mine. I look up to see the smiling face of a senior nursing officer, who was not dressed in traditional QARNNS nurse's uniform, but was in the standard navy issue blue trousers, shirt and obligatory blue woolly pulley with epaulettes that told me her rank. She was still a beautiful sight though with her short blond hair, bright blue eyes and broad beaming smile.

'Sergeant Glass isn't it?' she asked.

'Yes Mam.' I mumbled through clenched teeth as the pain was again getting a good grip on me.

'I am Sister Owen and I will be looking after you with my team for a while. You have got yourself shot up a bit haven't you Sergeant? But don't worry we will have you properly cleaned up and sorted out very shortly. I promise you.'

She paused for a moment and then continued before I could say anything.

'I can see you are in some pain, but I don't want to give you anything right now as the surgeons will be giving you a general anaesthetic very soon. Do you understand that Sergeant?'

'OK.' I said.

'Let's get you cleaned up then.' The Sister nodded at a couple of, I assumed nurses, standing close by. One of the 'nurses' was a young fresh faced guy who looked like he hadn't been out of training long, but I didn't care because I knew I was in the best place, and in safe hands. The young female nurse spoke first.

'Sergeant,' she said.

'Call me Harry, please, let's drop the Sergeant bit for a while,' I said.

'OK Harry, I'm Lorraine and this is Neil. Neil is not a nurse, as you will quickly find out,' she said with a broad smile.

Neil returned the smile and said.

'Harry, I'm a Lab technician sorting out blood testing and infection screening so this lot can fill you up again with the right blood type and hopefully give you the right medicines at the right levels.'

Something burst and a sudden wave of pain hit me like a steam train with the throttle wide open and then I felt the first trickle of warm blood running down the side of my leg. The leg dressing was sodden and fresh blood had started to leak out of the side of it.

Lorraine saw it immediately.

'Harry, we are going to get you ready as quickly as possible and get you down to theatre.'

Lorraine quickly left the room as Neil started to cut away what was left of my minging combats and my even more minging underpants. Lorraine came back with a bowl of hot water and some sponges. I didn't care if my dick was flopping about for all the world to see, but even in my shit state I was glad it was Lorraine who sorted out that particular area. Stupid I know.

Within a few minutes, I was cleaner than I had been for days and was feeling much better just for that. The only thing left from the field hospital was the new dressings on my left side that Ken had put on the night before. This, I assumed, would be taken off at the last minute when I was in theatre.

Lorraine, Neil and a couple of other new people had successfully moved me onto the trolley and the next thing I know I'm being wheeled down the passageway. Strong overhead lights blinded me temporarily as I'm pushed into a small anteroom. I have to blink a few times to focus properly on the face of the guy who was carefully sliding the needle into the back of my left hand ready for the general anaesthetic.

'You'll be OK very soon Sergeant.' I don't know who said it but then I felt the freezing cold liquid filling my hand and I knew I was heading off into the deep fantastic abyss of an anaesthetised sleep.

24

I wake slowly and after a few minutes I realise that I'm not hurting as much as I thought I should be. Some good old soul has also left a Sun newspaper by my bed. It was several days old, but I didn't care. I flick straight to the back page and it was great to see that Manchester City were ending their season with a winning streak. Page 3 was pretty good too and that made me feel much better.

I take a moment to study intensely a beautiful 21 year-old Liverpool girl's fabulous tits and I get completely lost in my own happy thoughts. I didn't notice Sister Owen standing by my bed and almost crapped myself when I hear her say.

'You're feeling better then, Sergeant Glass.'

Fuck! I had been well and truly pinged and I feel my neck instantly getting warmer and then the heat radiating up to my cheeks. Royal Marine Sergeants aren't supposed to blush, but I knew I was doing exactly that right now.

'Sergeant, you will be getting a visit later today from Surgeon Lieutenant Commander Hugh Bowdich. He's the surgeon who plugged all the holes in you and patched you up, so be good when he comes in. And don't spend too much time studying that page either, you need all the blood that's left in your body to be feeding your vital organs, and that's not one of them right now,' she said pointing at my groin with a wicked smile on her face.

Hugh Bowdich arrived at 1503. He was a bald, stocky guy with a smiley face and a strong Welsh valleys accent. He explained that the wounds to my head, face and nose had been redone by another surgeon on board, who luckily for me was a specialist in cosmetic surgery. I would still end up though with a fairly brutal, but neat scar, on the back of my head and a slightly lumpy area of skin where the bullet had creased the left side of my head. The cut through my right cheek would also leave a small but noticeable scar. All he said about the nose was it was straight again and I had clear airways on both sides, but I wouldn't want to look at it right now. He was smiling when he said it.

The wounds to my left side and right leg had been cleaned out again and the last few bits of dirt and grit that the guys in Ajax Bay had not been able to see in the dull light of the old refrigeration plant were now also gone. Hugh Bowdich told me they had excised some more tissue from both wounds to ensure it would not affect the growth of healthy new tissue during the next few days.

'If it is all looking good we'll close you up before you go home. You are going to be OK Sergeant, but you were very lucky they found you when they did and got you to Ajax Bay otherwise you would be dead.' He said and smiled again.

Nice way to finish off a conversation I thought, but he was right.

I spend three more comfortable days onboard Uganda drifting in and out of drug-induced sleeps. I know there was a heavy duty amount of pain relief, antibiotics and whatever else being pumped into my body and I also know it was for my own good. On the fourth day, I was told that the wounds to my side and right leg were greatly improved and could now be closed up for the journey home. That had been a good news day.

I am lying in the same room that I was brought to on the first day on board Uganda, waiting to start the next stage of my journey back to the UK. The nursing Sister, whom I quickly had found out was called Mary and who had been a lot of fun since catching me studying Page 3 intensely, was carrying out a final check that all the dressings are good and that I am properly secured to the stretcher ready for the transfer to HMS Hydra. It would then be a short sail to Montevideo where I would be put on an RAF VC10 for the long flight home to Brize Norton.

'Patient transfer will begin in five minutes,' boomed out of the ship's tannoy system.

Mary kneeled down beside my stretcher and looks down at me, her eyes are moist with tears. I wondered what was wrong but before I could ask she said.

'You have been very brave Harry and have done a fantastic job out here. I'm so proud of you and all the others who are fighting for the people of the Falkland Islands, but you now must take care of yourself. Your body has taken quite a beating and has suffered potential life threatening injuries, but more importantly you must not ignore or downplay the mental traumas you have also endured. I feel these will be your greatest challenge in the coming weeks and months so take all the help and support that is offered. Please look after yourself and get well soon.'

She squeezed my hand gently and then she stood up and walked away without waiting for any response.

I suddenly thought that would be the last time I saw her and I was surprisingly and instantly saddened by that for some strange reason. I had only known her for a few days, but there was something special about her and the care she had given to the many injured men on board.

Time to go home now.

Part Two

Falklands Aftermath

1

The days at sea heading towards Montevideo had given me the time to think a lot about all the events of recent weeks and about the people who had saved my life.

I was able to say thank you and goodbye properly to Neil, Lorraine and Mary before our last meeting. All of them had been brilliant, as had all the others in Ajax Bay and without their care I knew, as the surgeon commander had said; I would be dead. My life had to mean something now, didn't it? This was a pressing thought right now and something inside me was telling me I had been kept alive for a reason. What that reason was I didn't know right now, but maybe soon I would.

I also thought a lot about my friends and how they had died, especially Tom, John and Bob. Jimmy had been killed in action and there was nothing any of us could do about that. That's war. But the others, from what Reynoso had said, were executed for some macho bullshit reason by Colonel Muscardin and his henchmen.

That was something they would have to pay for; with their lives preferably.

It is a cool but sunny Tuesday morning when we arrive in Montevideo. There are lots of people fussing around as I'm carried down the gangway headfirst on a stretcher. I lift my head to see uniformed Uruguayan soldiers and sailors getting ready to take over from our medics. It was their job to get us into the waiting ambulances. I see the intrigue and interest on their faces as we are handed over. Everyone was trying to get a glimpse of our wounds, but fortunately the blankets draped over the stretchers frustrated those prying eyes and the scrum of photographers and press were forcibly being corralled at the end of the dock and kept well away from us.

The short transfer to the airport and to the waiting RAF VC10 was completed efficiently and within a couple of hours of docking at the quayside I was being strapped down in the aircraft's converted cabin ready for take-off. There was room for 20 or more stretchers as well as plenty of seats for the walking wounded. Once in the air there was not much to do except read the latest newspapers and sleep, which the medical team had covered and shortly after a couple of their tablets I was on my way.

The VC10 landed smoothly at Brize Norton in Oxfordshire late on Wednesday evening. It was a quiet affair really with just the essential people waiting. As I'm carried down the steps I can see relatives, wives and girlfriends of the wounded guys on board ready for a brief reunion. Then it will be off to another hospital somewhere. I had managed to speak to Kathy and Gerri when I was on the Uganda to let them know I was alive and all right. But I wasn't sure if either, or both of them, would be able to meet the flight.

I am carried into the arrivals hall to be booked in by four strong airmen – who were never going to drop me. I wasn't able to sit up due to the restraining straps still holding me onto the stretcher. I lift my head as much as I can to scan the sea of faces in the small arrivals hall. I see them. Kathy was there with Gerri standing beside her. My emotions go into overdrive and my heart is beating faster than it has for days.

She was a sight for sore eyes and looked completely gorgeous in her knee length boots, tight jeans and fitted burgundy jumper. I closed my eyes for a moment just to capture that image. I did have moments in the past weeks where I didn't know if I would ever see her again, but there she was. Today was a good day.

All the relatives were standing behind the rope that was creating the holding area for those of us on stretchers. They must have been asked to wait behind it until we had been processed. But that was never going to happen today – even on a military base. The first under the rope was Kathy striding purposely over to where I had been laid down on the floor. The RAF airman 'guarding' the rope didn't try very hard to stop her – or the tide of people that followed her. I don't think he needed telling what was the best thing to do. He took a sensible step back and watched the unfolding joy on people's faces and the cascade of tears as they reached their still breathing loved ones.

Kathy got down on both knees next to me. Gerri went round the other side and did the same. Kathy looked me up and down slowly. She could only see the bumps of the large dressings covering the wounds under the blanket, but the heavy white bandages covering the top half of my head couldn't really be missed.

'You are in a mess aren't you Harry Glass. I let you out of my sight for one minute and this is what you do to yourself.' Tears were streaming down her face now making her mascara run a little onto her flushed cheeks. She leaned forward and kissed me softly on the lips then moved over to my uncovered right ear and whispered,

'I love you Harry.'

The tears started to creep out of the corner of my eyes now and roll down the side of my face. I couldn't do anything to stop them as Kathy was hugging me gently. My arms were still pinned down beside me by the restraints – which was very frustrating as all I wanted to do was hug her tightly. We stayed like that for a good minute until I felt Gerri squeezing my right hand a little harder. She was still kneeling next to me – tears falling freely down her cheeks, as well.

'I'm so happy you are home Harry. We all missed you and were very worried about you and all the rest of the boys.' Gerri squeezed my hand even harder when she paused.

'I know,' I said. 'But I'm back now and I will be OK in a little while. And I will have two lovely homemade nurses to look after me.' I added a quick wink as I finished talking.

'You are OK, aren't you?' Kathy said as she leaned back on her heels. She smiled again at me before continuing. 'There's not much that a little time won't heal and a bit of TLC I'm sure.'

'Sergeant Glass.' A man in a white coat was standing over us.

'We have to move you now. You are going to be taken to the base sick bay tonight and then you will be moved to the Royal Naval Hospital Stonehouse in Plymouth tomorrow. Ladies you are welcome to accompany us, but I'm afraid you cannot stay on the base tonight.'

Gerri spoke first.

'We know that, it was in the briefing pack, so we will be going home later.' The same four airmen picked me up and carried me out of the arrivals hall and put me into a waiting RAF ambulance. Gerri and Kathy jumped in the back with me.

An hour later and I was on my own again ready for sleep after another dose of pain killers and some more sleeping pills. Before they left Kathy and Gerri said that as soon as they knew the ward I was on in Plymouth, they would be down to see me. It was quiet when they had gone except for the low breathing noises of the other two wounded soldiers who had also been on the VC10 with me. They were sleeping soundly probably helped by the same stuff I had been given.

It was just before 1100 when I woke to find myself alone in the four bed ward. The sun was shining in my face through the small lead paned square windows. It was bright and warm and it felt very good. A voice came from the doorway.

'Sergeant Glass, here is some breakfast for you. You need to eat something before your transfer to Plymouth.'

On the tray was some cereal and a glass of fruit juice. I think it was apple, but I didn't care, I had a mouth like the inside of a Chinese ditch digger's ju ju bag, and that isn't a pleasant thing.

'Would you like some bacon and eggs as well?'

The young nurse was busying herself around the bed straightening and sorting out corners and such like.

'Yes I would like that very much,' I replied.

'OK,' she said and hurried off through the door.

I had just finished my cereal and juice when she returned with a plate of bacon, eggs and beans. That will do for me, I thought to myself, especially as I just about got rid of the fur balls and gunk that was in my gob earlier.

An hour later as I am being sorted for the onward journey, I had a visit from the RAF Station Commander, an Army General and a Royal Navy Commodore. They were all very nice and said the right things.

'You served your country with honour and can be very proud of what you did,' blah, blah, blah.

All I wanted to do was get to Plymouth, see some mates and start to get better. But it was a good show by the top brass and people just saying thanks and recognising you personally for what you did, does go a long way in my book.

2

I was brought down to the waiting Royal Navy ambulance and was getting strapped in place by the young Navy medic who was going to be sitting with me for the journey.

'What's the date mate?' I asked.

'It's the 14th of June Sergeant.'

'It's Harry for this trip, OK?'

'OK Harry,' he said, 'let's get you back home.'

On the trip down, Gary Wetson, my new best Navy mate, said he was going to fill me in on the news from the Falklands. I was keen to know what was going on. News filtering onboard the Uganda was only partial and really the last couple of days had been just a blur anyway.

The old charabanc of an ambulance was shaking and rattling as we trundled down the country roads heading for the M5 and then the A38 to Plymouth. It was a grey day, but I could see the tops of lush green trees and English sky; there had been moments I thought that I would never see those again. I was a very happy man right now.

Gary began to fill me in on recent events.

'A few days ago, around the 11th or 12th June, I think it was 3 Para that were in the thick of the action again. They fought their way up Mount Longdon over some very difficult terrain and were up against some really well dug in Argentine defensive positions. The Argies put up some very heavy resistance and in some places it had come to hand to hand combat. I think the Argies came off worst though.' He said with a grin before carrying on.

'It had been really difficult to get up Longdon because the Argies had used every crevasse and small caves to hole up in. The Paras also had to fight their way through the maze of alleys that cut naturally through the rocks just to find them. You probably saw things like this yourself, didn't you Harry?' Gary asked.

'Yeah,' I replied. 'It's very tough terrain down there.'

Gary continued the story.

'45 Commando and the Welsh Guards did something to help 42 Commando take Mount Harriet.'

'A start line,' I said.

Gary had looked at me completely blankly, shrugged his shoulders and carried on.

'I also heard that a couple of squadrons from the SAS had attacked and taken the Murrell Heights. This was supposed to be an important place, I think.'

'I think you will find they are all important Gary,' I smiled.

'Yeah, you're right I'm sure of that, but the Navy did also get in on the act,' Gary continued. 'They fired hundreds, maybe even thousands of rounds from the ships to support all these actions.'

Somebody else, but he couldn't remember who, had taken Two Sisters. But he did know 45 Commando had been moving on Sapper Hill at around the same time.

'Yesterday was a big day though and a good one for our boys.' Gary was in full flow now.

'The Scots Guards had a hell of a fight with the Argentine 5th Marines to capture Tumbledown, the news people are saying that the 5th Marines are supposed to be some of their best soldiers. Anyway, it was an 11 or 12 hour battle but the Guards got there in the end. The Gurkhas have been in action too and took Mount William, but they were very pissed off because the Argies didn't stick around long enough for a good fight.'

'Gary, how do you know all this stuff,' I interrupted him as he was taking a breath.

'Oh,' he said. 'My cousin is down there. He's a medic in the Ajax Bay field hospital.' 'And.' he picked up his flow again. '2 Para have been at it again and got stuck into a place called Wireless Ridge. They can now see Port Stanley from there. They are completely mad that lot, but a fucking great bunch of soldiers, as are Royal Marines of course, Harry.' We both smiled.

'Nice escape out of that one,' I said. 'Phew,' was the sound that came back from Gary.

'Anything else happened that I should l know about Gary?'

'Well as you asked. Some more of your boys and the Welsh Guards took Sapper Hill, so pretty much now we have all the high ground around Stanley and are getting ready for the final push. The last thing I heard last night was a joint operation involving the SBS and SAS had gone a bit tits up. They were blasting up a place called Hurden Water and started to take fire from all over the place. Apparently, they were lucky to get out with only a couple of the guys getting minor injuries. And that's about all the news I have right now Harry but there should be more updates when we get back to Plymouth and RNH.'

I lay back and tried to get more comfortable, trying not to stiffen up by pre-judging the bumps and holes in the road that seemed to be attracting the old ambulance to them. Every time we hit one of them a sharp jab of pain would travel up and down my body and then quickly subside just in time for the next one. I didn't want any more drugs swilling around me right now so I decided just to grit my teeth.

I was thinking about the SAS and SBS operation Gary had just told me about and wondered if Bill and his team were involved. I also thought about what he had said at Ajax Bay. We did need to do something about what had happened to Tom, Bob, John and Jimmy, but that was for another day. I just prayed that Bill and the rest of the boys were OK.

'Gary.'

'What's up Harry, do you need anything?'

'No, no, I was just wondering what's the name of your cousin in Ajax Bay.' 'Oh, he's called Ken, Ken Parkin, he's a tall skinny guy who is losing his hair, what he had, and he's pig ugly too, but a good guy though.'

We both laughed at the final comment.

'I know,' I said. 'He looked after me in Ajax Bay and he is a bloody good guy.'

It's a small world, I thought to myself.

3

RNH Stonehouse, Plymouth 14th June 1982

1400 hrs and I'm looking around and feeling very privileged to be lying in my own private hospital room. These are usually reserved for Ruperts, but I think they must be making an exception for those of us coming back wounded from the Falklands. It's a compact room with a view overlooking the internal courtyard. The courtyard was nothing special, but it had a couple of trees and today you could hear the birds chirping through the slightly open window. The rest of the room was furnished with the usual set of drawers and a chair, plus various bits of equipment that beep at odd moments and a red button to attract the attention of nurses during the day – or night.

There was also a wardrobe on my right that at this moment had nothing at all in it. I hadn't exactly had much of a chance to pick up my kit before I left, but I'm sure it would find me again one day or I would get issued a full set of new stuff when I get out of here. Above the chair in the corner was my very own television suspended on a bracket from the wall. This is real luxury I thought to myself.

It was also really good in here because I could completely darken the room at any time of the day. Every window and the glass part at the top of the door were fitted with heavy grey plastic Venetian blinds. Not very attractive, as Kathy would definitely say when she saw them, but very functional and did the job just fine for me as I hated seeing any light when I was trying to go to sleep.

Sleep was hard to come by as from the moment I arrived I was prodded and poked by a whole host of people in medical uniforms and white coats, all wanting to inspect the various holes and operation sites on my body. There was a lot of umming and arring, nodding of heads and furrowing of brows, but none of them actually seemed displeased at what they saw. I think it was the first time any of them had actually seen what a bullet, or two, or three do to a human body. And then the questions and the forms that had to be filled in. Boy was I glad when they all fucked off and let me sleep.

4

I wake up on my second morning at RNH just in time for another visit from a whole gang of doctors. One last check-up and body inspection – more prodding and probing – before I have to go down to theatre for a few last bits of surgery.

'Just tidying up a couple of things. Nothing for you to worry about Sergeant. You will be fighting fit again in no time.' The Surgeon Commander said in a nonchalant voice.

'Thank you sir.' I replied.

The lights above my head are much brighter that anything in Ajax or on Uganda as I am wheeled down the corridor to the operating theatre. I have no fear anymore. I know I am in great hands and I'm hoping this will be the last time I do this for a while.

I watch the fully gowned anaesthetist push the plunger on the syringe and then feel the cold milky coloured liquid filling the back of my hand and then start to travel up my left arm. I knew that before the feeling of the cold liquid got anywhere near my elbow I would be in that wonderful pain-free drug-induced sleep again. I wasn't wrong.

I wake a few hours later from the surgery and all I can hear is loud noises. There is the sound of clapping and cheering coming from the corridors and other rooms close by.

A young nurse rushes into my room.

'We've just seen it on the news. There are white flags flying over Port Stanley. The Argentines have surrendered.' I lay back on my bed and smiled. No one else needs to die, us or them. I'd had a bellyfull of that for now and I knew it.

I watch the early evening news and the nurse had been right. There were white flags flying over Stanley, but no surrender had been signed yet, that was actually being sorted out as the news was being broadcast. I know I go to sleep with a smile on my face and my wounds didn't seem to hurt that much anymore either.

The next morning – day three at RNH Stonehouse – I wake up to hear it's all over. 2 Para were the first to get into Stanley just in front of the Royal Marines. My boys wouldn't have been happy about that but for all the fighting 2 Para had done it was probably the right thing.

General Menendez had signed the surrender document at 2359 the night before in front of Major General J. J. Moore. I turn on the TV and the newsreader confirmed that 'on the 15th of June 1982, our troops had moved into

Stanley to sort out the Argentine prisoners and make sure the civilian population were all OK.'

I smile again – it's another great day to be alive.

5

As the days and weeks passed by I watched the great scenes of joy and happiness from all over the country as the victorious soldiers, sailors and airmen came home. There were also many stories that started to filter out of the incredible bravery and courage from individuals in all the armed forces. The negative side was the terrible sight of the badly burned men from Sir Galahad and from other naval warships being brought home.

The pictures of young men with fresh air where limbs used to be, others swathed in bandages and being carried from the aircraft brought it home to the vast majority of people. This was the true sight of war.

A week after I had arrived in Plymouth I had a special visit from someone that I really hadn't expected to see. My dad Ron turned up with Gerri. I was still in a bit of a shit state at that point but seeing him was the best tonic I could have asked for. He looked mean and fit with his US Navy SEAL regulation haircut, shaved at the sides of his head with a quarter inch flat top on top. He would never change it. He had blagged his way onto a transatlantic US military flight to Brize Norton as soon as he had received the call from Gerri. They had spent the day before together just catching up on things and by the looks of it they had had a really good time!

We spent the whole afternoon together, it was a great boost for me to have them both there laughing and joking just as we had all done on his 'special' visits to the UK over the years. I took the piss out of Ron telling him he was getting old and past it because I had won my first arm wrestling contest with him only last year when he had come over on another one of his short visits.

He was still a Master Sergeant in the US Navy SEALs but told us he was being commissioned later that month due to his long and exceptional service. The next three years as a Lieutenant would do great things for his pension, he had said.

We reminisced about the past and how they had met. A story I had listened to a hundred times before but I always enjoyed hearing them tell it again. Gerri had been Gerri Axle then and had been a UK athletics track star representing Great Britain in the 1952 Helsinki Summer Olympics. Or as she always used to correct me, the XV Olympiad in Helsinki, Finland, to use its proper name.

She had run the 100 metres final in 12 seconds dead only to be beaten into fourth place by Shirley Strickland de la Hunty of Australia by one hundredth of a second. Worse was to come when she was injured shortly after the race, which meant she couldn't be part of the British 4 x 100 relay team that actually came third behind Germany and won themselves the bronze medals. Gerri was an independent, intelligent and determined woman who had studied physics at the Manchester Municipal College of Technology at the same time as she was developing her track career. After the Olympics, she ended her athletics career to study full time and went on to gain a Doctorate in Nuclear Physics, which was still a very new subject at that time.

The other great event for Gerri at the Olympics was meeting Ron. I noticed she still giggled when she recalled the moment and she still blushed a little. Ron was a US Navy man already but was also an Olympian representing the USA. He had just celebrated his 21st birthday before boarding the plane for the Olympics having made the weight to fight in the 81kg light heavyweight class.

His great disappointment was that he went all that way to Helsinki but never fought a single round in the Olympics. He was denied that honour by an injury to his right hand when a sparring session with his 'team mate' Lee Norvel, got brutal. There had been bad blood between them for a while so when the 'light sparring session' turned into a full on punching fight, and before the trainers could get in and separate the two men, Ron had swung a huge right that had got past Norvel's guard and was heading towards his temple. Norvel had ducked and twisted at the last moment and Ron's fist smashed into the top of his skull. He broke two bones in his hand. Even seeing Norvel slump to the ground was not enough to take away an even greater pain than was coming from his hand, it was the realisation that his Olympic dream was over.

Norvel went on to win the Gold against a tough Argentine opponent, which did nothing but make Ron even more determined to beat the guy up one day. I loved the part of the story when he tells us that he achieved it twice in later years knocking him out both times. That same wry smile always appears on his face at this point.

It still never made up for not being able to fight for the Gold medal and a chance to fight the great Henry Cooper who was in the same class at those Olympics. As everybody knows Cooper went on to become a great fighter and ambassador for the sport, and was someone who was able to knock Ali down on his arse as well, and not many had done that.

The next part of the story had Ron and Gerri play punching and poking each other with their fingers on the end of my bed. They were just like a couple kids as they fought to win the battle to tell the next part of the story.

They first met at the Olympic Village medical centre and then shared the ambulance that would take them to the local hospital for their respective x-rays. The next bit always made me cringe as they both blurted out 'the attraction between us was immediate and became passionate and physical very quickly.'

'No more, please don't tell me anymore.' I always joked with them at this point. No son ever wants to think about his mum and dad 'doing it'.

A great afternoon came to an end. The nurse hovering at the doorway had made it clear it was time for them to go. We promised to all get together with Kathy once I was out of the hospital and I could move around a bit more. I was really hoping it might be sooner than all the doctors had been telling me though.

6

Saturday 24th July – RNH Stonehouse Plymouth

Five weeks had gone by and I felt the anger building and the dark depression invading my brain and senses every day. I lay on my pit for hours and hours blaming myself for the deaths of my friends and comrades. Why couldn't I have saved them? What could I have done differently? Why did I survive and not them? I kept asking myself the same questions over and over again.

My main thoughts always came back to the same thing. Where were that fucking arsehole Colonel Muscardin and his henchmen? I wanted to kill him. I wanted to kill all of them who were involved.

I also thought a lot about SAS Captain Bill Dye and what he had said to me in Ajax. I pondered a lot about what we could do about what happened if we ever saw each other again. Even in my darkest moments I never thought negatively of the young Argentine Lieutenant who had been beaten up so badly, both by his own people – and us. I wondered if his nose would ever be straight again.

On good days, I even hoped he would be able to follow his true vocation into law. He could then help the people of Argentina come out of this very dark period in their country's history.

In the early weeks in hospital, the only thing to lift me out of my black moods were the visits from Kathy and Gerri. My spirits were lifted every time I saw them – especially Kathy.

It was at the end of the fifth week since arriving in Plymouth and I was getting up and moving about now. Kathy was due for a visit today so I had got myself up, shaved and washed early and so I didn't look like some minging tramp camping out on the London Underground.

I also needed a haircut desperately as I was beginning to look like Jimmy. Selfishly I didn't want to think about him today though – if I could help it.

Kathy was going to be on her own today, Gerri had to work. It will be great just having the two of us together for a while although visiting times were still being strictly enforced, even for me and the other wounded from the Falklands. There was no letting up on hospital rules and if Matron came round and found anyone still there after hours, there was hell to pay. She was a right old bag and a strict disciplinarian – even the Surgeon Commander didn't mess with her.

I had a bit of a secret weapon now though. Two weeks earlier a lovely face, that I recognised instantly, had appeared around the door. It was a sight that lifted me out of another black mood instantly.

'Hello Harry.' Mary Owen said from the door with a smile that went from ear to ear. I didn't know what I had done to deserve this attention, but I wasn't going to complain.

'How are you feeling now, Sergeant Glass?'

'I'm OK,' I had replied.

'Well, you are looking much better than the last time I saw you, that's for sure and everything still in good working order.' She winked and smiled broadly.

'Thanks – everything is,' I said, smiled and blushed a bit because I knew exactly what she was referring to.

It was really good to have a friendly face around and be able to talk to someone about the bad things I was experiencing. Mary had learned more about what had happened to me and the death of Tom and the rest of the boys. She also knew about the depression and black moods that suddenly overwhelmed me.

During the past couple of weeks, she had been to see me on most days and we had talked a lot about what I had seen. She had also told me about some of the horrific sights that had landed in front of her, especially after the bombing of the Sir Galahad. She told me with real sorrow in her voice:

'I felt completely useless when we received some of those Welsh boys who had been wounded by the fire. Their wounds were horrific. Some had no skin at all on legs, arms, hands and even their faces. The unbelievable pain they were in and the pitiful noises coming from burnt and swollen lips is something I will never forget.'

During her visits, we talked a lot about the future and what it would hold for both of us. I even told her that what I wanted more than anything was to kill the men who had murdered my friends and comrades in cold blood. She never judged me, but always gave me good council on what was right and what was wrong.

We talked a lot about Kathy and what I hoped for in the future. I also talked about not staying in the Marines – but that I wasn't sure what else I could do right now.

'Take your time,' she said. 'It will be at least a three or four months before you can start any physical training again. You also need to get some time and distance from the events of May and June of this year before making any decisions.' She was right of course and I knew it deep down.

It was just after 1600hrs on Saturday afternoon when Kathy slipped in quietly through the door. Mary was sitting on the bed with her back to the door too busy concentrating on removing the dressing on my leg wound to notice that Kathy had come in.

'This is looking much better now Harry. It's healing very well. This is the last one we have to do today so you can have some uninterrupted time with Kathy.'

Mary gave me a nudge in the ribs and a naughty wink. My head was already swathed in a clean white bandage and a new one had also been wrapped firmly around my gut earlier in the day.

Mary almost jumped out of her skin when Kathy said hello from the doorway. I grinned as I saw Mary's face flush knowing that Kathy must have seen the nudge and heard what she said. She didn't mention it at all though as the two women introduced themselves. They both said at the same time how much they had heard about each other and how nice it was to meet in person.

'I can't help it if I like talking about beautiful women,' I said.

They both gave me one of those looks only women can when they want you to stop talking immediately.

Kathy thanked Mary for taking care of me. Mary said I was an easy patient to look after and that it was a pleasure. I think she was lying just a little bit – I wouldn't have called me an easy patient on any day. They continued to talk to each other for 20 minutes, Kathy sitting on the end the bed whilst Mary finished sorting out the bandage on my leg. That process took an age due to the chattering between them and it always surprised me how personal women's discussions got, especially after just first meeting.

They talked about me and what went on recently, their personal experiences and all sorts of other stuff. All I could do was just lie there and listen. I learned early on that there's not much else any bloke can do when girls go off on one.

Mary finished sorting me out and got up to leave. She paused for a moment and said.

'Matron is not here tonight so stay as long as you want to, Kathy; he's in pretty good shape now. I will brief the nursing staff on my way out to leave you both in peace.' She then looked straight at me, smiled and gave me that naughty wink again.

When she got to the door she pulled the cord to close the door blinds tightly shut. These now matched the rest of them in the room. Mary gave a little wave and then closed the door behind her.

I don't think Mary heard, but Kathy said quietly. 'Thank you Mary.'

I said thank you Mary quietly to myself as well as I could feel a tingling sensation in just the right place and my gut was starting to knot up with the anticipation of what I hoped might happen next.

'Can I get up there with you for a while?' Kathy asked.

She was looking directly into my eyes and I could see straight away there was a little glint of something in hers.

'Sure you can.'

'What side would be best?'

'Left side,' I said, hardly able to contain the excitement I was feeling inside. The wound there was not really painful at all now and was healing well just like the rest of them.

I shuffled over to my right a bit and Kathy carefully eased herself onto the bed beside me. It had been a warm day and she was wearing just a short denim skirt, no tights. She had kicked off her white summer sandals a while ago now – which had gone under the bed somewhere.

She was wearing a crisp white cotton blouse that was unbuttoned just enough to show the cleavage of her small but beautiful firm breasts. They were captured in a pretty white lace bra and when I looked at her now lying down by my side, I could see the tops of them clearly through the opening. Christ, I thought to myself, it really was a long time since we had lain down together on the same bed. In fact, this was the first time we had been this close physically since I had left to go to the Mediterranean on the Brilliant in January.

We lay there together in the quiet for over an hour. It was just the right thing to do. The TV was on low in the corner of the room, but we hadn't been watching it at all. Now though there was a big shark or killer whale bouncing some poor unfortunate seal off its nose and then biting huge chunks of flesh from its body. I didn't really want to see any more blood and guts so I reached for the chunky silver remote on the bedside table and turned it off.

Kathy was resting her head on my chest when the TV went off – she lifted her head up and looked at me.

'I'm sorry, I didn't think you were watching that,' I said.

'I wasn't, I was just listening to your heart beating, it's such a wonderful sound and one I thought I might never hear again,' she replied – her voice cracked a little and I know I heard a little sob.

Her left arm stretched across my chest and tightened to give me a good hug. I was beginning to feel a bit emotional myself now but overriding everything else was the desire to make love to this wonderful woman. I couldn't have loved her any more than I did right at this moment.

Her head came off my chest and moved up towards my face. She paused for a second and looked into my eyes – and then I screwed up. I spoke.

'I bet I look like a right twat with this big white bandage on my head.'

'Shut up Harry Glass,' she said with just a touch of annoyance in her voice and it showed on her face. The annoyance only lasted for a fleeting moment though before her expression and eyes softened again. She leaned forward and kissed me gently on the mouth. She didn't pull away at all but stayed there to gently suck and nibble the thick parts of my lips.

It felt so good that she was this close to me again, kissing me like this. The feelings that were surging through my body were like multiple electric shocks and I felt more alive than I had done in weeks – months. Her left hand moved down slowly over the clean white bandage wrapped around my stomach and towards the electric blue M & S cotton boxer shorts that she had given me on her last visit. They had been the most comfortable thing I could wear and very easy to slide over the dressing and bandage on my right leg. All I wanted right now though was for Kathy's hand to carry on the path it was taking.

I didn't have to wait long.

Her small hand wrapped around my bone hard erect penis that was desperately trying to burst out of the cotton boxers that were holding it down. Both my hands held her face as I kissed her very passionately now. I could feel the blood charging around my veins and as I pulled back for a second to look into her eyes. I could see Kathy's face and neck beginning to flush to a deep red colour. Her hand was still inside my boxers gripping my throbbing penis tightly.

I kissed her passionately again as she released her grip very slightly and started to slowly move her hand up and down the length of the shaft. I thought I was going to explode there and then, but I desperately held on. I wanted so much for Kathy to feel me inside her right then but as I couldn't exactly start leaping around the bed and do all the things I wanted to, I knew I had to leave it to her.

I was writhing around now as she continued to massage the shaft of my penis. It was so full of blood that it was actually beginning to hurt. Not that I cared.

'Steady on tiger,' was the next thing I heard. 'It's been too long for us both Harry and we know it's not going to last long but I want to feel you inside me again now.'

Kathy rolled off the bed and stood a couple of feet away from me. My heart is pounding like a base drum and my breathing is fast and shallow as I watch Kathy slowly unbutton her blouse to reveal the pretty lacy white bra I had only glimpsed earlier. She threw it towards the chair in the corner of the room, but it missed and ended up on the floor. She didn't care. Next came the short denim skirt. It was sliding down her legs within a second of her undoing the waist button and sliding down the zip on her left side.

She was standing there in just her sexy bra and pants. Her beautiful slim body was perfectly in shape from her many days spent in the gym. Seeing her like this only made my heart beat even faster than it was already doing. She put both arms behind her back and expertly unclipped her bra and then seductively held it in place with her left arm, only letting it fall off her right shoulder slowly to gradually expose her right breast.

A second later both breasts were fully exposed and the bra had gone the same way as the blouse and skirt, straight to the floor. Her nipples were a deep red colour and hard. She obviously had had enough of this now and her pants came off without any further teasing or delay. I could hardly believe my eyes, Kathy was standing there completely naked right in front of me in my private Royal Navy hospital room. She looked so beautiful and so damn sexy I don't know how I didn't come right there and then.

I was trying to push down my boxers, but they were stuck.

'Little Harry not coming out to play then.' Kathy was smiling from ear to ear as she spoke. 'I will have him out of there in a jiffy just lift up your backside for a second,' she said.

Why women sometimes have to name these things, God only knows. But I really didn't care right at this minute and I got my arse off the bed as instructed. She had the boxers down and off before I could say boo to a goose.

Kathy eased herself back onto the bed next to me and then carefully moved her left leg over my hips so she was astride me but raised up on her knees so there was no pressure on the wound in my side. There was no more talking to be done as Kathy reached down and grasped my hard penis. She moved the head purposely into position and used it to slowly ease apart the moist lips of her vagina. As I looked down I saw the head disappear slowly inside her and then the rest of the shaft as she eased herself almost fully down on its length. She was so wet inside it only needed a couple of slow rocking movements before Kathy was filled by me.

I was in a place of ecstasy that you would only usually find in your dreams or fantasies. I loved Kathy so much right at this moment nothing could surpass my feeling for her.

We both let out a low moan at the same time as my hands reached up and cupped her beautiful small breasts. Kathy slowly moved her hips backwards and forwards and couple more times and then using her strong thighs she lifted herself upwards almost to the head of my penis before relaxing and letting herself slide back down the shaft. She began to increase the tempo with every stroke.

I tried in vain to help by thrusting upwards with my hips, but the right leg wasn't strong enough yet or properly healed. It let me know it too by giving me a couple of stabs of sharp pain, which Kathy saw as my face screwed up from the pain.

'Stop trying to help Harry – leave everything to me,' she whispered; slightly out of breath now.

I relaxed immediately and refocused on the total and absolute sexual pleasure coursing through my body and as much as I wanted this moment to last much longer, I just couldn't stop myself from exploding inside her seconds later. Kathy ignored my groans and continued to rock back and forward in increasingly rhythmic movements until I felt her suddenly tense up and then let go as her orgasm sent multiple shock waves through her body. Both our orgasms were so intense it felt like they carried on for minutes. Of course they didn't, but they were fantastic for every second of the time they were with us.

Kathy was still astride me with her head resting gently on my chest; her strong vaginal muscles still holding me inside her. Kathy took her hands away from my chest and put them on the sides of my face and then gently squeezed them together making my lips push out into a funny shape. She was looking down at me now with a mischievous look on her face. Her body was covered in a fine sheen of sweat that was running down her breasts and over her still erect nipples, I started to reach up to cup her breasts, but she pulled away and shook her head.

'They are too sensitive now for your great mitts to be playing with them,' she said. 'Just give me a hug please.'

She didn't have to ask twice.

She leaned forward and freed herself of 'little Harry' and then lay down next to me with her head resting on my chest. As I put my arm around her I managed to grab the corner of the sheet and blanket and pull it over us. Her head was just under my chin now and I could smell the lavender shampoo she had used that morning. It was a wonderful womanly smell. We didn't move or say anything and that was where we stayed until the early hours of the following morning.

The red digital screen on the bedside clock read 0546. Kathy was sleeping soundly beside me with the sheet and thick woollen service issue blanket covering her naked body. I didn't want to disturb her, but boy I needed a piss desperately. I tried to quietly sidle out of the bed, but she woke as soon as my feet hit the deck.

'What time is it Harry?'

'0546,' I told her.

'Shit,' she said alarmingly. 'I'm sorry Harry, I have to go. I need to get back home and pack as I've got to go to Sweden tonight with work. I forgot to tell you yesterday because we got distracted.'

Her face broke into a huge smile as she jumped out of the bed on the other side and faced me. She was still looking absolutely fantastic standing there with nothing on at all.

'You can put that away as well, Harry Glass. I really have got to go.' She was pointing straight at the huge erection protruding from my groin.

'Its OK Kathy, I'm just busting for a pee that's all, but are you sure you have to go?' I winked at her and smiled.

'Yes I do. Go and have your pee.'

Bugger it, I thought. But I had to go.

When I got back into the room Kathy was fully dressed, trying to smooth out the wrinkles in her blouse. She then began smoothing out her hair with a huge brush that miraculously appeared from her handbag that really didn't look big enough to hold it.

A couple of minutes later we said our goodbyes. We had a full body hug and I had slipped in a quick grope of her right breast, which got me a playful slap on the good side of my head. She said she would be back next Saturday. I said I couldn't wait and then she was gone. God how I loved this woman and although I knew the guilt would still be there, I was very happy that I had survived.

7

Time passed slowly even with the daily visits to the physiotherapist and the now twice weekly check-ups with the Surgeon Commander. I was feeling pretty good though as everything was healing really well – walking was becoming a lot easier as well with minimal pain now.

'I do believe we can be thinking about getting you away on sick leave very soon.' I heard the Surgeon Commander say. I was still thinking about Saturday.

'Excuse me, what did you say sir,' I said.

'Sick leave Sergeant Glass at the end of next week if everything continues as it is now.'

'Brilliant; thank you sir,' I said with a huge smile across my face; I needed to get out of his office now and call Kathy and Gerri.

'I could be coming home at the end of next week,' I blurted down the phone when Gerri answered. I had already tried to ring Kathy, but she must still be in Sweden.

'Just let me know the day you can come home and I will come and get you.'

'Thanks Mum.' I said smiling all the time.

We chatted for a couple more minutes, but then she had to go so we said our goodbyes and hung up. Things were improving every day for me and I was still getting news about what went on during the conflict from the boys in the squadron. They had been very frequent visitors since I got back.

It had taken a few weeks to get Bob's body released and I knew there was a lot of anger about that, but I had been ordered not to say anything about what had really happened until the formal inquiry had been completed. It was very hard not being able to tell the truth to Jeannie when she had complained to me about the delay in the return of Bob's body. One day she would know it all.

A number of memorial services were held for Bob after he had been buried. The squadron church had one. Plymouth Cathedral held one for him and all the other local servicemen who had died. The Cathedral was full of politicians and local dignitaries so he wouldn't have liked that one much.

The most important day was when Bob had been buried at his local church in the small seaside resort town of Bude in Cornwall. His mum, dad, Jeannie and the kids had been treated very well by the whole village. Everyone had turned out to say their goodbyes to a guy who was well known and liked very much.

I remember the first visit from Jeannie just a few days after I had got back to Plymouth. It had been more painful and emotional than anything else I had ever experienced. I hadn't known what to say except that he died doing a great professional job, trying to protect me and the rest of the guys. He was also a very brave man and a great friend who I knew loved her and the kids more than anything else in the world.

We had both cried a lot and even though the pains from my wounds were still pretty severe at that time, it was nothing compared to what she must have been feeling then. I had found it very hard to resist saying that I wanted to get the men who had killed him. Mainly because I couldn't; but also because I didn't know if I would be able to, or how I would go about it right now.

Today had been a good day for news, plus another visit from the boys in the squadron had done nothing but make my day even better. I had just finished off my roast chicken and veg supper when Mary put her head around the door. She had been giving me that knowing smile ever since Kathy's 'sleepover' and taking the piss saying things like; 'everything perky in here?' And, 'still got some blood left in your head then?' We had grinned at each other a lot.

'Hello Sister and what little quip are you going to leave me with tonight?' 'Sergeant Glass, whatever do you mean?' There was that smile again. 'I have someone who wants to say hello to you.'

A tall skinny shape appeared in the doorway whose smiling face was instantly recognisable.

'Hi Harry, looking better than the last time I saw you.'

'Ken Parkin,' I said. 'Well, I was wondering when you would be linking up with your cousin again. He said you would be back here at some point.'

'He's full of shit. Oh! Sorry Sister.' Ken remembered who he was standing next to.

'I've heard worse,' she said. 'I think I will leave you two to catch up but I'll be back later to check on you, Sergeant Glass.'

When Mary had gone, Ken went into great detail about the end of the conflict and how certain prisoners had been kept back for further questioning by the special interrogators. They had been sent down especially from the UK to back up those already on the Islands. Lieutenant Fernando Reynoso had been one of the prisoners kept behind.

'That SAS Captain.'

'Bill Dye,' I reminded Ken of his name.

'And one of the other SAS men in the room that day at Ajax and the Royal Marine you called Sparky I think, had been wounded on a combined SAS and SBS mission somewhere near Stanley the day before the surrender. All their wounds had come from grenade shrapnel and were fairly superficial, but still needed a good clean out and a few stitches. They all just came in, got patched up and insisted on getting back into action straight away, but they missed the end of the fighting as it was all over by the time they had hitched a ride back to Stanley. I bet they were pissed off at that.'

Ken was in full flow now.

'That Captain Dye was a scary fellow though when he came back in. His eyes were cold and staring and he didn't speak very much at all to anyone. There was also a serious amount of menace and anger about him, but I reckon if you had lost your brother in the same circumstances you would feel the same. I did hear most of the conversation when they brought in that Argie Lieutenant to see you,' Ken said.

'Anyway I know that Captain Dye stayed on to help interrogate the prisoners, and so the rumours go, he was a tough motherfucker who used some pretty hard and brutal methods to get them to talk. When we received the order on the 13th of July to say these 'special category' POW's could go back to Argentina, I was seconded to the MV St Edmund as some of them were not in good shape, we had to send a medical team back with them, which included me. That's why I've only just got back to work today after my leave.'

I had been listening intently; so Bill Dye was alive at least. I wondered if he got anything more out of Reynoso about Muscardin, or any of the other POW's for that matter.

Ken and I chewed the fat for a while longer and then we said our goodbyes. Before he went I said, 'Thanks again for sorting me out down there.'

'No worries Harry; you're welcome. I'll come and see you again before you go home next week.'

It was dark when Ken left and when I was alone I wondered if Bill would be searching me out or would I have to go and find him.

What I did know was I needed and wanted to get out of here ASAP now.

8

Tuesday 24th August 1982

10 weeks and one day after arriving at RNH Stonehouse and I'm walking, slowly, still with the aid of a stick, out of the hospital main doors to the car they had allowed Gerri and Kathy to pull up right outside. A small crowd had gathered to see me off. Everyone who had looked after me and had been around these past weeks seemed to be there. Nurses, doctors and other patients all clapping as I exit the building.

I took some time to stop and thank the Surgeon Commander who had done a great job of patching me up, physically and mentally to a degree. The nurses who all at some point had fussed over me and embarrassingly for me, but not for them it seemed, even had to wipe my arse in the early days. Ken and Gary are in the line smiling broadly. They have been real stars in every way for the duration of my stay. They have kept me furnished with a good supply of great movies, and even a porno or two when I was feeling better. I hadn't told Kathy that. They would definitely be coming to the Sergeant's Mess for a beer or two when I was back on active duty. That was going to be an excellent heavy night on the piss.

Even Matron was there in her pristine uniform puffing her ample chest out and trying to look stern and serious as she always did. I had got through to her though and although she called me a rough and a cheeky young sergeant, she now said it with a smile. I also knew now that under that prickly exterior, she was a magnificent and caring woman. Still someone definitely not to fuck around with but who absolutely knew how to run a hospital properly. I gave her a big hug and planted a big kiss on the cheek, which she didn't pull away from. She responded with a gentle hug of her own and a small rub on my back. Once we were apart she could feel the looks and hear the sniggers from the assembled group. It only took one fierce glance in their direction and nobody sniggered anymore. Not even the surgeons. She looked at me and cracked just the smallest of smiles, there was no doubt she cared a lot for all her patients and I knew I would miss her.

Then there was Mary. The beautiful Mary standing by the car door next to Kathy. She had been a constant presence and companion on my journey from the Falklands 8000 miles away, where I almost met my maker, to this moment of being able to walk almost unaided back to something like a normal life. She had seen me through some very dark times but had never judged me even when

I had snapped at her in anger just because she was the only one there. She had also made me laugh when I hadn't wanted to and talked seriously to me about wanting to kill more people. I think she now understood completely the pain I felt from losing my friends and comrades and why I wanted to do something about it.

She was someone whom I would never forget. We embraced probably a little bit longer than we should have, but what the hell. I knew Kathy understood how special this woman was and how she had taken such great care of me. I believed they had become real friends now as well. I had a feeling this would not be the last time I would be seeing her, or the new Navy boyfriend she had excitedly told me about that morning. I kissed her on the cheek and we said our goodbyes. Finally, I turned to the assembled group and just said, 'thank you.'

We left Plymouth and headed north towards home in Gloucestershire. It was just after 1300hrs so the traffic wasn't bad at all and pretty soon we were cruising past Exeter at 80 mph. Gerri didn't really bother with motorway speed limits much. Kathy had been unusually quiet so far on the journey home. I wondered for a moment if she was a bit pissed off or worried about the kiss and hug I had given Mary.

'Are you all right sweetheart?' I asked.

'I'm just glad to have you coming home with us,' she said whilst glancing over at Gerri momentarily.

'It's great to be coming home too,' I said, as I leaned forward and rubbed her right shoulder. I was sitting up on the back seat with my legs stretched across the back seats.

A couple of hours later and we were coming off junction 13 of the M5 and heading for Nigglesworth. It was only a few miles to home now, but we had to stop off at Tesco's and pick up something for tea. I stayed in the car just taking in the scenery as Gerri and Kathy wandered off into the shop. It was nice to see familiar places again and it even smelled like home.

The girls returned 25 minutes later laden with bags of stuff that must have filled the boot of the car. I thought we only needed something for tea and were not feeding the whole neighbourhood.

'Need to build your strength up,' was all Gerri said

Ten minutes later and we were driving past the Jovials pub and up the lane to Gerri's small but comfortable cottage. There were no welcome home banners or balloons tied to fences. These were all gone now. I was a few weeks late for all that although Gerri did say that the Jovials was planning a little homecoming party sometime soon, but only when I was ready for it.

They cooked me one of my favourite foods, chicken pasta. But the best thing of all was to be at home and just be with Gerri and Kathy. A bottle of good Pinot just topped everything off.

Kathy and I finally collapsed into bed around midnight, there was no sex. We were just too knackered. It had been such a long and emotional day. In the morning, it was different though once Gerri had gone off to work, but I still sensed something wasn't right.

9

I had been home for nearly a month and getting stronger every day, but I was beginning to get worried. Gerri and Kathy have been acting very strangely at times, getting into huddles and whispering in the kitchen or bedroom. I'm sure I'd seen tears as well but when I asked what was wrong I got a short sharp rebuke from one or both of them. I'm thinking maybe it's best just to stay quiet for a bit. Something was going on today though as Kathy has not been herself from the moment we woke up.

Does she want to end the relationship? Is she going to ditch me? These were the dreadful thoughts that were suddenly invading my brain. Maybe she can't do it because I'm banged up right now. Maybe me getting shot up is just too much for her to deal with. Maybe she has found someone else. All I know is I will have to get to the bottom of this tonight because I can't carry on like this. It's really beginning to do my head in right now.

The food on the table is good old British comfort food, cottage pie, peas, carrots and gravy but there is a definite tension in the room and nobody is smiling or talking as we usually did over supper. Even though I feel very tense and not really that hungry I still get stuck in. I know I'm only trying to delay the inevitable conversation really. A minute or two after tucking in and I noticed a couple of sly glances between Gerri and Kathy but immediately their eyes met they dropped to the plates of food in front of them. Kathy wasn't really eating anyway and was just pushing things around her plate.

She was very quiet now, much quieter than I had ever known her. Gerri wasn't much better either. Now is the time I thought. I rested my knife and fork on each side of my plate, deliberately making a noise at just the right level to distract them both.

'OK,' I said a loud voice. 'Enough is enough, what's going on here?'

They both look at me in complete shock as I never usually shout, especially at them. Then to my complete surprise Kathy burst into a flood of tears. I'm scared now. This is it, she really does want to dump me. I know it now. Gerri walked around the table and put her arm around Kathy trying to console her. I am more scared now than at any time since I was getting shot at in the Falklands.

'Harry, Kathy needs to tell you something important. You just need to sit there and listen. Don't say anything, just listen.'

This is definitely it, she has found someone else. The tears stopped for a moment and Gerri returned to her seat. Kathy was looking straight at me through those lovely blue eyes both now a bit bloodshot and starting to go puffy. Black mascara streaked both cheeks. As Kathy opened her mouth to speak, my heart was dropping through the floor.

'Harry,' she reached over and grabbed my right hand. 'You know I love you more than anything in the world.'

I'm listening, but I'm numb all over and waiting for the next bit.

'I am afraid I have to tell you something that was not in your plans for us right now.'

What the hell is coming? I'm thinking and panicking at the same time. There was a pause and then Kathy spoke quietly.

'Harry, I'm pregnant.'

Tears are falling again in buckets and Gerri is crying too. I just sit there stunned. Did I hear that correctly? All the air in the room seemed to have been sucked out and been replaced by a vacuum. Everything has gone fuzzy in my head. Did I hear her correctly? I asked myself again. Did she say she was pregnant? She isn't going to ditch me then? Fuck me I'm going to be a dad! How brilliant is that?

'Harry, Harry, say something.'

Kathy is tugging at my wrist looking straight at my face trying to suss out my reaction, tears still streaming down her cheeks.

'Harry, say something please.'

She now had such a pained expression on her face I knew I had never seen her looking so sad. The fog then cleared and the brain finally took in what she had said.

'I'm going to be a dad,' I said.

'Yes you are Harry.'

'Brilliant, just bloody brilliant,' was all I could think of saying.

Tears were now running freely down my cheeks, as well.

'I'm really going to be a dad,' I said again.

'Harry are you all right with it?' Kathy was gripping my wrist even tighter now.

'All right with it, are you crazy? This is the greatest news I could ever have wished for. A baby with you. There has to be a God up there somewhere.'

Everyone is bawling now but smiling uncontrollably. I couldn't believe it, I was going to be a dad. What had all that fuss and tension been about? What did they think, I wasn't going to be happy?

It took several minutes for all of us to regain a bit of composure and that was when I told Kathy that I thought she was going to ditch me.

'Stupid idiot,' she retorted and cuffed me around the back of my head.

Gerri and Kathy had been in cahoots for weeks ever since Kathy had missed her second period in August. For some reason, which I couldn't fathom, they had been worried that I might not want this right now after what had happened to me and because I still wanted to stay in the Royal Marines. How wrong they both were. This was the best news I had ever had.

The three of us spent the evening sat in front of the TV not watching anything in particular, it was just background noise really. We spent the time talking about the events leading up to today.

'It was that night in the hospital that did it,' Kathy said.

'Well at least some parts of me were working OK that night.'

Kathy giggled.

'Harry!' Gerri said in a mocking stern voice just like she had done when I was in trouble as a kid.

I went to bed and was still smiling as I cuddled up to Kathy. All the tensions were gone and I knew both of us couldn't be happier right now. I'm sure Gerri would be planning a wedding very soon even though nobody had spoken about that. I would do that part the right way, but for now everything was calm and I needed to sleep.

I reached over and gently stroked Kathy's belly and soon her hand was in mine gripping it softly.

10

Wednesday 10th November 1982

I'm pushing myself up the final 100 yards to the house. I'm blowing like an old whale, but it had only been a couple of weeks since I have been cleared to get back into full training so I don't think I'm doing too badly after five miles on the road. I should have been back running weeks ago really, but a small problem with the skin graft on my leg in September had put me back a bit. Pain in the arse it was, but not to worry about that now as I'm in the last 50 yards of my morning run.

At the crest of the hill, I clock a car on the drive that I don't recognise. Who's the fuck's that? I need a shower and some breakfast. I don't need to talk to one of Gerri's mates or some numpty about double glazing and new doors. I stop running and I can clearly see the shape of a man sitting in the driver's seat. I still cannot see who it is as all I can see is the back of his head but his hair is a bit long for a Marine buddy.

Old Mr Ray appears around the corner 30 yards ahead, his two ancient poodles walking closely alongside him as usual. At this time of the morning, it must be their first walk of three for today. I had better not catch his eye or I will be hearing about the 'real' war again. As our paths cross I just say a quick, 'Morning Ray,' get my head down and carry on walking towards the car.

It was a brand new white sporty Ford Escort RS1600i. The man in the car must have seen me coming and was now exiting the driver's door. I recognised him immediately.

'Hello sir,' I said.

'Hello Sergeant,' replied Captain Bill Dye of the SAS.

He stood there dressed casually in jeans, open neck shirt and a bomber style jacket hooked on one finger over his left shoulder. You would have never known this was a man in the toughest regiment in the world and who had just spent the past few months on covert and overt operations on the Falkland Islands doing what SAS men do and then when it was all over had spent some considerable time interrogating the Argentine prisoners who were of specific interest to the UK government.

'It's good to see you sir, how are things?' I asked.

'Things are OK Harry, but let's drop the sir whilst I'm here, it's Bill. Good to see you are back in training although it did look like those last 100 yards were a bit of a struggle.' Bill smiled and so did I.

'Shouldn't be long before I'm back in good shape though Bill.'

'Good, I'm counting on it,' he said with a surprisingly hard tone in his voice.

Strange response I thought, but I let it go for now.

'Let's go inside and I'll get a brew going Bill, this is obviously not just a social call is it?' No more was said until we got into the kitchen and the kettle had started to make the rumbling sounds of something getting ready to boil.

'How are the wounds Harry?'

'They're fine, I'm not getting any twinges from either the side or leg now and as you saw I am back running twice a day and will start with full weights next week.'

'Good news Harry.' Bill said and then went quiet for a few seconds before he spoke in a low voice.

'I know exactly what happened to Tom and the others Harry and I know who murdered them, and why, which is the most sickening part of it.' Bill took a long breath and continued. 'You may, or may not know, I stayed on after it all finished to 'look after' some of the 'special' prisoners. One of them was our Lieutenant Reynoso. You remember him?'

I nodded.

'Reynoso told me about the events at Rincon, plus a lot of other stuff. We also managed to get hold of his Sergeant and Corporal just as they were boarding the boat for home. They were not best pleased at being manhandled off it, but when Reynoso spoke to them they calmed down and then they confirmed it was them that had carried the beaten up and semiconscious Reynoso away from the hollow that Tom and the rest of you were trapped in. They also witnessed the killings and identified the men who actually fired the shots that killed Tom and the others. You were so lucky,' Bill concluded.

'I know,' I said quietly.

'Who was it then?' I asked, although I knew the answer to that question already.

Bill spoke clearly.

'It was Colonel Octavio Muscardin. Reynoso confirmed the name he had given us in Ajax Bay along with his Sergeant whose name is Jorge Manuel Astiz. A very nasty fucker by all accounts. Plus three other as yet unnamed soldiers from his little private army.'

We sat in silence for a couple of minutes just looking across the kitchen table at each other. My blood was boiling and my anger increasing with every breath I took. Murdering fucking bastards, we had surrendered, we were no threat to them anymore. Why, I asked myself again. Then I asked Bill the same questions.

'We believe it was done purely for some macho reasons and bragging rights back in Argentina.'

I was getting even angrier now, if that was possible. I knew we had to do something about it and Bill must have been reading my mind before speaking again quietly.

'In the past couple of months we have been trying to get to them through official Argentine Government channels. We haven't told them everything, just that we want to question certain individuals about 'incidents' during their occupation of the Falkland Islands. So far they have ignored every communication that has been sent to them. The military junta is having a bit of a tough time of it right now, as you probably know from the news. Ordinary Argentineans are demanding change and answers from the dirty war that has been waged against them since 1976. We know the junta are still fighting for their lives so we don't believe they will be giving up anybody.'

'You keep saying we,' I said. 'Who is we?'

'I'm coming to that now Harry; and why I'm here.'

'It was quite a few weeks after the war ended that I was able to bury my brother along with John and Jimmy. There was a good turnout, but questions are being asked by many within the Regiment, and outside, as to why it took so long to be able to put them to rest. The conclusions of the second autopsies and the red tape that then wrapped itself around the whole issue have caused a lot of people a lot of pain. In the end, it took one of the Joint Chiefs of Staff to tender his resignation to the Prime Minister to get the bodies released back to us and the families for burial. Since my return to the UK, I have been in London at Northwood and back in Hereford debriefing politicians and senior officers on the events of the war and the interrogations of Argentine prisoners. One of the main subjects of deliberation, and key to the delays in releasing the bodies was the murder of POW's by the Argentines, in particular Tom, Bob and John. It was clear from your statement, Harry, that Jimmy was already dead before the murders so he was formally classified as a legitimate casualty of war and that was why he could be buried before the rest of the guys.'

Bill paused for a second to take a swig out of his now cold coffee.

'Basically our so-called politicians are fucking the whole thing up with their pontificating and irrelevant posturing, whilst the killers are living it up back in Argentina.'

'Maybe we should put them in a fucking hole and let Muscardin and his henchmen have five minutes with them. That would have focused their minds and speeded them up a bit,' I said.

'Yes, pity we couldn't do that,' Bill said without a smile.

Bill continued.

'Harry we had got nowhere in getting any information about the other men involved, or in fact getting any answers at all from Argentina, until,' Bill paused and looked straight at me.

'Until, what do you mean, until?' I asked.

'Harry, what I am going to tell you now has to stay in this room and I mean in this room just between you and me; no one else, do you understand?' Bill continued before I could say anything. 'When I say you and me Harry that is exactly what I mean. No family, girlfriend, Marine buddies, no fucking body and if you cannot swear to that now I will be gone and won't be back. I have to know I can trust you.'

My head is spinning and I'm looking directly across at Bill over the small kitchen table thinking what the fuck is he going to come out with next? Before I can think anymore I hear myself saying,

'Of course I swear, you can trust me with anything you want to say.'

135

There was a pause in the discussion as Bill appeared to be checking out the small wooden carvings of chickens and pigs scattered around the shelves of the home-made pine kitchen units. Something that Gerri had been collecting for years and some of them were very old and you would probably say cute, if you were one of Gerri's ladies that lunched. I couldn't give a shit what they looked like right at this moment I wanted to hear what Bill had to say.

'Harry, I received a letter from Lieutenant Fernando Reynoso last week.'

I hadn't expected that.

'How?' I asked.

'The letter was posted in Canada by his friend and was addressed to Captain W. Dye, SAS Regiment, Hereford, England, UK and topped with 'Private and Confidential'. Of course, it was screened and sampled for any traces of explosives before I was able to open it; which I did in the company of my CO.'

Bill then placed the letter on the table in front of me.

'You need to read it Harry, Take the time you need, I'm going to make another brew if that's OK with you. I think I can find everything.'

With that Bill got up and wandered over to the Gerri's new Kenwood silver and green kettle that was sitting by the neatly arranged labelled jars of coffee, tea and sugar in the corner of the marbled-effect Formica worktop. Gerri liked things squared away. Just like me.

I flipped open the envelope flap that had been carefully eased open at Hereford with something very sharp to check for wires or any other sort of trigger. The letter was handwritten on very fine good quality paper and it was dated 1st November 1982. The handwriting was exceptionally neat and was obviously done with an equally excellent quality fountain pen. Not a smudge anywhere.

I laid the two pages down on the table, brushed them flat and began to read.

11

Dear Captain Dye,

You will no doubt remember who I am, but to be sure, my name is Fernando Alberto Reynoso and I am the Lieutenant you and your men captured at Rincon Grande along with a number of other Argentine soldiers.

Following my capture, you took me to Ajax Bay and to the building that was being used as a field hospital to see the surviving Sergeant from the atrocity that occurred at Rincon Grande. It was there that Sergeant Glass confirmed my involvement in the crime that was committed that night by soldiers of the Argentine Army. It was because of the honesty of that brave soldier that you and your men understood and accepted my story. You also interrogated me, twice, at Port Stanley prior to my repatriation to Argentina in July. I hope by that time you had concluded that my honour and integrity would not allow me to be part of any such crime and if I could have stopped it, I would have.

I am sure you would have been suspicious when this letter arrived from whatever country it finally gets posted from. If my friend has been caught smuggling this out of Argentina, he and I will surely be dead by now. However, if you are reading this letter I should still be alive and wish to help you avenge the death of your brother and the other men. I also want to help rid Argentina of the criminals who not only murdered the men on the Malvinas, but have abused and terrorised my own people for many years.

The Muscardin family are one of the worst perpetrators of violence against the ordinary people of Argentina and during the Malvinas war it was the younger brother Octavio who was on the islands from the first day. You almost caught him at Rincon Grande as I have found out since I returned home, but he just managed to escape you and get back to Argentina with his four bodyguards. His brother, General Don Juan Angel Muscardin, went to the Malvinas after the initial occupation, but returned to Argentina after only a few days. There is a strong rivalry between the two brothers and I now know it was a challenge laid down by the General to his younger brother that he would not kill anyone during the war.

Since I have been back in Buenos Aires, I have heard about the Colonel bragging that he killed many soldiers in combat and that some of them were Special Forces. I have also been visited personally by Muscardin and his men where he has threatened to kill me and members of my family if I ever talk about what happened at Rincon Grande.

Obviously I have not spoken out yet, so as of today nothing has happened to us. This is not to say it won't as I feel they are getting very nervous about the enquiries from England regarding the actions of particular individuals during the occupation and the worsening situation for the military junta here in Argentina.

I do not know what will happen in the future, but these men are evil and have brought shame and disgrace to my country. If nothing is done they will continue to threaten, rape, murder and steal from the good people of Argentina. If you wish to find the men who carried out the crimes at Rincon Grande and deliver justice, I can and will help you with whatever you need.

I will be in contact again via another route shortly to confirm you have received this communication.

Yours respectfully

Fernando Alberto Reynoso

12

I was staring down at the pages and thinking about this man. He had put himself at risk again to do the right thing, just as he had done at Rincon Grande.

'What are your thoughts Harry?' Bill was leaning against the kitchen worktop cradling his mug of hot coffee in both hands.

'It sounds like if we do nothing now it could be years before any justice is done, or never, and I don't like the thought of that.'

'No one does Harry and we heard from Reynoso again yesterday, which is why I'm here. He made contact through the US Embassy in Buenos Aires where apparently the US Ambassador is a good friend of his father so he was able to see him without much trouble and without raising suspicions. The US Ambassador then spoke to his counterpart in London, who contacted his friend Sir Mathew Wilkins at the Foreign Office. Sir Mathew then got the message to me via a former SAS Colonel who is now a Brigadier and is currently advising the Government and the Foreign Office on security matters.'

Bill passed over another piece of paper from the back pocket of his jeans. I unfolded it and pressed it down over the other two on the table and started reading the typed text.

Message for SAS Captain W Dye – Hereford

Muscardin still in Buenos Aires with his soldiers. Have secure comms route via US Embassy. I am ready to help. I wait for your response.

Fernando Reynoso.

It was very quiet in the kitchen and my mind was working overtime thinking about what next. I'm suddenly distracted by one of Gerri's pesky cats rubbing up against my leg. Feeding time no doubt.

'What can we do Bill? Can we get down there and do something? Would it be legal? Can we get weapons down there?' I didn't mean to blurt out all those questions but as I thought about them I just let them out.

'Whoa Harry, slow down, slow down. We need to talk about a few things first don't you think?'

The next hour was spent covering a few details. Firstly, I confirmed I wanted to be part of any operation, if there was one. That didn't need any further discussion. We then agreed the next steps we needed to take.

It was just after 1300hrs when Bill's white Escort pulled out of the drive and headed off down the lane. It was a minute or two before I wandered back inside as I was taking in the view across the valley and mulling over the past couple of hours' conversations. Could we actually go to Argentina and take revenge on these bastards? God knows they deserved it and not just from their actions in the Falklands by the sound of it.

A couple hours later I was still in my sports kit sat in the kitchen and having massive pangs of guilt regarding my instant response to Bill about definitely wanting to go and kill these bastards even though it probably meant going to Argentina to do it. A suicide mission if there ever was one. At no point had I thought about Kathy and my unborn child, now at 16 weeks and going strong. What the hell was I thinking? How could I go and risk not coming back to Kathy? I would have to call Bill in the morning and tell him I couldn't do it.

I sat at the kitchen table with more cold coffee for another hour wrestling with myself and now feeling even more guilty about not wanting to go because of Kathy. What about the murder of Tom, John and Jimmy? None of them should have died the way they did and then been left to rot in a hollow in the ground by those bastards. What about my best mate Bob, as well? My thoughts were broken with the sound of a car pulling into the drive. Christ, it's 1630 already and Gerri's home from work.

I leg it up the stairs for a shower after a brief hello and making the excuse that I had just finished my second run of the day. I didn't give her enough time to spot there were no sweat patches on me anywhere. I think I got away with it.

On the short walk down to the local pub, the Jovial Foresters, I'm still agonising over my hasty decision and agreement to go on a potential suicide mission to Argentina. What the fuck have I done?

Several pints later and some darts and pool with the locals I wobble out of the pub and wander back up the hill towards home. Through the beer goggles, I had no doubts now that I had made the right decision to do whatever it was Bill and I were going to do. But I also knew I had to make sure I got things in order, financially, so that Kathy would have everything I had if I didn't come back.

The morning run almost killed me I pounded the road on a short eight miler. The headache was nearly gone by the sixth mile and nothing had changed from my final drunken thoughts the previous night. I knew I had to go and do the job because I would never forgive myself if I stood back and passed up this chance to take revenge for what they did.

Muscardin and his cronies had to pay with their lives.

13

Two days later the doorbell rang at exactly 0900. The military driver was dressed in civvies and greeted me with a cheery, 'Morning Sarge.'

He grabbed my overcoat before telling me, 'I'm Corporal Jones, your driver for the day. It will take a good hour or so to get to camp but it should be pretty clear now all the work traffic has gone.'

Steve Jones opened the rear door for me to get in the back, but I declined and jumped into the passenger seat in the front.

'I'm not a General yet,' I said, 'the front seat will do fine.'

The journey took us down to the A46 towards Stroud and then left to the A38 at Whitminster. The route through Gloucester was always fun, but we only got held up a bit by the old docks that were looking very sorry for themselves these days. The A40 Ross-on-Wye road was moving well as we passed through the villages of Huntley and Longhope. This was nice countryside around here although my thoughts were firmly on the next few hours and how they could change the course of my life completely.

I had had to tell Gerri and Kathy a small white lie by saying that I was going to the nearest army camp to have my wounds checked over. I had to dissuade them from taking time off work to come and sit with me. In the end, they were fine though especially when I told them I was being picked up.

We pass through Much Birch and I briefly catch sight of the signpost. Hereford A49 straight on.

'Only a few miles now,' Steve informed me. He must have seen me looking at the sign.

We skirted to the south of the town and then motored on a couple of miles until branching off right towards Credenhill, our final destination and the home of the SAS.

After the usual security checks, we are through the gates and heading towards one of the old brick buildings. I don't see many people around and it all seems very quiet. That didn't last for long though as a green Jungley passed only 30 feet above the car with lots of bodies standing in the open doorways, the significant downdraft from the rotors buffeting the car as it went by. The Sea King helicopter then went into the hover just behind the buildings we were heading for. A dozen men and kit descend quickly down the hastily dropped ropes and then the noise increased by quite a few decibels as the Jungley rose into the sky and headed off across the fields.

'Morning Sergeant.'

'Morning sir,' I reply with a quick salute to Bill as he meets me outside the main door.

It has to be formal now as we are both in working combats and my Green Beret is on my head for the first time officially since the Falklands. Bill ushers me inside and then down a white painted brick corridor to an empty room. It's quite a large room with a decent conference room table, white board, projector screen and all the other bits you need to carry out operational briefings, or just to teach.

'Good trip Harry?'

'Yes sir.'

'OK Harry drop the sir in here, it's Bill when we are on our own.'

'OK. Bill.'

In the corner of the room there was a coffee pot, cups, saucers, sugar and spoons. There were biscuits as well. Chocolate ones.

'Shall we get one?' Bill saw me looking over at the cups,

'Yeah why not,' I said.

We didn't have to wait long until the door opened again, I only had a chance to drink half of the very decent boiling hot coffee.

Two men walked in and Bill and I stood up quickly and to attention. Colonel Colin Shaw, the current Colonel Commandant of the SAS, was a big man and carried himself in a way that said public schoolboy even before he opened his mouth. Next to him stood Brigadier Brian Whistonhall, the former SAS Commandant and now Foreign Office advisor. He was a very regal looking man standing bolt upright in his smart uniform that looked like it had just come out of the press, or been pressed by his batman.

The hat and gloves were placed on the table and the Brigadier's hand outstretched towards me. 'Stand easy Sergeant Glass, Harry. Excellent to see you are getting back to good health after your injuries.'

'Thank you sir,' I replied.

There would be no first names with these two even if he did call me Harry. Colonel Shaw also shook my hand and then gestured for Bill and me to sit down. The Brigadier went to get himself and the Colonel a coffee. I almost offered to do it as I was the most junior rank in the room, but managed to stop myself just in time as that would have been a right knobhead thing to do.

'Harry, I know Captain Dye has filled you in on events over the past few months and the recent communications from Argentina.'

I nodded and Colonel Shaw carried on.

'Brigadier Whistonhall and I are deeply unhappy about the murder of any soldiers, but especially three of our own. Brigadier Whistonhall is a former SAS Commander as I think you know.' The Brigadier had taken a seat opposite me now so I just nodded to him to indicate I did. 'We are getting nowhere through the official channels and it seems increasingly unlikely that we will achieve anything this way. We are also concerned that if there are changes in Argentina and the Junta is removed; very quickly the perpetrators of these crimes will just disappear into the pampas, or elsewhere, and we will never get to them. This is why we are here today.'

I didn't feel the need for me to say anything at this point so I just stayed quiet. The Colonel looked over at Bill indicating he was to speak.

'Harry, we had another communication from Reynoso yesterday. He says he has received information that the Muscardin brothers are planning to eliminate him and the other witnesses to the killings at Rincon Grande. He also fears for the rest of his family if something cannot be done, and soon. He could be dead before we can do anything. Reynoso says he has made arrangements to defend himself and his family, but if he is executed we could not rely on any support from within the country if that happened. I have been in discussions with Colonel Shaw and Brigadier Whistonhall ever since we received the first communication from Reynoso and I now have agreement for us to go and do something about these bastards.'

I nodded to indicate that I was listening. Colonel Shaw stood up before he spoke again.

'Sergeant Glass, we are talking about a black operation in Argentina that would be totally deniable by the UK government and of course this Regiment, and the Royal Marines. Both of you would be on your own and if any of the Muscardin family or their allies catch you I believe you would be executed after significant amounts of torture and pain.'

Nice thought for me to ponder on!

'What I and Brigadier Whistonhall want if you are willing to volunteer of course, is for both of you to get into Buenos Aires and find, with the assistance of Fernando Reynoso; Colonel Muscardin, Sergeant Astiz and the other three as yet unidentified soldiers, and eliminate them.'

I had agonised over this moment and what I should do because of Kathy and our baby, but I needed to do something and I badly wanted revenge for what they did.

'Where do I sign up,' was my reply.

Bill grasped my offered right hand and said.

'Let's do this for Tom, Bob Jimmy and John.'

'I'm with you Bill, 100%.'

Both the Colonel and Brigadier stood up and offered us their hands. After firm handshakes were exchanged it was down to business. The rest of the day was spent planning and sorting out lists of kit and supplies we were going to need. How we were going to get into the country, what maps we would want, money, documents, RV points, ERV points and most importantly, weapons. The car finally came to take me home just after 1900hrs. It was a quiet ride home as I had lots to think about. I had just volunteered to kill myself.

But not before I took some of those bastards with me.

14

Three weeks, five further messages from Reynoso and several planning meetings with Bill later, all of them now taking place in a rented house a few miles from Credenhill, and we were nearly ready to go. Two weeks earlier when I was signed off from sick leave, I had been called into the CO's office in Poole and told I had been seconded to the SAS for three months to carry out elite training with some of their Boat Troop. It was deemed a good job to ease myself back into operational life. No one had blinked an eye although it was a complete sham arranged by Colonel Shaw.

'It will also give you more time to heal properly and be closer to Kathy, blah, blah, blah,' my CO had said.

Gerri and Kathy were both happy that I wouldn't be too far away as they wanted to keep their eyes on me. They were even happier when I told them that I would be home at the weekends for the next three weeks at least, but after that I would be away on exercises for a couple of weeks. I didn't like lying to them, but I was committed now to what Bill and I were going to do.

Bill and I worked every day on the plans. He pushed me hard on the fitness training, often ending up at the base gym at 2000 for a final hour on the weights. We had been pushing out 13 mile runs daily for the past week and I felt really strong and in top shape now with no after-effects at all from any of the wounds. Some early mornings were spent at the range honing our small arms accuracy and refreshing some sniper training and weapon handling. It was as good as it was going to get by the second week of December. Bill and I were completely in tune and had learned a lot about each other in a very short time. I knew I could depend on him, and he on me.

15

0900 hrs Friday 17th December 1982 – Credenhill

I was back in the same room that I had come to a few weeks earlier and was standing in front of the same two men, Colonel Shaw and Brigadier Whistonhall. Bill was on my right and after a cordial welcome it was straight down to business. There was a serious air to proceedings today and a very definite tension in the room.

'Captain Dye, Sergeant Glass, are you ready?' Brigadier Whistonhall spoke directly to both of us.

'We are sir,' replied Bill.

'I'm sure I don't have to remind you both that this is a deniable operation and if you are compromised you will be on your own. We or the British Government will not be able to intervene on your behalf.'

'We understand sir.'

'You leave tonight on the scheduled flight to New York, correct?'

'Yes sir.'

'I assume all the documents you were given yesterday are in order?

'Yes sir they were,' Bill replied.

'And I doubt anyone anywhere would know they are not authentic as we still have some very talented, although misguided people, who are more than willing to help when threatened with expulsion from the UK.'

The Brigadier and Colonel were both smiling now and I knew why. Bill had told me of an illegal Eastern European living in Manchester that the security forces and the Regiment squeezed sometimes when they needed passports and documents for black ops. The items on the table in front of us were as near to perfect as you could get, but completely untraceable back to the source if we got caught.

Bill had paid Ivan, the individual in question, a visit a couple of weeks earlier with the shopping list of stuff we needed. It had all turned up yesterday via two couriers and a very obscure route starting in Manchester then via Oxford and finally Gloucester. Finally, Corporal Steve Jones had got his hands on the package at the front entrance of the beautiful Cathedral in Gloucester city centre.

When Steve had buggered off after delivering the package to the house, Bill had emptied the contents out onto the table in front of us. There were two passports, one Canadian and one US. Bill's cover was William Lowe, a Canadian journalist working at the Toronto Star Newspaper and I was Harry

Finch a US journalist working for the New York Post. There were also covering documents backing up who we were and letters from the current editors. They were excellently forged of course, giving the details of our collaborative assignment for our respective newspapers as conducting post Falklands War reactions from the people of Buenos Aires.

Also enclosed were reference articles we had supposedly written and the names of two key people, one at each newspaper, who could be called if there was a need for further clarification on anything. This was the biggest hole in our story because they didn't exist and we couldn't get anyone else involved from across the pond because essentially what we were about to do is illegal. It would just be a case of fronting up and if you act as if you are who you say you are and that you should be there, 99% of the time you can blag your way through it.

We had everything except the plane tickets.

'You will need these now.' Colonel Shaw placed six envelopes on the table.

'Inside the first two envelopes are two return business class tickets from London to New York in your real names. These have been booked separately so it will appear you are travelling independently. The return tickets to London are open for one month so you will be able to catch any available flight back here when you want to. The next two envelopes contain return open economy tickets from New York to Buenos Aires in the names of Lowe and Finch. These were booked at the same time to indicate you are travelling together on your journalistic assignment. In the final two envelopes there is $500 US currency and 5000 Argentine Pesos in cash for each of you. If you need any more you will either have to steal it or get it from Reynoso.'

Colonel Shaw then reached into his inside jacket pocket and produced a folded piece of paper.

'I received this message last night from Reynoso – it reads:

Message understood. Pick up and transfer to hotel from airport arranged Sunday 19 Dec. Will make contact Monday AM. Stay in hotel.

Reynoso'

Brigadier Whistonhall had been sitting there quietly, just watching us and listening to us go through the documents, flight details and the note from Reynoso.

'Captain Dye, have any details of the plans changed,' he asked.

'No sir,' Bill answered. 'Although no doubt we will have to improvise when we are on the ground.'

Brigadier Whistonhall relaxed, sat back in his seat and took a sip of coffee before speaking.

'Let's hear it one last time please Captain.'

'Sir,' Bill started to talk. 'The route into Argentina is via New York as you have heard. We will be on the ground in Buenos Aires Sunday afternoon around 1600hrs when we will be picked up by one of Reynoso's men. He is called Thomas. He will be in the arrivals lounge and have a board with our names on it.

Sunday night we stay in the hotel and wait for contact with Reynoso on Monday. We will then be taken somewhere, as yet unknown, to pick up the weapons we have requested. All will be Argentine military and untraceable to any individuals. I have asked for two Mauser M1909 Snipers rifles, which will have been modified from the German Gewehr 98 model, so we know they are good bits of kit. Two Pistola Brownings, which are based exactly on the UK version of the Browning pistol but manufactured in Argentina, and finally two P.A.M. 9mm machine guns that will put down some heavy fire if we need to get really noisy.'

Bill paused to check the Brigadier was up to speed; he was.

'After picking up the weapons we will then need to travel approximately 45 minutes to get eyes on the target's home. We will do a drive-by, if safe to do so, avoiding the attention of the estate security guards that we know are there. We intend to recce as much of the area as we can and will then return to the hotel. Later that night we will go back to the estate and hopefully get eyes on the target when the family sits down for the main evening meal; which is after their second visit of the day to the local Catholic church.'

Bill looked over and gestured for me to take over.

'Sir, the following morning Reynoso is going to provide another car plus two men if we require it, but the man who is picking us up at the airport plus another will be with us for the duration. Both of these men Reynoso trusts implicitly as they are fathers of children who have 'disappeared' and obviously have a deep hatred for the junta and members of the Muscardin family who they believe are responsible for what happened to their children. We plan to follow Octavio Muscardin as he leaves for Buenos Aires on Tuesday morning and that is when we will assess the situation and take our chance if one presents itself. But, if we get an opportunity on Monday at any point, we will take it and kill the men who murdered our friends and comrades. We have a couple of days to create an opportunity to complete the job if nothing presents itself on Monday, but whatever happens we need to be out of there by Thursday at the latest.'

I check the Brigadier is still with me. He nodded indicating he was so I carried on.

'According to Reynoso intelligence, Octavio Muscardin visits a gentleman's club in the centre of Buenos Aires at least three times during the working week, but he always goes there on a Monday. This is a place that could provide us with a good opportunity later in the week if we don't take him somewhere in open ground.'

Brigadier Whistonhall stood up and then spoke quietly; but with firm resolve in his voice.

'Well gentlemen, I have to be getting back to London. Let's make this bastard and those others pay for what they did. Good luck.'

Bill and I both saluted as he turned away from us and left the room. We could hear him talking to Colonel Shaw as he headed out of the building. A couple of minutes later we heard a car pull away from the front door. We assumed it was him.

Colin Shaw re-entered the room a minute later.

'Anything else we need to go through?'

'No sir, we both replied.'

'Ok, I'm sure you both have things to tidy up before the off. Corporal Jones will pick you up at the house at 1400hrs. Good luck gentlemen.'

'Thank you sir,' we said in unison.

We all left the room and went our separate ways. No one else knew where we were going next and what we were going to do, which was definitely the right thing for everyone's sake.

Part Three

Black Operation – Argentina

1

I had said my goodbyes to Gerri and Kathy the night before. Gerri had been working, but Kathy had managed to skive off and spend the whole day with me. I hated telling her lies about going off on exercise for two weeks. My gut churned up every time she mentioned it, but I think I deflected most of the questions easily enough, although I'm not sure she was totally convinced. I'm a crap liar.

After Gerri had gone off to work we had got up and had a leisurely breakfast just chilling out and listening to the morning show on the radio. Things then got a little silly when Kathy started flicking rice crispies at me over the kitchen table. I started to chase her around the house before finally catching her at the bottom of the stairs. I picked her up in both arms and carried her back up to the bedroom. She did put up a little bit of a fight when we got there, but not much of one.

The next hour we spent exploring each other's bodies and making love gently; so as not to frighten the baby as I had so delicately put it. Kathy was not so impressed by that comment and had playfully screwed up her face in mock annoyance. She was very happy though when I spent lots of time rubbing her back and her ever increasing belly bump. I was torn between being incredibly happy with my lot right at that moment to being in utter despair at the thought of never being able to hold this beautiful woman close to my body again. I did my best to force the doubts, and a significant amount of fear for what I was about to do, to the back of my brain; but I couldn't stop the gnawing sensation in my guts, whatever I did. I almost went into a blubbing fit when she told me 'she loved me so much' for the umpteenth time during the day. But I held it together; like a man.

The rest of the day we just did some shopping, for girl's shoes no less. There could be no doubts now how much I loved her too. Then we did an afternoon movie, I have no idea what it was about or even the name of it. It was just great to be in the dark holding hands and having Kathy cuddling up to me.

1900 hrs had come too fast and it was time for me to leave for Hereford. I had my big tough face on and didn't cry when I left Gerri and Kathy on the doorstep waving happily thinking I was off to play a few war games with my buddies, but I did ball my fucking eyes out for a good couple of minutes in a lay-by half a mile outside Nigglesworth. Hopefully nobody saw me.

The overriding thought in my head was what the fuck was I doing leaving Kathy and my unborn child to go to Argentina of all places? It is one of the most volatile and dangerous places on the planet right now especially for a British

SAS Captain and Royal Marine SBS Sergeant who had both been killing Argies on their beloved Malvinas only a few months before.

I had no illusions or doubts on the risks of the mission, I never did, or that there was a higher percentage probability that I wouldn't be coming back alive; especially if we got rumbled or into a fire fight with Muscardin and his men. I was scared and I knew it; not about the actual getting stuck into the Argies or killing Muscardin, it was all about never seeing Kathy ever again, or my kid, ever.

My biggest regret was that I couldn't get her to marry me before I left. She had been adamant that she wasn't going to get married while she was pregnant and when Gerri had agreed and sided with her I knew I was never going to win so I had given up on that one straight away. 'There's no hurry' she had said innocently.

It had taken a while to pull myself together in the lay-by, but I knew there was no going back on my word or my commitment to avenge Bob's death and the other guys', plus everyone whose lives had been so cruelly affected by those bastards. I was fit, healthy, and now had been trained by one of the best soldiers I had ever come across. I was ready to take my revenge and Bill needed me so I couldn't let him down now.

2

I was ready to go dressed in casual chinos, a blue shirt with no tie, and a well lived in brown sports jacket. Bill was similarly dressed but with blue cords.

'Do we look like journalists?' I said to Bill.

'We are probably too smart. We should have said we worked for the Canadian or American version of the 'Sun' then we could have just been scruffy.'

We both laughed out loud, but Bill's comment did momentarily take me back to the tremendous job that particular newspaper had done during the Falklands conflict. It had kept up our morale with the great coverage of what was going on, loads of sport, news and the most beautiful women with fantastic tits on Page 3. Nothing better to keep a man's spirits up.

Steve Jones knocked on the front door at exactly 1400hrs.

'Heathrow Airport it is then. Going somewhere nice?'

He knew he wasn't going to get an answer for that question so when Bill gave him that stare he knew not to say anything else for a minute or two. I knew it wouldn't last though and football would be the topic of conversation very shortly and most likely be about his beloved Manchester United. I was pretty sure Bill would be telling him to shut the fuck up, but not in quite those words, in less than an hour.

He did.

Bill actually succeeded in shutting up the gabbling Steve Jones within 30 minutes by telling him to 'Concentrate on the road Corporal. We need some quiet for a while.'

'Yes sir,' had been the swift reply.

The miles began to close as we steadily progressed towards Heathrow. The car was quiet except for the low hum of road noise and the occasional honk of a horn from some irate driver trying to get someone to move from the outside lane of the M5, even though they were clearly doing over 80mph. At Bristol, we swung left onto the M4 and by the time we reached Reading we had both read everything in the final briefing packs again. Everything was returned to the briefcase that Steve Jones would be taking back with him.

The journey was going well and it wouldn't be too long before we saw the signs for the airport terminals. Bill closed his eyes after Reading and had dozed off. A few minutes later I was digesting the information we had just read when I saw my first plane descending over the factories and nearby houses on its approach to its specified runway at Heathrow. I watched the plane dropping lower and lower until it eventually got so far into the distance it became just a speck in the sky. I was feeling a little tired so I thought the best thing to do was try and rest my eyelids as Bill was doing; and before Corporal Jones started talking about bloody Manchester United again.

The rest of the journey was uneventful. The M4 was flowing smoothly for a change and I was brought back from my dozing when I hear,

'Sarge, we will be there in about five minutes.'

Steve had turned his head back towards us momentarily from the driver's seat to tell me.

'Thanks,' I replied as Bill opened his eyes.

'Are we there?'

'Yes sir, we will be there in a minute,' Steve answered him.

There was no queue outside Terminal 3 and once our bags were removed Steve secured the briefcase containing the confidential briefing packs in the boot. We said our goodbyes and Steve was heading back to the motorway in less than two minutes from the time he had dropped us at the front of the terminal.

Once inside we had a quick look at the flight departures board for the early evening flight to New York. We found it and then headed off through the milling crowds to Desk 15 to check in and dump the bags.

After clearing security, Bill said.

'Let's find the lounge so we can have a beer and some quiet.'

Steve Jones hadn't been completely silent on the journey up and I had engaged in some football conversation, but not much as it really wasn't my game.

'I don't know about you but I need a beer right now.' Bill was already heading off in the direction of the 'business lounges' sign before I could respond properly.

'I'm with you Bill,' I muttered to myself and headed off after him.

The airport was not too busy at this time of night. A few old dears were clustered together by the perfume stand in the duty free, giggling and laughing like a bunch of sweaty teenagers out on their first school trip. One of them was spraying great clouds of some pungent smelling stuff into the air and then getting the others to walk through it. I only hoped they wouldn't be sitting too close to me on our flight as they were going to stink. I heard another fit of laughter from the group as I left them 20 yards behind me.

The terminal was looking a bit shabby, but I could see they were trying to upgrade it and were expanding the area we were walking through quite significantly. Probably more retail outlets to prise even more money out of us poor saps with nothing else to do for an hour or two.

Bill was waiting by the door of the lounge.

'Did you need to get anything from duty free?' He asked.

'Sorry Harry I just wanted to get somewhere out of the way and buggered off without thinking.'

'No worries Bill, I don't need anything except that beer you spoke about. It must be my round.'

'You're only saying that because it's free.'

We both smiled. We also knew this would be the only time we had to savour a nice cold beer because it would be our last until the job was done.

Just over two hours later the Boeing 747 thundered down the runway for our seven hour flight across the Atlantic. Life in business class was very nice and as I settled into my big seat drinking my glass of freshly squeezed orange juice I had to crack a smile as I watched the same bunch of old dears wander past me, stinking of a vast mixture of exotic perfumes and still giggling and jostling each other on their way back to their seats in cattle class.

This was a first for me, great food and lots of free wine and beer, if you wanted it, and great attention from the stewardesses; even the male ones. Lovely boys they were too.

This is something I could get very used to, but I knew I probably wouldn't.

3

2000hrs Friday 17th December 1982 – Hurlingham Club

Buenos Aires Province, Argentina

Colonel Octavio Muscardin was in the centre of a crowd of men leaning on the large oak bar in the comfortable main seating area of the clubhouse.

He was holding court with his faithful bodyguard Sergeant Jorge Astiz standing nearby looking menacingly at anyone who got too close. The place had a very distinctive English feel to it with oak wood panelling all around the room and sturdy oak columns holding up more fine oak panels that decorated the ceilings throughout the club.

Fresh flowers cut that morning adorned every corner of the room and most of the tables. The sweet scented aroma allegedly had the effect of making the members relax as soon as they entered the rooms.

The polo club was in Hurlingham, an affluent province of Buenos Aires and was set in 73 hectares of a beautiful and rich landscape. The beauty of the place was only enhanced, for its horse-loving members, as its fine stables were also home to many of the top polo thoroughbreds from all over the country. There were cultivated polo fields spread across large areas of the land; tennis courts, squash courts, a gym and many other first class facilities for its very exclusive and wealthy members. It even had a full size cricket pitch.

It was named after the Hurlingham club in Fulham, London and was set up in 1888 by the local Anglo-Argentine community; since then it has been 'the place to be seen,' for all its years in existence.

There was quite a crowd in tonight for Grandma Muscardin's 70th birthday. Even the elusive and secretive General Don Juan Angel Muscardin, the older brother and chief tormentor of Colonel Octavio Muscardin was there quietly sipping a glass of fine Malbec from the Luján de Cuyo region. His eyes though were firmly fixed on his increasingly louder little brother who was guzzling Dom Pérignon like it was fizzy water. The General knew he would have to quieten him down shortly before his tongue got too loose.

The General had escaped all the hatchets after the Falklands War because he had only spent a week on the islands just after the invasion. He and Major General Mario Menendez, the Islands' new military Governor, did not see eye to eye on many aspects of how the Argentine forces and Island civilians should be treated. The British politicians and military had known it would have been a whole lot worse for the civilian population of the Falklands and any POW's if General Muscardin had been in command.

Both during and after the war General Muscardin had been very vocal about the lack of leadership and professionalism of the commanders on the Malvinas. He had on a couple of occasions even uttered the words 'cowards' in public with regard to the Argentine senior military officers who had tried in vain to stop the British humiliating the Argentine forces and taking back the Islands.

This had gone down well in many quarters and because of this he now held even more power than before the war. This actually meant to him and his family even more money coming in from the corrupt activities he sponsored and also greater freedom from prosecution for his violent methods of controlling and dealing with any vocal opponents or dissidents.

The volume of the laughter and general joviality rose a couple of decibels as the Colonel, in a loud and booming voice, recounted the moment he killed the 'so called elite SAS men.'

'We had them trapped in a hole after tracking them through the day to their hiding place,' he said in an excited voice. 'At nightfall we waited on the route to their boat that we had found earlier that day and then,' he paused only to allow his gathering to draw in closer before continuing his boast, 'we cornered them and tried to get them to surrender. But they wouldn't. So when those that were still alive raised their weapons at us we had no choice, did we Sergeant?'

'No sir,' was Astiz's prompt reply.'

'What happened next?' Came the excited question from one of the throng surrounding the Colonel.

'We had to take evasive action as they fired at us but we were too quick for them. Then we just blew their fucking heads off, didn't we Sergeant?' He laughed as he finished.

'Yes sir, we did. Then Ricardo, Jorge and Costa filled them up with a few more bullets to make sure they would never come back to fight us again.'

The roar of approvals reached new levels from the assembled group and glasses were clinked together celebrating the bravery of their Colonel standing before them. Octavio Muscardin was lapping it all up and failed to notice Alan Patrice in the far corner of the room.

Alan Patrice was a good friend of Fernando Reynoso from law school. He was also an accomplished polo player as had been his father. He had been a member of this club all his life. The Patrice family had been seen as bleeding liberals by the Muscardin family and had been political targets for them in the past.

No one in this room right now was a friend of Alan Patrice.

Alan Patrice though was taking in what was being said and trying to pick up on any information that could be useful for his friend Fernando. In particular he had been asked to listen for any travel plans for Octavio during the coming week.

Alan narrowed his eyes enabling him to focus clearly on the General who was now approaching the group of pissed up men surrounding his younger brother.

'Time to eat Colonel,' he spoke in a very formal and stern voice.

The responding, 'yes sir,' was said with the cockiness that only drink and brotherhood would allow when addressing such a senior officer; even in this environment. They were both in full dress uniform so military discipline had to be upheld.

Alan sat quietly in the corner of the room in a heavy dark brown leather chair, a large cigar slowly burning in the white marble ashtray next to a strong black coffee on the table beside him as he watched intensely the Muscardin family and their arse-kissing buddies.

His intense hatred for the Muscardin family, but in particular for the two brothers in front of him, was always with him. It became almost unbearable when he saw them in the flesh, as he could right at this moment. His heart was beating very fast so he was taking slow deep breaths, his hands and face were clammy and trickles of sweat ran down the back of his neck wetting the crisp white collar of his shirt.

If he had had a decent weapon in his hand he would have used it to kill them both, just as they had done to his father and brother two years previously. He was absolutely certain one of the brothers had done it, or ordered someone else to do it, but not surprisingly no evidence or witnesses could be found so the case file went into the same black hole as the thousands had done before it. Alan Patrice brushed away a tear of frustration as he dropped his newspaper onto his lap for a moment and picked up his coffee for a sip of the now cold black liquid.

The rest of the evening was going as planned for the Muscardin family. The private dining room was full, everyone was there, Grandma, uncles, aunties, sisters, brothers, cousins, nieces, nephews and the newest addition, three month-old Caroline, new daughter to Don Juan and Octavio's first cousin, Julia.

Eva Muscardin, the sister who had been born three years after Don Juan and two before Octavio, was holding baby Caroline out at arm's length like she was an alien or something. Her face was contorted into a scowl that said to any onlooker, 'Get this thing away from me.' Baby Caroline was retrieved seconds later by a worried looking Julia.

The vast majority of the family's enemies believed that Eva was the most evil of all the three Muscardin siblings. Octavio certainly never messed with her. She had also reached a very senior rank within the 'security' services and was known for being an expert at female torture, but wasn't averse to slicing off a man's balls if he pissed her off; even after they had spilled their guts.

All together there were 27 members of the Muscardin clan in one room. To the rich, famous and those in the seats of power the Muscardin family were a good Catholic family. The mother and father had attended church every Sunday until they were both killed when their private jet had mysteriously crashed three years earlier. The family never discovered how the crash happened although many outsiders believed members of the family were involved somehow in order to seize the power their father would never have relinquished.

Don Juan had taken up the role as head of the family and had kept up the good Catholic family image by taking up where his father had left off. He had ordered every family member to attend church with him on Sundays and the special family dinners held on those evenings. The family held lavish dinners every evening of the week, but attendance was not compulsory as it was on Sundays; although most did attend the midweek dinners through fear of displeasing Don Juan.

Dinner always started at 2100 with scores of maids and butlers busying themselves making sure everything was just right. The consequences if it was not, just did not bear thinking about.

Don Juan took care of the family and their businesses. He even did the whole charity thing giving away little bits of their legitimate fortune whilst at the same time squirreling away 10 times more from corrupt deals and from what they just stole from other people by using intimidation and violence.

Alan Patrice sat quietly boiling with rage as he watched them all having a great time. Octavio was still boasting about his conquests and heroic actions during the war and was getting even louder than he was before. Alan could see that Don Juan was getting more pissed off with it all especially as he was the one who had goaded his little brother at the start of the Malvinas war telling him that he wouldn't have the guts to go and fight and kill like a real soldier; as he had done for his country.

Don Juan knew that Octavio had volunteered to go out to the Rincon Grande settlement just to have some sport with the cowardly Reynoso boy. He had not known then that he would get the opportunity to silence his brother's goading. Don Juan also knew that the SAS and SBS soldiers were finished and had already surrendered when his brother and Astiz had killed them in cold blood. He didn't care about that though because at least Octavio had had the guts to do it. Silently he was very proud of his little brother although he would never show it openly.

The party began to wind up as the mums whisked kids away to the waiting cars that were parked neatly in a row outside the front entrance. It was shortly after midnight when Alan Patrice got up and left the remainder of the cold coffee he had been nursing for the past hour or two. No more snippets of information had come his way as he passed by the private dining area on his frequent visits to the restrooms.

He did though have some news to relay to Fernando regarding the movements of Octavio and his henchmen during the next few days. He would also tell him of the boasting that would surely make the two British Special Forces soldiers arriving on Sunday morning even more determined to kill these murdering bastards.

'Revenge is a dish best served cold and you will be cold soon enough Don Juan.' Alan Patrice muttered under his breath as he watched the General disappear out of the front door and into the bulletproof black Mercedes limousine.

Alan got into his car and was about to pull away when he saw Octavio Muscardin was being helped out of the front door and down the steps by Jorge Astiz and Ricardo, one of the other bodyguards. He was eased gently into the back of another large black Mercedes and then Astiz jumped into the driver's seat ready to take him back to the palatial family home only a short distance away.

Alan rounded the corner on the driveway heading towards the main entrance gate so couldn't see them anymore in his rear view mirror. Had they seen him they would have noticed he was smiling. He was looking forward to the next few days and the significant amount of pain that would be inflicted on that murderous family.

4

2000hrs Friday 17th December – New York JFK

We arrive at JFK on time but have 12 hours to kill. First job was to sort an airport locker for the drop bag with all our British kit in it. Passports, plane tickets and anything else that could remotely link us to the UK went in there and then the key was forced into a block of blue tack and stuck behind a pipe completely out of sight in the roof space above the third trap of the gents' bog just to the left of the lockers.

Bill and I headed off to one of the many faceless and soulless hotels that surround all the major airports. Passports checked and reservations in the names of Lowe and Finch are confirmed at the Marriott check-in desk so room keys are handed over. One room on the first floor and the other on the second. There was no need to make a fuss or bring any attention our way for not being next to each other, as was requested.

We both headed to my room on the second floor so we could take some time to run through the plan again from memory. Bill left an hour and a half later. I cracked another coke from the mini bar and watched the late night New York news. After the third murder story and umpteenth police siren blasting out the television, I turned it off. Time to get my head down for a few hours.

0800 and the waiters and waitresses are busying themselves in the noisy hotel restaurant filling up coffee cups, taking orders for toast, bacon, sausage and eggs over easy. I wouldn't call it bacon though and eggs over easy, what the hell was that all about? What I wouldn't give for one of Billy's bacon and egg banjo's right now with loads of HP brown sauce on it. I wondered where Billy and the Brilliant were right now; probably still in Plymouth having all the holes filled in.

I was still pondering about the Brilliant's breakfasts when Bill tapped me on the shoulder.

'Morning Harry get some kip?'

'Yeah Bill, I got a good six hours. You?'

'About the same I think so we are good to go, as they say here.' I grinned.

'This lingo must be second nature to you though with your dad being a Yank.'

'You know Bill, I can get into the yank mode pretty quickly because the US is actually a brilliant place to be. There are plenty of great people here and I always loved coming back here as a kid. Ron always took me to some very cool places and we did some pretty wild things, without Gerri knowing of course, especially when it involved being with his buddies in the SEALS.'

'Well Harry, when this job is done and our lives get back to some form of normality you will be able to get yourself back here for a decent holiday with Kathy – I think you are going to need it.'

I was sure Bill was right, but there was no time to chat as my two over easy eggs arrived sitting next to four pieces of brick hard overcooked streaky 'bacon' and two tiny pieces of white buttered toast.

We sat in silence on the rusty old red airport transfer bus that billowed clouds of black diesel smoke from its exhaust as we headed back to the main terminal an hour later. I think the driver deliberately hit every pothole he could find just so he could rattle the bones of every passenger on the bus for the 15 minute journey from the hotel. Every time we stop the compressed air lines activating the hydraulics hiss loudly like a bunch of angry vipers on heat.

Both of us stood up as the doors hissed open for our final time but were unable to get off straight away as some overly large American females bundled themselves onto the bus dragging enormous suitcases behind them. One very sweaty foul-mouthed woman got jammed in the doorway, but the eagerness of the other inflatables behind her wanting to get onto the bus and into a seat; forced her in. The air was blue as we stood aside and let the gobbing off hulk squeeze past us. She was still making a loud fuss as we finally stepped off and walked away towards the departure hall. I felt sorry for the poor sods still left on the bus.

'American Airlines flight 006 is on time and will be leaving at 1105,' the female check-in clerk beamed across at us.

'Thanks,' I said in my best New York accent.

'You have a nice day sir,' she said with that beaming face again.

Bill and I watched as our bags got hauled onto the main conveyor and then disappear through the thick plastic curtain sheets at the end of the row of desks. I always think to myself at this point – will I ever see it again?

With the bags gone we now just have to navigate security and passport control. The airport is full of people hustling and bustling as they make their way down to the screened off area in front of the entrance to security. If the big signs at the entrance could speak they would be shouting at you and telling you to get into the right lines and have your tickets and passports ready, or else.

So many instructions to follow in so little time. This could be the fun part though as most of these guys either don't give a shit and let you just walk straight through, or they have a complete sense of humour failure and want to fuck up your whole day just because of the metal belt buckle you happen to be wearing, or because of the coins you have left in your pocket before passing through the metal detection machine.

The security guards and cops were standing in all the right places, weapons in full view, but not much else was going on. They still didn't move even when the noise level increased a few decibels as the throngs got squeezed tighter and tighter into the lanes ready for the walk through. They didn't seem to want to move at all from their posts and were just chatting and nonchalantly looking around.

'We have got the 'couldn't give a shit' watch,' I whispered to Bill.

That was fine as far as we were concerned.

We passed through both security and passport control without incident. The security guys and their baggage checks in particular were pretty shoddy. I wasn't here to audit their systems and procedures though so I just kept my head down. At the next hurdle, I just said thank you to the chisel jawed passport control officer in his immaculately pressed blue uniform as my false US passport was handed back to me; without a smile.

We sat in the transit lounge of Miami airport for two hours on the one stopover to Buenos Aries, some of the time just thinking about who had chosen this route and the flights. There must have been a better way. I hated just kicking my heels. I could feel myself getting more nervous and tense as the time passed. I was sure it would be even worse once we got closer to our final destination. It was like the time waiting to get onto the raider in the Falklands, but once you are on your way you always feel much better.

This was a whole new experience for me and I just hope I didn't blow it. Not that I will I keep telling myself. All I want is the opportunity to take out either Muscardin or Astiz, or both, and avenge Bob's death. I look across at Bill and he seemed to be really chilled out.

'You OK Bill?'

'Yep, but could do without the waiting.'

Good, it's not only me then.

We had a bit more time to kill so the only thing left to do is read. I open up my book, Argentina and its rich history. I had found it in one of the many charity shops in Stroud a couple of weeks ago. It was a bit beaten up with a few pages bent over in the corners. I think it had been to Argentina with its previous owner so I hoped it would give me a bit more knowledge of what we might expect when we got on the ground. I hadn't shown it to Bill yet, I had just squirreled it away ready for this day and I knew it wouldn't look suspicious if anyone wanted to search my bags.

The pack of typewritten notes that Colonel Shaw had given us to read in the car had detailed the recent years of turmoil and the atrocities the Argentine military government had inflicted on its own people. Brigadier Whistonhall had been very busy on our behalf gathering all the history and up to date intel. The notes had detailed the 'state terrorism' or dirty war that was being waged against Argentina's own people right now. The dirty war had been going on since the military coup in 1976 and thousands of people since then had just disappeared. The Army claimed they were fighting communist revolutionaries and they were just casualties of war. The real truth was; if you questioned the military junta in any way you would be brutally dealt with and your family and your friends.

The men would usually be tortured and killed quickly, but the women would be sent to 'detention' camps where they would be subject to multiple rapes and torture. After the guards had finished 'using' them the majority of the women were also murdered. It was well known that some of these so called guards really enjoyed the brutality and had been compared on numerous occasions to the SS guards assigned to the Nazi concentration camps in WWII.

The younger children faired a little better, if you could call it that. They would be farmed out for adoption to people who couldn't have kids of their own, but who could pay very well. These were usually high ranking officials in the current brutal government or had connections to someone within it. It was all interesting stuff, but there were no real surprises from previous briefings on Argentina, except for really understanding the sheer brutality of what certain individuals could do to their own people.

I got my head back into my book and even after just reading the introduction to the history of Argentina it was clear it had been a struggle for the people of that country. It had started with the first settlement in Buenos Aires dating back to 1536 but as I read on I'm not sure I agreed with some of the text that talked about 'Argentina's rich history.' I think it might be more appropriate, and factually correct, to describe it as more of a 'chequered history.' But what do I know, as a few months ago I was happily killing some of the poor sods fighting for their 'motherland'.

I look up to see if there is any more info on our flight. Nothing had changed. Bill had wandered off to the coffee stand. He still looked very cool and calm, unlike how I was feeling inside.

I get my head back into the book and I find the point on the page where I left it and read on. It tells me that even before 1536 the quest for power had started with the indigenous Querandi natives who killed all the early Spanish settlers in 1516. The Spanish don't give up that easily though and came back years later to win the battle to colonise Buenos Aires where they firmly established themselves in the seat of power over the course of that century. As the years passed they became incredibly strong and could not be ousted by anyone. Although many tried.

Over time though the Spanish did 'merge' with the indigenous Indian population across large parts of the country creating a whole new 'home grown' Argentine people. It was in 1776 that Spain named Buenos Aires as the capital of the new Viceroyalty, which effectively acknowledged the fact that Buenos Aires had outgrown Spain's political and economic domination. It still took a few more years though before full independence from Spain could be finally achieved. During the Napoleonic wars, the British had two unsuccessful attempts at seizing control of the city in 1806 and 1807 when Spanish colonies were the key objectives for British forces.

I have a quick look to see where Bill was before turning over to the next page. He was still standing by the coffee stand talking to a pretty, normal sized, American girl. Well we have to pass the time somehow, so I read on.

Full independence from Spain came in 1816, but there was still more trouble to come when the provinces were only really united in name only. With no effective central authority, a new order rose in the regions called Caudillos, or local strongmen, who resented and resisted Buenos Aires as strongly as Buenos Aires had resisted Spain.

It was all becoming a bit blah blah blah now and I'm getting bored. How much of this stuff will I really need to know and how useful will it be? I spend the next couple of minutes turning over the pages trying to find something more interesting when my eye scanned over a paragraph that amuses the hell out of me. Apparently the Welsh are there in numbers. My gran will be pleased, I thought.

About 150 of them turned up in a boat in 1865 and decided to stay. They formed a colony in Chubut, wherever that is. I will have to stay clear of that place. I am smiling to myself now and hoping that Bill doesn't come back and see me grinning to myself like some big dickhead. He will think I've gone loony tunes or something. I don't think I want to run into any distant ancestors on this trip as there won't be much time to chew the fat.

I quickly scan the next few pages. It's all about the economy booming, which obviously is not happening in these current times. It also tells me about the huge influx of immigrants, including loads of Brits, Italians and Spanish who came into the country at the end of the 19th century and who were the catalyst for the boom times. I flick through a few more pages and I am just about to put the book down when I read the first short paragraph about Juan Domingo Peron, an obscure Colonel who became Argentina's first leader. He was the first politician to actually try and get to grips with the economic crisis that had plagued the country for many years. He didn't do a particularly good job though and eventually fell victim to a coup in 1955 before being exiled for 18 years.

Bill was still chatting up the girl by the coffee stand so I start to read more about Eva and Juan Perón from the beginning of the chapter. The first line started 'Juan Perón became Argentina's most revered, as well as the most despised, political figure in its history,' This could be a bit more interesting, I thought to myself.

Only another hour to wait.

5

The overnight flight to Buenos Aires took off at 2030. We would be landing at 0630 Sunday 19th December and if everything goes to plan, a man named Thomas will be waiting for us. Hopefully, he will be holding up a board with our names on it so we won't have to wander around the airport like a couple of lemons. All being well we would both be back here in five days' time on Thursday 23rd December and on a direct flight back to New York with the job done.

It was bedlam in the crowded arrivals area. It was not a big space and pretty shabby with it. It looked as if the posters hanging off the dirty walls had not been changed for at least 10 years. There was also an underlying musty damp smell in the place. 'Welcome to Buenos Aires,' the sign said in five languages. Although what the last language was I didn't know due to the total fading of the words on that part of the poster.

I'm sure they would not be welcoming Bill and me if they knew what we were doing only a few months ago. Immediately behind us the noise level increased another decibel, or ten, as a group of middle-aged well dressed women with big hair, big glasses and even bigger handbags got into a right argy bargy over their places in the passport control queue. Fingers are pointed, arms are flailing about and it looked like it was about to descend into a full on shoving competition between two of the feistiest characters in the bunch.

Bill and I moved as far forward as we could and then watched, in some amazement, as the scene behind us unfolded. Some of the men had now become involved and fists started to be thrown. Bodies were flying everywhere, some of them ending up on the deck close by. The noise level was definitely now up at least another ten decibels. Next thing we see is the exit doors flying open and several burly police officers come wading into the melee.

One of the feisty women gets whacked on the side of her head with a short baton, blood instantly spilling down her white frilly blouse and over her smart tweed jacket. The man in front of her didn't fare any better. He got one right across the bridge of his nose, spreading it across his face. Lots of people got the benefit from that one, as blood sprayed over the front couple of rows of the circling crowd. More screams came as another woman got a short baton. It was like a fucking war zone out there. I was glad we were up the front of the queue and away from the majority of it.

A few more whacks and a lot of shouting from the senior officer and it was all over. The crowd moved back into line allowing just enough space for the people who were bleeding to sort themselves out. No one was making eye contact with the remaining police officers – if they could possibly help it. The man and woman who had got whacked and were bleeding the most were being manhandled out of the arrivals hall each between four officers. The remainder of their group looked shit scared as the senior officer continued to shout at them and wave his baton close to their faces.

Bill gave me a nudge to divert my attention away from the scene. Only a few seconds more and it would be our turn at passport control. Just be calm Harry, I tell myself, let's not fuck this bit up. There were still some people arguing in the queue, but nothing like what had gone on earlier. A man had appeared from somewhere to mop the blood up off the floor. He did it without batting an eyelid. Just as if it was a normal event.

I check my small leather carryon bag again; my notebooks, pens, pencils and a guide book of Buenos Aires are all still there. All the things you would expect a journo to have. We move forward a bit in our designated isle for non-Argentine nationals and wait patiently for our turn. The officer sitting at his desk on passport control was massive. Not in a muscular way, but in a greasy fat fucker with a nasty face way; and with a temperament to match, no doubt.

There were four people in front of us now, two businessmen in smart suits and a very smartly dressed man and his elegant wife, or maybe mistress. The two smartly dressed businessmen breezed through with hardly a glance from greaseball. Bill and I both saw the banknotes that had been folded into the passport photo pages. A deft sleight of hand from the fat fucker and the notes were slipped into the right pocket of his uniform trousers. I wondered then if we shouldn't have done the same. Bill and I exchanged glances both knowing we had no time to sort it.

The elegant woman was already at the counter being leered at by the greaseball who was obviously slowing undressing her with his bulbous red bloodshot eyes. The man had obviously been here before and without any real concealment moved past the women and placed his hand flat onto the top of the counter and said something quietly to greaseball. Greaseball's fat sweaty hand covered the man's hand just for a fleeting moment and after the man had drawn it away again, a wad of notes was being slid back off the counter and heading for the same trouser pocket. With that, the two passports were stamped and handed back. With a dismissive wave of his fat fingers, he indicated that they should move through. He just couldn't resist one more look at the woman's backside after she had passed him. He had a sick grin on his face when he waved his hand in our direction. I was up first.

'American.' He almost spat at me.

'Yes,' I said in my best New York accent.

'Why you here? Business or pleasure?'

'Business. I'm here to write a piece for the New York Post about the war in the Malvinas.' I knew it would be better not to say the Falklands as that would have definitely got them riled up.

'You been to Argentina before?'

'No sir.'

'How long you here?' He spat at me again. I'm sure I felt spittle land on my cheek this time. I resisted wiping it off.

'Four or five days only,' I replied.

'You have some dollars for immigration tax?'

The fat fucker had my passport held firmly in his hand. He was looking directly at me with a sneer that had appeared instantly when I had made a bit of a face. He was after money, no doubt at all. Otherwise, it was going to be a long drawn out day. It was made even clearer to me as his mate, who was standing just to the rear of the counter, took one step forward.

I put my hand in my pocket where I knew I had some bills. I should have checked what was in there, but I really hadn't expected to be fleeced this soon. I pulled out a $10, $20 and a $5 dollar bill and then placed them on the counter.

The bills were gone in a flash and without any further discussion the stamping machine was thumping down on a fresh, clean page of my forged passport. The date was scribbled in the appropriate space at the top of the new stamp and with the same indifference he slapped my passport on the counter and waved his fat fingers at me to indicate that I could walk through. His mate had gone back to his previous position, one step back away from the counter.

Bill had been watching the whole thing unfold and saw the $35 bucks changing hands and the final outcome. The lowest denomination note Bill could find quickly was a $50, which he slipped inside the photo page of his false Canadian passport. I didn't look around until I reached the doors that led out into the main baggage area. As I looked back I could see Bill smiling at the fat fucker and the stamp was already out thumping down on an empty page. A few seconds later Bill was striding purposely towards me and the same exit door.

The baggage area was filling rapidly with people and not just from our flight. There were only four carousels so there was definitely going to be a bun fight in a minute. I wondered if the Argies in the passport queue would be kicking off again in here.

Bill spotted our carousel number on the board first. It was number three so we made our way through the growing crowds and parked ourselves next to the belt, which we hoped would deliver our bags shortly. They were in the first lot to come through the dirty plastic curtains and were together so it allowed us to quickly get away from the increasing melee around the carousel. It was time for customs now and with $40 each tucked under the customs form we were dealt with quickly and were through without any questions being asked. There was just a small smile and a wave of the customs man's free hand whilst the other one was stuffing the dollars into his pocket.

I think I was getting the measure of this place.

6

We eased the door open to the arrivals concourse and the noise hit us like a steam train. The high pitched shrill of squealing women and kids was unbelievable. There were hundreds of them out there jostling and pushing for a good position by the barrier all waiting for their loved ones to come through. We became caught up in the throng of people heading towards the left hand exit of the cordoned off area. Everyone was pushing and shoving their way past the uniformed police who were doing a pretty crappy job of keeping order. I sensed though that they wouldn't put up with being shoved around for too long and the batons would surely be out again in a minute.

'Bill there's a clear space over there to the right of the main exit door,' I shouted over the noise.

We force our way through the masses whilst at the same time scanning the sea of faces in front of us for someone with a board with our names on it.

'I'll go and see if I can locate our friend Thomas. You OK to stay here with the bags Harry?' I nodded and Bill walked off back into the heaving crowd.

It took a couple of minutes for Bill to locate our man Thomas. He was a short stocky man of native Indian origins, his body rippling with hard heavy muscle. He had deeply weathered brown skin and a battered face that sat under a thick mop of dark black hair. These visible attributes told the story instantly about how this man had spent all of his life outside looking after the land and cattle. He was a Gaucho with a mean looking face. I thought immediately, you wouldn't want to meet this guy down a dark alley holding his *'facón.'* The *'facón'* is a huge dagger that these men carry and use in their daily working lives. They are also razor sharp and would slice you open in seconds.

When he smiled his face changed completely into one of a welcoming friend, even with the large gap where one of his right molars should have been.

'Buenas tardes hombres, me llamo Thomas, nada.' Then in pretty good English he said. 'Welcome Mr. Lowe, Mr. Finch. My name is Thomas and I will be taking you to your hotel. Signor Reynoso greets you tomorrow morning.'

'Thank you Thomas.' I said, as he firmly shook my hand and then it was Bill's turn to feel his iron grip.

'The car is outside and only a short distance away, please follow me.' Thomas said.

We exited the main doors of the terminal and the muggy heat hit us. It was sunny and must have been at least 28°C, but there were some dark stormy clouds moving in from the West.

'We will have a storm later today. It will arrive after you have got to your hotel though. In three or four hours' time.'

Thomas was talking as he led us around the edge of what I assumed to be a short stay car park. We stayed right and walked past another large rectangular building and then did a quick dash across the main road to a large circular car park. This was in the centre of the airport complex and was surrounded by the terminal entrances and exit roads at both ends.

Thomas led us through the maze of sturdy looking box type cars. Renaults, Volkswagens, Fords plus a smattering of pre-1960s American looking classic cars. We stopped next to a very clean and tidy version of one of these. Its red body, white roof and loads of chrome, plus the white walled tyres hardly made it inconspicuous, but Thomas seemed very pleased with it.

'Your car Thomas?' I asked.

'Si Senor Finch, I rebuild it after my father gave it to me. It is a very fine car built in Argentina.'

'What is it?' Bill asked as he joined in the petrol head discussions.

'It is an IKA Kaiser Carabela built in 1959 by Industrias Kaiser Argentina. That is what the IKA stands for.'

'She's a beauty Thomas,' I said.

'Thomas I agree with Senor Finch but don't you think we should be getting out of here now?' Bill spoke politely to Thomas and he was right we needed to be moving away from here and soon.

Bill had one last look around the car park to see if anyone was watching us or had followed us out of the terminal. I had been scanning the area as well and so far had seen nothing untoward.

'Harry you go in the front, I'll keep a lookout behind us.'

'OK Bill.'

Thomas edged his way out of the car park slowly, he was now behind the queue that had built up whilst we had been admiring the Kaiser. We were moving slowly and are on the wrong side of the road for us. I remembered something in one of the reports about the changes the Argies had inflicted on the Falkland Islanders during the occupation. One of the first things they did was to have them start driving on the right side of the road. That hadn't gone down well at all.

Thomas forced his way into the flow of traffic heading towards the exit toll booths and was ready with his cash. We hardly stopped as the cash was handed over with a grunt from the very pissed off looking attendant. Clear of the booths, Thomas sped off down the Au. Teniente General Pablo Ricchieri, a good road which was basically the same as the M6 Motorway – but in Argentina. This would take us most of the 14 miles into the main town centre of Buenos Aires. The 'City of Fair Winds' or 'Paris of the South' as it has also been known.

We spot what looks like a commercial air terminal on our right, although I can see there are a few private planes parked outside one of the main hangers. Some people are obviously not being hurt by the country's economic difficulties. Same as in every country, I muse to myself as we pass by. Huge trees and large woodlands break up the landscape once we are clear of the airport buildings. It's quite green around here and not what I expected, although

I'm not sure what I expected really. Bill is quiet in the backseat of the Kaiser, but I see him occasionally turn around and scan the road again through the rear window. Thomas is also quiet and doing the same through the rear view mirror.

The next few miles we pass more woodlands and open green fields before coming to a few individual houses that have a few acres on the side. Further on we pass clusters of houses sitting on smaller plots of land before finally hitting the main suburbs of Buenos Aires. It's not long before we see a huge waste treatment plant and long single storey factory units taking up acres of flat land. The houses are now all squashed into small square blocks stretching for miles and miles.

Thomas is oblivious to it all and keeps the Kaiser speeding towards our final destination in downtown Buenos Aires. I've got the street map out now and as we cross the Av Gral Paz I ask Thomas,

'Do we stay on Av Luis Dellepiance all the way to the city?'

'No Senor, we will take some of the Au 25 de Mayo and then leave it at Avenida 9 De Julio. This will take us straight to the Hotel Crown Plaza Panamericano. It will not take us long now.'

'OK, you're in charge Thomas,' I said smiling at him. He smiled back, gap and all.

There is nothing but buildings now. Millions of people are squeezed into the North East corner of this vast country. Tomorrow we will see the real effects of being in this environment when we go into one of the Villas to collect the weapons. Reynoso will have paved the way for us, but both Bill and I were nervous about this part of the operation because from what we have read they are pretty mean and lawless places.

Five minutes later, Thomas swung off the motorway and down the left side ramp. We pass under the South exit road before climbing and swinging left again over the main motorway we have just left. Thomas then steers the Kaiser down into the seven lanes of Avenida 9 De Julio avoiding the throngs of cars we now find ourselves in. The guide book said it is the widest avenue, or Avenida in Argentinean, in the world. I can absolutely believe it as it is chaos down here.

Cars are coming at us from all sides, horns are blaring, arms and fists are being waved. And that was just the women. Angry men are hanging out their driver's windows, some with fags in their gobs shouting, 'get out the fucking way you tosser,' or something akin to that. The profanities in these situations are the same the world over. Thomas takes it in his stride though and guides the Kaiser through it all until he gets us safely into lane four.

'The drivers in Buenos Aires are fucking crazy, no?' Thomas said looking over his shoulder at Bill.'

'Yes Thomas they are even worse than New York.' We all smiled and I wonder briefly how the famous yellow cab drivers would cope with this lot. Probably very well I decide just as Thomas throws the Kaiser hard left to avoid the car that drifted into our lane without any signal or care it seemed.

That little incident slows us down a lot, but then Thomas put on a burst of speed as we tried to beat the lights at the next junction. We just get across Avenida Independencia stopping the progress of the last two lines of the several lines of traffic on our right. More horns are blaring, at us this time. Tall mature trees line the whole length of Avenida 9 de Julio, although I couldn't believe they would have any effect on trying to keep the smog at bay. Thousands of tons of exhaust fumes must billow into the sky every day from this city of a couple of million people. My guide book told me there were several million more people in greater Buenos Aires. And it was still growing by the look of it too.

Some of the buildings look very grand and spectacular. They are a mixture of the finest architecture from all over the world, but mainly European, as it said in my useful little book. How can these people be so fucked up when they can build things of beauty like this, I ask myself.

We race through another intersection with the lights with us this time. Thomas leaned back over his seat as we cleared the intersection and tells us.

'On your right, this is the famous Avenida De Mayo, the grand boulevard of Buenos Aires. Along there are some of the finest buildings and Plazas in the city. Maybe tomorrow we will go past some of them.'

Bill and I aren't here to be tourists, but don't want offend our new buddy so I just nod my head and smile. He was right though because just from the brief glance I had down it, I could see more very spectacular buildings lining each side of the road.

The pavements had started to fill with people now all heading for their morning coffees and newspapers no doubt. I should be calling them sidewalks here, I tell myself, and then give myself a silent bollocking. Stupid mistakes like that could fuck us up.

I look back through the Kaiser's ample rear window to make sure we still have no tail. I check that no car is the same as 10, 15 or 20 minutes ago. When I am satisfied I turn back to look ahead through the spotlessly clean windscreen. Just ahead of us now and right in the middle of the boulevard is a huge Obelisk rising well over 200 feet in the air. Bill tapped me on the shoulder and pointed ahead.

'Yes I see it, it's pretty impressive isn't it? I remember seeing it on a news programme when the Argentine people were celebrating their 'victory' in the Malvinas and again when they lost them; although that time it wasn't quite so pretty.'

We both smiled and although Thomas didn't acknowledge our conversation, I know he knew what we were saying from the look on his face.

I reached into my bag and retrieved my guidebook again. I opened it up at the page that said 'Obelisco' and started reading just as it was temporarily obscured by a large cloud of black diesel smoke that spewed out of an old City bus that had just cut us up. Thomas braked hard throwing me forward towards the windscreen, but I managed to stop myself with my left hand before hitting the dashboard.

'Sorry Senor.' Thomas said as he leaned on his horn for longer than both Bill and I would have wanted. The last thing we needed was to get in a ruckus in the first hour on the ground especially as we had avoided it very well at the airport. I started my reading again as Thomas backed off the horn. I read out loud so Bill could hear.

'The obelisk was built to commemorate the 400th anniversary of the foundation of the City but has now become a key meeting place for political demonstrations. Which is why we saw it so much on the news. They also use it for public celebrations as well like New Year's Eve.'

Bill was looking at me from the back seat lightly shaking his head from side to side. I bet he's thinking: you knobhead, but I can't help it; I like the detail. Bill did have a wry smile on his face though so I'm not going to feel too bad about spouting off historical facts occasionally.

The Kaiser was well boxed in behind the bus and getting the full treatment from its choking black exhaust fumes. If we could see or even hear the bus driver, I'd put money on it that he would be laughing his cock off at Thomas. This would be payback for earlier leaning on his horn and giving him the finger gesture. Thomas was muttering something unpleasant under his breath as his prized Kaiser was engulfed again in acrid black smoke. I was sure the bus driver was purposely revving up the old engine to push out more crap from the exhaust.

Everybody moved in unison as the lights changed. The bus gave us one last cloud of choking black death to deal with before cutting up someone else as he moved over into the outside lane. More horns and hand signals. I doubted he gave a fuck. Twenty seconds later we turned right into the entrance of the Crown Plaza Panamericano.

I didn't notice at first that we had arrived at our destination as I was busy looking at the impressive Colon Theatre directly across the road. It was a huge stone coloured block building with tall rectangular windows on the ground floor and large round windows on either side of the carved facade over the main entrance. The building was topped by a massive pitched roof. Three chimneys sat at each corner of the triangular frontage that held the half-mooned window that dominated the entire space. The theatre covered almost a whole square block on its own. God knows how many people they must get in there. Harry, this is an impressive place, I said to myself. Kathy would love it here was my next thought; but not right now.

'We are here Senor Finch, Senor Lowe.'

'Thank you Thomas and please it's Bill and Harry from now on.'

'OK, Bill and Harry,' he answered and then displayed that beaming gapped smile again.

'Senor Reynoso will meet with you in Mr. Lowe's room at 9.00am tomorrow morning. My brother and me will take you to wherever you need to go after your meeting with Senor Reynoso.'

We retrieve our bags from the boot and then I gave it a couple of taps. Thomas then raised his left hand out of the Kaiser's open window and gave a wave as he pulled away. Bill was already heading for the hotel entrance as I raised my own hand to acknowledge Thomas. He was going to be a good asset on this job I had no doubt about that.

The Crown Plaza was a typical US style hotel, but this one was in serious need of some significant cash being spent on it. The reception area was dark, musty and stained from years of being filled with smoke from a large fireplace directly across from the desk. The thousands of cigarettes and cigars that people had puffed on from the huge leather armchairs and settees hadn't helped either.

I am back on plan now and scanning the room for any signs of us being pinged. All was clear so far. A short fat guy with a bald head and a big smile directed us towards a smart pin-stripe-suited man at one specific counter.

'Gentlemen, good morning. I am Jorge Martine, the hotel assistant manager.' He said in perfect English. His shiny brass name badge confirming who he was and his position.

We placed our passports on the counter and after a quick scan Jorge leaned forward slightly.

'Mr. Lowe, Mr. Finch, your suites are ready for you. You are on the third floor of Tower One at the back of the building. It is very quiet there and away from the road.' He said.

'Thank you,' Bill said looking quizzically at Jorge. 'Did you say suites?'

'Yes Mr. Lowe, I did.' He said now in a hushed voice. Compliments of my great friend, Senor Fernando Reynoso.

Our newest friend Jorge quickly finished the paperwork and handed us our keys. The lift was noisy and rattled a lot, but it got us to the third floor OK. My suite was 304, right next to Bill in 306.

My suite was bigger than every house I had lived in up to now.

7

Crown Plaza Panamericano Hotel Buenos Aires

Monday 20th December – 0830

Fernando Reynoso slipped quickly and quietly through the emergency exit door in the basement of the Crown Plaza Panamericano hotel, his hands firmly clutching the battered old brown briefcase to his chest. He knew that if this briefcase and its contents fell into the wrong hands it would undoubtedly mean execution for him, his family; and many others. His friend Jorge Martine held the door open for the few brief seconds he needed to get through. After the agreed three knocks.

Jorge led him down the cluttered corridor that was filled with the boxes of old plates, cutlery, glasses, table linen and all sorts of other items that were not now required upstairs. They both heard the commotion before rounding the blind corner ahead of them. They both peer through one of the two porthole style windows in the double swing doors but couldn't see anyone in their direct line of sight. Fernando pushed open his door first and stepped straight into what should have been the lunchtime's fresh cream of tomato soup. Fernando's left foot went away from him immediately and it was only Jorge's lightening quick reactions and his strong hands grabbing Fernando's jacket that stopped him sitting in the middle of about five gallons of the stuff.

The two junior cooks who had been given the responsibility of moving the big pot of soup from one of the stoves to a thirty gallon steam copper were now getting a severe bollocking in the corner of the kitchen. Their faces were already flushed with fear but then turned crimson red when the head chef, a huge man with a belly to match, stormed around the corner ready to add his fearsome anger and weight to the senior chefs who were already berating the two unfortunate cooks.

The head chef's face changed and the anger dissipated instantly when he clapped eyes on Fernando; who was still being supported by Jorge as they navigated themselves out of the puddle of soup. Fernando was a man the head chef had never expected to see down here in his kitchen.

Instructions from the head chef were bellowed at another senior chef to get the mess sorted out and then a beckoning of the hand was the signal for the

Jorge and Fernando to follow him. Once through a second set of identical double doors and clear of the general noises that emanate from any large kitchen, the three of them found themselves in the service corridor that housed the Head Chef's office. The huge man rounded on Fernando and placed his shovel sized hands on his shoulders.

'You are well my friend?'

'Yes Sebastian I am, thank you.' Fernando answered his old friend.

'I heard that you were badly hurt in the Malvinas war?' Sebastian had a deep furrow on his brow as he spoke. 'And that 'the little Muscardin bastardo' has been saying bad things about you.'

The insult was clear in the way he said 'little.'

'They are all evil in that family Fernando. You have to be careful.'

'Yes I know and I thank you again Sebastian, but I am completely well again now and I know what he has been saying, but he is not saying anything anymore. That has been resolved.'

'Good. So why are you sneaking through my kitchen with our old friend Jorge?'

'It's a long story Sebastian, but I have a business meeting here with two men that I do not need my competitors to know about right now.'

'Say no more my friend and if you come through my kitchen again you must stay for some food. And not what was on the floor,' Sebastian laughed heartily and then they all laughed together.

Jorge then led Fernando out to the staff elevator just a few yards further down the corridor. They passed two young waitresses giggling like a couple of schoolgirls after casting their eyes on the handsome Fernando.

'I must leave you here now. I have to be back at the main desk in 10 minutes; Mr. Lowe is in suite 306 where they will meet you as requested. Mr. Finch is in 304. They are expecting you at 9.00am and I will be back here at 10.00am to take you back through the kitchen to the exit.' The doors to the staff elevator opened in front of them.

'Thank you Jorge.' Fernando said with his hand on his friend's arm. He knew that Jorge and many others, were taking huge risks for him right now, but Fernando had prayed many times they would all be successful in their mission and that none of his friends or family would be hurt. He also knew the risks were very high, but the rewards for many people outweighed these. Fernando stepped inside the elevator and pressed the button for the third floor.

The old elevator slowly made its way upwards, creaking and groaning all the way. The lights dimmed twice and flickered as if they were going to fail at any moment. Jorge had warned him that this might happen so he wasn't worried. The doors opened onto the dimly lit corridor next to the third floor linen cupboard. More importantly it was only 20 yards from Suite 306 just around the first corner.

Fernando checked his watch. It was 0859 exactly. He was now standing in the brightly lit corridor outside the door of suite 306. He was feeling nervous for the first time that morning. He told himself again he was doing the right thing, but was still deeply scared of the potential consequences if things went wrong. It was really a bit too late to be thinking about that now though, Fernando said to himself for the tenth time today.

We both heard the knock. Bill got up from his chair and went to the door, taking a second to look through the security eye piece. When it opened Fernando Reynoso walked in. He was dressed smartly in a brown two piece suit, white shirt and a plain beige tie. His expensive looking brown shoes looked wet and had some spots of discoloration on them. I was pretty sure they shouldn't have looked like that but then blanked that from my mind.

His face had healed completely. The last time I had seen him was in Ajax Bay hospital, bloodied and battered by Muscardin and his boys. And Bill. With the door now closed his hand extended to meet Bill's.

'Captain Dye it is good to see you again,' he said in that perfect English accent. Bill just nodded slightly.

'Sergeant Glass,' he said as he walked over to me with his hand open and arm outstretched. 'It is also very good to see you looking so well and healthy, unlike the last time I saw you in Ajax Bay.'

'I was just thinking the same about you too.' I said as a knowing smile spread across our faces, our hands still firmly clamped together.

The knock on the door broke our handshake instantly. We both tensed not knowing what was coming next.

'I've ordered coffee and toast,' Bill said, 'I thought we might need something before we go out.'

Fernando moved quickly into the other room and out of sight before Bill opened the door. A large jug of coffee and several pieces of toast were laid down on the table. With the man tipped and the door closed again, we each took a chair around the table in the lounge area of the room.

'I have to apologise for getting out of sight so abruptly just then.' Fernando looked a little worried and had a furrowed brow as he spoke. 'The Muscardin family have many spies and many friends who are trying to trap me and members of my family. The situation in Argentina is changing day by day and the Muscardin family are getting worried, even a little paranoid. We know they are already behind the disappearance of a number of people during the past three months, including some high ranking officials. Nobody is safe and we cannot get the proof we need whilst they hold the power that they do.'

'OK, how long do we have?' I stop for a second and then ask another question before waiting for the first answer. 'What do we call you?'

'Please call me Fernando, Sergeant.'

I nodded and said, 'It's Harry then for me.'

'And it's Bill for me. Shall we get on now?'

'We have an hour,' Fernando now answered my question. 'I think it is best I update you on the latest intelligence and then you can tell me of your plans.' We both nodded before Fernando continued. 'You have met Thomas already. He will be with you from now on to drive you and to support you in whatever you need. Today you will meet his brother Alejandro who will also accompany you. They have a particular need to assist you in your mission and cannot be swayed. They may look like common Gauchos now, but they have both done their time and served their country in the 5th Marine Corps. These are

176

honourable men who served with me before the Malvinas war. You can trust them with your lives.'

'We can definitely use the local support. Thank you.' Bill said.

Fernando looked very confident as he concluded, 'They will prove themselves to you, I have no doubts.'

We spent the next 50 minutes hearing about the Muscardin family. The bragging of Octavio about his heroics in the Falklands War and how he killed the SAS soldiers in battle. The best part of the story was his escape after fighting off hundreds of troops. All complete bullshit we knew, but the words ignited an inner rage in me and an immovable determination to see this through to the end. There was no doubt in my mind now that I needed to be here and the look in Bill's eyes said it all. It was a mixture of pain and rage that I had seen only once before in Ajax Bay when he had pummelled the man's face who was sitting in front of us.

It was not directed at Fernando this time though.

We heard in detail about the personal threats made by Octavio Muscardin and his henchmen at Fernando's home and his new law business premises. Threats of personal violence against him, his family and friends, the building catching fire and blowing up, etcetera, etcetera. We got the picture.

The ultimate threat was that people, including him, could still just disappear without trace. The added threat that Muscardin's sister would have fun 'playing with him' was a little perplexing until he explained how much pleasure this women extracted from hurting men in ways that made your eyes water just hearing about it.

We had maps and photos of the Muscardin family home, the Hurlingham club where Octavio spent quite a lot of time, his Mercedes and personal station wagon. Fernando also had more photos and the address of his guarded Buenos Aires apartment and the Richmond Gentlemen's club and Spa he frequented at least three times a week.

Fernando then produced more photos and home addresses of Octavio's 'favourite' three girls. When he laid them on the table we could be sure the only way the little fat fucker could have these women would be either to pay them or rape them.

The last five photos were dropped onto the table. Sergeant Jorge Astiz still looked a mean fuck and the other three men who were with him on the Falklands didn't exactly look like pussycats either. All were supposed to be serving soldiers but were, in fact, Muscardin's private bodyguards. The final photo placed onto the table was of the big brother, General Don Juan Angel Muscardin. Fernando then told us of the publicly made goad to his little brother prior to him leaving for the Malvinas.

This prompted a discussion about the possibilities of taking him out as well because it was clear now that he was the main instigator of the atrocities that Octavio Muscardin had carried out. We concluded it was unlikely we would get them all together at the same time and as it was Octavio Muscardin, Jorge Astiz and the other three who had pulled the triggers we decided they would stay the main focus of the mission.

'Thomas and Alejandro will be waiting for you outside at 1015,' Fernando said. 'They will take you the short distance to pick up the weapons you will need. It is very important that you allow Thomas and Alejandro to complete the transaction once you have checked over the weapons and agree the price. These people you will be dealing with do not like strangers or foreigners.'

Fernando's stern expression said everything. We would definitely be letting Thomas and Alejandro sort this bit out.

Fernando produced a large brown envelope from inside his briefcase and placed it on the table. It was full of cash.

'There should be enough money here to cover all your needs. The weapons, bribes, whatever you need.' Fernando was speaking to both of us as he pulled out the notes from the envelope. 'If you need any more just let Thomas know and it will be supplied.'

Bill spent the next 15 minutes briefing Fernando on the plans to recce the homes, clubs, surrounding areas, establish RV's, and ERV's if we got separated, and all possible exit routes. We would make the final call on the hit point within the next 48 hours and agreed to meet him back in the hotel suite at the same time on Wednesday 22nd December.

'It's 0950 and I have to go.' Fernando said as he got up and flipped over the top of his now empty briefcase.

I looked directly into his face and I could see he was more than a little afraid; much like the rest of us. I shook his hand and he said, 'Good luck.'

Bill was alongside him as they reached the door but before he could open it Fernando turned to Bill and then looked at me.

'Thank you both for being here. It was not right and cowardly what those men did to your brother and your comrades in the Malvinas and they do deserve to die for it. They also have to answer for their crimes against the honourable and decent people of Argentina and you will be doing them a great service as well. I only wish I could be with you when they pay for their crimes.'

'That would be suicide for you and you know it,' Bill said. 'Your work is only just starting and we know there are many things to resolve in this country, both now and in the future. Argentina needs men like you, strong leaders with integrity who can make things change and bring justice to the perpetrators of the violence against your people. Leave us to do what we came to do.'

Fernando nodded and didn't say anything else before slipping out the door and back around the corner to the staff elevator.

'Let's go find those murdering bastards Harry,' Bill said when the door finally closed.

'Fucking right,' I replied.

I am very ready to do this now.

8

Crown Plaza Panamericano Hotel Buenos Aires

Monday 20th December – 1000

Jorge Martine had been standing outside the elevator doors when the creaky old thing finally came to rest at sub level one with a large jolt. He swiftly ushered Fernando on the reverse route through the kitchen to the emergency exit door, via the cluttered corridor, making a mental note to have the corridor cleared up very soon.

On the way through the kitchen, head chef Sebastian was giving some poor junior cook a real roasting over something in a large pot. He only stopped briefly to raise his hand and smile at Fernando, then it was back to the bollocking. A quick conversation with Jorge about the arrangements for Wednesday, a shake of the hand and Fernando was out the door and heading across the tarmac to his car.

The old white Mercedes slowly pulled out of the service yard at the back of the hotel, Fernando sitting in the front passenger seat next to his friend; who knew nothing of what had transpired inside. He was just doing his friend a favour. Fernando knew it was better that way as the fewer people who knew what was going on, the better for everyone. After thanking his friend and asking him to take him straight to his office, Fernando stayed quiet just thinking about the next few days.

I am in front of Bill as we exit the busy lobby of the hotel and walk over to where Thomas is waiting by a different car.

'Hey Thomas,' I said. 'What's this, where has the Kaiser gone?'

'Senor Harry we have to go to a very bad place now and the beautiful Kaiser would be taken apart in only a few minutes and then sold in many pieces. The Torino Grand Routier is much better for where we go now. Nobody will notice us and no one wants to steal these!'

We stood looking at a fairly new but battered beige four-door Renault of some sort. We had seen thousands of them as we travelled into the city yesterday.

'Senors, she may look a little scruffy but this is better for today. She has a very good and powerful engine that will make us hard to catch.' The big gapped smile was there again.

A man appeared from the passenger side of the car and Thomas introduced him to us.

'This is my ugly brother Alejandro,' Thomas said with a big smile on his face.

We shook hands before getting into the car. He was the spitting image of Thomas, but had all his teeth. Within a minute, we were moving away from the hotel and heading North on the Carlos Pellegrini that ran parallel to the seven lane Avenida 9 de Julio we had come down yesterday from the motorway.

Bill and I had checked out the maps for distances to the key places that we needed to see in daylight. We knew the distance to our first meet was no more than a couple of miles. We also knew this would be very different to the other places that we would be doing 'recces' on today. Even after the rush hour, the traffic was still backing up on all carriageways.

'How long do you think it will take to get through this traffic Thomas?'

'Perhaps 10 or 15 minutes Senor Harry. It could be less though.'

'You don't know then,' I replied. The gapped smile appeared again.

'This is Buenos Aires Senor, things change every minute.'

I smiled back at him and sat back in my seat and let him get on with it.

On our side of the road the large oak trees and long shadows from the buildings meant we were driving in low light, whilst 30 feet away the cars, buses and buildings opposite were bathed in warm, bright sunshine. The journey was stop start all the way and it seemed we were never going to get two green lights simultaneously. But then everything moved and we had a good run. The trees began to thin out a bit so we could see the mass of traffic spread out across all the carriageways. It was going to be difficult to tail anyone in this lot, I thought. You could lose your target in a second.

Thomas swung right and heading due East at the next lights onto Avenida Santa Fe. More impressive grand European style buildings filled the avenida. Within two blocks, we were completely enveloped by trees before breaking out into a huge plaza. Facing us was the monument of San Martin, whoever he was, sitting proudly in the Plaza de San Martin. Well it would be called that, wouldn't it, I thought. They certainly hadn't done things by half in this city, that's for sure.

Thomas guided the car around the right side of the plaza just missing another one of those crazy bus drivers. The obligatory finger was thrust out of the bus window as Thomas leaned on his horn again. As we drove past the next open space of ground Bill gives me a nudge and pointed to his left. Across open fields and a small lake, we could see what could have been an English clock tower, standing proudly in the middle of Buenos Aires.

'A fine symbol of their colonial past,' Bill said.

The road began to clear again and I can see the main railway station stacked with trains just waiting to go somewhere.

'Thomas how long until we get there?' I asked.

'Only a couple of minutes now Senor Harry. We have one more turn to make and then we will walk.'

Thomas parked the Torino on the corner just off Carlos H Perette, a narrow rubbish strewn street that borders the infamous Villa 31. As we get out of the car

I count seven unsavoury looking characters in their mid-twenties hanging about just across the street. Their attention is drawn immediately to the small day sacks we were carrying. They wouldn't know they were both containing a significant amount of cash that we had transferred into them for the weapons, but that wouldn't matter as they would have 'something' in them hopefully worth stealing. Alejandro had supplied the day sacks and had passed them over to us from the front footwell of the Torino as soon as we had got in. Because of these we would have both hands free to fight with, if we needed to.

There had been no pictures of this place in the guide book and as soon as we crossed the road I could see why.

'We think we have bad slums in the UK,' Bill whispered in my ear.

'Fuck me, how many people do you think live in one of those?' I whispered back.

In front of us there were hundreds of square red brick and concrete block boxes about the same size of one of the smaller freight containers that are carried all over the World on the back of massive ships, usually stacked on top of one another three or four high. Some of the boxes had been painted white, cream, blue, or just left 'au naturel' red brick or grey breeze block coloured.

Hundreds of lashed up electrical wires fan out from single poles to the boxes. I scan ahead and see ramshackle vehicles and trashed pushbikes littering the curbs of the rough roads that lead deeper into this sorry place. The traffic noise from the Arturo Illia motorway above us is loud. Very loud. Cars, lorries and huge 16 wheelers navigate a severe 45 degree turn and then sweep off to the North West directly through the middle of Villa 31 that stretched at least another half a mile in front of us.

We move in further past more multi-coloured square blocks, clean washing hanging precariously off lines lashed across the gaps to neighbours' homes. After 100 yards Alejandro turned left off the main road and into a narrower street that was only one car wide and dark and gloomy from being in the shade. Alejandro is leading, Bill is in front of me with Thomas acting as rearguard. There were a few shouts behind us now, which I assume are abuse or threats from people who have obviously clocked our foreign white faces.

Alejandro paid no attention to the noises or the people who were now appearing at their doorways to peer at us. He just carried on heading deeper into the Villa dodging more washing hanging across the gaps and a snarling vicious looking dog tethered by a not very strong looking rope. The smell of piss and shit and God knows what else was definitely getting stronger as we moved further into the heart of the Villa. Around the next corner, it was hard not to chuck up there and then, as we stepped over a river of human and animal waste that was barely moving down the middle of the street. Even Thomas looked a bit green as he rushed past me to talk to his brother.

We all had heard the noise behind us. 10, maybe 15, pairs of feet walking quickly the way we had just come.

'Hurry Senors we must get to the man quickly.'

'Lead on then,' Bill snapped at Thomas.

We both knew we were very exposed in here right now especially without any weapons to defend ourselves. Thomas broke into a run now but with one hand gripping the handle of his concealed facón. I had also clocked that Alejandro had a matching large dagger carefully concealed under his jacket when we met him outside the hotel.

The smell that had penetrated my nostrils from the open sewer had no effect on me now as we legged it down another narrow alleyway. Adrenalin was pumping through my veins heightening my senses and getting me ready to fight. We needed to find our contact soon and hope he would be able to control the fuckers behind us otherwise we would be in the shit big time.

We exited the street and ran out onto a small piece of open ground that was masquerading as a football field. It was probably about three quarters the size of a proper one.

We were just over halfway across the field when a single shot from a revolver whistled over our heads. It distracted Alejandro enough for him to lose his footing and send him crashing to the ground throwing up a cloud of choking red dust in the process. Bill managed to stop just before ploughing into the now prone Alejandro and turned quickly to face the way we had come. Thomas also stumbled and fell onto the ground next to Alejandro, producing another cloud of choking red dust. I stop next to Bill and turn to face the throng of men, well boys really, who are closing the gap quickly across the field. The majority are wearing their football colours. A royal blue shirt with a wide bright yellow band wrapped around the middle of it.

'Dossay,' I hear from over my left shoulder.

'What, what was that?' I ask Alejandro.

'They are members of a very violent gang, fans of Boca Juniors, very bad people.' Alejandro was looking a little worried.

'What do they want apart from wanting to kick the shit out of us,' Bill asked.

'They want what's in the bags Senor Bill,' Thomas answered the question.

'Well, they can't fucking have them Thomas. Talk to them,' Bill said.

The dust kicked up around us as the gang came to a swift halt five yards in front of us. Bill and I were ready to fight, standing tall, fists clenched, looking directly into the eyes of the leading group. Thomas and Alejandro were ready too and had both drawn their facóns that glinted in the morning sun. I count 16 bodies slowly spreading into a half moon in front of us. I can see two guns and lots of knives in all shapes and sizes, some small some large, but all potentially lethal.

Thomas started shouting something at the obvious leader of the gang. He in turn screamed back at him and waved the gun in his right hand around wildly whilst pointing at us with his other hand. The heated exchanges carry on for another 40 or 50 seconds more. Alejandro had joined in moving next to his brother on his right side. There was fuck all me and Bill could do except watch as the rest of the gang started to creep forward kicking up the dirt as they moved their bodies from side to side in an increasingly aggressive swagger.

Knives are being waved at us like in some pre-fight ritual. All were waiting for their leader to say the word. Thomas was now angrily gesticulating at the gang leader whose face was now contorted with rage. Spittle from his gob almost reaching Thomas every time he threw out a tirade of whatever the fuck he was saying. The leader was one pace in front of everyone else and was inching closer to Thomas with every movement of his body. Thomas had his facón gripped tightly in his right hand ready to strike.

I whispered to Bill.

'I'll take Curly with the gun and you take his mate on his left. We're going to need their weapons to stand any chance here. Hopefully, Thomas or Alejandro can distract them long enough for us to close the gap.' Bill nodded slightly so I knew he understood.

People began to appear from all corners of the Villa, some of them slowly moving closer to the standoff in the middle of the pitch. The younger scrawny kid with the other gun was getting very agitated and his voice getting higher and higher each time he screamed some obscenity or other at us. The gang was only seven or eight feet away from us now. Bill was getting ready to go and I had my man lined up. Thomas and Alejandro were also ready for a fight. They were hard men and were not going to back away from this lot even if it cost them their lives.

Scrawny had lost the plot now and was dancing from one foot to the other. The revolver, a replica Colt 45 it looked like, was brought up and levelled ready for a shot at Bill's chest. We both had started to move forward, but right then the kid's head exploded in front of us. Bits of what was his brain and deep red blood splattering the majority of his mates on his left. The bullet had entered his head dead centre of the right temple and exited through the left. I hadn't realised in that split second that the bullet had continued on a deflected path and embedded itself in another kid's neck. He hit the deck at the same time as his dead mate screaming as he did so.

Bill made it across the small gap and caught the falling Colt 45 before the kid's head bounced off the dusty ground. I leapt forward and smashed the kid, with the facón look-alike, dead centre of his nose with my right fist, my left hand clamping down on his right wrist before twisting as hard as I could. He went down quickly blood pouring over his lips and chin from his newly broken nose. He squealed like a young pig, blood spraying over my left boot as his wrist snapped in my hand. The huge dagger was in my hand now as I backed away to get next to Bill who was now holding the Colt in front of him waiting for any of the gang to make a move.

Their leader was lying on his side in a crumpled mess on the dusty ground. His Boca shirt now had a front vent in it running diagonally from his left shoulder blade to just under his right nipple. Unfortunately for the kid, matching that vent was a deep cut that went down as far as his rib cage. The vented football shirt was trying unsuccessfully to absorb the blood now oozing from the wound, but there was just too much of it.

Thomas was also now holding the 9mm Browning that had seconds earlier been in the leader's hand. It was levelled at the confused and scared looking remaining gang members. I noticed that the gang leader was gripping his right wrist that was also pouring blood from a deep laceration caused from the upward stroke of Thomas's facón before he had brought it down across the kid's chest. He had severed the tendons and nerves causing the kid's hand to open and drop the weapon. Exactly what Thomas had wanted to achieve. The kid was in a shit state and wouldn't be fighting anyone else for a long time; if at all ever, as he would bleed out within a few minutes, I calculated.

Everything had happened so quickly I hadn't noticed the group of six men approaching us from behind plus another two coming from the direction of the rifle shot that killed the first kid. I could see now they were all armed, five with various rifles and three with handguns. One of the two men closing in on us from our left was carrying a German Gewehr sniper rifle, an old piece of kit but still very good. The crowds around the field had already started to vanish back down their shitty streets and I could see only the occasional head peeking out from the windows in the boxes at the edge of the field now.

The remaining gang members were not moving an inch. They all looked shit scared as they watched the group of men approaching.

'Lower the weapons,' Thomas said to both of us. He was looking relaxed now and cracked another one of those gapped smiles.

The big man leading the 'new gang' of mean looking men made a beeline towards Thomas and Alejandro. Their facóns were back in their belts before they arrived. Thomas just had the Browning hanging loosely in his left hand leaving his right hand free to swing over his cousin's right shoulder as they embraced. The big man did the same to Alejandro.

The 'Dossay' were surrounded by the men with guns now and looking very very scared. The big man walked over to where their leader lay crumpled on the ground, moaning as his blood oozed slowly out of him and into the dust. He let out a sickening cry of pain as the heavy kick to the kid's guts knocked out whatever wind there was left in him.

Thomas's 'cousin' angrily addressed the kid on the ground and then the rest of the gang. Thomas and Alejandro had backed away and motioned for us to join them. More shouting and gesticulating from 'cousin' now, his own Colt 45 waving wildly towards the gang, all were cringing and ducking as the gun was waved in their direction. Then in a split second he took one step back and fired off a single shot into the head of the prone gang leader.

Nobody moved until after a few more words from 'cousin'. His men then opened up a route for the gang to go back to where they had come from. Six of them stooping to pick up the bodies of their former gang members, as they had been instructed. The whole gang then started to retreat quietly back across the dusty football field.

'Senor Bill, Senor Harry this is my cousin Juan, he is the man with the guns.' That smile appeared again.

'Hello Juan,' Bill and I said in unison.

'Glad you turned up when you did,' I followed up.

'Yes the little fuckers would have skinned you and stolen everything you had,' Juan said.

'But they made the mistake of coming into my Villa again. They had been warned so now it was time for someone to die.'

No shit, I thought.

'We must be going now though, the police will not come in here but we need to get you your weapons so you can leave this place. The little fuckers will be back so I know I will have to kill a lot more of them next time.'

Cousin Juan finished talking and turned and led us off the blood soaked field, down more shit and rat infested alleyways until he stopped outside a smart collection of the boxes. These were three high and five wide all painted the same colour with trees around the edges that threw shade over some of the lower windows. This was Juan's gaff and was palatial in comparison to 99% of the rest. More of his men were standing on each side of the main doors. Both had new P.A.M. 9mm machine guns strapped across their chests. They didn't move from their posts as we entered Juan's lair.

Thirty minutes later we were leaving the building with two Mauser M1909 Snipers' rifles, two Pistola 9mm Brownings that were manufactured in Argentina and four P.A.M. 9mm machine guns. Bill wanted to cover all options so he got a couple more of the P.A.M.'s for Thomas and Alejandro. We also kept the Colt 45 and extra Browning taken from the Dossay.

'You can have them for free.' Juan said with a grin.

The last things in the bags were the two modified short wave ex-military radios.

Juan allocated six of his men to escort us back to the car, two of them carrying the long heavy box of assorted ammunition that was enough to start a small war. The cash Reynoso had given us was more than enough to cover all the purchases, in fact, we only actually needed a third of it and we still had all the cash we had brought in ourselves.

No one came near us on the way out of the Villa and with the gear stowed in the boot of the Torino, Thomas headed back the way we had come, past the bus and railway station and onto Avenue 9 de Julio. The traffic was still bad but at least was moving.

'We are going to stay off the motorways,' Thomas said. 'We are going the longer route, it will be easier to see if we have anyone following.'

'Very good Thomas you know where we need to go.' Bill said as we both relaxed back in the seat. It was the first time I had felt a bit relaxed since I got here and was a lot to do with seeing both our new friends in action. These guys knew how to handle themselves and absolutely knew what they were doing.

We drove past Santa Fe Avenue to the next, Cordoba. We hung a right, all traffic on the six lanes heading one way, West. We would still have to stop at almost every intersection because of the traffic lights so this would be taking us a little while.

'How far to Hurlingham Thomas?' I asked.

'About 30 kilometres Senor Harry.' I was doing a quick calculation in my head when Bill said, '18½ miles Harry,' without looking in my direction as he was still scanning the streets and vehicles behind us.

'Thanks Bill, I was just doing that.'

I could see the smile on his mouth in the reflection on the rear door window. 'Smart arse,' I thought quietly to myself.

'It will take us 45 – 50 minutes to get there,' Alejandro said as he looked back from over his front seat.

This avenue was similar to the others we had passed. Lots of impressive buildings with cafés scattered across the sidewalks. Not so many of the highbrow shops here but still doing a brisk trade from what I could see. It was incredible to think that we were only a mile or so from Villa 31, but we could have been on another planet.

Once over Avenue 9 de Julio we started to move quicker and the further away we got from the centre the better it got. After a couple of right and left turns we were on another main avenue, 'Alvarez Thomas,' passing another heavily populated Villa about the same size as 31. Twenty minutes later and we pass through Billinghurst and then Villa Bosch. Both don't look bad places at all compared with 31.

Five minutes later and we are back onto a major road heading due East. The Torino was covering the ground easily and in some comfort. A short time later we see a private airfield on our left covering hundreds of hectares with several very expensive looking private jets parked neatly outside the hangars. Alejandro sneered as he spotted something.

'See the one with the big M on its tail and eagle wings on either side? That belongs to the Muscardin family. Some of our people have 'fallen' out of it over the Atlantic Ocean or Los Andes mountain ranges close to the border of Chile.' Nothing more needed to be said.

After the airfield, we forked right onto the Gral Julio A. Roca and shortly after pass a sign saying 'Partido de Hurlingham.'

'We are here,' Thomas said from the driver's seat. 'We will drive past the grounds of the Hurlingham Club in about two minutes. You will see the clubhouse on the right as we come to the fields. It is then only minutes to the Muscardin estate on the North side of the Club.'

'Thomas let's do the drive by nice and steady when we get there,' Bill had his left hand resting on Thomas's shoulder as he spoke.

'Si Senor Bill, I have done this before, do not worry.'

Bill relaxed back into his seat just as the famous Hurlingham Club appeared before us. There were swimming pools, four tennis courts and two full size Polo fields on our right. Further back I could make out the golf course and some more open space. More Polo fields I surmised. The clubhouse itself was grand and imposing, just what you would expect really.

We will have a closer look at that later but first we need to do the drive by of Muscardin's estate.

9

Hurlingham, Buenos Aires

Monday 20th December – 1514

We pass under one of the major motorways onto Avenue Pres. Arturo U. Illia.

'The Muscardin family estate is very close now, on the right.' Thomas was talking to no one in particular.

On our right, we pass some huge properties on very large plots. Most were only partially visible because all we could see was the red roof tops peeking out above the dense copse of trees that surrounded them. On our left were smaller sized plots but still with large individual styled executive homes with pools and trees and lots of green bits around them. Flash cars and 4 x 4's littered the driveways some of which would have cost more than most people in Villa 31 would earn in their entire lives.

Thomas slowed the car down, turned his head and said over his shoulder.

'This is where the estate starts. The main gate, which is guarded 24 hours a day, is 1000 yards further on the right.'

I can see sod all because of the high wall and the large mature trees behind it. The main gates were equally high and the line of sight into the grounds was mostly obscured by the guard room. The wall carried on another couple of thousand metres until Thomas pointed and then spoke again.

'That is where it ends, but it is the same distance to the next corner, all contained by the same type of wall; except in the corner of the new executive retirement complex we are coming to now.'

Thomas slowed and stopped several feet from the front of the brand new set of high ornate iron gates. A security guard stepped out from a small hut at the side of the road and sauntered towards the car, pissed with power and looking for trouble.

Thomas and Alejandro went into full flow about looking for a property for their parents and then threw in lots of stories about having to look after the old people with some obligatory jokes about them thrown in for good measure. The guard nodded sagely and laughed at the appropriate times so was completely chilled when he waved us through the gates and then headed back into his box by the side of the road. Bill and me just kept our heads down and stayed quiet throughout the whole performance.

A new white Mercedes had pulled around us whilst Thomas was delivering one of his stories. The guard had recognised the occupants of the car and just raised his hand to say hello. It was 40 yards in front of us now heading off to the right around the cultivated lawn and the mini obelisk that stood proudly in the centre.

We followed the Mercedes around the corner where the main building of the complex appeared. It was a huge place, two separate buildings, three storeys high, with what looked like large apartments in them on both sides of the courtyard. The reddy-orange coloured roof was glistening brightly in the sunlight and everything else was immaculate and in its place.

Something you would pay a serious amount of dosh for, I thought.

The Mercedes slowed and turned right into a smart and elegant cul-de-sac and then parked up on the drive of the second house on the left that was partially hidden behind the large trees that shaded the fronts of each of these substantial homes.

Thomas drove the Torino around the next bend and then turned right, we pass a brand new sports complex with an indoor swimming pool that looked like you could hold the Olympics in it. Further along was a single tennis court, which seemed out of place, and then we saw a gap in the trees that had been cut for the temporary gate. The gate blocked the access road that ran alongside an open field that Thomas had briefed us was being used for the construction traffic for the new complex.

Bill and I got out of the Torino and walked over to the closed gate. On the right of the rough road, a new wall was being built in the same stone used all around the Muscardin estate.

'We have our way in for the recce tonight.' Bill said as he pointed to the corner of the field 600 feet away directly in front of some dense woodland.

For the next couple of hours, we cruised around the area until we found a good drop off point for later that night. It was on a rough narrow track that cut through the woodland and was completely out of anyone's sight. But, it was only 1000 yards away from the entry point that Bill had chosen earlier. RV and ERV points were fixed now and Thomas and Alejandro knew their positions and times to be at each place. Thomas would be coming through the woods to the entry point with us and would be our rearguard if it got noisy. Alejandro was doing the driving tonight.

Later that afternoon Thomas and Bill got into the Hurlingham Club without any challenge from the uniformed doorman. Bill had specified that both Thomas and Alejandro should bring some casual business attire today as well as their Gaucho gear they were wearing that morning. Bill had brought his journo kit from the flight over but with a brand new freshly pressed crisp white shirt. Thomas had done most of the talking initially but the immaculately dressed haughty female standing behind the reception counter took a bit of a shine to Bill and once she found out he was 'Canadian,' she had spoken to him in excellent English from then on.

Bill and Thomas posed as businessmen and said they had been recommended to the club by one of Thomas's cousins. Bill asked if it was possible to play a round of golf at the end of the week and have some dinner at the club after the game.

'I do not believe that will a problem Senor Lowe.'

The haughty female had made a bit of a show of it as she called the professional shop and booked a tee-time for them at 2.00pm on Friday and a dinner reservation for 7.00pm that evening.

Neither would be taken up as we hoped to be back in New York at the latest on Friday.

Maria, the haughty female, volunteered her services instantly when Bill asked if they could have a quick look around the club. An hour later and they had seen every part of it and were back in the car. Alejandro and I had gone for a drive and had got back to the car park five minutes before they had reappeared and even then Alejandro had had to fend off a couple of zealous security guards who asked what we were doing there in 'that piece of crap car.'

I kept my head down under my cap just in case Octavio Muscardin or any of his henchmen decided to appear at the club. It was best not to take any more chances than Bill had already done by doing a personal recce. But it had to be done to give us every possible option to eliminate our targets.

'The place is crawling with security and personal bodyguards. We had a security guard with us all the way through the tour as well as the lovely Maria,' Bill said as he got back into the car; both he and Thomas were smiling.

'I think you might be in trouble if you came back on Friday, in more ways than one.' Thomas smiled at his last quip and then so did Bill. Alejandro and I just looked at each other and shrugged our shoulders. A private joke about the 'lovely Maria' that we would find out about later maybe. It succeeded in breaking the tension of the past few hours so not a bad thing as we drove slowly out of the beautifully manicured car park and surrounding gardens.

10

Muscardin Estate, Hurlingham, Buenos Aires

Monday 20th December – 2040

Thomas had taken us to the town of Pilar to get some grub. A fairly modern affluent town from the look of things with many up to date shops and no shortage of decent restaurants. The clouds had come in quickly whilst we were eating and then dumped a shed load of water onto the buildings and the street outside. For a few minutes, there were loud claps of thunder and vivid lightning bolts crashing to the ground somewhere out of sight. It was quite a show but thankfully it all stopped after 15 minutes. We were definitely going to get wet now and we would be slowed down a bit because of it.

We had eaten well on some local beef stew and crusty bread. Our bellies were full and aided by a couple of full strength coffees we were ready to go. Civvy style green combats that Fernando had supplied us with were put on in the car. Day sacks were filled with all the kit we would need including NVG's and extra rounds for the weapons. I had a rifle and a Browning, Bill had one of the P.A.M.'s and the colt he took off the kid. Thomas was kitted out with one of the other P.A.M.'s.

'2040 check.'

'Check.' I confirmed with Bill.

Thomas nodded his confirmation.

Alejandro pulled away from the drop off point taking the Torino to the position we had agreed earlier, just off the track and about 10 yards into the woodland at the back of the new estate. We had found entry to the construction service road 20 minutes after leaving the estate earlier, and fortunately it wasn't guarded. Alejandro could be with us within 30 seconds at this RV point.

Although the rain had stopped a couple of hours earlier there was still a good breeze that was wafting the smell of fresh woodland into our nostrils. We entered the woodland quickly and quietly and although the ground was a bit soggy it was surprisingly firm underfoot.

Large droplets of water started to fall on our exposed heads and run down the back of our necks, soaking our shirt collars in seconds. We moved further into the wood slowly letting our eyes get accustomed to the gloom and giving us a chance to slow down our breathing and relax the tension a bit. Bill was in the lead several steps ahead of me, I could see him OK but nothing else except the shadows of the trees. The soft sound of the high leaves rustling in the breeze was the only other noise apart from the occasional squelch of a boot on the soggy ground. In fleeting moments, I can see a deep black sky and bright stars that were intermittently being masked by wispy clouds. I wouldn't have minded a few more clouds right now as we really didn't need to be silhouetted by bright moonlight tonight.

Ten minutes later we were at the entry point to the estate. Bill stopped at the edge of the woodland and whispered.

'I'll go and see if anything has changed from earlier, then I'll give you the signal to come ahead if it's clear.'

Bill moved over the open ground quickly towards the base of the 10 foot wall. It was only 20 feet away so he covered it in a couple of seconds. He disappeared around the break of the wall. He would be heading to the temporary wire fencing we had seen stretching across the field from the housing complex that afternoon. A few seconds later, from his crouched position at the corner of the wall, Bill gave me the OK sign with his thumb and forefinger.

I ran across the divide leaving Thomas hidden in the trees. It took less than a minute to dismantle the fencing, undoing the wire ties carefully rather than cutting them and leaving any sign, something we wanted to avoid at all costs right now.

Once through and into the Muscardin estate we moved southeast hugging the high wall and using the trees for cover. On this part of the land, the trees were in clumps of three or four separated by 30 yard gaps, rather than in the long straight lines we could make out further on. I could just hear the occasional sounds of cars passing by on the main road 1000 yards away. Any sound was deadened by the high wall and the large mature trees that lined the whole of the front of the estate by the road.

After 600 yards of crouched running we came to the solid line of trees, three and four deep that ran southwest to the centre of the one million square yards of land that made up the whole estate.

'Harry move up and keep your eyes right, I'll take the left.'

I didn't need to answer Bill as I was already moving into the cover of the trees. There was a 10 yard gap between the wall and a new line of trees with fresh tractor and 4x4 wheel tracks evident. No sign of any vehicles yet though. I moved again and put my back into a wider tree so I can scan the area from a better position. I needed to take a deep breath as my heart is banging on at full tilt. 20 seconds and it's slowed a bit so I tune my ears in and listen. It was pitch dark and very quiet so Bill came across the divide as soon as I gave the signal.

'No dogs yet Bill,' I said.

'No, we may be lucky and they are with the family for dinner. It's something they like to do apparently.' Bill whispered.

'There doesn't appear to be any security out on this part of the estate, they must be feeling secure with all the goons they have positioned close to the main house. We will just need to keep our eyes peeled as we close in, Harry.'

We came up through the trees, stopping every 10 or 15 yards to listen and look for moments. The clouds are clearing now and light from the half moon is bathing the ground ahead of us outside the tree line. We stop again at a clearing that after a closer look was a full sized perfectly flat polo field and manicured so it resembled a crown bowling green. A minute later another immaculate field appeared on our right surrounded by mature trees. It had its own covered stand that would hold a couple of hundred people. I can see by the new moonlight it was freshly painted in brilliant white.

A sudden noise spooked us both as we approached a single storey line of buildings. I was on the deck in a heartbeat. Bill did the same two yards from me. Moisture from the ground instantly soaking through the pretend combats I was wearing. It was cold too. The noise came again louder and clearer this time. Horses, more than one by the sounds of it. Of course, there had to be some here. I knew that. You dumb arse, I thought to myself as I got up from the wet ground. Bill moved in close and whispered.

'Stables directly in front, 30 yards. You can't see the corner from here, but they stretch 100 yards left to right from there.' Bill was pointing to the corner of the stable blocks as he spoke.

We both heard the sound of a man's voice at the same time and hit the deck again. It was coming from inside the stables. Someone was talking to a horse, as no human response was forthcoming. We needed to push on quickly and get to cover so Bill moved first to the corner of the oak framed, tin roofed, stable block. It was constructed better than some houses that I have seen people living in very recently. Money was obviously no object with this family. I was right behind Bill as we legged it across 20 yards of open ground.

We were now in another row of trees that ran parallel to a huge paddock, which was half the size of one of the polo fields. Some horses were inside, I could see them under the lights in the stables. The lights creating small shadows in front of the plant pots that lined the hard standing next to the main arched double doorway.

I then see our man moving across the open doorway. He was dressed in traditional Gaucho gear carrying a feed bucket to a stable away from the corner we had just passed. His facón was clearly visible hanging from his belt. As he disappeared from view we moved on quickly through the trees, not stopping until we came to another wall that bordered the main property. It was only a six footer, more for show than security.

We were over it and down on the other side before we needed to think about it. More trees ahead of us masked the point where we had come over the wall. Once we made it to the edge of the tree line we could see the cover was going to get a bit sparse from here as there were now only a few perfectly positioned mature trees within the immaculately manicured grass and landscaped garden.

On our right was a tennis court with its own changing rooms and shower building. The 30 yard swimming pool was only 80 yards away in the left hand corner of the gardens. I can see the main house now. It was lit up like a Christmas tree. Almost every light was on upstairs and downstairs. Had we picked the night of a party? That would be just our fucking luck.

Bill already had his field glasses out and was scanning the back of the property. It was a very elegant colonial styled brick building with a red tiled roof. It was at least couple of hundred feet long and 70 to 80 feet in width at the ends although it had a much bigger central block. A very impressive place indeed although I was planning that that little fucker wouldn't have much more time to enjoy it.

The bright lights within the property illuminated an array of fine art, sculptures and very expensive looking furniture, all matching the deco of each room. Each appeared to have a theme with a colour to match it. I was checking out the pink room at the far edge of the right wing. It looked like a kids' room. This was confirmed for me when a hefty woman dressed in a nanny type uniform leaned out of the window and pulled together a pair of large wooden shutters completely blocking out any light that would now be trying to escape from the room.

'Harry, take a look.'

I move my glasses from the pink room and re-focus on the right hand corner of the ground floor.

'It's the dining room,' Bill whispered.

With a slight adjustment on the focus, I could clearly see people sitting and others moving along the outside of a huge highly polished wooden table. Four massive crystal chandeliers hung, evenly spaced, down the length of the room. Two were directly above the table. The light from them illuminating two huge pieces of artwork hanging from the walls behind the table.

I focused on one of the smartly dressed men who looked very imposing and stern. The head butler I presumed. Two very large vases filled with all sorts of fine flowers adorned the table. More people entered the room and sat down at the table. Servants leapt into action easing the chairs in under some quite fat arses, and some fine ones as well, I noted.

'Let's move Harry, to those trees about 50 yards from the house.' Bill pointed to a row of mature trees to the right of the dining room. I nodded.

A couple of minutes later we reached our objective from two sides. I went left past the tennis court, through more trees and crawled across the grass until I found good cover behind a large oak tree. Bill crawled over the final few feet to join me as I peered around the side of the tree through the half decent telescopic sight we had acquired from cousin Juan. Moments later we were both watching the Muscardin family gathered for their evening dinner. Fernando had told us that this was a big family tradition for most Argentine Catholic families, especially on Sundays.

I count 26 adults and nine older looking kids. All over twelve I would have guessed. I assumed the younger ones must have been put into their beds by now. A couple more minutes went by with most of the family seated now. The small army of butlers and maids fussing over them as soon as they were sat down.

I clamp my jaws together tightly and grind my teeth together as I fix my eyes on him and his big brother for the first time since Rincon Grande. The little fat fucker, Octavio Muscardin and Don Juan were carefully guiding a very elderly old dear through the huge double doors into the dining room. She had to be either the mother or grandmother. Following close behind them came a striking and formidable looking woman dressed in a long blue evening dress that swept down across from her right shoulder to under her left armpit. It hugged her ample breasts that were held up by a very good support bra, or silicone!

Bill had also spotted the Muscardin brothers but was focused particularly on Octavio. This was the first time he had laid his eyes on him for real. This was the man who had murdered his brother in cold blood and there he was in his fine dinner jacket smiling, laughing and having a great time with his family.

I rested my hand on Bill's shoulder to try and ease a little of the tension and anger I could feel building with every second he had his eyes on him.

Finally through those huge doors came the fucker I wanted, Sergeant Jorge Manuel Astiz. He slowly and purposely closed the double doors behind him and then took up station in front of them.

'2156, Harry.'

I illuminated my Casio. 'Check Bill.'

It had taken nearly an hour to get across the estate and into position and we still hadn't seen any patrolling guards or heard any dogs yet, which was fucking astounding when we both knew of the enemies this family had in their own country.

We watched them in silence for a further hour, the cold and damp from the ground seeping deeper into our bones with every minute that passed.

I had a clear shot at both of them on four occasions, but I knew I couldn't take it. That would be suicide for both of us, but it did take every fucking ounce of self-control not to blow their fucking heads off right then. We both knew we were going to have to do this somewhere quieter than here because we needed time to exit the country once we tapped them.

'Let's move Harry, I think we've seen enough of this place. It's too open for a hit and there's too much distance to the RV in open ground. They would cut us down for sure. Let's hope we have more luck with the club tomorrow.'

'It's 2316 Bill, we only have 44 minutes to get back to the RV. It shouldn't be a problem because we can go directly away from the house towards the pool. We will be in tree cover for most of the way,' I whispered.

'I was thinking the same,' Bill answered.

We kept low and moved fast away from the house skirting around the side of the pool before finding the wall again. This time we went straight over it and landed on the far side of the first polo field we had seen on the way in.

More clouds had come in so it was almost completely black now. Bill and I moved quickly through the trees and over the small bits of open ground using the night vision goggles that did exactly what they were designed for in this light. I could see everything in front of me but could hear nothing at all. It was deathly quiet.

Across the field the lights had gone out at the stables, everyone had packed up for the night. We kept going straight and had our backs against the 10 foot boundary wall a couple of minutes later. Using the darkness and shadows of the wall we covered the 900 yards back to the break in the fence without incident.

Bill put the fence back as he had found it earlier. My eyes scanned the field and the temporary road to our right for any movement or activity whilst he did it. There was none. The night was still and quiet. The drizzle had started again a couple of minutes earlier, but it was now getting heavier. I just hoped that we could get back to Alejandro and the car before another cloudburst like we had experienced earlier even though it didn't really matter as I was soaked through to the skin anyway.

Thomas appeared 20 feet away from his hiding position in the woods and whispered just loud enough for us to hear.

'Senor Harry, Senor Bill, we have to move quickly to be at the RV in time.' Bill motioned for me to move across the open ground and join Thomas. The last metal tie was done and Bill was with us seconds later.

'OK Thomas, let's get the fuck out of here, you lead,' Bill had his hand on Thomas's shoulder as he spoke. He gave it a short tap and we moved off quickly into the deep cover in the trees. We made it to the RV with two minutes to spare.

There was no sign of Alejandro yet.

'Did you see them? Were they there?' Thomas asked. His eyes ablaze with hatred.

'Yes they were,' Bill replied.

I could tell from Thomas's face he was wondering why we hadn't taken them out there and then. We would have our chance to debrief him later, but not right now. We were crouched low in the gulley at the side of the road waiting and ready to go when we saw the lights of the Torino flash on and off once. Alejandro switched them on fully as we pulled away and headed back towards the main road.

Ten minutes later we turned left back onto the Avenue Pres. Arturo U. Illia and drove steadily past the guarded front entrance to the Muscardin estate in silence.

11

We left the Hurlingham Club behind us and soon were cruising past the darkened airfield with only the odd red beacon visible in the distance and a few lights on in the terminal. Alejandro headed South after the airfield. We were going to take the faster and shorter route back down the Guillermo Marconi to the motorway Acceso Oeste, then across onto the Perito Moreno and finally the Au 25 De Mayo straight into Buenos Aires.

'30 minutes and we will be there.' Alejandro said from the driver's seat.

On the way back, we debriefed Thomas and Alejandro. Thomas was not happy, but he understood. We then went through the plans for later today. Thomas and Bill would be coming back to Hurlingham at 0500 to pick up and tail Octavio Muscardin and Jorge Astiz after they leave the estate. They would be using the Torino and Alejandro and I would be taking the Kaiser to 'The Richmond Club.' This was the very exclusive gentlemen's club frequented by many senior politicians, military leaders and the very wealthy of the Argentine capital city.

At the club, we would be meeting Maria Argibay a former 'favourite' of Octavio. She had been beaten to a pulp by him in the dungeon room a couple of weeks after he had returned from the Malvinas because 'she hadn't given him pleasure.' When she returned to the club several weeks later, the bruises had gone but the two inch raw scar left on her forehead was still there from the substantial gold and diamond ring that Octavio always wore on his right hand.

The scar was now carefully concealed by a new fringed hairstyle.

She hated the man with a vengeance and she was not the only one. Many of the girls who worked at the club both past and present had hoped someone would kill the bastard in the Malvinas war, so when she had been approached by Alejandro and told there were people who wanted to 'take care of him now,' it had been an easy decision for her when asked to help. The detailed descriptions of the building and the hand drawn layout maps of the floors she had supplied to Alejandro had been excellent.

We started to go through them again now.

The club is what's left of the Richmond Hotel, an Argentine-British hybrid opened in 1917. It was only four blocks away from the Presidential Palace that's now commonly called Casa Rosada because of the pink overtones on the sides of the building. It sits there in all its glory facing the magnificent Plaza de Mayo and is a place for Argentines that invokes memories of historical events in colonial times and vivid images of recent times from the ill-fated Malvinas war.

The Richmond Club is situated in a five storey building in one of the best parts of Buenos Aires. Built in fine white stone blocks with hand crafted arches and huge windows in the centre of each floor, which looked down onto Calle Florida and the throngs of people that are always rushing to wherever they need to be. The top floor was used for club administration and had members' meeting rooms and office spaces. All were very well appointed.

The exclusive restaurant on the fourth floor served the finest traditional Argentine cuisine accompanied by some of the best wines and cognac available anywhere in the world. Sometimes the 'hostesses' would join their men for dinner before the 'main event.' On the third floor was the 'long bar' fully stocked with any drink the members had requested. They could stand and chat and smoke their grand cigars for as long as they wished. It never closed.

Through another set of doors was the billiard room with three beautifully crafted tables arranged in a perfect line. The balls always ready stacked so that members could just pick up one of the many high quality cues and play. On the second floor is the 'Gentlemen's room.' No ladies were allowed in there at any time, on any day. Any member who broke this rule would lose his privilege to enter the club for the rest of his life. No one had ever broken this rule, not even any members of the Muscardin family.

The room was long with four high square ceilings separated by huge single oak beams. In the middle of each ceiling hung the finest Italian crystal chandeliers that would be envied by many palaces across the world. The walls were covered in the finest antique carved wood panelling. Sturdy oak coffee tables were carefully placed on plush soft carpets so they were not touching the red leather upholstery that covered the deep armchairs. Some chairs had high backs for the elderly members and several long low sofas were perfectly aligned each side of three huge open fireplaces. Highly polished brass edgings and ornaments were evident throughout the room. The large round cigar ashtrays were a feature on every table.

This was the room where many despicable plans had been hatched and corrupt deals sealed over the years. Billions of pesos had changed hands in this room. Two large knobs with ornate surrounds stand out proudly from the massive oak doors at the end of this room. Once through the doors there is a lift and stairway that connects all floors. The stairs run the height of the building in a spiral around the encased lift shaft.

The stairs down to the first floor take the members into a brightly lit reception room with lightly coloured soft furnishings and a deep soft neutral carpet. Many ornate mirrors adorn the walls in this very feminine room. Behind the wall on the left at the bottom of the stairs is the main entrance, reception and cloakroom for 'The Richmond Club'. There is no door to the main reception from this room and the wall has been fully sound-proofed to ensure complete privacy for the members. The only way in, and out of this area, is via the stairs and through the club itself.

This room is the viewing area where members choose their hostess or hostesses for the evening. A very smart and elegant lady runs this part of the club with a rod of iron. She had the bearing of a military officer and mannerisms to match. None of the girls ever fucked with her.

Once chosen, each hostess would lead their member to the suite that had been allocated or chosen by him for the evening. Each suite had a sitting area, fully stocked bar and a huge bed. All the rooms had been decorated in a different style and members could request and book any one of these depending on their mood. Some were light and bright with lots of cushions and fluffy things, including 'toys.' Other were themed in Western, Hawaiian and old style music hall. The most popular though for certain members were the 'S & M room' and 'the Dungeon room.'

The lower ground floor of the Richmond Club was used for deliveries and storage of old furniture. All the emergency exit doors and main entry door were heavily bolted, and alarmed, as were the roller doors for the delivery trucks. There was a separate service elevator with open caged doors within the building that accessed all floors. The exterior elevator doors on the lower ground floor were always secured with a large padlock and club staff were only permitted to sign the keys out for this lock from the main reception when there was an actual delivery. The only other entrance and access down to the lower ground floor was next to the main reception desk on the ground floor, which was double locked on the reception side.

This was Octavio Muscardin's bolt hole. He came here at least three times a week, sometimes in the very early hours of the morning when he just wanted to 'fuck' someone. He usually wanted one of his three favourites ready in the S & M or Dungeon room. If anyone was 'doing' the one he wanted they would be given the word he was coming. There were few people, if any, who would stick around to argue. Pretty much everyone was afraid of the Muscardin family in this city.

We walked into the hotel lobby at 0050 local time; the other four clocks showed the times in London, New York, Tokyo and Madrid. It was 1850 in London. No one was sitting in the comfortable armchairs or settees at this time of the morning. There was just the solitary cleaning lady mopping the marble tiled floor by the lift doors. Her industrial Hoover parked on the edge of the brown patterned carpet was just waiting to be flashed up and manoeuvred around all the heavy furniture in the lobby.

'Harry we need to talk.' Bill wanted a quick discussion in the privacy of his room before we got our heads down for a couple of hours.

As soon as the room door was closed, Bill spoke quietly.

'The house is out Harry, too many guards, people and kids. You saw those spotlights around the polo fields and on top of the walls.'

'Yes I did,' I replied.

'If they were switched on we would have been fucked. We would have been lit up all the way to the wall and anyone with a rifle and scope would have had two easy targets. Also, the distance to cover on open ground was too much, even at full tilt. It has to be somewhere else. Either in his car or at the club. Do you agree?'

I paused for a few seconds before answering.

'I had been thinking the same all the way back Bill. I could have taken a shot with no trouble, but the glass could have deflected the round or it could even have been bullet-proofed. Reynoso had not been able to confirm or deny that but seeing the place I would put my money on that it was bullet-proof glass. Let's do our work tomorrow and see what comes out of it, but I'm definitely with you, the house is out.'

12

Hurlingham

Tuesday 21st December – 0550

Bill and Thomas were sitting on the corner of Mariano Moreno just off the Arturo U. Illia 30 kilometres away from the Grand Plaza that Alejandro had just left. We knew the roads would be busy at both locations even at this time of the morning, and they would get even busier as the rush hour got into full swing.

Bill had a clear view of the oncoming traffic heading towards Buenos Aires. They had been parked for 10 minutes.

'We won't have missed him Thomas, would we?'

'No Senor Bill, at 0620 the black Mercedes will pass by this street. I have seen it several mornings at exactly the same time. They do not alter their schedule, only their route sometimes.'

Thomas had the car started and engine warmed up so at exactly 0620 when the large black Mercedes appeared 100 yards up the road, they were ready to go. It was boxed in by another Mercedes and an old but immaculate classic Jaguar.

Out of nowhere a big new 4x4 of some sort overtook them all at speed; Bill barely caught sight of the driver or the person sitting next to him. He knew instantly though it was Astiz driving, but the other one he couldn't make out clearly. Thomas could see the frown on Bill's face as he racked his brain for an answer as to who it was.

'Jorge Astiz was the driver Senor Bill and the other one is also named Jorge. He likes to cut people with knives, especially when they can't fight back. Octavio will be behind the dark glass windows in the back of the second Mercedes.' Thomas assured Bill.

Several flash cars were bumper to bumper following the Mercedes. Ninety percent of the cars around here were the latest and most expensive new models. Bill remembered the last time he had seen so many shiny new cars. It was on Rodeo Drive in Los Angeles a couple of years ago when he was over there doing some training with the Delta boys.

Thomas forced his way out and into the traffic. A horn was leaned on excessively by some dickhead behind us so Thomas thrust a finger out of the driver's side window. It was all over in seconds with a final gesture of the arms in the windscreen behind. No one batted an eyelid. It was such a common occurrence on these roads.

The second Mercedes carrying Octavio was now directly behind Astiz's 4x4 and was following the route that Thomas had taken only a few hours before down to the Acceso Oeste motorway. It was 0630 when Thomas eased the Torino into the heavy motorway traffic that was moving steadily east towards the capital. He placed the Torino four cars back for most of the way, but he crept forward a couple of times to reduce the gap to two or three cars to change the view in the Mercedes' mirrors for a minute or two. He then allowed a few cars to pass us, but he always had the Merc in sight. He had obviously done this a few times before.

It took 20 minutes to get to the outskirts of the city. The Au. 25 de Mayo was steady all the way to the junction at Avenue 9 de Julio. Astiz led the Merc into the pull off lane without indicating. Thomas exited three cars behind him. Astiz then turned immediately right onto Av San Juan heading towards the port. The other Merc and Jag peeled off the other way.

'He will turn left onto Av. Paseo Colon in 1000 metres,' Thomas said with conviction. And so they did.

'Where next, Thomas?' Bill asked.

'He will go to the Casa Rosada then left past the Plaza de Mayo and onto Av De Mayo. The Muscardin offices are in the Palacio Barolo building. They have the whole of the 21st and 22nd floors. It is one of the finest buildings in Buenos Aires and was designed by the Italian architect Mario Palanti in the 1920s.

'Thanks for the history lesson Thomas, but let's keep our focus on that Mercedes.'

Thomas screwed his face up in annoyance at Bill's remark.

'Senor Bill do not worry I have done my work well.'

Bill sensed he had pissed him off big time, but he wanted the details.

'Ok, Thomas what happens next?' Bill asked.

'They will not stop at the Palacio first time. He will continue all the way up Avenue de Mayo then past Plaza Mariano, which is only 150 metres from the offices. He will then go to the Plaza del Congreso before turning right by the Palacio del Congreso. He will then double back down Bartolome Mitre before turning right and then right again back into Avenue de Mayo. This is one of three routes they alternate every day.'

'I apologise Thomas. I should know by now that you would have all this covered.'

Bill was feeling a bit of a twat for doubting Thomas's abilities, but it was his life at stake as well.

The Torino pulled up at the traffic lights on the corner of Rivadavia and Callao six cars behind the Merc. There were no signs that they had been spotted. Bill watched the Merc but also took in the impressive Palacio del Congreso ahead of them. It was an imposing building that had the look and feel of Capitol Hill in Washington DC. It had the same huge domed top with an impressive spire and a copper facade that had turned an earthy green colour with the passage of time. Massive circular stone blocks with deep lines carved vertically in them were joined together to make the huge columns that supported the building and its entrance roof. Thousands more huge and precisely placed carved stone blocks made up the core of the building behind the columns.

Bill shook his head and asked Thomas whilst pointing at the building.

'How can your country be so fucked up when you have built such a beautiful thing as that?'

Thomas shrugged his shoulders but didn't answer as he moved the Torino forward, his eyes fixed firmly on the 4x4 and Mercedes that had pulled away and turned right. Thomas knew it would turn right again immediately so turned right into the next street losing contact with the cars one street ahead. Bill was not going to question him this time.

Two minutes later the Torino was parked 50 yards up the road from the Palacio Barolo. It was out of sight of the Av de Mayo, but close enough to get out quickly if Thomas had got it wrong. He hadn't. Bill and Thomas were strolling back down the street when they both saw the black Mercedes pull across the pavement in front of them and down into the private garages under the building.

Bill casually walked by the car park entrance but inclined his head slightly so he could see the camera above the top right corner of the long roller shutter door, which was now closing.

'We need a coffee Thomas and somewhere we can see this entrance, there's no way to get in there without the right vehicle,' Bill said in a low voice as they crossed the point on the pavement where the Mercedes had disappeared down the runway into the garages.

Thomas led Bill to the next corner and then crossed to the other side of the road, cutting back on themselves until they were almost directly opposite the garage entrance. The small cafe was already doing a good trade. It was 0730. On entering the cafe the smell of freshly ground coffee and bagels fired up the senses in their noses. They both realised they were hungry.

Thomas indicated to Bill that he should grab a table by the window and that he would get the drinks and food. They sat there for an hour and a half just watching, drinking and eating. Both felt refreshed and were ready to go even though they had only had three hours sleep in the past 24.

'We have to get in there,' Bill said quietly.

'Si, we go now,' Thomas replied. 'There is a distribution company in the building where I will make enquiries about shipment costs for animal feed. This will give you time to look around.' Whilst they had been sitting down the cafe had become very crowded and there was quite a scrum for their seats as they made a move to leave.

They entered the Palacio Barolo building and walked up to the security desk situated in the centre of the luxurious foyer. Thomas gave the name of his company and our business there. Bill kept quiet and looked around being disinterested, but all the time was scanning the room for other entry and exit points and the strengths and alertness of the guards. They were alert enough and all had side arms clamped firmly to their right hips in polished leather holsters. They all looked like they knew how to use them too.

As they were being ushered to the elevators on the left side of the foyer, Bill spotted that one of them was exclusively for the 21st and 22nd floor and was opened with a special key.

They travelled up to the 18th Floor where Thomas got out.

'See you in 10 minutes,' Bill said as the doors closed and he carried on to the 20th floor.

Bill had picked up an information brochure at the front desk and was casually reading it when he stepped out of the lift and walked down the carpeted corridor. He got fleeting glimpses through open doors of the palatial offices and work spaces. Each one was a little bit more ostentatious than the previous one.

Bill made his way to the farthest corner from the lift to the only fire exit door on the floor. Two electrical plates opposite each other on the opening corner of the door told him it was alarmed. If he pushed it the shit would definitely hit the fan.

There was no way up from here quietly and going noisy would not be an option. The place would be crawling with guns in minutes. The lifts were too slow and discharged you into open areas and the fire escape would take too long to get down. Bill also now knew that the building's security guards were well armed and looked well trained, add to that Muscardin's private bodyguards and this place is a nonstarter unless they wanted to commit suicide. It was time to get back to the elevator.

Thomas had timed the 10 minutes to perfection and was standing by the doors on the 18th floor as they opened. Just Bill was inside.

'There are too many negatives here for a hit, it would be suicide for us all.' Bill said as the lift made its way slowly back to the ground floor.

Thomas was quiet until they were back out into the morning air.

'I hope Senor Harry and Alejandro have better fortune with Maria at the Richmond Club,' he said.

'Yes so do I. We are running out of options and time, Thomas,' Bill replied. They turned left and walked in silence to the car a short distance away.

13

Buenos Aires

Tuesday 21st December – 0600

Bill had gone an hour ago. I had been awake and heard the door closing at 0455. I entered the hotel lobby at exactly 0600. No signs of any Hoovers or mops now. Alejandro was outside in the Kaiser Carabela, I could see him in the driver's seat through the large clear glass doors that had been meticulously cleaned of fingerprints and any other grubby marks during the night. The car looked as magnificent as it did the first time I saw it.

Our new friend, Jorge Martine, the hotel assistant manager was behind the reception desk as I walked by. He looked up smiled, waved and then tilted his head slightly in a knowing nod as if he knew where I was going and what I was going to do. Had Reynoso told him? If he had he was in as much danger as the rest of us.

Alejandro unlocked the car door from the inside and pushed it open.

'Good morning Senor Harry,' he said as I reached behind him and put my day sack on the back seat.

'Morning Alejandro. Let's go and meet Maria shall we?'

'Si Senor Harry. We do not have to go far to the Richmond Club. It will take only a few minutes. We will drive past the front of the building first and then we will park nearby at a place away from any eyes and where Maria will meet us at 0630.'

Maria was about 5' 6" with dark straight auburn hair that just covered her shoulders. Her eyes were deep blue and she had high cheekbones and baby smooth skin. She was beautiful and looked sophisticated and elegant. The short fur collared coat was not buttoned so that when she walked towards us it opened a little exposing a clean white blouse that hugged her shapely full breasts. I moved my eyes down this vision of beauty as she got closer. The blouse was tucked into a tight fitted black skirt that fell from the tiniest waist then flared out over lovely curved hips. I couldn't see all of her legs or her bottom at this point but I had no doubt they would be perfect too. Maria glided up to the car in her 4" black stilettos, which perfectly finished off her attire. Inappropriate thoughts about how Kathy would look equally as gorgeous in that kit and how I would like to take it off her briefly flashed across my brain.

She opened the back door and slid onto the seat without speaking. I could see the fear in her eyes now and the worry lines on her face. She lightly brushed the hair from her face and I saw briefly the ugly red scar on her forehead that was a long way from fully healing.

'Maria, this is Senor Harry, the man I talked to you about.' I twisted around in my seat so my head and upper body was facing her.

'Hello Maria, I know what Octavio Muscardin did to you. He did atrocious things to my friends as well and has also brought great shame on your country.'

She looked straight at me, her eyes glassy and tearful but filled with rage and hatred.

'He is a fucking bastard who deserves to die and I am not the only one to want this.' She paused for a second taking in a big breath to steady herself, she was shaking now but not through fear.

'You will kill him, won't you?'

I took in a big breath myself and considered how far this had come from the meeting at my home in Gloucestershire a few short weeks ago.

'We will kill him. Yes.' I said.

'Promise me you will, Senor Harry. Please promise me because if you don't and he finds out I have helped you he will kill me for sure. But before I die he will kill my family and my friends in front of me. He has threatened me with this before when I haven't pleased him. I know he would do it.'

'He will die very soon Maria I do promise you that.' I said.

What else could I say? First though we had to get into the Richmond Club to see if it would be the right place for a hit.

I wondered how Bill was getting on.

14

The Richmond Club

Tuesday 21st December – Buenos Aires – 0700

Alejandro turned further around in his seat and asked Maria.

'Is the delivery door unlocked?'

'It will be at 7:15,' she said. 'There will be a delivery of bread and pastries. Also, today at 7:45 the beer, wines and spirits are delivered so the door stays open. My cousin Rafel has to stay down there to check and sign everything in. He will signal you from the door.'

'I take it you know Rafel, Alejandro?' I asked.

'Yes Senor Harry. He is my cousin too, a distant cousin, but still a cousin.'

'Yeah OK,' I said. 'So we are still in good hands.'

A positive nod from both of them was enough. I was feeling nervous now about how many people were getting involved in this and who knew what we were here to do. It only took one word out of place and we would be done for but what could Bill and I do? Everyone wanted this fucker dead and a few others – especially us.

Maria told us she would be outside the lift on the ground floor at 0730. It would be quiet as no girls would be working then. We would have no longer than 10 minutes before having to go back down in the lift and be let out the back door before the beer delivery was finished. We studied again the layout of the rooms on the first floor from the map drawn by Maria. We knew we had to move quickly from the lift to the first room on the right. That was critical.

Maria got out of the Kaiser and walked to the entrance of the Claridge Hotel car park. Alejandro had parked the Kaiser in the far corner of the car park so it was a full minute before she disappeared onto Ave Tucuman. We had a clear view of the exit and the main road so could be back at the Crown Plaza hotel in less than five minutes, if we needed to. The Richmond Club was only 1000 yards away and would only take us a couple of minutes to get there. We were all set.

It was 0655 when we left the car and followed in Maria's footsteps. She would be half way there now. Traffic was still fairly light, as were the sidewalks, and nobody took any notice of us as we walked the few hundred yards along Tucuman and turned left down Calle Florida. I was casually dressed in jeans and t-shirt with a short bomber jacket on. Alejandro was similarly dressed. Our day sacks on our backs with all the things we might need; guns, ammo, wire cutters, lock picks and a camera.

We crossed over the road at Lavalle and walked into the small delivery yard at the back of the Richmond Club. We were in a good position at 0708 crouched behind a low wall 25 feet away from the large roller door that Rafel would hopefully be opening for us soon.

The door started to open at 0715, electric motors hummed and gears clanked together as the heavy door rolled up. A face appeared around the doorframe. I assumed this was Rafel. It was. He beckoned us forward with a couple of sharp moments of this hand. I followed Alejandro keeping low against the wall until we were only 10 feet from the door. Five seconds later we were inside.

Rafel quickly ushered us into a space between two old oak wardrobes that had obviously been gathering dust for some time. It was an ideal place to hide just inside the door and was only 10 feet from the service lift we needed to get into very shortly. Alejandro and Rafel exchanged a few words then Rafel disappeared for a few seconds. I heard Rafel unlock the padlock and remove the metal box covering the controls for the lift that I had pinged as I came through the door. He then pressed one of the buttons and the service lift motors sprang into life bringing it down from whichever floor it had last stopped at.

I stepped into the service lift at 0729, my finger hovering over the first floor button on the control panel. Alejandro joined me a second later.

I press the button and with a quick jolt we were on the move. I had already retrieved my Argentinean 9mm Browning from my day sack, it was in my hand now. Alejandro had done the same. Side by side we were ready to shoot any fucker who wasn't Maria when the doors opened.

She was there and within seconds we were both out of the lift and into the first room on the right. Maria was scared, very scared, it wasn't hard to see that.

We all were in fact.

After a little coaxing Maria found her bravery muscles again and led us down the corridor towards the various 'play' rooms. The room layouts on either side of the corridor were exactly as Maria had described them. They were all similar in size but had different decoration and themes. I make a few mental notes about each room just in case I have to hide in one. It was five strides, about 15 feet from the entry door through the lounge area to the double doors that led to the bedrooms. All had huge oversized beds three paces from the doors, about nine feet. On the right or left depending which side of the corridor we were, there was another door to the bathrooms. All had large Jacuzzis, showers, toilet and a bidet.

Once the main door was shut Maria confirmed that each of the 'normal' rooms were almost completely soundproofed. The members need to close the bedroom doors to ensure no sounds could be heard from the corridor.

'The last two rooms on the corridor are completely soundproofed,' Maria whispered as we made our way to them.

The entry to both of the rooms was through a padded and soundproofed 'ante room.' The first was the 'S & M room.' There were chains and straps hanging off the walls and several pieces of 'equipment' that could only be used to badly hurt someone. There was a leather topped bench full of neatly laid out 'toys.' Maria told us this room was not in use last night, which is why everything was in its place. I counted six whips with different types of flails at the ends.

Some other weird items that could be strapped around the victim's heads were hanging off the back wall. One had a soft leather ball that obviously went in your gob, although the metal studs and rings on the straps that held it in place could easily rip the recipients face if enough pressure was applied. A selection of full leather face masks with holes for the eyes and mouth hung next to the assorted handcuffs and leather wrist and ankle straps.

Other 'toys' on the bench looked more like torture implements rather than sex toys. In someone like Muscardin's hands, I was certain a lot of pain could be inflicted on the unfortunate 'hostess' chosen to entertain him for the evening. Maria interrupted my scan of the room.

'This is not his favourite room. It is the last one, but we have to be quick now. The cleaners who service the rooms daily will be here at 8.00am. They would not understand you being here. It would be very suspicious.'

'OK, Maria lead on let's see it quickly,' I said.

I went through the door after Maria and then stood bolt upright and still. My hands trembled slightly and my gob was open but no words came out.

'This is a sick place. What men would take enjoyment from such a place?' Alejandro spoke for the first time since our recce of the rooms.

The room felt warm, but everything else about it made your blood chill. It was bigger than all the others, Maria told us that there had been additional sound proofing added a couple of years ago because other members complained they could still hear the screams from inside and it put them off what they were doing!

The room looked and felt like a medieval dungeon. Several dark alcoves, quite shallow in depth, were equally spread around the edges of the room. All had shackle rings in them. In the centre of the room, there was a long stained thick wooden table with several shackling points on either end. Above the table hung a wooden frame that a human being could be shackled to and where all, or individual limbs, could be raised or lowered to any required height. Deep slits and chucks of wood had been cut or chopped out of the frame on different occasions from the colour and staining of the wood.

Knives of all shapes and sizes and more whips with metal studs on the end of the flails hung from the wall. On my right in between two of the alcoves was a shorter metal table where knuckledusters, needles, clubs and a short police type baton were neatly arranged alongside several medieval looking instruments that obviously got inserted into whatever orifice they would inflict the most pain.

This table wasn't covered with leather. The top was solid stainless steel with a hole in each corner. I didn't need to see the drain below to know why it was made of stainless steel and with holes, they were there to enable the washing away of the blood and other bodily fluids that remained on the table after the event. Maria walked over when she saw my focus was on the table and the things around it.

'They bring girls in here off the streets or from the detention centres to 'play with'. They do not use us, we are too 'valuable.' The sarcasm, anger and sadness could not be hidden.

'We sometimes hear them crying when they bring them in if the drugs have worn off. They arrive in body bags over the shoulder of one of the bodyguards and are taken first into a small room across the corridor where they are prepared.'

'Prepared? What do you mean by that Maria?' I asked.

Alejandro was standing next to me now listening intently although I think we both knew what was coming.

'They are given medicine to empty their bowels before having a forced irrigation with water. It is so that when two members want to fuck at the same time the back passage is clean.'

'Fuck me these people are calculating animals.'

'Yes Senor Harry and they are Argentineans, but that is not all.' Maria took a deep breath before continuing.

'They drug the girls to calm them before they are made to shower and put on a simple peasant dress. They are then brought in here blindfolded and shackled to that chair or in the first alcove to await their fate.'

I turn and look in the first alcove and see four leather straps securely bolted to the wall. The top two straps would have the girl's arms secured high above their heads and the two around the ankles would have the legs secured about 18 inches apart.

'We never hear them leave and yet we have done nothing about this.' Maria started sobbing as she finished talking, her tears rolling freely down her cheeks.

'Until now,' I said.

I put my arm around her shoulder and she nestled briefly into my left shoulder before pulling away, embarrassed. She wiped her face with the sleeve of her blouse trying to remove the tears. She didn't quite succeed.

'We have to go now,' she said.

A last look around the room and my thoughts turn to the atrocities that must have taken place in here. I can feel my blood begin to boil with rage and anger. Alejandro grabbed Maria roughly by the arm that made her yelp in pain and surprise. He was as angry as me.

'Do you prepare these women for slaughter?' 'What role do you and the other whores play in this?' he growled at her.

Maria was struggling to free herself from his vice grip, wriggling and twisting her arm, but Alejandro was having none of it. She was on her knees now crying freely.

'Nothing, nothing,' she sobbed. 'We only hear them coming in sometimes. We have been ordered to stay out of the way and not to look. Olga prepares them herself, she is the only one. She is a vicious woman whom Octavio and the other members rely on solely to get the girls ready. We have never been

209

involved in any of the things that happen in here. We would be killed just for looking.'

Alejandro let her go, instantly regretting manhandling her in that way, but he knew his sister who had 'disappeared' 18 months previously could have ended up in this room, or one just like it somewhere else. Alejandro suddenly gagged, but held it and swallowed hard to push the vomit back down to his gut. His eyes watered but still had a murderous look in them. I was in no doubt he wanted to kill someone and that someone was Octavio Muscardin.

Maria began to get up off the floor so I put my arm under hers and helped her up the rest of the way.

'I'm sorry Maria,' Alejandro said. 'This place has made me very angry. I know you would not be part of this.'

Maria straightened her clothes, but didn't answer Alejandro directly.

'We must go quickly,' she pleaded looking straight towards me.

There was real fear in her eyes now because she knew time was running out for us. My Casio said 0749.

'Shit we have to move Alejandro, we have to get out of here – now.' I almost shouted.

We had seen everything we needed to and didn't need to be caught now. The corridor was still quiet. Some of the doors still ajar as we had found them ready for the cleaning team. The others were closed, but no one was in there as all the members had gone home to their wives, or whoever.

Maria got to the lift first and pressed the button. It hadn't moved so the doors opened straight away.

'Rafel will be waiting for you, but if there is a problem the doors will not open. You will have to wait.' Maria said.

'One question Maria. Who is Olga?' I asked.

'She runs this part of the club for the members and has done so for many years. She comes from Eastern Europe or Scandinavia we think, but she is very evil and no one has ever talked back to her. She would kill you if you did.'

The lift doors closed as Maria turned away to go to 'her' room to pick up something that she had left behind the previous evening. That was the cover story if anyone asked. We would meet her back in the car park shortly.

'I have seen the Olga woman,' Alejandro said. 'She is a small thin blond woman with a pointed nose and narrow eyes. She was probably quite attractive once although now her face has deep lines and her skin is wrinkled from years in the sun. She looked like an evil bitch when I saw her before, but now I know she is.'

We got to the bottom and the lift doors didn't open.

Shit there must be a problem so I turn the emergency key to kill the power so we can't be sent back up to the other floors and then I press my ear hard against the door. I couldn't hear anything.

'Fuck it what's wrong?' I said to no one at all.

Nothing happened for a full minute and then I heard the loud hiss of air brakes being released and men's voices shouting their goodbyes. The sound of the engine revs picking up to take the truck out of the loading bay came next. It was another 30 seconds before it was fully quiet again and the slap on the doors we had been waiting for.

'Alejandro, it's me Rafel. Put the power back on so I can open the doors.'

I turned the key back to its original position and the lift doors opened immediately. A minute later and we are back outside and behind the wall watching the roller door close. We waited for a couple of minutes to let everything go quiet again and then made our way to the point where we could cross the car park and out onto Calle Florida.

Alejandro opened the door of the Kaiser several minutes later. No one had paid any attention to us on the way back so all we had to do now was wait for Maria. She arrived at the car 35 minutes later looking a lot calmer than we had seen her earlier. She told us that Rafel had come back upstairs as soon as the roller door was closed. He had signed the keys back in and then met Maria on the first floor to check she was all right and that no one had seen us.

They hadn't.

He then told her there was another unscheduled delivery that afternoon and two planned for the following morning.

She was gone again within 5 minutes.

15

Panamericano Hotel, Buenos Aires

Tuesday 21st December – 1205pm

Maria arrived back at the Panamericano Hotel just before midday where she was greeted affectionately by Jorge Martine as she entered the packed foyer. They had first got to know each other shortly after she had started 'in the business.' That was a few years ago now, but Jorge was always hopeful that she would be able to move on to other things and as he walked her to the elevator he asked her the same question he always did; 'Are you still in the same business Maria?' In a soft voice she replied, 'Yes.' Jorge could only feel sadness for her, as always, but he understood the difficulties and risks of exiting the 'business' she had found herself in.

Bill had arrived back with Thomas 25 minutes earlier and we had shared the events of the morning. Whatever plans we had were not looking good; the estate was out – too much collateral damage, the office was heavily guarded and inaccessible plus getting out quickly would be just about impossible. We reviewed the option of hitting the car on the way back to Hurlingham, but there were too many risks of failure and still we both wanted to see the looks in their eyes when we tapped them.

Maria saved the day with her news.

'He is coming tonight at 7:30pm' she said.

'They are bringing a girl this afternoon to be prepared by Olga. Rafel has to open the roller door at 4:00pm and wait for them to arrive.

'Which room Maria?' I asked, already knowing the answer.

'He is going to use the last room. It is booked for the whole night.' Tears welled up again in her eyes as she spoke.

I filled Bill in on the 'last room.' He was a man not easily shocked, but this did it.

'What, they do that for fun? The fucking arseholes,' he said.

'We have to do this tonight Bill, this is the best opportunity I think we are going to get. The way in is good and all we need is Maria to tell Rafel to leave the door open for just a few seconds longer. We have a place we can hide while they unload the girl and then Rafel can just bugger off and leave the rest to us.

We can take Muscardin in the 'last' room, it's completely soundproofed so it won't matter how many times we tap him.'

'Whoa Harry,' Bill held his hands up. 'Let's sit down and go through this line by line. We haven't much time so we need to be sure that some or all of us don't end up dead because we didn't plan.'

An hour later all five of us were sitting back in our chairs sipping the warm coffee that Jorge Martine has personally brought us 15 minutes earlier. We had a plan, and it was for tonight.

Thomas and Alejandro left first to find Reynoso so they could brief him on the plans and the timeframe. They also had to cancel our meeting for tomorrow morning at 0900, because if everything went right we would have landed in New York by then. We also asked Thomas to bring us both a complete change of clothes so that we could change into them as soon as we were out of the club. They would be bloodstained.

Maria left to return to the Richmond Club. She would brief Rafel as soon as she got there. It was going to be dangerous for everyone, but the people staying behind in Argentina had some real guts, there was no doubt about that.

As soon as Maria was gone, Bill rang the American Airlines desk at the airport and booked two first class tickets to New York on the 2200 direct flight. We would arrive in New York at 0805.

Travelling First Class was a key part of our exit plans if we get to the airport without any dramas because the last thing we needed was to be slowed down by any crowds at the airport. It was important to get through security and passport control fast and straight onto the plane if possible. If we had to wait for any reason we could get ourselves out of the way in the lounge.

Jorge arrived with the clothes that Thomas had dropped off for us at 1500, and some fresh coffee. Bill asked him to hang around for a minute whilst we both did a quick change into new underpants, jeans, t-shirts, socks, trainers and a light zip up jacket that had good deep pockets for extra ammo. Thomas would make sure these clothes would be burned by the time we were in the air tonight.

Bill produced an envelope full of cash and asked Jorge to use it to cover the hotel bill and any extras. Jorge stated there wasn't any need for it because everything had been covered, but Bill insisted that Reynoso's name was cleared from any records that could link him to our rooms, and us. Jorge nodded and confirmed he understood and that he would see to it himself.

I handed Jorge two white plastic laundry bags that contained everything we needed to bin. Inside were the clothes we had just taken off and the useless combats and boots we had used the night before. It would all be incinerated within the hour.

Our suitcases still had all the clothes we had brought with us, but were now screwed up and crumpled in the case just like they had been worn. The clothes and shoes we need for the flight sat on top in a separate plastic bag. The carry-on bags held the same stuff, but the notebooks contained lots of scribbles and notes from imaginary people we had penned on the first afternoon. These would be going in the Kaiser.

In our individual day sacks, there was a P.A.M. 9mm machine gun with four full clips, a Browning with two further clips, an Argentine Army combat knife and a smaller four inch flick knife. Bill also had the Colt 45 he had nicked from the Dossay. The rifles and other weapons were already in the Torino's boot.

We were about to open the door to leave when the phone started ringing. We all looked at each other wondering whether we should answer it or not. Three rings later and Bill picked it up.

It was Fernando Reynoso.

'Good luck Captain. You do your countrymen a great service tonight and the people of this country. I hope we meet again in different circumstances in the future.'

'Just make sure you have a good alibi for tonight and good luck to you as well,' Bill said as he put the phone back down on its cradle ending the brief call.

The big head chef Sebastian poked his head out of his office door as we passed. He saw two strange men, but we were with Jorge so he just smiled, half waved and went back to whatever he was doing. The kitchen was completely empty and quiet except for a large pot of something gently simmering on one of the large gas ranges. It smelled good whatever it was.

We exited the hotel at 1520 using the same emergency exit door that Reynoso had used the previous day. Thomas was waiting for us in the Kaiser and Alejandro in the Torino, both with engines running. All the luggage for the airport went in the boot of the Kaiser. The plastic bags containing our travelling clothes, shoes, clean pants and socks, were stowed under the front seat ready to put on when we finished the job tonight.

The day sacks were taken with us to the Torino. The brothers had decided it would be Thomas who would be with us inside the Club with Alejandro waiting with the Torino to get us away from there fast if we needed to. They each had a short wave radio to stay in communication just in case we needed to change our plans quickly and come out the front door with all guns blazing.

16

Richmond Club, Buenos Aires

Tuesday 21st December – 1555

Alejandro tucked the Torino away in the corner of the Grand King Hotel car park a short distance from the delivery yard for the Richmond Club. He could be in the delivery yard within 20 seconds from his position. The Kaiser was ready to go in the Crown Plaza Panamericano car park just a few blocks away.

'I make it 1605, Harry. Where the fuck is Rafel?'

Before I could answer Bill the clanging of a large padlock against the metal door could be clearly heard and then the whine of motors as the door slowly began to rise. Rafel appeared and took one step forward as he scanned the courtyard. Once he was happy he beckoned us as he had done earlier in the day. Ten seconds later Bill, Thomas and I were all hidden behind the two old wardrobes in the delivery bay. Rafel had already unlocked the box over the service lift controls so it was ready to take its next human cargo.

The brand new Silver Mercedes van stopped inside the bay five minutes later just 10 feet away from us. Bill nudged me as he recognised the driver straight away. It was the other Jorge, the man who was with Sergeant Jorge Astiz on the drive to Muscardin's office that morning. Jorge switched the engine off as Rafel was closing the roller door.

Bill was in the best place to see what was happening in the van. I could only listen. I heard the side door slid open and then talking. Bill watched as two goons jumped out of the back and then reached inside to drag a full size canvas body bag into the doorway. She was not very big from the look of how the bag flopped over at the top by a good couple of feet. She must have been bound, gagged and drugged because she didn't struggle at all as the two goons hauled out the bag and carried it to the lift.

The lift doors closed. Jorge, the two goons, Rafel and the bag went up to the next floor and we were left in silence again.

'That was Ricardo and Costa the other two personal bodyguards of Octavio Muscardin,' Thomas whispered.

I got a fleeting glimpse of the first one carrying the bag as they entered the lift and I knew had seen him before. He was definitely one of the fuckers with a gun in his hand standing on the edge of that hollow on East Falklands.

The lift came back down several minutes later. I had changed positions with Thomas so I could get a clear view of them all. Rafel got out first and stood to the side. There was no acknowledgement from any of the other men, he was just a piece of shit to them, a busboy.

Rafel closed the roller door behind them after the van had cleared the doorway, but this time he didn't apply the inner padlocks. We just had to wait now until Maria rang down to tell us to come up.

Ten minutes later we got into the lift and took the short ride to the next floor. Rafel took the stairs to sign the keys back in as usual. Maria was waiting for us when the doors opened. She didn't say anything and just turned quickly and hurried away from us down the corridor, the three of us right on her heels. We entered one of the suites that was only 10 feet from the dungeon room door. I had seen this room earlier, it was being refurbished so wouldn't be used tonight.

The room was dark and quiet when we entered, but not for long. Thomas crashed into a pair of stepladders knocking them to the floor. The can of paint that had been sitting on the top step hit the deck with a thud. Fortunately the cover sheet and thick carpet deadened the sound almost completely. But we were not quick enough to prevent the paint spilling out of the can as the lid popped off. Not much spilt but it would be enough fuck up the carpet. Fuck it I thought they can blame it on the painters. Stupid thought but the tension in the room was electric and this is now shit scary stuff. If we are found and not killed, Muscardin and his goons will take great pleasure in seriously fucking us up before we died. He was a powerful, mean and psychotic mother fucker who would kill a lot of people if we fail. I feel a bit shaky and my gut is tied up in the tightest knot it has ever been in but my resolve is absolute and Muscardin, or his goons, will have to kill me now to stop me avenging my friend and comrades.

Bill had the door shut before the ladders had hit the deck and was now surveying the scene with his back against it.

'Fucking hell Thomas be quiet and be more careful.' Bill whispered but loud enough for everyone to hear.

Thomas didn't need to answer him, he knew that was a potential big fuck-up.

'The rooms are all soundproofed,' Maria said looking very scared.

'Olga is two doors away with the girl. She would not have heard anything from inside that room I'm sure. She is the only one here apart from me and she is expecting me to be getting ready for tonight because I have been asked for. I must leave you now though. Please kill him.' She said quietly.

'We will Maria, thank you for everything. You go now.' I said and gave her a little push towards the door. She didn't need asking twice.

The smell of the spilt paint eased off after an hour, but I had one hell of a headache now from the fumes, the tension, fear and everything else. I illuminated my Casio again,1855. It won't be long now. We occasionally heard muffled sounds coming from the corridor. Nothing intelligible but definitely girl's voices.

Bill cracked the door open Five minutes later. I was standing over him looking through the small gap as well. We were just in time to see Olga guiding a pretty young girl across the corridor and through the door into the dungeon room. Her hands were tied behind her back and she was blindfolded. She was dressed in a simple peasant cotton dress, her hair had been freshly washed and brushed. The tears were visible on her cheeks and her mouth was moving saying something neither of us could make out or understand. It was a picture of fear and utter desperation as if she knew what was going to happen next.

There was now a single chair by the door of the dungeon room indicating that there would probably be a goon on guard outside whilst their master played. I would have to sort him first and I hoped it would be Astiz. Bill was going to tap Muscardin as we had agreed right at the start of this because he was the one who had murdered Tom.

At 1925, Bill cracked the door again. The chair was still empty and the corridor quiet, no sound or movements from anywhere. Soft red light now illuminated the corridor giving the place an eerie feel. The silence was suddenly broken by the sound of the lift doors opening. Muffled voices shared greetings and then the conversation grew louder as they moved down the corridor towards us.

The woman Olga was talking to Octavio Muscardin and then he said something to her and they both laughed loudly. I had heard his laugh before. Her shrill laugh was like something out of a bad witch movie, I fully expected to see a woman with a green face, black hat and long hooked nose as they passed by the door. Almost, but not quite, as I got a side view of her through the crack in the door. She was an evil nasty looking bitch though, that was for sure.

Jorge Astiz followed them two paces behind. He was going to be the man on the chair but first his job was to open the dungeon door for them. Octavio and Olga entered the room leaving Astiz outside. He was a big ugly man, but I had no worries about taking him down now. Pure adrenaline is pumping through my veins, tightening my muscles and heightening my senses. I am ready, he is going to die tonight for killing my friends, especially Bob. I owed Jeannie and the kids that at the very least.

Olga pulled the outer door closed behind her as she left a minute later. She said something to Astiz then walked back up the corridor to her 'reception' desk. She was smiling as she was walked past, the fucking bitch. I couldn't believe she was actually enjoying her part in this horror story. But she was.

Bill watched Astiz take his seat before gently closing the door.

'We cannot leave the girl in there long, we have to do this now.' I whispered.

'I agree Harry. Thomas, you ready?'

'Si Senor Bill.'

'Right then, as soon as you have Astiz in here Harry I'm going for Muscardin. Thomas you go and fuck that bitch up.'

Bill went back to the door and cracked it open again, a little further this time. It made no noise and so Astiz didn't look up from the book he was reading. He looked quite comfortable on his seat and I assumed he had done this many times before.

Thomas pushed over the steps again, planned this time, they hit the paint cans and tools that we had placed in the corner of the room opposite the door.

The steps sent the cans of paint and the long handled brushes for painting the ceilings flying. That level of noise coming from the partially open door would definitely get Astiz's attention.

I watch Astiz raise his head and then stand up. He reached inside his short leather jacket to produce an ornate silver Browning that definitely wasn't a replica manufactured in Argentina. Bill is on the left behind the door, combat knife in his right hand. I am three feet back on the opening right side of the door, my Browning ready in my right hand. Thomas was kneeling on the floor several feet away out of the line of fire and out of sight but with his P.A.M. pointing directly at the door.

Astiz's massive frame blocked out the dull corridor lights in the door crack as he stood in front of it. He slowly began to push the door open with his free left hand, his Browning pointing straight into the gloom of the room as the door opened halfway, his left hand searching for the light switch on the wall.

I came out of the darkness in one step and simultaneously gripped his right arm just above the wrist with my left hand and rammed the muzzle of my Browning into his left temple. I got in real close so the force of the Browning pushed his head against the edge of the door.

'Drop the fucking weapon,' I snarled into his ear.

He knew when he was fucked and didn't move, his left arm was still outstretched though and potentially dangerous. He hadn't dropped the weapon either.

He had been taken completely by surprise, but I knew he was now calculating his next move. He wasn't expecting the combat knife though when it penetrated the back of his clenched right hand and exited dead centre of his palm hitting the butt of the weapon. The silver Browning dropped to the floor as Bill twisted the blade. Astiz roared like a wounded bull as I dragged him further into the room at the same time smashing my Browning down into his temple. He still wouldn't go down though, but Bill now had the door closed and the lights on.

Thomas was up on his feet and took the one step he needed to deliver a perfect right boot into the bastard's nuts. Astiz's knees buckled immediately and he was down, but definitely not out. I lost my grip on his right arm as he went down. Bill had pulled the knife free of Astiz's hand as he fell forward and was now back at the door. Thomas swung another kick that connected above the kneeling Astiz's right temple sending him sprawling sideways knocking me off my feet.

Astiz was lying on his back, his hulking body trapping me by my legs. The kick had dazed him considerably, but he still was not going to let that beat him. He released his hold on his bleeding right hand and swung his clenched left fist in a big arch backwards that connected squarely on the bridge of my nose, breaking it instantly. Blood pissed out of it straight away and I am now the one that's dazed, my eyes watering as I push myself up into a sitting position, a stream of blood rolling down over my top lip and into my mouth as I did so.

Astiz moved quickly and rolled up my body pushing me back onto the floor, his full weight pinning me there. Both his hands are free trying to reach for the Browning that's still clenched in my right hand but I know what he's going for and with every ounce of force I can muster I ram my left fist directly into his right kidney. It made him briefly arch his back and grunt loudly from the pain, I knew this is my moment. I planted another hard punch, and then another, into the side of his face, which stopped him grabbing at the gun for just enough time for me to arch my back and push up hard with my legs that are now free of his weight.

It took a huge effort to get him off my body, but I did. Thomas had been waiting for the right moment to get another boot into Astiz's body or his head and this was it. Astiz tried to sit up, but the force of Thomas's boot in his face threw him backwards and towards the entrance door. Blood exploded from his mouth, teeth were shattered, lips were split wide open. Most men would have been fucked by now, but not Astiz. I'm getting back on my feet and took my eyes off him for a fraction of a second.

'Gun.' Bill shouted from the doorway.

Astiz threw himself towards the bloody ornate silver Browning that was lying where it had fallen moments earlier. He got it in his hand before Bill or Thomas could get to him and had the weapon several inches off the floor heading for a chest or head shot at Thomas who was right next to me.

The round from my own Browning penetrated Astiz's left temple next to the still visible red ring where I had pushed the gun into his head when he entered the room. The exit hole was bigger of course sending bits of skull and brains splattering onto the door and the plush carpet before his dead body crumpled into it.

Thomas was already stepping over him and heading to the door. The smell of cordite was heavy in the room and the sound was still reverberating around it. I wondered briefly just how good these sound-proofed rooms were. No time to find out though as Thomas and Bill were already moving into the corridor.

Thomas headed out right at speed. He was going after Olga. Bill headed left and across the corridor. I was only a couple of seconds behind him, blood still pissing out of my nose and falling freely down my chin and onto my shirt and jeans. The carpet in the corridor got a good splattering now too.

I pinned myself flat against the wall on the opening side of the door that led into the dungeon room. Bill pressed his ear hard against the door and then shook his head. He couldn't hear fuck all. Bill's eyes then fixed on something behind me. I glanced back down the corridor to see Thomas 15 feet away with Olga pinned up against the wall. Her feet six inches off the ground and trying to kick out at Thomas. He ignored the blows to his shins and kept his left hand firmly clamped around Olga's throat to stop her screaming. Her eyes were filled with terror, but there was still defiance in them.

Olga thrust her clenched left fist into Thomas's face deeply embedding the huge diamond solitaire into his right cheek. Using all her strength, she then dragged it down his cheek tearing flesh as she did so. Thomas still didn't release the grip on her neck though, he increased it momentarily before thrusting the facón into her body. It entered under her sternum and then Thomas forced it upwards slicing through her heart and destroying other major organs as it went further in. He pushed the blade all the way up to the hilt and then slowly twisted it inside her staring straight into her eyes and watching the life slowly drain out of them. Thomas whispered something in her ear as the life finally drained out of her, urine running down her skinny legs and over her expensive shoes.

Thomas was still holding her up and then he did something neither Bill or I expected. He pulled the facón out of her chest and let it drop to the floor. Blood poured from the wound, but there was one final act of vengeance to deliver. Thomas let Olga's body slump down onto her knees. He moved behind her holding the back of her head with his left hand and then gripped her chin with his right. In one swift, violent movement Olga's head was twisted right, her neck snapping instantly.

She was already dead, but this act was Neanderthal in its execution. Thomas looked like he was in a trance as he let the lifeless body finally fall to the ground. There was pure hatred for this woman in his eyes but a small smile cracked his lips as drops of his own blood from the wound on his cheek fell onto her forehead and into the now ragged bleached blond hair.

My attention and focus are back firmly with Bill as he slowly turned the door handle. The ante room was small with just enough space to get three or four people in there and be able to close the outer door behind you. I closed the outer door as soon as we were both in. The small overhead light barely lit the small space, but it was enough to see the second door handle that Bill now had his hand on.

Bill paused for a second.

'Harry, for my brother and the others.' he said quietly.

I didn't need to reply.

Bill eased the door open. No sound came from it. I had clocked the two dead bolts on the inside of the door earlier, but Muscardin was either too excited about what he was going to do and forgot to slide them across, or would have assumed Astiz would be able to stop anybody wanting to come in, or get out.

The lighting in the room was dull, but bright enough to see everything in there. Muscardin had his back to us, his shirt was off but he still had his trousers on. He stood in front of the terrified girl who was handcuffed to the chair I had also seen earlier. An eight inch strip had been ripped from the front of her dress all the way from her neck to the hemline. A little blood was oozing from a small cut on her right shoulder blade from where he had cut the dress before he ripped it.

Her small breasts were both exposed and she was shaking uncontrollably through fear and sheer terror. I spotted another small cut just inside her right thigh two inches away from her neatly trimmed pubic hair. Her knickers had either been cut off or she had not been wearing any under the dress. I couldn't see them anywhere right now. Maria had told us the neat pubic hair thing was something Muscardin always demanded.

The girl's knees could not close properly. Her private parts slightly exposed because of the restraining straps securing her ankles to opposite legs of the sturdy wooden chair. She had obviously wet herself as well from the small puddle of yellow liquid evident under the chair. Muscardin was probing the gap between her legs with a silver facón as we burst in through the door.

Muscardin was taken completely by surprise. At first he looked at us quizzically, but then it dawned on him what was happening and his face changed instantly. His eyes were wide and fear spread across his face.

'Jorge, Jorge,' he screamed.

'Shout all you like you fucker, he isn't going to help you anymore,' I snarled at him.

Muscardin looked at me in puzzlement for a moment. Maybe because of the accent, maybe it was my face, I don't know and I didn't care. His eyes moved to the Browning that was held firmly in my right hand and now pointing directly at his head. Bill moved a step closer to him and into more light.

'Move away from the girl Muscardin or I'll kill you where you stand,' Bill snarled at him.

Muscardin's eyes almost popped out of his head as his eyes moved from me to Bill.

'You are dead I killed you,' he screamed. Spittle spraying from his fat gob.

'No, you murdered my brother in cold fucking blood and now you will pay for what you did,' Bill snarled at him again through gritted teeth.

Muscardin stood up straight and screwed his eyes together focusing intently on Bill.

'You think you can get away with this,' Muscardin said with a sneer and mocking smile.

The initial shock was gone and his confidence was returning.

'You will be killed within minutes of leaving here if you do anything to me. You think the two of you are a match for my men and my family. You are arrogant fools. Go now before I kill you myself,' he said raising the facón in a defiant gesture.

Bang, Bang.

A small wisp of smoke rose from the barrel of Bill's Browning. He made no mistakes using the SAS way to close kill your target. Always a double tap, just to be sure.

Blood began to ooze out of the two neat holes one inch apart on Muscardin's bare chest, precisely over his heart. Muscardin was dead before he hit the floor, the facón dropping beside him as he went down.

Bill had already moved towards the sobbing young girl, his Browning tucked into his jeans behind his back. I went to Muscardin's body and placed my three fingers on the side of his neck to check for a pulse. I wanted to be sure because I didn't want this fucker coming back. There was no pulse. He was dead all right.

Bill freed the girl and grabbed Muscardin's shirt to cover her up. She was too traumatised to fully understand what was going on and was very submissive because of this. I looked at her and the frail body that was now tucked under Bill's left arm and thought of what horrors she would have faced in this room. I was sure she would have never seen the light of day again if we were not here today. I also thought about the countless others who had been tortured, raped and murdered by the despicable individual at my feet.

I only wished then we had come sooner.

I could hear Bill calling me from the door, but everything went into a blur for a moment. I stood over the body of Octavio Muscardin looking down at the ugly, arrogant face of the cold-blooded murderer who had tried to kill me all those months ago. Three rounds left my Browning in quick succession obliterating the top of his head. One for each the boys.

'You are never coming back now,' I said quietly over the corpse of Octavio Muscardin, and then I smiled.

Thomas was waiting for us in the corridor next to the wide bloody smear on the carpet where he had killed Olga. He had dragged her body back into her office where she was laid on her back, legs together and arms dumped by her side.

There was a flicker of recognition from the girl, but no reaction, as we briefly stopped to look at Olga and retrieve our day sacks that Thomas had placed outside the office door. Thomas pressed the lift button and the doors opened immediately. Before the doors closed I caught the faint whiff of cordite, we had done what we came here to do.

Now all we had to do was get the fuck out of here.

Thomas turned the short wave radio on as soon as we exited the lift on the lower ground floor. The girl was still tucked under Bill's arm not wanting to move an inch away from him.

'Pablo One, this is Pablo Two. We are coming out in 30 seconds.' Thomas spoke clearly into the handset.

A short crackle and Alejandro's voice came through low, but clear.

'Do not exit. Do not exit. The driver, Jorge, is smoking outside of the car. He has just walked over to the roller door and is looking at something. Wait I will fix this.'

'Alejandro no,' Thomas instantly let go of the send button. He was furious with himself for saying his brother's name as it was possible that someone could be listening on the radio's wavelength.

'Pablo One, no,' Thomas growled into the microphone on the handset.

He was only trying to protect his brother, but it was too late. The receiving radio was off. Thomas was agitated now.

'What can we do Senor Bill, Jorge is a very dangerous man and expert with the knife. He has cut a lot of people.'

Bill was thinking on his feet whilst still keeping a tight hold of the girl.

'Harry kill the lights,' Bill said.

'Thomas when they are out hit the roller door button and get out of sight. Let's see if we can lure him into here before Alejandro has to go hand to hand with him.'

The door motors kicked into life as soon as I knocked the lights out. The door jumped the first couple of inches before settling into a steady rhythm, sliding up the guide tracks easily. Jorge was startled by the sudden noise of the door opening and quickly reached inside his jacket to produce his own personal favourite weapon, a matt black Colt 45.

Alejandro ducked behind an industrial waste bin halfway across the car park without Jorge spotting him. He could clearly see him though, and his drawn Colt, he was peering into the gloom of the Richmond Club loading bay. The door was fully open now, but no one had emerged. Jorge took a couple of tentative steps forward searching the loading bay for signs of life.

I've got myself tucked in behind some empty beer kegs by the door and Bill is in between the wardrobes, his hand clamped firmly over the girl's mouth. Thomas was standing three feet back from the loading bay opening on the left hand side.

Jorge sensed something was not right and went into defensive mode. He ran to the other side of the doorway opposite to where Thomas was standing. Bill gently let the girl go and put his finger to his lips and made a shushing sound. He then took two paces forward so he was standing at the front of the gap between the wardrobes with both arms outstretched. His left hand supporting his right that gripped the butt of the Browning, the index finger on his right hand taking first pressure on the trigger. Jorge then made his last and fatal move by stepping around the front of the door and into full view.

Bang, Bang. One round each from the two of us.

Bill tapped him in the head and I got him through the heart. He dropped like a stone, dead before he hit the deck. Alejandro was already running back to the Torino with us not far behind him. A quick check on the crumpled body of driver Jorge as we left the loading bay confirmed he was dead.

The door at the far end of the loading bay opened before we could disappear from view. Two security guards had been despatched from reception when the roller door alarm had gone off. There was an old fat one blowing hard who looked like he had never chased anything in his life. The younger one of the two was a little different, he looked ex-military, tough and ready for a fight. He already had his weapon drawn and when he came through the door he took up a defensive position immediately.

I fired off two quick rounds in the general direction of the young guard just to keep his head down. My quarrel was not with him so I didn't want to kill him unless I had to. Bill, Thomas and the girl were already moving quickly across the tarmac towards the Torino. I started legging it after them.

The first round fizzed by the right side of my head. A second and then a third pinging off the tarmac on my left. Two more shots were fired before I hit the deck and turn to face the loading bay. Lying in a prone position I let rip with my Browning. Thomas got down beside me in the same position three feet to my left and opened up with the P.A.M. The young guard didn't stand a chance. Thomas hit him with several rounds in the chest and head. I got him at least a couple of times with the Browning as he disappeared backwards into the gloomy loading bay. No more rounds came our way; after that fat boy was nowhere to be seen.

Alejandro had the Torino alongside us 10 seconds later. Bill was cradling the young girl in his arms, her head limp on his shoulder. His hands were covered in blood from the two holes that had punctured her back. She was dead when I pulled her away from him.

'Bill we need to get the fuck out of here now.' I said quietly.

There was no time for goodbyes or regrets as Alejandro eased the car out into the light northbound traffic on Florida as though it was just a normal day.

Four guys in a Torino just finishing a shift and going for a beer. Nobody looked and nobody bothered with us.

No one could see the blood.

17

Buenos Aires

Tuesday 21st December – 2021

We heard the sirens before seeing the two police cars that blocked the road at Lavalle and Florida. Two more police cars entered the car park that we had left a minute before and several others simultaneously screeched to a stop outside of the front door of the Richmond Club. All officers had their weapons drawn as they exited their vehicles. We lost sight of all the commotion when we turned left onto Tucuman.

The traffic was light at this time of night and getting up Carlos Pellegrini to the Crown Plaza Panamericano only took a few minutes.

'Fuck me that was close, Bill,' I said as I dumped my bloodied shirt into the plastic bag.

'You're not fucking wrong Harry. All we need to do now is get rid of this kit and get the hell out of here. It's not over yet though, we still have to get checked in at the airport and through the gate.'

Neither of us believed that was going to be as easy as it sounded.

By the time Alejandro had got us to the Kaiser all three of us had washed ourselves down with wet towels, dried off and changed into the kit we had stowed under the seats of the Torino earlier. The blood-stained clothes were stuffed back into the bags ready for burning.

The Kaiser pulled out of the hotel car park at 2034 and onto Av 9 De Julio. A firm shake of the hand and a nod was all we had time for with Alejandro. He had important things to do, ditching weapons and burning kit far away. It took us eight minutes to get to the Au.25 de Mayo motorway. A frustratingly long eight minutes with most of the traffic lights on red again.

As other cars pull up alongside us at the traffic lights I can see in my peripheral vision the inhabitants staring across at us. This makes me feel even more nervous and tense every time we have to stop.

'They only admire the car, Senor Harry. They do not know who you are or what we have done.' Thomas must have spotted my nervousness.

I didn't answer, I just kept my head down. As Bill was also doing.

Once on the motorway it was plain sailing all the way to the airport. Thomas kept up a steady pace not wanting to attract any unwanted attention.

Several police cars and army jeeps with lights flashing and sirens wailing raced down the other carriageway into the city. Good for us I thought.

I lifted our two bags out of the boot of the Kaiser at 2106.

'Thank you.' Thomas said as he shook each of our hands in turn.

There was no time to linger as we had to pick up the tickets from the American Airlines desk before checking in and Thomas also wanted to get back to his brother as soon as he could. Thomas pulled away from the kerb giving us one last smile and a wave before heading for the exit lane. He was out of sight before we got to the terminal entrance door.

Our first class tickets were waiting for us at the desk. A very pretty young woman behind the counter told us that we were very late and would have to be really quick to get through check in and security in time. Boarding would start in less than five minutes. Bill made our excuses about being late and apologised. We had cut it very fine so Bill decided to try and turn on the charm.

'Please miss,' He said with the broadest smile. 'Is there anything you can do to help us get our flight? We have to back in New York tomorrow for a very important meeting. We will be in really deep trouble if we miss this flight.'

She huffed and paused for a moment. We both smiled at her.

'Wait here please Mr. Lowe, Mr. Finch,' she said and then disappeared through a door at the back of the counter.

Fifteen seconds later and she was beside us.

'I don't usually do this, but if I don't you will miss your flight and there is no refund on those tickets. Please follow me,' she said smiling at Bill.

'Thank you. Thank you,' we both said in unison as we all ran across the terminal to the first class American Airlines check in desk. No one was in the queue so that part of the process was sorted quickly. Our bags were taken away by a man who was going to put them on the plane himself. Bill's new friend had sorted that with another one of her beaming smiles.

Passport control next. A neatly folded US $50 note next to the entry visa ensured a swift passage through there. The presence of a pretty young woman at passport control certainly helped as the lecherous old officer scanned her up and down whilst deftly slipping the two notes into his left hand jacket pocket. He barely glanced at us as he thumped down the exit stamp on the appropriate page of our false passports. He had one obvious last stare at her arse as we were ushered through with a dismissive wave of his hand. We were on our way to the plane with minutes to spare.

The aircraft doors closed a minute after we sat down in our large single seats, one in front of the other. No time for champagne or any pleasantries with the stewardess we just had to strap ourselves in and wait until after take-off for that. Neither of us spoke until the seat belt sign was off and we were at 33000 feet on our way back to New York. The stewardess had already brought me the glass of champagne I had missed earlier.

Bill crouched down by my seat with his glass of champagne in his left hand.

'Thanks Harry, I couldn't have done it without you. I know my brother would be proud of us,' he said quietly.

'I think John, Jimmy and Bob would be too,' I said.

Our right hands wrapped around each other's in a firm grasp. We held them there long enough to look at each other's faces and know this meant everything to both of us after the nightmares of that night on East Falkland.

18

New York JFK

Wednesday 22nd December – 0830

We dumped the bags in left luggage at JFK after arriving on time. The flight from Buenos Aires had been quiet. Most of the time I'd spent trying to sleep on my full sized flat bed but not very successfully. I had turned down the offer of my very own pyjamas this time. Pyjamas on a plane, what the fuck will be next, personal massages and full length bars no doubt. I scoffed at the idea.

We had 10 hours to kill once we had purchased our business class flight tickets back to London. Bill said we needed to use up the cash, I wasn't going to argue with him. The next few hours we spent quietly in a great bar I knew off Times Square. The beer went down very well as Bill and I talked a little about the past few days but more about life in general. Kathy, families, babies, sport and plans for the future all went onto the table.

I thought we would have to spend loads of time in debriefings when we got back, but I was put right on that one.

'It will very likely be only a one to one with Colonel Shaw and Brigadier Whistonhall. We will need to make sure that all records, correspondence and notes relating to this operation disappear and then we can go back to our normal lives.' Bill told me.

What was normal after this I wondered, but all I wanted to do now was get back home and see Kathy.

We caught up with the early evening news in the airport business lounge. It was mostly about murders in New York, traffic problems, teenage pregnancies and a big sale at Macy's. The international news grabbed our attention though as we watched in silence at the piece on multiple deaths at the Richmond Club in Buenos Aires. The most high-profile victim was Colonel Octavio Muscardin from one of the most powerful and influential families in Argentina.

There was a slight delay on the English subtitles coming up as General Muscardin spoke outside the front of the Richmond Club. I started to read.

"These murders are the actions of terrorists who were trying to undermine the important work of the Government."

Where had I heard that before?

The General continued talking and more lines appeared on the bottom of the screen.

"My brother, Octavio Muscardin, was striving for change," it read. "But the perpetrators of these crimes do not want change." Another pause. "The Muscardin family and this Government will not stop working or change our plans until Argentina recovers from the recent military and current economic crisis."

The news piece then showed pictures of five body bags being wheeled out the front door to the waiting vans. The newsreader was back on screen now standing in front of the Richmond Club spouting off about ongoing police investigations and suspects being questioned and important leads being followed up.

The screen then changed to a picture of a huge truck on its side with the text underneath telling us there was a serious RTA on the New Jersey Turnpike that was blocking three lanes.

It was all bullshit from the General of course, but they seemed to be looking inside the country rather than outside, which was good for us. My thoughts immediately went to Fernando, Thomas, Alejandro, and Maria especially. They were in incredible danger and all I could do was hope they would all survive.

Argentina needed strong people to break the hateful and powerful grip on the country that Muscardin and others had on it right now.

People started to move in the lounge as our flight was called. A few business suited gents were the first to move followed by a couple of powerfully dressed women who then joined the queue to leave the lounge, their big shoulder pads bumping the men in suits as they pushed in. I did smile.

Bill had sorted us two seats together on the left side of the plane. My thoughts drifted off to the good people of Argentina we had met over the past few days. I doubted I would ever see any of them again as I would not be going back there in a hurry, that's for sure.

Time to get back to the 'normal' life Bill spoke about.

Part Four

Safe – Home in England

1

England

0740 Thursday 23rd December 1982

Corporal Steve Jones was standing at the end of the cordoned off area outside the exit doors from the baggage reclaim hall.

'Morning sir, Morning Sergeant. I have instructions to take you into London. Brigadier Whistonhall and Colonel Shaw will be waiting for you. We have to be there at 1030, so we have plenty of time,' he said as we reached him.

An hour and a half later the car pulled up at the back of St James's Palace. Steve Jones showed his service identity badge to the armed soldier on the gate; Bill and I did the same after retrieving ours from the two envelopes that had been left on the back seat of the car.

Colonel Shaw was in civilian clothes, as we all were, standing between a high stone archway leading through to the officer's quarters currently being occupied by the 2nd Battalion Coldstream Guards. One of the Queen Mother's 'favourites' by all accounts although the 'Black Watch' probably took top spot when it came down to it.

'Captain Dye, Sergeant Glass, follow me,' Ian Shaw said after handshakes rather than salutes.

We were led past a number of open doors. Soldiers were talking on radios, getting their kit ready or just had their heads down poring over mounds of paper. We walked in silence until we came to two huge wooden doors, they must have been 10 feet high and covering a gap of eight feet across. The left-hand door opened as if on cue and a smartly dressed military steward stood back to let us in.

Brigadier Brian Whistonhall was sat in the Queen Mother's private dining room at the head of the long oak table. He was dressed in a very smart city pinstripe suit.

'Gentlemen, welcome home,' he said as he rose from his seat and then strode over to us with his hand outstretched.

'Well done Captain,' he beamed at Bill shaking his hand firmly.

'And you Sergeant,' he said as he gripped mine.

'One hell of a good job. It has been all over the news and is causing quite a stir in Buenos Aires. The general public have not bought the story that the

General put out about terrorists being responsible. The families of the 'disappeared' are saying it was some of their own that killed Octavio Muscardin and they are very happy about it. Thousands are back out on the streets screaming for others to be brought to trial and hanged when they are found guilty. They are naming them as well. General Muscardin and his sister Eva, who I understand is probably the worst of all of them, are very high on their hit list. The Army is now involved trying to quieten things down, but you have stirred up one hell of a rat's nest,' he then laughed.

'A truly excellent operation gentlemen, your comrades would be proud of you. Now, let's hear all about it.'

We went through every detail of the mission, who we met, where we went and what Reynoso was like. We told them about Maria and Thomas and Alejandro and their connections to Fernando. We also mentioned the others who had helped us and confirmed that nothing we left there could be traced back to the UK.

The debrief went on for hours and hours and even with a good supply of bacon butties and steak pies for lunch and a shit load of coffee, I was completely knackered by 1500 and just wanted to get the hell out of there and go home.

It was 1650 when we finally got up to leave. We wrapped it up with our close call at Buenos Aires airport and how the pretty young American Airlines girl had made the difference. I was happy to be out of there and I know Bill was as well from his facial expression when we got back into the car.

Steve Jones informed me that my car had been delivered back to my home and I was going to be dropped off first. Bill was going back to our temporary digs in Hereford where he was going to crash for the night before going off to his parents for Christmas. We had been given the good news that we didn't have to report back to Credenhill until the 10th January.

Colonel Shaw had some final words before we drove off.

'Have a safe and happy Christmas with your families and friends. You have earned this break. You have done your country and our fallen comrades a great service.'

As we pulled away I felt a deep sense of pride in what we had both achieved but I'd seen enough dead bodies now to last me a lifetime. I needed some peace for a while.

2

Nigglesworth, England

1930 Thursday 23rd December 1982

Kathy at 21 weeks pregnant had more than just a little bump showing as she ran down the drive and jumped into my arms.

'When did you get back? Why didn't you call? Where have you been? What happened to your nose?'

'Oh,' she said putting her hand to her mouth.

'I can't ask you all that can I? You look so tired, but you are here and home for Christmas. You are home for Christmas aren't you?'

It was like a barrage of guns going off but then she stopped, her arms wrapped a bit tighter around my neck and she kissed me once on the ear and then snuggled in.

'I am home for Christmas,' I whispered.

She gave me another squeeze but the moment was broken when she heard the low cough from behind me. Kathy looked up to see a man standing by the car door.

'Oh,' she said, a little bit embarrassed as she released her legs from around my waist and slid back down to the ground.

I grabbed her hand and guided her towards Bill who was smiling broadly.

'This is Captain Dye. I have been working with him these past few weeks. He is the brother of Tom who died in the Falklands.'

Bill put his open hand forward towards Kathy.

'It's Bill, and you must be the Kathy that I have heard so much about. I think Harry has undersold you.' Bill smiled again and Kathy blushed.

I nudged her in the ribs and winked when she looked at me. I got a slap on the arm for that.

'It is very nice to meet you Bill I have heard lots of good things about you as well.'

'All lies, I'm afraid,' Bill replied.

'Would you like to come in for a coffee or something Bill?' Kathy asked.

'No thank you Kathy I need to get back home myself. Another time though.' Bill then turned to me.

'Have a great Christmas Harry, I'll see you in January.'

233

We shook hands and he got back into the car. Kathy's arms were wrapped tightly around my waist with my own arm around her shoulders as the car disappeared at the end of the lane. It was good to be home.

Christmas was a happy time spent with good friends and down the pub with the boys. One night after having a couple too many Kathy had to slip in alongside Gerri because, in her words, 'I was snoring like a pig.' She did let me off though when I blamed it on the fat nose I still had. Christmas Day there were just the three of us eating far too much as everyone does and then crashing out in front of the television to listen to the Queen.

Days were spent just chilling out and going for walks together, doing the cinema, eating out, going to the pub, it was a great time. On occasions, we caught sight of the news and particularly the unrest in Buenos Aires. The Army was using considerable force to control the huge crowds that had gathered in many places in the capital. It was hard not to say anything especially when I saw shots of the Pink Palace at Plaza de Mayo and the Obelisk on Av 9 de Julio. It wouldn't be right to tell Kathy what I had been doing over there and she hadn't asked again where I had been, so I let it drop.

This was our time.

3

Credenhill – 10th January 1983

The guardhouse at Credenhill came into view and I wondered for the umpteenth this morning what was next for me as I hadn't been given any orders, I just had to report here on the 10th January. I parked up outside the building that housed Colonel Shaw's office and wandered in. The place was bustling with people, it was manic, I'd never seen it like this before. Officers and NCO's were shouting orders down the phones and out of the windows. Something big was kicking off.

The door to Colonel Shaw's office was open so I knocked twice on the doorframe. He was on the phone so waved me to a chair in front of his desk. More shouting from another room as a lieutenant went past the doorway at the rush. Colonel Shaw put the phone down and walked past me to close the door.

'Morning Sergeant how was your leave?' he asked.

'Very good sir, just what was needed.'

'Excellent and how is the nose now Sergeant?'

'Fine sir, thank you.'

'Good. You will have to excuse the commotion here. We have a hostage situation in London that we have to deal with. It only came through 10 minutes ago.'

'Do you need me to leave sir?'

'No Sergeant, we need to talk. Everything is under control here,' he said as he sat down again behind his desk.

'Captain Dye tells me you handled yourself very well in Argentina and by all accounts in the Falklands too. You have an exemplary record in the Marines and you have had your papers raised for officer selection for two years now, but this is something you seem reluctant to take forward from what I have read. Why is that Sergeant?'

'Sir, I'm not sure how long I want to stay in the Marines, especially now with a baby on the way. I also want to finish the degree I started and possibly specialise in Nuclear Science, which is a field my mother has some expertise and experience in. There appears to be the potential for a good career and future opportunities in that specialist field. I've also seen and been involved in a lot of killing recently and I'm not sure that is what I want to do for the next 20 years, and....' I was stopped mid-flow by a loud knock on the door.

'Come in,' Colonel Shaw was obviously expecting someone, from his relaxed response.

Bill entered the room and walked over to shake my hand.

'Morning Sergeant,' he said with a smile.

'Morning sir,' he said whilst shaking the Colonel's hand.

'Have you discussed anything with the Sergeant yet sir?'

'No Bill, I was just coming to that.'

The knowing looks they were giving each other slightly worried me about what was coming next.

'Sergeant,' Colonel Shaw started. 'We have a proposal for you that may also fulfil your ambitions with respect to the degree you wish to obtain and specialising in Nuclear Science. There is an increasing threat from so-called dirty bombs, which not only kill from the initial blasts, but could also contaminate huge areas of land and the people from the radioactive fallout. There are a few experts who are spread around the country, but like your mother they are all currently civilian. The worrying thing is that inside the military, we have little or no actual expertise in this field and this is something we need to address as a priority. Thoughts Sergeant?'

I was completely taken by surprise and didn't know how to answer.

'It's a lot to take in I'm sure and you will need some time to digest what the Colonel has proposed,' Bill said as he lifted a brown A4 envelope off the Colonel's desk.

'In here are full details of the objectives we want to achieve. Take it away and read it carefully. Unfortunately, we cannot go through it now as we have this situation to deal with.'

'I know sir,' I said.

I was still reeling from the conversation. Were they really talking about me? This could be everything I have ever wanted, use my brain, stay in the Marines and I might not have to kill any more people either.

'There is one critical thing though Sergeant.' Colonel Shaw paused and looked at me.

'What's that sir?'

'Sergeant, if everything in that envelope is what you want for your future, you will have to become a commissioned officer.'

I was stunned at what was happening, I could hardly believe my ears.

Colonel Shaw continued.

'You need to go away now Sergeant and think very hard about this. In the envelope, you will find a positive endorsement from your Commanding Officer approving your place at the Admiralty Interview Board at HMS Sultan next Monday. If you are successful after the three days, and we believe you will be, you will join an officer training programme at the Commando training centre at Lympstone. You will have missed the first 16 weeks of initial training, but this has been waived. You will also find details of the degree programme that we have selected. We will meet here at 0900 on Thursday for your decision.'

The phone rang just as Colonel Shaw finished speaking and after listening to the muffled voice on the line for a few seconds he dropped the phone back on its cradle.

'Captain we have to go. Sergeant we will see you here on Thursday. Sorry, we can't spend more time on this now.'

They left me alone in the office contemplating what the fuck had just happened. I had come in here thinking I was back off to my unit, and my mates, and now this time next week I could be on the commissioned officer's training course for the next six months. I would then be going back to university to complete the science degree course I had dropped out of to join the Royal Marines. I needed to get out of here and sit down quietly and read all this stuff and then talk to Kathy.

The next couple of days I talked endlessly about the written offer at great length with Kathy and Gerri. I also talked to Ron in the US who said I would be mad to pass up the chance. He said I should just go for it and if it didn't work out I could still go back to my unit, or leave anyway and do my degree as I was originally planning. I know he made a lot of sense, but what about Kathy and the baby?

Of course when I had asked that question Kathy had given me one of those cutting looks that only women can when they think you are being a complete dickhead. The hands on her hips either side of the growing bump finished it off.

'You should absolutely do it. You will make a great officer and then be able to do something really positive for the Services once you have your degree. You love the Marines, and the life, so what's stopping you? And don't you dare say me and the baby, because we will be fine.' Kathy had left nothing in doubt.

Gerri had then got in on the act.

'I will help you with your degree and anything else you need to know about Nuclear Science, you know I will.' She was definitely on Kathy's side.

They had both stood there in Gerri's small kitchen staring at me and poking me, figuratively speaking, to say yes. I know I wanted to do it and now the two, and a half, most important people in my life gave me the endorsement and all the encouragement I needed.

'I'm going to do it,' I had said finally.

Lots of hugs and tears later and I was ready for a pint, or two, or three, down the local Jovial Foresters pub.

The next morning I was back in the Colonel's office telling him yes. He was very pleased and the first thing he did was call Bill. I stood there in the office listening to their short conversation knowing I was about to start a completely new phase in my life; it was a bit of a scary thought but I was just glad it wouldn't involve killing any more people for a while.

I was excited and sad at the same time as I put my head down on the pillow next to Kathy's that evening as I knew I wouldn't be doing it much over the next few months whilst I was on my training course at Lympstone.

4

Nigglesworth, St Georges' Parish Church

1300 Saturday 4th June 1983

Harry Robert Glass Jr had been born on Saturday April 23rd in Gloucester Royal Hospital. The delivery room was immaculately scrubbed and smelling of fresh disinfectant. Everything had been ready for the birth in the boxes at the side of the room and on the trays. The midwife and nurses had all been brilliant and were especially happy when they did not have to call a surgeon to do an emergency caesarean. It had got close, though.

Harry Jr weighed in at 7lbs 10ozs, he was a chunky little bugger. He had Kathy cursing like a true Royal Marine Commando and swearing she was never going to let 'little Harry' near her again. Everyone in the room instantly knew who 'little Harry' was; their tell-tale smirks confirmed that. The deep nail marks in the palm of my right hand would remain there for days as would the scratches on my forearm. But what a moment when he popped out, it was worth all the pain, for me.

The relief on Kathy's face after seven hours of labour was clear for me and everyone else to see. Then there was the moment of indescribable joy when Harry Jr was put into her arms for the first time where he made his first gurgling sounds quickly followed by a full on wail. There had been a few times in recent months on the officers' training course that had brought me, and many other strong men around me, close to tears from pain, agony and exhaustion, but at that moment I couldn't have given a shit who saw me as I looked down at my son through great blobs of water that had cascaded freely down my face. I managed to get it back together and had dried my face when I held him for the first time. I couldn't have my new son's first view of Dad being one of him with leaking eyes, could I?

Here he was now six weeks later and a lot chunkier and usually much louder, but right now in the calm and serene surroundings of this great old church he was quiet and gurgling happily in Kathy's arms. No doubt that would change when he got doused in cold water. Everyone who was invited had turned up. Even Ron had blagged his way onto another free transatlantic Military flight.

After the Christening and all the usual stuff that goes with these things, it was time for a party. Gerri's house was really buzzing by 1600. Uncle Keith got pissed as usual but was full of fun and good banter until the big chair called him. He was snoring by 1700. Auntie Val just patted him on the head, 'Bless him,' she said and then wandered off to find Harry to have another cuddle.

Kids were everywhere with most of them careering around the garden screaming.

'You'll wake the baby, play quietly.' Numerous mums said to their respective excited siblings after grabbing hold of them as they tried to whizz by. Two minutes later though and it would all kick off again.

A bus load of my SBS mates and others from the various Commando units I had served in had also come up for the day. I hadn't seen some of them since collecting my kit from Plymouth in January before heading off to Lympstone. They still gave me tons of stick even though I was almost an officer. 'Almost' was enough to still take the piss mercilessly, the bastards. Steve and Mike, two new buddies from Lympstone also coming from the non-commissioned ranks, didn't get let off lightly either. It was all in good fun though.

Jeannie and the kids had come up as well. They were obviously still missing Bob very much. Jeannie had gripped me by the arm and taken me to a quiet corner for a word!

'Bob would be very proud of you Harry, you're a good man but you just make sure you take care of Kathy and little Harry, or I will be after you,' she said in a motherly kind of way.

I could feel myself blushing slightly and grinning stupidly knowing we will have to find another name for the other 'little Harry' very soon. It was at that moment I decided to tell Jeannie that I had given Harry Jr the middle name Robert after Bob. She almost broke my neck from the squeeze she put on it. Tears streamed down her face before she rested her head against my chest for a moment. All I could do was place my hand on her head and hold her.

'So you have told Jeannie about Harry's middle name then?'

I looked up and through my own glazed eyes there was Kathy cradling Harry Jr softly in her arms. I nodded as Jeannie lifted her head from my chest and reached out to hold the baby. There were lots of hugs and more tears from the assembled group of wives and girlfriends as they led Jeannie away to the girls' corner. I needed to dry off my shirt so headed to the kitchen where most of the blokes were steadily demolishing the stack of cans of lager and beer.

I got interrupted by the doorbell right in the middle of a sordid run ashore story that was just about to get even more sordid. Kathy called out that she had the baby and could someone else get the door. No one was going to move from the girls' corner there was too much cooing and baby cuddling going on as Harry Jr was being passed around.

'Hi Harry, how's the new dad?' Bill asked as we shook hands.

'I'm fine Bill, thanks for coming, it's great to see you.'

'Well, I couldn't not come and see the new improved Harry Glass could I, and of course the new mum. Where is she?'

'I'm here Bill.' Kathy stepped past me and gave him a big hug and kiss on the cheek.

'I've been telling all the girls about you.'

She winked at me and then grabbed his hand and led him into the girl's corner to see the now fast asleep Harry Glass Jr. When Bill looked back, I just raised my hand and gestured, when he could escape the booze was in the kitchen on my left.

'OK.' Bill mouthed.

A little over an hour later and after much mingling and aversion of cooing eyes from the assembled females in the house, Bill got himself free and came to find me.

'Harry can we go somewhere quiet, we need to talk.'

His face had changed and was looking serious as we headed out into the garden. A couple of the kids were still running around like crazy things and a couple of adults were just mooching around inspecting Gerri's flower beds. The garden table and chairs were free though and far enough away from the doors and the other occupants of the garden to have a private conversation.

'Harry we've had some news from Buenos Aires,' Bill said.

Fuck, I thought, this is obviously not good from the look on his face.

'As you will know Harry the country has been in turmoil since the conflict and we did a good job of stirring things up when we took out Octavio Muscardin and some of his crew. The first part of the bad news is that his older brother, General Muscardin, is fighting his corner and is still hanging on in there. He still holds significant power and influence with people at the very top of the Government even though others are openly after him.'

'OK Bill, so what's the second bit of bad news?'

'Fernando Reynoso has contacted me again through the Embassy. I haven't brought the actual text with me, but what he told me was, Maria and Rafel, the butler at the Richmond Club, 'disappeared' several weeks ago. There was no trace of them until five days ago when Maria's mutilated and bloated body was found in the water by fishermen five miles offshore. Reynoso catalogued her injuries, which were horrific. One breast had been sliced off, both legs had been broken and had drill holes in both knees and ankles. Both arms were pulled out of their sockets and also broken in several places from repeated blunt force traumas, probably a baseball bat or something similar he had surmised. There was also evidence of significant trauma to her private parts and back passage.'

Bill looked so sorrowful when he finished speaking. That beautiful girl who had already suffered so much in her life, but had been so brave, had now been subjected to horrendous torture delivered by some real savage fuckers by the sound of it.

'If she wasn't dead already,' Bill paused and took a deep breath, 'her brain had been punctured by something red hot that had been inserted through her left eye.' I gagged a little at this point; beer, cake and a story like this did not mix well, but Bill continued.

'An attempt was also made on Fernando Reynoso's life on Tuesday morning, which prompted the contact via letter to London. The letter said we must assume that General Muscardin knows everything that Maria knew. She wouldn't have been able to take that much punishment without disclosing what she knew about the two foreign men who were involved in the murders at the club. I don't think it would have taken them long to figure out where we came from either.'

'Fuck.'

It seemed an inadequate and inappropriate response from me, but that was all I had right now. Bill spoke again quietly with his head looking down at his feet.

'General Muscardin most likely knows about our movements in Argentina, has a description of us and knows the false names we used. I don't think it will be too long either before he knows that our final destination after New York was London; if he doesn't know that already.'

'Shit,' I said this time.

'Shit indeed Harry, but Reynoso will be in contact again as soon as he has more intel. He and his family have battened down the hatches for the minute but are using all their contacts to get us more information. We have to be vigilant Harry and make sure our families are safe, I would not want to bet against the General or his sister, or someone else coming after us; even in the UK.'

'Harry, Bill, come on in here, you're not talking work today are you?'

Kathy was standing by the patio doors with Harry Jr asleep against her shoulder.

'No, no, we were just catching up.' I said and tried my best to get rid of any concern and worry from my face as we walked back inside.

The rest of the day went according to plan and everyone seemed to have a good time wetting the baby's head, especially the boys from Poole and Plymouth. Their minibus came to collect them at 1900. I would have put money on that most of them would be crashed out by the time they got to the motorway less than five miles away. Bill had left an hour earlier saying he would be in touch as soon as he had more news.

Finally at 1915 there were just the five of us left. Harry Jr was asleep in his cot, Gerri and Kathy slumped in the chairs whilst Ron and I cleared the last of the debris out of the kitchen. By 1930, we were all sat down with a cup of tea in front of the TV. Not that I noticed what was on because I was thinking about Maria and Rafel. I doubted anyone would ever see Rafel alive again, or in one piece. I also thought a lot about Fernando Reynoso and the danger he and his family must be in right now. I worried about Thomas and Alejandro who had risked so much and hoped they wouldn't have to pay the ultimate price as well. I was sure they wouldn't go down without a fight and would take out a few of them on the way if it came to that.

It was time though to beef up the security at home and get an alarm fitted, some new locks and definitely a new front and back door. All things we had already discussed but had not got around to, so it shouldn't ring alarm bells when I get them sorted tomorrow.

5

Nigglesworth, St Georges' Parish Church

1400 Saturday 22nd October 1983

Where did five months go? That was the last time I sat in this very seat on the front pew of this magnificent 14th century church. Its high vaulted ceiling was held up by the massive curved oak beams that still looked as strong as they did when the old craftsmen of that time originally put them there. The horse hair plaster was flaking in quite a few places and could do with a fresh coat of paint now. I hoped the flaky bits would all stay up there today as I didn't want anything to fall onto my brand new 2nd Lieutenant's uniform fresh from my passing out parade at Lympstone three days earlier.

My head was clear now, but it should have still been numb from the excesses of alcohol at that party. Thankfully no alcohol had passed my lips in the previous 24 hours so I was feeling pretty good for my wedding day.

There had been a lot of classroom work to deal with during the last few months of the officer training course, which did get a bit tedious at times. It was all over now though and after today I had a whole week's leave before reporting to 42 Commando, briefly. I would then be heading up to Manchester to start the science degree course.

Kathy and I had decided to spend just a couple of nights in Wales at Saundersfoot for a mini honeymoon after today was over. We had stayed in a little hotel there three times before. It was comfortable, quiet and great for walking along the coast. Gerri was going to have 'little Harry' and Ron had elected to stay for the week to 'help.'

I was looking forward to hearing about that.

'I think Kathy is here,' Bill whispered in my right ear interrupting my thoughts.

'There's no backing out now Harry. Not that you would want to of course,' he said with a grin.

'Of course,' I replied with confidence, but secretly I was a bit nervous about the occasion as most men are I believe. But I had no doubts about what was going to happen in the next 45 minutes or that Kathy was the only woman for me. I think I knew that from the very first time I ever set my eyes on her.

It had been a tough choice on who would be my best man. If Bob had been alive there would have been no question, but since our Argentine adventure Bill and I had become great friends. He had followed closely my path through the Lympstone course often giving me tips and hints on both the practical and physical aspects of getting through. Bill had also pushed me very hard over the Brecon Beacons, building up extra fitness, honing map reading skills and doing search and evade survival training on three of my weekends off.

On the first weekend's training he had taken the piss mercilessly when he caught me twice on one day, ambushing me with a huge wet sod of grass the second time, which he had dropped onto my head. How I had missed him I didn't know but I made sure he didn't get me the next day and he only succeeded once on the following two weekends in the allotted time.

Bill taught me some great evasion skills and when it came to doing that part of my training course for real, I eventually had to turn myself in once the exercise was completed because they hadn't captured me. Apparently that hadn't happened in a while but I wasn't going to let on about my extracurricular training with a senior SAS officer. I said it was just luck.

On those weekends, we often talked about Reynoso, Maria and the others. We also went through our own security arrangements checking and double checking everything was in place and operational, especially with respect to Kathy and 'little Harry.'

Rafel's tortured and mutilated body had been discovered by accident in woods 50 miles south of Buenos Aires. It had been a complete fluke apparently as the dog had only found him from tugging at a small piece of cloth from the leg of his trousers. It was the only piece of him that was visible, but had been enough for the pooch to grab hold of and tug, which then exposed a lot more of his body by the time the dog's owner had reached him.

Reynoso had known about finding a body two hours later. The next day he had confirmation it was Rafel. Bill knew two days later. Thomas, Alejandro and the hotel manager Jorge Martine had been squirreled away somewhere by Reynoso that same day. They were alive and safe the last time Bill had heard from Reynoso, which had been five weeks ago. Of course we were both worried we hadn't heard any more from him since then but it wasn't unusual from past experience and we were pretty sure we would have been contacted by someone if he had 'disappeared'.

Rupert, another brand new 2nd Lieutenant, had been delighted to act as one of my ushers and had just made the thumbs up sign. He now had his hands up by his face clicking an imaginary camera to tell me Kathy was outside the door having her photo taken. She would be standing in front of a classic stone archway with the two very substantial oak doors pushed open and locked to the sides. It had been a little chilly earlier, but she would now be bathed in warm autumn sunshine on the Church steps.

The Bridal March started and the rustle of bodies standing up filled the church. A couple of seconds into the der derderder der derderder and I couldn't help stealing a quick look over my left shoulder. Kathy looked absolutely fabulous in a traditional long white strapless wedding dress. It was tapered in at the sides so it hugged her now slim waist. The wide white ribbon around her waist led to a large silk bow fixed at the back of her dress. I couldn't see all of the bow, but Gerri had let that little secret slip. Below the bow, the silk splayed out like an old Victorian dress, its long white train being expertly held up by two young page-boys and the two flower girls behind her.

Four smiling bridesmaids in long satin blue dresses holding tightly their own posies followed close behind. Her veil was down, but I could see the smile on her face and sparkle in her eyes as she walked slowly towards me. I puffed my chest out involuntarily with pride. My campaign medals clinking briefly on the left side of my chest.

Kathy was standing next to me now lifting her veil, her father gently put her hand in mine and winked. We turned to face the vicar, the music had stopped now. Silence descended over the church only to be briefly interrupted by the gurgling sounds of Harry Jr and another little tot a few rows back.

The service was done before we knew it, rings and vows were exchanged, register was signed and pictures taken. Before we knew it, we were walking back down the aisle and out through the large stone porch into the bright sunlight. I patted the carved stone head that stuck out from the left hand column as we left. There was an identical one on the other side that I had patted a few months earlier when we had come out after Harry Jr's christening. Superstition and folklore said it would bring good fortune and good luck so I thought it was worth a pat or two.

The rented white Ford Escort was tucked out of sight behind two other cars down the lane. Inside the car, three pairs of eyes watched the traditional English wedding day scene outside the church. It was tense and silent in the car.

Kids chased each other around the lawn now they were free. Anxious mothers trying unsuccessfully to control them so they didn't trash their new specially made suits or get completely covered in crap before the photographer had got all the important photos.

Uncles, aunts, friends and other relatives who hadn't seen each other since the last wedding, or funeral, were mingling around catching up on old news and general gossip. I watched with much amusement as the boys from Plymouth moved in on the bridesmaids. I knew I should warn the girls when Kathy whispered in my ear.

'They are big girls and can look after themselves.'

Kathy's huge smile joined the many out on the lawn in front of the church, everyone waiting patiently for their part in this great day to be captured on film.

There were no smiles from inside the car though, Ricardo and Costa needlessly scanned the area for police, or other security. Not that they expected any, but that was what they had been told to do by the other passenger in the car. Eva Muscardin was barely able to contain her rage and loathing from the back seat of the Escort, her ice cold eyes filled with hatred and fixed firmly on the blushing new bride and her Royal Marine Officer husband.

Eva had studied thoroughly the intel gained from the torture of Maria and Rafel. They had taken a little while to break, but she had extracted what she needed to lead her to the Reynoso family and these two British soldiers. She knew there had been others involved in the execution of her brother, but she would get to them later. Her eyes widened further as she now had them fixed on both of the key players as she watched Bill walk up and give the new bride a gentle hug and a kiss on the cheek.

Kathy responded to Bill's touch by turning to face him and putting her arms around his neck and then whispered in his left ear.

'Thank you Bill for taking care of Harry. I know how much you have done for him and how you have supported him through his course.' She then kissed him gently on the cheek.

'I haven't done anything.' Bill protested mockingly with his arms out wide.

'He can look after himself well enough, I can tell you.'

Kathy gave Bill a knowing look and then hooked her left arm through his whilst her other found her new husband's hand before guiding them both over to where the photographer was waiting patiently for them.

Eva sneered at the three of them from the back seat. 'Make the most of it bitch, because you're not going to be happy for long,' she muttered to herself. Eva had fantasised every day since she had found out about them and about how much pain she was going to inflict on Harry and Bill especially before she killed them. The girl and the kid would just be a bonus.

Eva had everything planned: once the goons had immobilised them, she would sever the femoral artery in the soldiers' legs so they would bleed to death in agony. But that was not before they would watch her two goons beat up and rape the lovely bride. She would then use her very special scalpel to slice through Kathy's soft pale white skin cutting her face, her throat, then her breasts and nipples before going to work on her genital area, if she had time.

Whilst they were all still alive and could watch her in action she would have more sport from smashing the baby's head into a wall, or doorframe, or something else until it was dead. Only when she couldn't have more fun with them would she put bullets into the dying or dead bodies of her brother's murderers. She only hoped they would stay alive long enough to watch everything she had planned for them, the only thing that was certain was they were all going to die very soon.

Eva refocused on the scene in front of her where the photo session was about to conclude. A few minutes later the new bride and groom stepped into the vintage white Rolls Royce for the short ride to the hotel and their reception. No one in the wedding party paid any attention to the white Escort as it pulled away shortly after the Rolls disappeared at the end of the lane.

Except Bill.

The Bear Hotel did a great job for the remainder of the day. Everyone was well fed and watered. Some were more watered than others, mainly the military personnel but everyone was going to dance until the DJ said, 'no more.'

Kathy and I were on the road being taken to our honeymoon suite in a secret location close by well before the end of the party. We both wanted to pop home the next day to see Harry Jr before heading off to Wales.

Harry Jr was going to stay with Gerri and Ron for the few days we were away. The deal I had to strike with Kathy just to get her to go away was if anything untoward happened we could be back home in two hours.

I was very happy with that deal too.

6

Nigglesworth, Sunday morning 23rd October 1983

Making love for the first time as man and wife was a funny affair and although we did eventually succeed it was after much giggling and messing about. Spooning was the order of the day and after a very gentle session we had fallen asleep in the position we finished in.

'Morning Mrs Glass. How are you this fine and lovely morning,' I said as I came through the bedroom door of our own house with a tray full of tea, toast, marmalade and orange juice.

Kathy gingerly looked over the top sheet and peered at me through sleepy eyes. She brushed her tousled hair out of her face and then said with a wicked smile on her face.

'Is that a present for me Husband?' looking at a slightly erect 'little Harry' who had been slowly coming to life as I prepared her breakfast. It was such a great feeling to think about how brilliant life was right now with my new gorgeous sexy wife upstairs. Plus we had no Harry Jr in the house this morning.

Making love was a lot more passionate and active than the night before. We explored every part of each other's bodies and somehow it did feel different, it was better in every way. I couldn't put my finger on it and say exactly what was different, but I did know I was the happiest I had ever been in my life, and I think Kathy was as well.

The white Escort had been parked 100 yards down the lane for a little over an hour, it was under the overhang of an old Magnolia tree that was full of shiny green leaves. Ricardo had done a walk by but didn't see any signs of life from inside the house, although he knew this was where the new bride and groom had spent last night.

Costa moved the Escort twice in the following two hours, both times moving to new positions but ones from where they could clearly see the front of the new small three bed-roomed detached house. It was one of several identical new houses in the cul-de-sac.

They watched silently as Kathy and Harry left the house at 1225, packing a couple of small suitcases in the boot of Kathy's car before pulling out of the drive. Costa moved instantly from his place under an old beech tree and started to follow. It wasn't far to Gerri's house where Kathy and Harry stopped for a little over an hour before heading down the hill to the main town and then west towards Junction 13 of the M5 motorway.

'Stay with them.' Eva instructed Costa as Kathy indicated to go down the slip road onto the M5.

They stayed a couple of hundred yards back, but the motorway was very quiet with light traffic at this time on a Sunday so they only had a couple of cars between them. Eva instructed Costa to back off further as the last thing she wanted was to be discovered now and spoil all her plans. She then told him to get off at the next junction as she was certain now they were heading to Wales and would not be back for a couple of days. There was plenty of time to get everything in place ready for their return, and for the fun to begin.

The blonde wig, large red glasses, jeans and big baggy jumper had been perfect to hide her face and body shape. No one had taken any notice of her as she had mingled with the crowds in the public bar of the Bear Hotel the night before. She had overheard two conversations telling her that the newlyweds were planning to escape for a couple of days without the kid and that they were going to somewhere in Wales where they had been to before. The one involving the group of bridesmaids was somewhat more graphic than the other with respect to what the newlyweds would be getting up to.

They sat quietly in the lay-by off junction 14 of the M5 for a couple of minutes to ensure there was a decent amount of space between Kathy, Harry and them. Eva roughly poked Costa on the shoulder and told him to rejoin the M5 motorway and head south to the M4. Costa kept his face neutral so Eva didn't see his annoyance at being poked by the fucking psychotic bitch. It was not the first time on this trip. He knew he had better get a move on though and not be late getting to their next destination even though they would be cutting it fine because of the delays of the morning having to wait for the man and woman to leave. He also knew he had no choice but to do everything she ordered as she, and the General, had made it clear that even though he was a trusted member of Octavio's inner circle, if he fucked up on this job, he, and every member of his family were as good as dead. It was the same for Ricardo.

Eva was on mission and didn't give a shit about the goons up front they just needed to do what she told them and right now all she needed was Costa to take them back to London to pick up the gear she had ordered when they arrived. They would be at the old Victorian town house in East London in a couple of hours.

When they were on the move again, she sat back in her seat and smiled at the thought of what was to come.

I was troubled by something, but I wasn't sure what. Kathy was tootling along the motorway doing about 55-60 mph, her safe speed as she always told me, chattering on about new curtains, wallpaper for Harry's room and the colour of the carpet in the small dining room and how it wasn't what she wanted for the long term. I had my best 'Yes dear' head on and just agreed to whatever she said. I didn't care as long as she was happy, I just loved the sound of her voice chattering away at ten to the dozen.

She caught me looking at her with a tell-tale smirk on my face.

'I can hear you Harry Glass. You have got your 'yes dear' voice on and I can see that grin on your face. You wait till I stop this car.' She then slapped my leg really hard stinging the skin under my jeans.

She knew I couldn't retaliate as she was driving, but I would get my revenge later. I sat back and looked out the windows watching the world go by occasionally looking back over my shoulder and in the wing mirror at the traffic behind.

As we turned off the M5 and onto the slip road towards the Severn Bridge and South Wales, I saw it again in the mirror. A new white Ford Escort speeding down the inside lane. I had pinged one yesterday by the church and again near the house this morning. It stood out because it was so clean and shiny. I was pretty sure I had seen the same car, or one very similar, shortly after we got onto the M5 when I reached over to grab my News of the World from the back seat.

I didn't want to alarm Kathy so I casually released my seat belt, turned around and leaned over the seat and began fumbling with my jacket. We were already down the slope and under the M4 before I could properly scan the road behind us. No white Escort was there.

It still wasn't there 20 seconds later. Was I imagining things? Maybe I imagined it and it was just the recent news from Argentina that had made me twitchy. I would be keeping my eye out for a white Escort all the way to Saundersfoot though, that's for sure. Kathy slapped my arse as it hung over the seat.

'Sit down you big lump you are blocking my view, and the sun,' she said mockingly.

At least she wasn't aware of anything going on in my head right now and that was the way I was going to keep it.

7

The four star hotel overlooking the bay and small harbour at Saundersfoot had pulled out all the stops. The room had been prepared with fresh flowers and a bottle of chilled champagne. A note said: With best wishes, Bill. There's another one waiting for you when this one is gone. The four poster bed had more cushions on it than you could shake a big stick at and a big teddy bear to boot.

Kathy ran full pelt and launched herself onto the bed scattering the teddy bear and cushions as she slid right across the deep burgundy silk bedcover and off the other side. I almost wet myself right there and then as Kathy lay on the floor on the other side of the bed laughing uncontrollably. I couldn't see her, but I could certainly hear her. I walked around the bed and she came into my view, I still had trouble focusing on her from the tears of laughter in my eyes. I sat down next to her on the floor after propping her up against the bed. We were still giggling like a couple of kids many minutes later.

In between the fits of laughter I popped the cork on the chilled champagne and plonked it on the floor between us. We just sat there with our backs against the bed smiling and enjoying the moment with a glass of good bubbly in our hands. The wallpaper in the room was a bit brash for me, deep reds and greys interwoven in a swirling pattern, very 'in' right now so I was reliably told by my new wife. The rest of the furniture was old and not that trendy, but it worked well in this room with its traditional four-poster bed.

Kathy put her glass down.

'I need the loo,' she said and wandered off into the bathroom.

I hadn't thought about the white Escort since we arrived, but it flashed through my head again now. I was sure I'd seen it at least twice on the motorway, but who would be in it? Was someone really following us or was it just my imagination?

I wasn't able to dwell on those questions any longer as Kathy appeared in my peripheral vision and got my attention immediately. She pulled the cord to close the curtains in the first big window and then sauntered slowly over to the other big window and did the same, winking at me as she crossed right in front of me. The look on her face was pure mischief.

She had changed into a sexy black basque that had small red ribbons and bows down the front of it. Small frilly black knickers hugged her pert bottom over the suspenders that held up sheer black stockings with lace tops. Kathy had finished off the outfit with bright red stiletto shoes.

She took my breath away, she looked so beautiful and confident. The basque fitted her toned body perfectly highlighting her slim waist and the curves of her hips. Her small breasts were pushed upwards just enough to form the perfect cleavage. Her hair was down and floating just over the tops of them.

'Like what you see husband?' She said playfully.

My mouth was open, but I didn't speak, I just nodded my head like some dumb beast.

'On the bed Harry Glass your wife wants to play with you.'

I went from sitting with my arse on the floor, legs fully outstretched, to the same position on the bed in less than a second.

'Not keen then?' Kathy said and grinned as I tried to put the glass of champagne down on the bedside table without taking my eyes off her. I almost slid off the damn silk bedcover whilst doing it.

Kathy slowly climbed onto the bed and then sat astride me. I moved my hands up to cup her breasts through the basque, but she grabbed my wrists and put them back down by my side.

'No. No. Harry Glass. No touching for you yet.'

I wasn't going to argue.

She slowly began to remove my shirt taking time to kiss my chest and nibble the hairs on it as each button was undone. With a bit of pulling and me lifting myself up briefly it was off but she didn't go straight for the jeans. Kathy teased me with soft kisses on my face and lips. She then nibbled my neck, chest and stomach, going down as far as the buckle on my jeans belt and then working her way back up again. She did this twice. Slowly.

'Little Harry' was aching now and bent up in my pants. She had been working on the top half of my body for several minutes when she slid down my legs and stood on the floor at the side of the bed. I had already kicked off my trainers so she slid off the socks one by one slapping my hand away from my belt buckle half way through. The softness of her touch on my feet that had taken such a battering over the past nine months was exquisite. She rubbed the soles of my feet slowly with her thumbs and usually I would have been kicking out from the tickle, but I just relaxed and enjoyed her sensual touch.

At the same time, she caressed the tops of each foot with her fingers gently moving the skin, tendons and muscles. It was a fantastic feeling. When she started nibbling and sucking the end of my big toe I almost lost it there and then. I was squirming around the bed, but she wouldn't let me get up. If this was what married life was like, I wanted more of it, for a very long time.

The toes didn't get too much more of the treatment as Kathy pulled my jeans and underpants off less than a minute later, she wasn't going to mess around anymore. I could see she was as aroused as I clearly was and was absolutely sure I would come as soon as Kathy came anywhere near my penis. I tried in vain to think about something else, I desperately needed to try and hold on. Kathy was not letting up even though I'm sure she knew of my dilemma as she ran her tongue up the inside of my right leg, kissing and nibbling the skin as she moved further towards my groin. I could see her beautifully shaped breasts that were held in place by the basque as she moved further up my legs.

Her right hand closed gently around my shaft and slowly began to move up and down, pulling back the foreskin off the throbbing head with each movement. Her mouth then closed around my right testicle gently sucking and playing with it with her tongue. The left one got the same treatment moments later. The gentle masturbation Kathy was performing with her right hand was doing its work and I could feel myself tensing up and getting ready to explode.

Kathy sensed this and gripped hard the base of my shaft blocking off temporarily the impending rush of hot semen. Kathy then let her mouth slide over the throbbing head and slowly moved down the length of the shaft, her forefinger and thumb still gripping the base of the shaft. She was licking, nibbling and sucking the shaft as she moved her head up and down it with increasing speed.

I couldn't hold on for a second longer. I exploded into her mouth, writhing and moaning on the bed as Kathy continued to move her hand up and down the shaft. She wouldn't release me until I had stopped thrashing around, her left arm and hand lying across my chest, holding me down. She finally released me and kissed the end as it started to soften.

I closed my eyes and blew out a long breath as Kathy slowly moved up the bed and put her head on my chest allowing me to kiss the top of her head.

'I love you Harry Glass with all my heart,' she said.

'And I you, Kathy Glass. Nothing will ever come between us, I won't let it.'

'No.' She replied, as I felt a single tear drop onto my chest and then another.

I know Marines are supposed to be tough and not do the tears thing but I couldn't help myself right at this moment as my eyes filled up and then spilled over the top. I snuggled in closer to Kathy just holding her and kissing her again on the top of her head. Life wasn't going to get any better than this.

We got under the covers and closed our eyes, just for a few minutes. We woke up a couple of hours later as it was starting to get dark. We weren't going anywhere for a while so I rang down to reception and asked for the second bottle of champagne to be delivered. I had to get out of bed to accept it as Kathy was still wearing her sexy kit.

We spent the next hour talking about the future and the things we wanted to do together. Number one on Kathy's list was to see the Taj Mahal and experience the culture of India and its people.

'I will take you there one day, I promise.' I said whilst giving her another big hug.

After a good sleep, champagne and honest talking about our future and dreams, I was definitely feeling good in more places than just my head. I lifted the covers to take a peek at Kathy in her sexy kit. She giggled that wonderful giggle only she had but went quiet as soon as I moved my hand across the front of her basque. My hand lightly brushing the tops of her breasts before I moved it down across her flat stomach to the top of her tiny black briefs. I paused briefly and with one finger gently stroked her pubic hair through the briefs.

I slipped my hand down inside her briefs and could feel the heat and moisture of her vagina as my finger entered her. Kathy let out a short moan and gripped my arm with all her strength as I used the back of my hand to pull away her briefs from between her legs. She helped me by lifting her knees and then used her left foot to remove them completely and casually flick them onto the floor.

Kathy had let the basque slip down just enough to expose her erect nipples. I let my tongue and lips caress and play with them before I moved my head down towards the neat patch of pubic hair that had been trimmed especially for our wedding day.

'The things us girls have to do for you boys.' Kathy had told me on the way down here to Saundersfoot. That wasn't a 'yes dear' moment, I was definitely listening then.

I wasn't going to rush things and wanted to spend the same amount of time on Kathy that she had spent on me earlier. I kissed the neat patch of hair and then moved down to caressed her feet and toes. Kathy writhed and squirmed on the bed especially when I placed one toe in my mouth and gently sucked and kissed it. I then moved onto all the others one by one.

I moved my hands upwards gently stroking her legs, excited by the smooth feel and look of the black silk stockings covering them. Kathy let out a small whimper as I kissed the exposed flesh at the top of her stockings, on both legs. I moved up a little further to nibble at the wisps of pubic hair and then down between her open legs. My nose embracing the beautiful sweet scent of an aroused woman before my tongue gently explored the soft folds between her moist lips.

Kathy was talking to me and tugging at my ear trying to pull me up.

'Harry make love to me now. I want you now Harry. Please don't make me wait any longer.'

I pulled my head back a few inches and put both my hands at the top of her thighs before gently using my thumbs to pull apart the top of her lips. Her juices were in full flow as her engorged clitoris filled my eyes. It was a beautiful sight, all shiny and glistening from her vaginal juices. I buried my head back between her legs and flicked my tongue across her clitoris a couple of times.

Kathy almost got away, but I held her tightly by her hips. I couldn't resist a small nibble before plunging my tongue deep inside her, rolling it from side to side trying to give her as much pleasure as was humanly possible.

Kathy could not hold on any longer and let out a loud moan as the orgasm exploded within her. Her body writhed and shook as she let the waves of pleasure wash over her. Beads of sweat appeared between her breasts forming little rivers of salty water that disappeared down the front of her basque.

Her eyes were still closed as I slowly moved up her body and positioned myself above her. My penis was so hard it hurt as I eased the head into her and then penetrating all the way inside in one smooth thrust. Her juices allowing the full length of the shaft go deep inside and then out again in easy controlled movements.

With each deep thrust, Kathy's moans grew louder and my own throaty noises and breathing got heavier. Kathy gripped my straight arms that were planted firmly on the pillow at each side of her head. After a short period of deep thrusting, we changed our rhythm and entwined our bodies to let us make love more slowly and gently. Kathy had climaxed twice more during the early part of our lovemaking but had pleaded with me not to stop. Moments later I exploded deep inside her, my body arching and shuddering from the release.

I stayed where I was holding my weight off Kathy for another minute or so until I was breathing normally again and then I eased myself carefully onto my left side next to Kathy. She snuggled in straight away as I put my left arm around her tiny waist and pulled her in closer to me. We lay there for a few moments holding onto each other in the quiet and peace of the room, our bodies covered in sweat and the sweet scent of lovemaking. It was a magical moment.

I felt her body begin to shake before I heard the soft sobs of Kathy crying. I pulled myself away from the pillow and rolled her onto her back so I could look at her face. A steady stream of tears rolled down her cheeks as she propped herself up against the headboard. I reached out for her left hand and held it softly.

'What is the matter Sweetheart?' I asked, my forehead furrowed with concern.

Kathy looked at me whilst hastily trying to brush away the tears from her face.

'Nothing Harry. I just love you and Harry Jr so much, I cannot believe how lucky I am to have you both in my life. I don't know what I would do if I ever lost either of you.'

Kathy started to cry again as soon as she finished speaking so I pulled her towards me and hugged her tightly.

'Well, that's not going to happen Kathy, so stop worrying now,' I said full of authority and confidence.

An image of a white Escort flashed through my mind as I said it.

8

Monday 24th October 1983

The white Escort was travelling at a steady pace in the inside lane of the M4, the 11 o'clock news had just finished and some unknown pop group was wailing something out of the radio. Nobody was really listening to it as Costa concentrated on keeping the speed of the car between 65 and 70 mph. The last thing they needed was any attention from the British police, especially with all the kit they had picked up in London in the boot. He also didn't need another bollocking like he had received from the bitch in the back for speeding on the way down to London, even though it was she who had given him the impossible deadline to get there.

Ricardo was sitting quietly next to Costa in the front passenger seat reflecting on the trip to London's West End.

Eva had been her usual nasty and demanding self, but it had been Costa who had been subjected to the full force of her wrath, this time. Sunday had not been a good day for him because firstly he had the bollocking for speeding and then Eva had given him a vicious slap across the face when he dropped the box of detonators onto the kitchen floor of Pepe Paez's spacious terraced house. She hadn't finished with him though and when he bent down to pick up the box she had kicked him so hard in the guts it had taken a good couple of minutes for him to get back on his feet.

'Stupid fucker, be careful.' She had screamed at him.

After helping his friend up, Ricardo had just kept his head down for the rest of the day and did whatever she asked him to do, immediately. He knew he had no choice, just like his friend Costa or that fat little fucker, Pepe Paez.

Pepe Paez had been working in London for three years at one of the major clearing banks. His job had been to move and clean money for not only the Muscardin family, but also for several other high ranking Argentine Government officials and senior military officers. He was a small portly man who blended into the city scene perfectly. No one took any notice of him tucked away in his little cubicle, but he was a very clever man and highly skilled at illegally squirreling away hundreds of millions of dollars for his paymasters.

He despised the people who worked around him. They were imbeciles as far as he was concerned and if any of them ever found his 'special' accounts, he was more than confident they wouldn't know what to do with them or who they belonged to. Only he, Robert Keys and Sir Richard Roses, the snobby English bastard he had to see each week to action the transactions he'd prepared, could access the Muscardin accounts. They could only access them when they were together because of the additional security he had put in place.

He was pleased he'd had a week without having to see the snobby git as Eva had been his number one priority. The relatively small amount of cash that she had demanded was extracted from the little slush fund he controlled so he didn't need the poncy English bastard's sign-off. In the past few days he had been doing something he really enjoyed, sourcing weapons, ammunitions and explosives for his countrymen. It was something he had done before and it made his dull, boring life much more interesting and exciting. It also made him feel a bit like an Argentine James Bond character, not that anyone would think that of course, looking at the size of his overfed belly.

When Pepe Paez had received a call from Eva Muscardin telling him she was coming to London and what she wanted, he knew he could be in deep trouble and had worried for weeks about achieving all her demands. He had met Eva once before at the Muscardin estate in Argentina so he knew very well it was in his best interests not to cross her, or fail her. He liked his balls intact and preferably still attached.

Eva's demands had been pretty straight forward though, £30,000 in cash, three Browning 9mm, two AK47's, three six-inch combat knives, 40lbs of high explosive, six manual detonators and one remote detonator kit. All of these items had not been difficult to source at all and she had been pleased with the quality of the weapons and explosives that had been placed in the boot of the hire car in his building's secure underground car park by the two goons at 10pm the previous evening. One of them was still visibly smarting from the kicking she had given him earlier.

Pepe had left for work early that morning in a grump though. Eva had decided they would stay Sunday night in his modest, but well-appointed two bedroom apartment, rather than book into a hotel. She wanted to leave as little trace of the three of them in the UK as possible so Pepe had had no choice but to give up his big bed in the main bedroom for her.

The single bed in the box room had been very uncomfortable and as he had tossed and turned throughout the night his only consolation was that it wasn't as uncomfortable as the sofa and the chair where the two goons had crashed out. Pepe was just thankful that it was only for one night and then Eva and her goons would be gone.

At 2300, he had told Eva that he would not be able to sort out breakfast for them unless they wanted it at 0600 as he had to leave by 0630 to go to his cubicle to clean and wash more money for the family. He smiled as he said it, but she hadn't laughed at his little joke and had just sneered at him before heading for the bedroom. He felt sick.

That was the last time he saw her before leaving for work and as she didn't ask him to call her in the morning he had left them all to it. There was no way he was going to disturb her at 0530 if she hadn't asked to be and anyway the goons were up and drinking coffee when he left so they could get her up. Mid-morning though, Pepe Paez was sitting in his cubicle, his head was in his hands, shitting himself as to whether or not he had offended her. He could only pray now he hadn't.

Eva tapped Costa hard on the shoulder making him flinch. She couldn't resist a smile to herself from the back seat.

'Pull in at the next services, I am hungry,' she ordered him.

She was still pissed off that the little fat fucker had not woken her and had not left her anything for breakfast. He would have to get a good kicking for that in the future, but right now she had more important things to do.

The Escort pulled into Reading Services at 1132. Eva's previous experience of the UK's grotty service stations had not been a good one and she had vowed never to step foot in one again. But, she really needed some food, a piss, and to make a phone call to her older brother, so when needs must.

At 1430, the Escort was parked 50 yards down the lane from Gerri's house. They were watching. The road was quiet and there was no car in the drive. Eva wanted to confirm that the kid was still with the bastard Glass's mother. She sat there with her eyes screwed together only wishing she could have lots of private time with him, which of course she knew she couldn't. Back home it would have been different when she would have skinned the fucker from head to toes and laugh as he screamed like that pathetic coward Rafel. The coward Fernando Reynoso was going to be her next victim and she was going to make sure he suffers a long, slow, painful death.

'There she is.' Costa said from the driver's seat as Gerri pulled into the drive half an hour later.

They watched Ron exit the passenger side first and then open the back door. A sleepy Harry Jr emerged cradled in Ron's arms, his head flopping about before Ron steadied it with his huge right hand.

The Escort's occupants watched and waited until dusk fell. The curtains at the cottage were drawn a little after 6:30pm as wood smoke began to billow out of the stone chimney. Eva made the decision to move as soon as she saw the smoke, she was pretty sure Ron and Gerri would not be moving again that night.

Costa got another hard tap on the shoulder from the back seat that made him flinch again. Eva smiled and then barked.

'Let's go.'

Costa started the engine feeling angry that he had flinched again and given that bitch in the back something else to smile about. He was a soldier and not her fucking bitch.

Why was he so afraid of her?

He knew only too well the answer to that question as he indicated to turn right at the end of the lane. He had witnessed first-hand what she was capable of and knew she wouldn't blink an eye if she decided to do the same to him.

It only took a couple of minutes to reach Harry and Kathy's new house. Costa parked the white Escort in the same place as they had the previous day when they watched the happy couple leave for their short honeymoon in South Wales.

9

Tuesday 25th October

Kathy was in full flow jabbering on about plans for the house, things she wanted to buy, getting back to work, taking Harry Jr to the swimming baths later. In the end, I had to say something.

'Sweetheart my ears are bleeding and we have only been on the road 30 minutes.' I got the sharp prod in the ribs for that.

'Are you suggesting husband that I talk too much?'

'No dear, but you might want to take a breath once in a while,' I said with a broad grin.

'Harry Glass you are being very brave all of a sudden. Just you wait until we get home.'

We talked all the way home and by the time we got to junction 14 on the M5, the new kitchen design was sorted, the colours, the style of the units, worktops, table and chairs, the whole thing. It was a great conversation to have, a proper married couple one and it did feel good.

Kathy had been quiet for a few minutes but as we drove through Wotton high street she said:

'Harry I want to see Harry Jr very much. But would you think I am a bad mother if I suggested we go home first and spend an hour or two on our own before going to your mum's to get him?'

I turned towards her and could tell that even though she had a mischievous look on her face she instantly felt guilty about suggesting such a thing.

'I think Mum and Ron will be fine for another hour or two. Do you have any more surprises waiting for me at home?' I said with a little hope in my voice.

Kathy blushed.

'Maybe,' she said.

I pushed the accelerator down hard as soon as we hit a clear patch of road, but only for a second or two. I wanted us both to get there in one piece especially after the fantastic experiences of the past two days. We had told Ron and Gerri that it would be nearer supper time when we got home so they wouldn't be expecting us until 1800 anyway. I quickly calculated our ETA at home to be around 1615; plenty of time for Mum and Dad to have some fun.

'Bugger.'

I was surprised to hear Kathy swear.

'What's the matter Kathy?'

'Milk and baby food, I forgot to ask you to stop on the way home.'

'You obviously had other things on your mind Kathy Glass. You bad girl.' 'Well, you need to go and get them now because I'm sure the shop closes at 5:00pm. You know the brand we need and anyway it will give me time to get ready for you,' she smiled at me with that knowing smile.

'I'll be back sooner than you can say jack flash,' I said whilst revving the car much too aggressively.

I pulled up next to the kerb outside the house rather than going onto the drive as I was keen to get to the shop and then back home again. No time to waste. With a glint in her eye and then a wink, she turned and got out of the car and walked towards the front door. I couldn't resist leaping out the car and chasing her up the path. I caught her by the front door and clasped my arms around her waist. She struggled as she tried to get the key in the shiny new Yale lock, but she couldn't break my grasp as I held her just far enough away from the lock.

Kathy turned around to face me and sighed in mock frustration and then kissed me passionately full on the lips. Her tongue darting inside my mouth rubbing along my lower teeth then up to the top layer. I responded with my own tongue gently flicking the end of hers when she grabbed it with her teeth. Not hard but just enough to hold it. I released my grip on her waist and then tickled her so she would release my tongue, which she did.

'Go and get the stuff from the shop, I'll still be here in five minutes Harry, you won't miss anything,' she said.

'I will,' I said. 'You.'

'Arrr,' she said and then smiled.

'Now go and get junior's food you soft bugger. I love you, Harry Glass.'

Kathy gave me a playful shove and turned to face the door. I looked back as I walked toward the car and saw she was having a little trouble with the new lock. I was about to go back when the key turned. I stopped and watched Kathy disappear into the house and the front door close. I took a moment to look at 'our' home and smiled at the thought of our future lives together in there.

I had just got around the front of the car when the searing heat of the explosion hit me. I was picked up like a twig and thrown across the road by the blast, the noise instantly deafening me. Kathy's car was tossed over and blown across the road with me. It hit the kerb on the other side before clipping a tree and flipping over onto its roof. It then crashed through a neighbour's wooden picket fence sliding on the grass and ended up resting against the front room wall.

The impact with the Cotswold stone wall was very hard, my shoulder took most of the force of the impact, my head the rest. I finished up in a shitty heap nearly 40 feet away from where the front door of the house used to be. Blood is pouring down my face from where I had split my head open on the wall. Then everything went black.

I was told that I had been unconscious for three or four minutes. Ivy, my elderly neighbour, was talking to me and holding a tea towel on my head to try and stop the flow of blood. It was another few seconds before my eyes started to focus properly on the carnage across the road. My mind flashed images of Kathy walking up to the front door and us embracing. The last image was of my hand reaching for the car door handle before I passed out again.

I come round and the first sensation I have is my face burning from the heat of the blast and the small razor cuts from flying glass and debris. I stay still for a few more seconds to try and let some of my hearing return. All I have for the moment is a buzzing sound in my ears, like tinnitus, but then the stabbing pains in my shoulder and in my head kick off big time.

I take a few more seconds to get some air into my lungs and then start to check my body parts and try to move them. I succeeded with most of them without too much pain, except for the right shoulder that was obviously dislocated. I was still trying to unscramble my brain when Ray knelt down and put his hand on my left shoulder. He looked at Ivy, his wife of 60 years, with tears in his eyes. They had seen us return home and knew that Kathy had gone into the house.

'I'm sorry Harry, there is nothing left over there,' Ray said solemnly.

I didn't comprehend what he was saying for a second. Then it hit me.

'Kathy,' I screamed and tried to get up.

Ray couldn't hold me down, but I only got as far as my knees when everything started spinning and I knew I was falling back onto the ground. As the world went black again and before any further noises penetrated my ear drums, I heard the dull sounds of police and fire engines' sirens getting closer and closer.

The white Escort had pulled away from the kerb almost immediately after the explosion. Eva placing the remote detonation switch back into the bag on the seat beside her. She was cursing to herself.

'The fucking kid was not with them. Fuck it, I wanted them all to die.' She punched the back of the driver's seat hard making Costa jump again.

'Let's get the hell out of here,' she growled.

I'm already moving you bitch, just because you fucked everything up by being trigger happy, Costa thought angrily to himself.

Costa knew the woman was dead and had seen the husband blown across the street, hitting the stone wall on the other side of the road with tremendous force. He saw his body slumped lifelessly against the wall and blood pouring from his head and down his face, but he was only able to observe the scene for a few seconds until Eva screamed at him to move. They could only assume he was dead.

'Fuck it. Let's go and get the kid and the bastard's parents,' Eva screamed from the back seat.

Her eyes were wide and scary and her face flushed red with rage and anger. She was out of control now, both Costa and Ricardo knew it. They also both knew it was madness to go after the family, but they wouldn't dare to go against her.

Two police cars hurtled past them on the road heading towards at least one completely obliterated house and many others that were seriously damaged.

Fatal casualties, definitely one, but most probably two.

10

The explosion rattled every window within a mile radius. Ron was sitting in Gerri's lounge when he heard the blast through the double glazed windows. His significant experience with explosives instantly told him that was no gas leak. That was a bomb of some sort.

They both peered out of the window and could see smoke starting to rise into the sky not very far away. They watched the smoke increase and get darker as the combustible material in what was left of Kathy's and Harry's house ignited and began to burn furiously.

It took them only a few seconds to realise that the smoke was coming from the direction of Harry and Kathy's house.

'I'll go and take a look, I won't be long,' Ron said as he reached for his coat on the settee.

Gerri was worried, she didn't know why, but she had a terrible feeling in her stomach that something wasn't right. Harry Jr started to grizzle so Gerri left the window and went over to his cot to pick him up. She knew it was his teeth that were bothering him so began to rub his gums with her little finger. She didn't notice the white Escort that had just pulled up outside the cottage.

Ron was in the hall tying up his boots, his coat lying by his feet ready to throw on.

'Hurry Ron,' Gerri shouted.

'Something isn't right, I can feel it.'

'I'm on my way now. I'll be back as soon as I can.' Ron said from the front door.

He finished tying his boots, paused and then walked back the few paces to the lounge door.

'Gerri, I won't be long, just look after Harry Jr. I'm sure everything's all right.' Ron knew he hadn't been very convincing but hoped Gerri would appreciate it just the same.

Ron was six feet from the front door when the doorframe splintered by the Yale lock cradle. It had been kicked out of its position from the force of the first blow, but the door was still closed and would need a second heavy boot to open it. Ron threw himself into the gap between the bottom of the stairs and the door before Ricardo's boot connected again. Ron's left leg connected with the radiator opposite the door and then trashed the umbrella stand next to it, but this only slowed him down momentarily and he was ready for whoever was coming through the door.

Ricardo came through the door first, his Browning 9mm straight out in front of him ready to take out any target that appeared, except for the baby, Eva wanted him just for herself. Ron was too quick for him though, his boot connected with the inside of the smashed door slamming it back into Ricardo's face. Ricardo was a big man though and recovered too quickly for Ron to take another kick at the door that could have trapped Ricardo's raised arm against the door frame.

Costa was directly behind Ricardo and had stopped him falling backwards out the doorway. In a split second, they regrouped and together they crashed through the broken door, Ricardo still in front. Ron's right boot smashed into the side of Ricardo's knee making him crumple into a heap on the floor. Costa's forward momentum couldn't stop him falling onto his back, winding him slightly. The fall knocking the Browning out of Ricardo's hand sending it sliding down the hallway.

Costa was quick and avoided Ron's first right-handed punch as he pushed himself up using Ricardo's back. He wasn't quick enough though to miss the left hook that swung in hard as Ron focused on his target. Costa's top lip split like a ripe tomato exposing the tops of both his front teeth.

Costa was almost knocked out by the force of the blow and fell backwards against the wall, his arse and legs pinning Ricardo to the floor as Ron swung another boot into Ricardo's ribs. Ron missed the ribs and connected mostly on his upper right arm. Ricardo howled in pain but was not giving up as he thrashed around trying to dislodge Costa off his legs and get back onto his feet.

The first 9mm round nicked Ron's neck. The second round missed completely but distracted Ron long enough for Ricardo to get fully back onto his feet. He turned to face Ron and swung his huge fist towards him. The punch knocked Ron backwards into the gap at the bottom of the stairs breaking the front door off its top hinge on the way through. Ricardo was on top of him in a second laying into him with a barrage of punches and elbows into his face and head.

Ron managed to get his arms up to deflect some of the blows, but he knew his opponent was a strong and well trained man. Ron also knew instantly he had to do something drastic and vicious to dislodge him, or he would be fucked. Ron caught a fleeting glimpse of a woman's shape stepping over the dazed figure of Costa whose blood-covered hands were fumbling around trying to push his top lip back in place.

Ron knew instantly the woman was heading for the front room and Gerri and Harry Jr. Seeing the gun in her right hand sent a massive surge of adrenaline through his body. He couldn't be any angrier than he was right at this moment and with every ounce of strength he possessed he thrust his left hand towards his attacker, his fingers gripping Ricardo's throat with such force he immediately stopped punching and put both hands on Ron's arm to try and pull him off.

This was all that Ron needed, Ricardo's head was now slightly tilted backwards and both his hands were down away from his face. With his free right hand, Ron smashed the heel of his palm under Ricardo's nose splintering the bone and ramming it up into his skull. As the bone penetrated the soft tissue at the front of his brain, Ricardo's eye's bulged out and fixed in a blank stare.

His grip on Ron's arm relaxed instantly allowing Ron to force him backwards and into the still sitting Costa. The back of Ricardo's limp head crashed into Costa's face inflicting more damage to his already fucked up lip. Ricardo was dead before the impact with Costa's head, his body now trapped Costa's legs beneath him.

Ron hauled himself up using the lowest stair rail and swung another right boot straight into Costa's face. It connected on the left side of his mouth snapping his head to the right and back against the wall. More blood flowed from his mouth where several teeth had been dislodged or just kicked straight out. His top lip was almost completely torn off and there was now a two inch strip of top lip flapping around his right cheek. His gums were exposed like a corpse that had all the fleshy bits of its lips gnawed off by unknown creatures.

That last boot had almost rendered Costa unconscious, but he was just hanging on, mainly because of the pain in his mashed up face. He was slumped on his right side, he couldn't fall any further due to Ricardo's body lying across his legs. Ron took quick advantage of this and placed another vicious kick directly into Costa's ribs. Blood spewed from his mouth as Costa violently exhaled from the blow. His blood spraying the hall's white wallpaper with a polka dot pattern of red.

Ron knew he had fucked him up for a minute, he also knew he had to get into the lounge right now. In one movement, Ron had the first guy's Browning off the floor and instinctively checked the safety was off as he took the couple of paces to the doorway. The gunshot was loud and close. Harry Jr let out a huge wail and then started that tortured crying of a baby that has been frightened out of his skin. Ron heard the crash of ornaments before seeing fragments bounce off the carpet as he reached the doorway.

Gerri had both hands around Eva's right hand forcing it up into the air. Eva had her Browning still clenched firmly within it. Gerri was not content with just that and in the couple of seconds it took for Ron to react to the scene before him, she had butted Eva twice in the face and brought her knee up hard into her crotch causing Eva to lose balance momentarily. This was all Gerri needed and she used all her strength and forward momentum to push Eva backwards towards the door where Ron was standing.

Eva started to punch Gerri anywhere she could with her free left hand but none of her blows had any effect on this immensely strong woman. Gerri's third head-butt as they were going backwards properly broke her nose. Eva's eyes watered as she continued to struggle to release her gun hand, she knew then she had a very significant opponent in front of her and it was now time to flee rather than fight. She needed those two fuck ups she had brought with her, but where were they?

Eva felt the solid bulk of Ron's body as she crashed into him going backwards through the doorway, but Gerri had already seen the opportunity to get rid of the gun. The back of Eva's right hand hit the doorframe with considerable force, the Browning fell from her hand and landed amongst the framed family photographs on the oak sideboard. Eva screamed as bones broke in her right hand, but she still carried on punching Gerri with her good hand.

The three of them fell backwards into the hallway. As he went down the back of Ron's head connected with an old cast iron hedgehog doorstop that was by the cubby-hole door under the stairs. The lumpy metal shell of the hedgehog's back split open the back of Ron's head instantly. Blood poured out of the two inch cut and started running down the back of his neck, soaking his t-shirt. The blow stunned him, but he was still conscious. The writhing and fighting bodies of Gerri and Eva still on top of him.

Gerri did not have to concentrate on the gun now so she pummelled Eva's face with her right fist. Eva reached up with her good left hand and grabbed hold of Gerri's right arm, stopping the blows to her face for a moment. Gerri then took her opportunity and buried her teeth into Eva's right cheek and bit down hard. Eva's blood mixed with her own saliva as she felt the cheek flesh tearing and ripping as she shook her head from side to side.

Costa was still slumped by the front door, but Eva's screams brought him back to life. His back-up weapon was a small colt 38 that fitted perfectly in the ankle holster Pepe had provided him on Sunday. He pulled it out and pointed it straight at the blurred shape of the woman on top of Eva. The bullet passed through the bottom part of Gerri right buttock check causing her to release her grip on Eva's face. Gerri screamed as the pain shot through her body, her right hand filling with blood as soon as she gripped the wound. Eva needed no second invitation to get free and landed a short left punch on Gerri's nose knocking her more off balance. Another punch and a shove and Gerri was off her.

This was Eva's chance and she took it, she was on her feet and racing to the door in seconds. Costa had barely dragged himself to his feet but had the colt pointing down the hallway as Eva reached him.

'Kill them. Kill them.' Eva screamed at him.

But before he could get a shot off a 9mm round embedded itself in the wall a couple of inches past his left ear. Ron, still very groggy, had fired in the general direction of the door hoping to hit either of them. The second round hit the doorframe, but Eva and Costa were already out of the door and heading up the path. Blood dripped down the doorframe from the bloody hands that had steadied themselves against it seconds earlier.

Gerri was already moving back into the lounge. Harry Jr was hysterical and thrashing around on his back on the settee. Gerri had literally thrown him there when she saw the woman coming through the doorway with a gun pointing straight out in front of her.

Ron got to the front door as the white Escort screeched away from the kerb and headed down the lane. Ron made it to the front gate only in time to see the tail lights disappear past old Tom's cottage at the end of the lane.

11

I had been admitted into a private room in Gloucester Royal Hospital after the accident and emergency department had stitched the gash in my head and put my dislocated shoulder back in place. Apart from the concussion and a bit of blood loss all the other superficial wounds had been cleaned and dressed and I was in surprisingly good physical shape after the effects of the explosion. Emotionally though, I was completely fucked up.

My head was still banging and numb from the impact with the wall and the shoulder ached like hell but the effects of the drugs I had been given earlier were now beginning to have some effect. I knew Kathy had been inside the house when the bomb went off, but no one had confirmed it yet so I still wasn't willing to accept that she was actually dead.

A senior police officer spoke to me before the full effects of the drugs took hold and told me that Gerri and Ron had been attacked by as yet unknown assailants, but Ron and Harry Jr were all right. Gerri would require surgery to fix the gunshot wounds she sustained, but she would be OK as well. I fell into a drug induced sleep shortly after that.

I was reunited with Harry Jr, and Ron the next morning. They were accompanied by an armed police officer and a woman constable who handed Harry to me. He was fast asleep. The officers left the room almost immediately but positioned themselves outside the windowed door once it was closed.

Ron explained that Gerri had already been to the operating theatre to have the hole in her right butt cheek cleaned out and packed.

'She is in no danger Harry, they just needed to clean out her wound of any residues from her clothes, and the bullet. She's a tough lady as you know and she will be back on her feet in no time being a pain in the arse as usual.' Ron smiled a little as he delivered the last line. I almost did too as it was always something he said about her in jest.

Ron slowly leaned forward to say something, I felt the room closing in on me and somehow darken around the peripherals. Ron was only inches from my face, his left hand now cradling the back of my head.

Ron's words came out as mumbles, but I knew what he was saying. Tears flowed freely from his eyes and down his craggy face. All that toughness disappearing in a split second as he struggled to finish each sentence.

'Kathy wouldn't have suffered, Harry, or known anything about the explosion, she was too close to it. The police took me to the house and there is nothing left. Kathy is gone son. I am so sorry. So very sorry.'

That was the moment my world caved in. Tears falling freely down both our faces now. Harry Jr began to cry as well and I just didn't know what to do with him, but at that moment the police woman came back into the room and reached over and took him off me. I didn't resist as she turned and left the room with him. I knew he was in good hands.

Ron pulled me up and buried his head into my shoulder. He hugged me for a long time until the uncontrollable sobbing and the tears subsided. Kathy had been my world and now she had been taken from me. I didn't know the full story about what had happened to Ron and Gerri, but I knew they were both OK. All I knew was Kathy wasn't.

'I want to see her,' I pleaded with Ron.

'No son, that's not possible, and if you try and get out of that bed you will fall down and hurt yourself some more. Leave it to the police, for now.'

The words 'for now' were emphasized and cut through the scramble that was going on in my brain. It took a good minute though before I had calmed down enough for Ron to let me go.

I slumped back down onto the bed as a senior looking female doctor walked into the room carrying a plastic tray. Tears were still rolling down my face as they were on Ron's. She didn't bat an eyelid but showed genuine concern for both of us in the way she spoke.

'Lieutenant Glass, I'm Doctor O'Hagan and I'm going to give you something to help you sleep for a few hours. You need to rest and so does your brain, it has taken quite a battering.'

I protested weakly that I was OK, but she was having none of it and quietly injected the contents of the pre-prepared syringe into the cannula in my arm. I know she was holding my hand as I drifted off to sleep.

It was dark outside the window and in the room when I slowly came out of my deep drug induced sleep. The only light penetrating the room was from the dimly lit corridor outside. There was now a drip attached to the cannula, but I couldn't read the writing on the label of the plastic bottle hanging from the stand, so didn't know what was going into me.

'Nurse, nurse,' I called out.

'Anyone there? Nurse.'

Before I could shout another word a new face appeared from around the open door.

'Good evening lieutenant,' the young constable said.

'There is no one around at the moment, but I will track someone down and tell them you are awake.'

'Thank you,' I said and fell back onto the pillow.

By 1900 I wished I hadn't called out. Nurses and doctors prodded and poked me expecting me to be suffering from some as yet unfound injury. They couldn't believe I could have got away with so few injuries after seeing the pictures of the destroyed house on the news.

The police asked me questions for well over an hour. Had I seen anything suspicious in the past few days? Why had my house and my parents been targets for these unknown assassins? Did I have any idea who the assailants could be?

Did I have any known enemies? It went on and on but I kept lying and told them I had seen nothing and I had no ideas.

I did have an idea though and a white Escort had something to do with it. I needed some Ron time now so I could get a description of the dead guy and the two that escaped although I knew who my money was on.

At 2000 the door opened again and I was about to groan at the intrusion thinking it was more doctors or police wanting to ask more questions, when Gerri appeared in a wheelchair being expertly driven by Ron. Harry Jr was cradled in her arms, fast asleep.

It took over an hour to get through the whole story starting with hearing the explosion, seeing the smoke and then the front door being smashed in. Ron didn't leave out anything and described the attackers in great detail. I couldn't hide my facial expressions from Ron and he knew straight away that I knew who they were. But, he didn't flinch and carried on to the end of the story. Gerri had missed the look as she was fussing with Harry Jr's blanket.

He finished by telling me the police had questioned him for three hours once Gerri had been taken to hospital, but when a neighbour had collaborated his story by telling them he had seen three people, two men and a woman, get out of a white Escort, go up the path, kick the door in and then the gunshots, they had let him go and said he would be questioned again in due course. He wasn't able now to leave the country as they had taken his passport. They also had found no ID on the dead man so he was still a mystery to them, but I knew his name was Ricardo.

When Gerri had told her side of the story she was particularly pleased that she had inflicted significant pain on the woman before being shot in the buttock. Even how bad I was feeling I still found it very hard not to crack a small smile at Ron's joke earlier.

The conversation had inevitably turned to Kathy soon after their arrival and just mentioning her name and knowing she was not with us any more hurt everyone so deeply it was impossible to contain our grief for more than just a few minutes at a time. I didn't know a grown man could cry as many times as I did in that hour. Harry Jr was oblivious to it all as he snuggled in close against Gerri's chest, but then she asked that question that I knew I would not be able to lie to her about.

'Harry, why did they attack us?'

It was another hour before I finished the whole story, warts and all. They both sat in complete silence, no questions asked, they just took it all in. More tears had flowed but not just from the sadness of recent events, they were for fallen comrades, and the anger that came from all the events leading up to today.

They left me shortly after 2200 and I was glad I had told them everything as there couldn't be any more secrets with what I was planning to do next.

12

'Harry. Harry wake up.' I recognised the voice immediately.

'Hello Bill,' I said before fully opening my eyes.

I sat up and then focused on the others in the room. Colonel Shaw and Brigadier Whistonhall were standing at the end of the bed. The door to the room was ajar but then a uniformed soldier and a policeman carried in additional chairs for the two senior officers.

The door closed.

'Harry.' Colonel Shaw spoke first. 'I know that I can speak for everyone in this room and tell you how sorry we are about Kathy.'

Just hearing her name spoken was enough to make the tears well up in my eyes again.

'Harry, it is a tragedy beyond comprehension. My sincerest condolences to you and your family.'

Brigadier Whistonhall was visibly shaken and looked gaunt as he spoke. His eyes had deep black rings around them, there had obviously been no sleep for him during the past 48 hours.

Bill put his hand on my arm before he spoke.

'Someone must have talked Harry, for them to find us so quickly. We are trying to get a message to Reynoso to see what he can find out.'

'If he is still alive of course,' the Brigadier interjected.

'It was that fucking murdering bitch, Eva Muscardin,' I spat out, hardly able to contain the burning anger and fierce rage building inside me.

'We know Harry, we missed them at Dublin airport last night,' Bill said. 'We got there too late and they were already on their way to Boston on the early evening Air Lingus flight to the US. They initially took the ferry from Rosslare to Cork and then dumped the Escort on a rough estate in the north of the city. By the time the Garda got there, it had been torched. We know someone helped them to get into Ireland, and do temporary repairs to some of the physical damage Ron and Gerri inflicted on them, but as yet we don't know who. There is a team working on that right now.' Bill looked downhearted as he finished talking but was obviously angry they had got away.

Brigadier Whistonhall then said something that made me listen intently.

'I have been talking to my friends on the other side of the pond and for now they have agreed to track Eva, and the other one, when they arrive. But they cannot intervene at this point.'

I leaned forward on the bed a bit too fast. A sharp pain instantly invaded the right side of my head and face.

'I don't want them to touch those fuckers, I want to take them down myself,' I spat out.

Colonel Shaw got up from his chair and stepped forward. He sat on the end of the bed before speaking.

'Harry there are very important things to take care of here before anyone takes anyone down. Gerri and Harry Jr need you very much right now and you have to take care of yourself and get fit again. You have a concussion, a small hairline fracture on your skull, as well as all the other cuts and bruises and they will need a little time to heal properly. You must deal with the important things right now Harry. Let Captain Dye and myself take care of the other business in the interim.'

I knew he was right but I just wanted to get out of here and kill them.

Over the next 20 minutes they told me how the situation with the police had been squared away. The bomb at the house was officially a gas leak now and Ricardo's body had been dealt with by one of the special crews from the Regiment. He would never be seen or heard of again.

Ron was also in the clear and didn't have to answer any more questions about Ricardo's death, or for that matter the manner in which he died. It was a clear case of self-defence anyway and MI5 had the case file now.

'Which will never be seen again,' Colonel Shaw said in a throwaway comment.

'You can be very proud of your father Harry. His actions, courage and skill saved Harry Jr and your mother's life. No doubt about it. He did a proper job on the dead Argie as well. A technique taught him by a member of the Regiment some years ago, I understand.' Colonel Shaw said with a wry smile before continuing. 'We currently have no intel on how they got into the UK, where the car came from or who supplied the explosive and weapons. But Bill is on it so we will have something very soon I'm sure.'

'Harry, I saw the white Escort at the church with three occupants just sitting there,' Bill said. 'Something about it wasn't right. I knew it, I absolutely knew it and If only I had followed my gut feeling, I could have stopped this.'

Bill was getting more angry with himself now, his face was bright red and fists clenched so tight the whites of his knuckles protruded from the back of his hands.

'I saw it too Bill and didn't do anything either.' I said. 'She was very smart using the events of the day to distract even the best of us from spotting them and doing anything about it.'

I needed Bill to stop blaming himself, it wasn't his fault.

'Please just be there for me and Harry Jr at the funeral,' I asked.

'You have my word Harry,' Bill replied.

The three men left a few minutes later after promising they would not let up until this was sorted.

I discharged myself at 1600. A fresh bandage and a box of pills for my head rattling around the bottom of the Sainsbury's bag one of the nurses had found for me. The protests from the doctors had been futile and they knew it. They understood that I needed to take care of things for Kathy but before I left I needed to see Ron, Gerri and Harry Jr.

I got a significant bollocking from both of them when I walked into Gerri's private room, but they also knew it was futile to argue with me about staying in. Ron told me he had temporarily fixed the door frame and latch at home so at least it could be secured. Gerri then told me that apparently 'a nice man' from the insurance company had been in to see her and said he was going to arrange for a new door and frame to be fitted within 48 hours. She laughed as she told me Ron had actually growled at him when he started to talk about getting a repair done on the original door. Apparently he said something like, "are you being fucking serious?"

The bullet holes in the wall were untouched but the hall carpet was gone and the wallpaper had been scrubbed. The smears of blood were still evident though but, "it will all be sorted as part of the insurance claim and a bunch of men will be in to do it all before I am released from hospital. I have been promised," Gerri said.

I tried in vain not to show my anger and pain after hearing about the damage caused by those Argie bastards and knowing how close they came to wiping me out and my whole family, in one day. Gerri reached out and pulled my head into her shoulder, her other arm around my back. She must have known what I was thinking. Ron joined us and put his arms around our shoulders but only for a moment because he had to break off when Harry Jr cried out from his cot by the side of Gerri's bed. Gerri began to sob quietly as we hugged. It started me off again as well, my heart breaking into a thousand pieces. I felt well and truly fucked up.

Ron and I had left Gerri and Harry Jr a couple of hours before when I had been discharged. The hospital had been fantastic and was letting Harry Jr stay with Gerri in her room for the next couple of days until she could come home as well.

We fed ourselves bought ham and cheese sandwiches before stepping out of Gerri's creaking front door into the light drizzle that had been falling for over an hour. It was 1800 so Ron and I still had enough daylight time to walk up the road and clearly see the devastation that was Kathy's and my first home together.

There was fuck all left. A small section of the back wall where the kitchen had been was the only thing left standing. Rubble had been stacked in large piles on the front lawn from where they had been searching through the wreckage for Kathy's body. Police tape was stretched taut right around both the adjacent houses. They looked completely fucked as well with most of walls closest to the explosion in pieces. All windows had been blown in and most of the roof tiles were either smashed, or just gone. They would all have to be demolished, there was no doubt about that.

Ron spoke to the police officer who had walked over to see what we wanted. The officer explained we couldn't enter the cordoned off area because the specialist teams hadn't finished their work and also because everything was so unstable and dangerous. Ron and I stood there for several minutes in silence, water running down our faces and into our eyes as we stared into the darkening mass of rubble, broken furniture and personal belongings.

It was a surreal moment. It was the moment when I realised my dreams of spending the rest of my life with Kathy were gone. Gone forever. It was now about Harry Jr and getting him sorted. Then it would be about revenge.

Revenge of a most personal kind.

My head hurt as we turned for home. Rage, anger and hatred had replaced the desperate sadness that had enveloped me since the explosion. I knew the sadness would be back, but for now I liked this feeling. I would make them pay for what they had done and at whatever cost to me personally. All of them would die, everyone involved in the murder of my beautiful Kathy, and I meant everyone. Ron knew it too.

13

Friday 4th November 1983

Nigglesworth, St George's Parish Church 1100

I looked up at the dull grey sky as I stepped onto the path. It was how I felt inside, dull and grey. The brand new front door of Gerri's cottage glistening from the light rain that had been falling all morning. It wasn't cold, just damp and drizzly and was set in for the day so the weather man on the television had said at 0600 that morning. No one had been asleep at that time.

The long sombre black hearse had pulled up outside a couple of minutes earlier. Kathy's coffin was already inside. It was closely followed by two extended black Fords that were going to carry us the short distance to the church and the cemetery. As I walked towards the hearse I knew that not all of Kathy was inside the coffin. Some body parts had been incinerated from the force of the blast and the fire that had started immediately afterwards.

The report from MI5 said Kathy had taken the full force of the explosion. They were pretty sure the bomb was hidden in the cubby-hole under the stairs and was triggered by a trip switch when the door had been opened. Or it had been triggered remotely if the attackers thought the switch hadn't worked. It would have killed her instantly because her body had been blown apart. It had taken five days to complete the search of the site and recover all the body parts from the rubble. When Ron and I had turned up we didn't know they still hadn't found her right foot and left hand.

The short ride to the church is the longest in my life. As we turn left up the narrow tree lined lane, horses are chasing around the field on my left with not a care in the world. Kathy would have smiled. As the car turned right into the churchyard I can see the car park is full, and the next field, which a local farmer had kindly let us use for today.

I take a moment to look at the church as the boys from Poole get ready to take Kathy's coffin out of the hearse. How many times in recent months have I been in this impressive 18th century building with its tall spires and arched stone windows, I asked myself. Each of the previous visits had been joyous occasions though, but not today. Even the ancient, but still intact, leaded stained glass windows seemed dark and uninviting today.

Kathy's coffin was carried into the church slowly, precisely and with dignity by six uniformed Royal Marines. My best mates. Nearly all the new officers from my course were present as were many others from every Commando unit I had served with. All were in uniform standing together making a guard of honour for Kathy. They lined up on each side of the path that led to the high stone archway at the entrance to the church. The light rain falling constantly on their bare heads and soaking their crisp No1 uniforms, not one of them cared a dot about that though.

Less than two weeks ago she was dancing and having fun with most of these men after our wedding in this very church. It is almost unbelievable that the sounds of joy and happiness on that occasion have been substituted so quickly by the solemn sounds of today. Harry Jr is cradled in my arms looking around at all the sights, shapes and colours. He seems fascinated by the men in green as we slowly walk by the guard. Gerri is beside me, her arm linked through mine, I'm not sure who is holding who up.

I'm distracted for a brief second as I look at the little stone carved face on the front of the arch. I was positive he was smiling on the last two occasions but now the mouth seems to curl downwards. The eyes looked heavy and the whole face was sad, but I knew it was all just in my imagination. I needed to get some sleep very soon.

The service was very traditional, just as Kathy would have wanted. My voice cracked throughout my reading about Kathy, but I only had to stop twice. I had been the happiest man alive less than two weeks ago and now this. It was hard to comprehend. Even the toughest of Marines and soldiers broke down along with aunties, uncles, friends and neighbours. Even the poor sods who had their homes destroyed by the bomb were there supporting me and Harry Jr.

The same six Marines carried the coffin out of the church and back out into the drizzle. The solid oak doors secured open by two heavy ornate black hooks. The slow, short walk to the grave took us past the huge Cotswold stone buttresses and the stone arched stained glass windows then around the edge of the car park and down a small slope to the plot.

The new grave was in a lovely spot just a couple of minutes' walk from the entrance to the church. It looked across the valley to the multi-coloured trees on the other side and although the grave was fairly close to the road below, at night it would be quiet and peaceful with only the rustle of the many trees surrounding the graveyard breaking the silence.

The small plot below the church was filled with people. Those who couldn't get down onto the neatly cut grass stood at the top of the rise by the car park to watch and listen to the last few words from the priest. The remains of Kathy Glass were lowered into the ground at 1215. My mates did me proud and lowered her to her final resting place with care and dignity.

I couldn't speak and say anything meaningful when I dropped the single pink rose onto the top of the coffin, followed by a handful of the sodden earth. I was barely holding myself together, but I knew I had to for Harry Jr who was resting quietly in the crook of my arm. Gerri was sobbing uncontrollably now. Ron by her side supporting her and loving her as he had always done.

It was well over half an hour before everyone moved away from the grave. The men with spades who would be finishing off the job stood and watched in silence at the edge of the car park. Waiting patiently for their time.

14

It was good to have Gerri's cottage back to ourselves. No one had outstayed their welcome. Bill was the last to go shortly before 1800 telling me he would be back on Monday to pick me up at 0900. I hadn't questioned him, no point, I had already received the letter from the Commanding Officer at Lympstone telling me I was on four weeks compassionate leave and a liaison officer would be in contact with me shortly.

Another hour of tidying up and Gerri, Ron and I were slumped on the settee in the lounge. The television was on but no one was paying it any attention.

'When are you flying back to the States Ron?' I asked.

'I have sorted another week son. I've got a flight out of Brize Norton next Thursday, but we will see how it's going shall we,' he replied. I knew exactly what he meant.

'Thanks,' I said.

I made my excuses around 2100 telling Gerri and Ron I needed some air. Harry Jr was sound asleep upstairs. The night was damp and cold and the fine drizzle hit my face as soon as I was out the door. I had taken the good powerful torch from under the stairs so seeing my way up the lanes to the graveyard would not be an issue. By taking the short cut across the field I was there in 20 minutes. My jeans were soaking, but the top half of me and my feet were dry. Not that I would have cared if they were wet.

The men at the graveyard had made a neat job of it. The white oblong marble gravestone was in place standing up perfectly straight and in line with the others in the row. The sodden brown earth was slightly raised but would be raked flat once everything had settled so that the grass could grow evenly across the plot. I knelt down on the left side of the headstone and shone the torch on the words highlighting her name first; Kathryn Rose Glass. I stared blankly at the stone knowing no one would be around to hear, I had to tell her something important. I paused for a long while steeling myself to explain.

'I'm so sorry Kathy. I shouldn't have gone to Argentina, I should have left it alone.' I said in a clear voice so she would hear me.

'You and Harry Jr were the most important things in my life and I failed you both.' I couldn't stop the tears starting again and didn't care as they mixed with the rain that was blowing steadily into my face now.

'I will never let anything happen to Harry Jr, I swear to you on my life Kathy. But, and it's a big but, I know you would not approve of this, but those people must pay the ultimate price for what they did to you. Harry will then be safe from them forever, I promise you.'

I was struggling with the words now but I hoped and prayed she would understand. I rested my head on the side of the headstone and stayed there for a while, I was thoroughly soaked now but I didn't care about the wet or cold.

I didn't know how long I had been there but I knew I had to get back soon as Gerri and Ron would be worrying and I didn't need them to have any more stress right now. I sat back on my heels and directed the torch beam so I could read the full inscription on the headstone:

IN LOVING MEMORY
OF A BEAUTIFUL WIFE
AND MOTHER TO HARRY

KATHRYN ROSE GLASS

14 JUNE 1954
25 OCTOBER 1983

In the left hand corner of the stone after the date she died was a four inch carving of a white dove in flight. Below that the words continued:

The Dove of Peace I have left for you
is a symbol of the undying love
I hold for you
It is not much I know I can say
but it will always be with you
until I join you one day

Kathy
You are in our thoughts every day and will be loved forever

'I will see you again Kathy my love. I will always love you,' I said out loud. No one would hear me in this rain and wind anyway, but I didn't say it for anyone except the woman who lay six feet beneath me. I reached into my coat pocket and pulled out a sodden piece of paper. It was the poem I had written in the first valentine card that I had given Kathy. The words had been changed slightly from those on the headstone but the message was still the same. I dug a small hole in the sodden earth with my hand and pushed the piece of paper into it as far as it would go then patted the ground down carefully once I was done.

I stood and turned away from the grave knowing that it may be the last time I would ever see it. My mood now changing and getting darker with every step I took away from her. By the time I reached Gerri's cottage not one part of me was dry. Gerri started fussing as soon as I walked through the door.

'Get those wet things off Harry. You must be freezing. I'll put the kettle on for you and make you a nice cup of tea.' She said and headed off to the kitchen.

The tea was hot and sweet and I was dry again sitting in the big armchair in a clean tee shirt and sailing pants. There was a strange atmosphere in the room everyone was quiet but I knew I had to tell them both what I had decided on my walk back tonight.

'I'm going after them,' I said quietly.

Ron and Gerri looked at me and then each other.

'We know son and I'm going to help you,' Ron said.

'What do you mean help me?' I asked.

'What it means Harry, is.' Ron continued. 'If we don't get these fuckers now they will be back and they will try to hurt you, Harry Jr, Gerri and me, because I killed one of their own. I cannot allow that. I also understand from Bill that they are in the United States, so they are on my turf now son and I have been in the covert operations business a long time so I know some pretty influential people. A few of them owe me a favour or two so I'm sure they will help me once they know the facts.'

'Harry Jr will be fine with me. I cannot go back to work yet and we have many friends who will help if I need it,' Gerri said leaning forward next to Ron.

'I know you son. Kathy didn't deserve to die and I agree with Ron those people will be back if nothing is done. I could tell from that woman's eyes she was evil and vicious and she will not give up on this, I know it.'

I didn't know what to say, they had both taken me completely by surprise. I really thought I was going to be in for a massive fight.

'I am going to ring Brize in the morning and see what I can do about getting an earlier flight back home. If nothing is on at Brize I will get a commercial flight back to New York from London as soon as I can. I need to start organising some people quickly,' Ron said.

'What about me Ron,' I asked.

'I think you will be following me shortly from what Bill tells me, that's why he is coming to get you on Monday.'

Things had been moving fast and I had been oblivious to all of it.

'More tea son?' Ron asked as he got up from the settee.

He was back in SEAL mode now, planning and organising, I could see it in his face clearly.

Part Five

East Coast – USA

1

Monday 7th November 1983

The weekend was a blur. Very kind people stopped by to pass on their condolences and to offer Gerri and me any help they could. Endless cups of tea and numerous jammy dodgers had been consumed. Harry Jr was passed around and cuddled constantly. He wasn't fussed until he lost sight of Gerri and then he had screamed his head off. I didn't know if he knew his mum was gone or not. I was definitely feeling a bit useless with regards to Harry Jr as my head was elsewhere. Gerri knew that and just gave me a knowing look as she, or some other doting female, sorted out the little guy.

Ron had left at 0500. He had got himself on a USAF mail plane that would get him to Philadelphia later today. One of his guys would collect him from there. Bill turned up shortly before 0900, just him, no driver. Bill got out of the car and walked up to me.

'Stupid question Harry, but how are you?' he asked as we shook hands.

'I'm OK Bill, thanks. I just need to get on a plane to the States as soon as we are done today.' Bill knew that I knew something.

'Ron's been talking hasn't he Harry?

'He has said something, but let's not fuck about Bill, you know what I have to do. I have four weeks compassionate leave, but I don't give a shit about the time. You know I will take as long as I need to get those fuckers, with or without, anyone's help.'

'Whoa, hold on Harry, I'm on your side, me and many others want to get them as much as you do.' Bill held his arms up as he spoke.

'Sorry Bill.' I realised then that I had been shouting at him, intense anger boiling up whenever I thought about them.

'I have to find them and kill them Bill even if it means going back to Argentina.' I said more calmly now.

'I know Harry, but we need to let Colonel Shaw talk to us before we do anything. We know Ron is on his way back to the US and that his guys have been tracking Eva and Costa since they landed in Boston. Expect more news when we get to base,' Bill said as he ushered me towards the car.

On the way, he told me that Eva and Costa were in New Jersey right now on the estate of a very wealthy Argentine businessman. Bill hadn't seen the latest intel yet, but again stressed it would be waiting for us this morning at Credenhill. We could be certain that the Muscardin family would have some very influential, rich and powerful friends all over the World, and they would be using them now.

Colonel Shaw was sitting behind his desk when we entered. He rose from his seat and came around to shake hands with us both.

'How are you and the little one Harry?' he asked.

'We're OK sir, thank you. My mother is making sure Harry Jr is getting everything he needs,' I replied.

'Good,' he said. 'Have a seat, the coffee will be here in a minute or two.'

Colonel Shaw waited until the uniformed soldier who had brought in the coffee closed the door behind himself.

'Harry, the last two weeks have been very tough for a lot of people, but especially you and your family. I am especially happy to know that your son is being so well taken care of.' Colin Shaw took a breath and paused for a few seconds. The silence in the room was deafening.

'We have been working hard during this period as it is clear from the events that your future safety, and that of Bill's here, is not secure. Intel on this Muscardin woman tells us that she is not likely to give up or forget about this either. She hates losing and you still being alive and the bungled attack on your family after the bombing would certainly constitute a failure in her eyes. Her brother, General Don Juan Muscardin, will certainly not let her forget it. We received a new message from Fernando Reynoso yesterday, via Brigadier Whistonhall. It said that the first democratic elections since the end of military rule have been a resounding success and that a great friend of his father has won the Presidency. The man who will take office before the end of the year is Raúl Ricardo Alfonsin. He is an influential politician, statesman and former lawyer who had been incarcerated for his opposition to Perón's Government in the 50s. He was also a man who was amongst a few prominent Argentine political figures to vocally oppose President Leopoldo Galtieri's invasion of the Falkland Islands last year. Most importantly though, he is a formidable opponent of the Muscardin family and everything they stand for.'

We broke for a few moments to refresh our coffees before Colonel Shaw started to talk again.

'Reynoso has been in hiding after two attempts on his life in recent weeks. His father has also been targeted, but he is now being guarded by troops and police loyal to the incoming new President. The message also says you will both be sorry to learn that Thomas and Alejandro were both killed in a car explosion.'

Bill and I looked over at each other for a moment, both of us were genuinely sad to hear the news about Thomas and Alejandro, they were good men.

Colonel Shaw continued.

'Moves are already under way to try and convince the current President, Reynaldo Bignone, to advance the inaugural by three months so Alfonsin can be in office before the New Year. Reynoso and his father have been asked to take up senior appointments in the new Government as soon as the inauguration has been completed. One of the first major legislative changes is going to be the rescission of Bignone's April 1983 blanket amnesty for those guilty of human rights abuses and will include identified war crimes that were committed during the Malvinas war. It will be Reynoso's job to find and prosecute those involved. Members of the Muscardin family are on top of the new President's list, which is why Eva Muscardin and the other fellow are still in the US.' Colonel Shaw finished speaking and placed his notes back onto his desk.

'It makes sense now,' Bill spoke first. 'They are using their contacts in the US to probably get the money out, get new identities, properties and everything else they need to escape. Eva is setting it up. They are going to do a runner before the end of the year. No doubt about it.'

'Sir, this is very interesting and I do not wish to offend you, or anyone, but I need to get out of here and onto a plane to New York so I can find the bastards who killed my wife and attacked my family.'

I was getting very frustrated just sitting there and had to speak out, but I knew immediately I had overstepped the mark with the Colonel from the look on his face. Colonel Shaw stood up.

'Lieutenant, I cannot imagine the pain you are in right now, but you are a serving officer in the Royal Marines and that is something you cannot just disregard, inside or outside of this room.'

I stood up so fast I knocked the chair backwards sending it crashing to the floor.

'Well Sir I will resign right here, right now. Eva Muscardin is going to pay for what she did.' I had lost control of myself and was shouting at him.

'Harry, Harry, calm down, we are both on your side,' Bill said. His hand gripping my arm tightly. I was sucking in air fast as rage overtook my senses.

'Sit down Harry. Please. Let's take a minute,' Colonel Shaw said as he sat down himself.

Bill lifted up the chair and with just enough force pushed it into the back of my knees making me park my arse. I knew I had to get myself back in control as behaving like this wasn't doing any of us any good. Bill stood on my right with his hand on my shoulder.

'Harry, let Colonel Shaw finish what he has to say please,' Bill said calmly.

'I'm sorry sir,' I blurted out, feeling like a right bloody idiot.

'It's OK Harry, but please let me finish this time. We are on your side as Bill said and we don't believe there would be any point in asking you, or even ordering you, not to pursue Eva Muscardin. Not that either of us would want to. So, we need to support you in this mission as you supported us when dealing with the murderers of Tom and the others. Bill has already volunteered and will accompany you to the United States. That is not for discussion, I think you will find.' Colonel Shaw was smiling, as was Bill now. 'Brigadier Whistonhall is organising some collaborations with specific US agencies and US Special Forces. They do not want the Muscardin clan ending up on their doorstep. It would be deeply embarrassing and detrimental to the 'special' relationship we have with the US. The Prime Minister has made that very clear already.' Colonel Shaw was smiling again as he recalled Brigadier Whistonhall's briefing about the conversation Margaret Thatcher had with the US President at which he was present.

'I understand your father is on his way back to the US although we know he has already begun to mobilise his team. You will not be short of support or allies on the ground, but you will have to deal with any interest from the local police force as they will not be involved. Just don't kill any of them will you.' Bill was smiling at me now as Colonel Shaw stopped talking.

'You see, I told you we were on your side,' he said.

'Thanks,' I replied to them both, which somehow just didn't seem adequate.

'We imagined you wouldn't want to be hanging around so you have two hours to get home and sort out your kit and deal with Harry Jr, and your mother.' Colonel Shaw said looking much more relaxed now.

'Bill will pick you up at 1300. You are on the evening British Airways flight to New York. You can go over the intel and the outline plans we have been working on over the weekend in the car.' I knew I shouldn't have doubted these men.

'Thank you Colonel. Thank you Bill, I really don't have any decent words to say how much I appreciate this.' I said.

'Just go and do what you need to. Your mother and Harry Jr will be looked after while you are away. Bill has put a good team on them and they will be safe I can assure you of that. Corporal Jones will be waiting for you outside, I'll see you when you get back. Good luck Harry.' Colonel Shaw reached out and shook my hand. His grip was strong and firm.

I nodded turned and shook Bill's hand without saying anything and left the room to the waiting Steve Jones.

'Nigglesworth then Sir,' he said.

'Thank you Corporal,' I replied with a smile.

I was thinking about Eva Muscardin and what I was going to do to her very shortly.

2

1100, Monday 7th November 1983

My pusser's grip was waiting for me on the bed with clean pants, socks, trainers, jeans, tee shirts, shirts, jacket and toiletries laid out next to it. Gerri knew I would be going today. I was greeted with a kiss.

'Your stuff is ready to pack upstairs; I'll bring you up a cup of tea in a minute. Harry Jr is sleeping in the front room so don't wake him,' she said.

Biil pulled up outside dead on 1300. I had already given the still sleeping Harry Jr and Gerri a kiss on the forehead and said my goodbyes, but as Gerri hung on to me in the doorway she whispered.

'Come back to us Harry, we both need you.'

'I will, I promise you,' I said.

'Oh, and look after your father as well, he not as young as he once was. But don't tell him I said that.'

I smiled as I walked up the path. She definitely still loved him, a lot.

Three hours later we were in the business lounge at Heathrow having gone through all the latest intel in the car. We had the address of the estate outside Hamilton Square in New Jersey and the offices of Eva's new best friend in New York.

Victor Armendáriz was a very rich man who had made his billions from suspicious real estate deals in the late 60s and 70s. He was known for using blackmail and extreme violence to achieve his objectives, but these were never proven. In more recent years he had distanced himself from the property business, his new passion and focus had been in horse-racing and breeding. His eldest son Dante was taking care of business now out of New York, but with a constant watching eye from his father.

Victor Armendáriz's stud was one of the finest on the East coast of the US. It was through this venture that he was connected all the way up to the President of the United States. Many senior congressmen, heads of industries and other powerful businessmen counted him as their friend. Little did they realise he had used every one of them to secure his position in the US and help him build his vast fortune. It had cost him a small fortune in the early days because of the millions of dollars he invested in individuals' campaign funds and the huge amounts in real estate deals with his new friends. Of course, everything had come back to him in spades in later years.

It was clear from the intel that to underestimate Victor Armendáriz and his family was as dangerous as underestimating the Muscardin clan. They were a vicious lot, well connected and feared even within the criminal world. They had always been just far enough away to avoid being implicated in anything bad. One New York District Attorney in the early 70s had got close to some damming evidence against Victor, but had 'disappeared' off the face of the earth one day, never to be seen or heard of again.

Latest intel on Eva's whereabouts confirmed that she was at the heavily guarded estate with Costa and although they had been getting out and about they had also spent many days just recovering from the injuries they sustained in the UK.

'We should try and get our heads down on the plane, then as soon as we land we can go and do a recce of the estate. We can do the offices in New York later,' Bill said.

We had been booked into the Holiday Inn on Broadway for our first night so that we had something to put down on the immigration forms, but it would depend on how the day panned out as to whether or not we would actually get there. The least amount of time we are on the ground the better as we needed to get this done and out of the country as fast as possible. Sleep would not be something we put in the plan for the next couple of days.

I had to wait a while for Bill on the other side of immigration controls. His Canadian passport was getting a good going over today. William Lowe of the Toronto Star smiled all he could at the beasty behind the counter, but she just wouldn't be nice. She gave him a good grilling as to why he was back in the US so soon after his last visit, how long was he staying, when was he leaving, where was he staying, who was he seeing in New York? He got the complete grilling, but the cover story and contacts would stand up, we had confidence in that. In the end, she slapped the passport onto the counter and in a tone of voice that meant she really didn't mean it, said, 'Welcome to the United States.' I had breezed through on my US passport. Even the copper standing there with his hand resting nonchalantly on his sidearm gave a courteous nod as I walked by. Harry Finch was home again.

It was 2100 and the arrivals hall was quiet except for those in cattle class off our flight who were now hustling past us to get to the baggage reclaim carousel first. Why, I had no fucking idea, as it would be a while before the bags start to come off, even at this time of the night.

Bill and I had only packed grips that we had carried onto the plane so we left the growing throng of people behind us and headed straight for customs. The officers didn't give us a second look after quickly scanning the forms. We were back in the US. The plan now was to head for the hire car booths and using our false licences get something decent and head off to New Jersey.

I was surprised to see Ron when we walked into the main terminal building, that wasn't in the plan. But there he was standing next to a hefty looking geezer who I recognized immediately. Master Sergeant Simon Steinway had been a US Navy SEAL with Ron, forever. He had taken care of me when I was a kid and then as a snotty teenager on my frequent visits.

'Fuck me you filled out Harry my boy,' he called over prompting some stern and disapproving looks from others in the waiting crowd.

Not that he cared about that and no one would be making an issue of it due to the size of him.

'I see the six-pack has turned into a bit of a party seven then,' I called back.

'Cheeky little fucker,' he said as he leaned over the rail to bear hug me.

'So sorry to hear about Kathy,' he whispered in my ear as he gave me a big squeeze and then gave the back of my shoulder a hefty slap as he released me.

'Leave him alone you big lug,' Ron said as he elbowed him out of the way. As I shook hands and hugged Ron, Bill introduced himself to Simon.

We dumped the grips in the back of the Ron's new AMC Eagle Wagon, which he had told me all about when he was in the UK. It was a real big ugly looking brute of a car but fitted us all in with acres of space to spare. We could have had a dance in it if we wanted. Ron gunned the 5.0l straight six engine out the car park, all four wheels screaming. Wherever we were going we would be getting there fast, that was for sure.

We left the hustle of the airport behind us as Ron headed up the JFK Expressway towards the Nassau Expressway and the Belt Parkway. There was little traffic so we covered the ground quickly. As soon as we got onto the Expressway I asked the question that I had been waiting to ask for a few minutes.

'Ron, what the fuck are you two doing here? I can guess how you found out from Gerri that I was arriving tonight.'

Yes,' he said.

Bill leaned forward and spoke directly to Ron.

'I know you know where they are from the direction you are driving. If you were taking us into New York we would be on the I-678 now wouldn't we?' Ron didn't answer.

'Ron we need to know where you are taking us or we need to get the fuck out of this vehicle.'

Although we were with friends, and very handy friends at that, Bill was agitated when he spoke because we had a plan of what we wanted to achieve in the next few hours and being highjacked by Ron was not part of it. Ron spoke for the first time since leaving the airport car park as we turned sharp left and down onto the Nassau Expressway touching 80mph. Ron was obviously not worried about the cops.

'Simon, and all the guys in my team want to help you after hearing about Kathy and the attack on Gerri and Harry Jr. They have been very busy in the past 48 hours since I called them from the UK. The Muscardin woman and the bodyguard are on the estate of Victor Armendariz; he is a billionaire property magnate and horse breeder who has been in the US for over 40 years. He is very well connected too, all the way up to the President.'

'Ron we know all that and we also know about the offices in New York, and that Eva has already been there,' I said.

'OK, OK,' Ron said. 'I know your people have been busy too. My buddy at the CIA told me that from the moment they landed in Boston some toff Limey has been on the phone constantly getting up to date intel on them both.'

Not a particularly flattering description of Brigadier Whistonhall, but pretty accurate. Not that you want to fuck with him, intellectually or physically with his background, I thought momentarily. Simon spoke now from the front passenger seat.

'Your Brigadier has also been briefed on Victor Armendariz. They have a large file on him at the CIA, but no one can seem to touch him. He is a nasty piece of work and so are his sons. There are few people who will go up against them because they know that in the past those that have do tend to disappear.'

We hit the ramp for the Belt Parkway still doing 80mph.

'Bill,' Ron spoke and made eye contact with him via the rear view mirror. 'I am taking you to the estate where one of my team is on the ground staking out the place. His last report was that all the family and their two guests were there. I'm sure you two will want to do a recce of the place yourselves, which is fine, but be aware it's heavily guarded with lots of electronic sensor equipment right around the entire perimeter. Dave has found a way in and he will show you if you want to go in, which I doubt from the intel so far. Dave will brief us when we arrive and you can make the call. Harry you will remember Dave Hine, he's the little guy that has had white hair ever since he started to grow pubes,' Ron then chuckled at his own joke. I did remember him.

'What are you and your team intending to do Ron? We didn't expect such direct support and I assumed you would be just feeding us intel and providing us with weapons. This operation is unofficially supported by the CIA, but politically this could cause serious ructions if US Special Forces are implicated in anything we do.' Bill said as he was leaning forward between the two front seats of the wagon.

'Bill, we know,' Ron answered. 'Me and the guys are officially off station, on leave until next week. My contact at the CIA is feeding me intel through a back door and only my CO knows anything about what we are up to. This is for Kathy, Harry, Harry Jr, and you. I also owe that fucker Costa a bit more personally, but we will stay in the background supporting you as much as you need us to. If it gets noisy though we have the kit to take out a few of them so that you can finish the job. This is your show so you guys call the shots from now on.'

We had agreed on the flight over that Bill was going to run the operation so as he sat back in the seat he seemed content with what Ron had said. It was very reassuring to have a team of SEALs with us, but the implications for Ron, Simon, Dave and the others in Ron's team, if they got caught, wounded, or killed, were more than serious. I knew it was pointless trying to change anyone's mind so I didn't bother.

Cross Bay Boulevard was still light with traffic as we headed out into Jamaica Bay and down towards Queens and Long Beach. It was a crystal clear night, the bright moonlight illuminating the calm waters of the bay as we headed South West past Long Island. Even from this distance the intensity of the lights from JFK airport was still lighting up the sky.

'How long till we reach the estate?' Bill asked.

'About 40, 45 minutes in this traffic,' Ron replied.

Everyone was quiet in the car as we passed Coney Island, Staten Island and Perth Amboy on our left. Five minutes later Ron had the Eagle Wagon heading South in the inside lane of the I 95 New Jersey Turnpike. The traffic was even lighter now, but Ron eased back to 65mph as the I 95 is notorious for black and whites nabbing speeders, even at this time of the night.

We left East Brunswick behind us on our way to Lakehurst. The lights of heavy industries operating 24 hour shifts burned brightly in the night sky behind us. I remembered this route from one of my visits when Ron had been stationed at the Naval Air Station at Lakehurst. It was a massive sprawling place with not much going on as I remember, but we had taken days out fishing, shooting, and going to the fantastic Ivy League university town of Princeton. Ron and I had explored the original 17th Century Nassau Hall building there and marvelled at the classic Neo-gothic archways and lanterns that were scattered all around the campus.

The Gothic University Chapel was as impressive as I remember and had one of the largest collections of precious stained glass in the US at that time. I loved wandering around the old buildings and sitting on the stone benches in the courtyard of East Pyne Hall just soaking up the history and atmosphere of such a great place of learning. The red stone was greying from years of wear and pollution generated from the numerous car and truck exhausts, but it had still been a magnificent thing to see.

The bump of cat's eyes brought me back to tonight as Ron exited the I 95 at the intersection with the I 195. It took less than a minute to reach Allentown centre before turning right on Main Street and past a row of new smart residential houses. Five minutes later and two miles out of town on the Old York Road, a white picket fence appeared on our left. It stretched as far as the eye could see in the early morning moonlight.

The first field was broken up by a large copse of elm trees a thousand or so yards from the road, but the rest of it was open ground. We travelled a mile further before coming across a triple line of elm trees and a wall that created a barrier between the road and the property.

'This is it,' Ron said. 'We pass the main entrance in 30 seconds.'

The heavy ornate metal gates hung from two huge pillars that supported a stone archway. A carved stone lion stood proudly on top looking down on whoever dared to approach. The nine foot wall on the left side of the gate with its sharp spikes protruding from the top stones ran a least half a mile back down the road inside the line of the elm trees. To the right of the gates the wall extended for at least the same distance before cutting back away from the road.

'The wall goes all the way around the main property,' Simon said. 'The actual house is tucked away in the far right corner where there is a second gate that leads to the stud farm, stables and gallops. The miles of white picket fence we saw border the whole property, and it's all wired.'

Dave was waiting for us in a big old RV at Crosswicks Creek, which was down a narrow track that led to a small woodland park three quarters of a mile from the main gates to the estate on the other side of the road. It was well away from prying eyes and completely devoid of people at this time of the night. After a handshake from Dave and a brief introduction to Bill, Dave placed a map and three enlarged photos on the bonnet of Ron's wagon.

'We are here,' Dave said as he pointed to a wooded area on the West of the Armendariz estate. 'The way in is at the corner of the East and South wall. It is a blind spot and far enough away from the paddock gate and stables not to be heard. You also get a clear view of the rear of the house from this point.' Dave moved his finger to a square he had drawn on the map. 'It's a gardener's shed full of sit-on mowers and other gardening kit. It's from there you get this view.'

Dave picked up the first photo. It was the rear view of a very grand and huge Gothic style mansion, built in a rich red stone similar to East Pyne Hall at Princeton. It must have at least 60 or 70 rooms in it.

'This is as close as I got, there are guard patrols every 30 minutes. All the ground floor entrances have heavy doors that are at least double bolted. All windows also have heavy bolts and latches, which definitely will be linked to the security system, and be alarmed.' Dave said.

Bill took the photo from Dave and I picked up the one showing the front of the building. It would house at least 100 students and contain several lecture theatres if it was in Princeton. The last photo was an aerial that showed the driveway from the gate to the house and the open spaces out to the perimeter walls. A few mature trees were scattered around, but none within 500 yards of the house, which was surrounded by mown grass lawns, cultivated plants and flower borders. There were also lights, hundreds of them, and cameras. Someone had taken a lot of time to plan the security on this place.

A couple of minutes passed, everyone silent studying the map and photos.

'Dave your assessment of the place would be what?' Bill asked breaking the silence.

'Not a good place for a hit, too many guards, too much open space, too many heavily secured doors and windows and a lot of ground to cover if you wanted to get the fuck out of there fast.' Dave said.

'I agree. Harry what do you think?' Bill asked.

'I agree with you both. It would be very difficult to get to the house undetected and it could get noisy very quickly with just one small fuck up. We can be sure they will have a significant arsenal of weapons in the house and they will know how to use them. We already know Eva and Costa can and then there would be the guards to contend with plus half the New Jersey police force in minutes, no doubt. This is no good,' I concluded.

Bill was studying the photos on the bonnet checking one last time if we had missed anything.

'Well, I for one need to get my head down, I'm fucked, and my head hurts. Let's go and have a look what happens when they leave in the morning. We can assess our options then as we already have their offices staked out,' Ron said as he rubbed the stitches on the two inch cut on the back of his head.

He did look shagged out, which was not surprising as he had got straight into the job as soon as he had arrived back in the US.

'I'll stay and keep stag tonight Ron,' Dave said. 'There is a place with good cover directly across from the main gate. I'm sure if what I saw this morning is repeated then we will get some activity around 0500 when the fresh food deliveries start to arrive. They all have breakfast at 0730 and the oldest son Dante is gone and on his way to the city by 0800. There were at least three people in the black limo he used this morning, the two bodyguards up front, plus I know there was someone else in the back with him because when they drove past me the nearside back window was open slightly and I saw another person sitting next to him. I couldn't tell if it was a man or woman. Roberto Armendariz, the 20 year old younger brother, leaves around 0850 and always goes by train from Trenton. He takes the Conrail, sorry the New Jersey Transit as it's now known, into New York rather than a limo.'

'Thanks Dave,' Ron said.

'Dave, why does Roberto take the Transit with so many cars and limos at his disposal,' I asked.

Simon answered as he had done the research on him.

'He was in a bad car crash when he was 11 and suffered serious head injuries that left him with some disabilities. He now suffers from fits and also has some minor speech and movement problems. Since the accident, he has lost his nerve with respect to being on the highways and doesn't travel distances in a car unless he has to. The short distance to the train he seems to handle OK, but for anything longer than that he will only travel with his father. He always travels with the same two bodyguards who are with him 24/7. He now 'works' with his brother in the City and has a nice office and a couple of pretty secretaries to look after him. But, he is prone to violent outbursts and has to be restrained sometimes and that is why the two goons are with him all the time. Eva Muscardin is also known to be very protective of him since his accident. They have always been close and she likes to spend a lot of time with him, when she is not with his brother.'

'Thanks Simon,' I said, my mind already starting to play out some different scenarios for the next day.

I crashed on one of the single bunks in the RV immediately after Dave headed off into the dark woodland towards the estate, my brain still buzzing.

3

0506, Tuesday 8th November 1983

We passed the main entrance to the estate heading towards Allentown at 0515, no one eyeballing the two armed guards that loitered next to their red stone gatehouse. Simon stopped the Eagle wagon half a mile further up the road from the entrance. The dense copse of elm trees on the opposite side of the road provided plenty of cover as we headed back towards Dave's position in a shallow gulley a few feet back in the copse opposite the gates. We crawled in next to him at 0540 and Dave told us that since the first delivery of fresh bread and pastries at 0506, two lorries and one more van had passed through the gates. Each one getting the full monty with respect to a security check. One guard gets the driver out of their cabs and gives them a full body search, the other checks the underside of the vehicle, inside of the cab and finally the back before letting them in. Two more guards do exactly the same again when they arrive at the house and once they are unloaded the vehicles are escorted off the property.

Moments after Dave had finished telling us we had missed the exit of the fresh meat, and the fresh veg lorries, bright headlights shone straight into our eyes buggering up our vision instantly. We all pressed ourselves hard into the dirt not daring to look up and risk being compromised by the guards who were only 40 feet away scanning the road for traffic. One of us needed to see what or who it was so I raised my head only a couple of inches off the deck and focused on the gates. 'Jeffries – The Freshest Fish delivered daily' was splashed across the side of the refrigerated van as it pulled out onto the main road in front of us.

There had been no more traffic in or out of the estate by the time it was getting light at 0700. The two guards had periodically come into view as they did a short circuit around the main entrance, but that was it.

Dante Armendariz left at exactly 0800. The long black limo turned right out of the estate being escorted by two heavies in a big black Lincoln.

'There will be at least one other bodyguard with him inside the limo,' Dave said clearly so we all could hear over the sound of the limo and Lincoln speeding away.

We couldn't see inside the limo so didn't know if Eva and/or Costa were travelling with Dante this morning. Ron had Gary, another one of his SEAL team, in Bryant Park, watching Dante's offices on 6th Avenue. We would find out at the RV at 1200 if anyone else was with him in the car. We had made the decision that we would wait until Roberto left on the off chance he might take some 'friends' along with him for the train ride. Simon could not confirm if Eva had made this journey with him before, but it was not inconceivable that she would. I could only pray that she would and if she did, Eva Muscardin was going to die today.

It was damp and cold in the trees but at least it wasn't raining. Forty minutes went by without any action, but the guards stayed alert and prowled in front of the gates every five minutes now it was light. Their M16 semi-automatic weapons hanging loosely across their chests, hands on grips and stocks, ready to go. Our own sterile M16s supplied by Ron at our sides.

'The gates are opening,' Dave whispered as he looked down at his watch. 'It's 0855, this will be Roberto,' he said.

The four of us pushed ourselves hard into the ground again, but with heads up. Ron had craned his neck backwards so he could fix his binos on the Silver SUV that was heading slowly up the driveway towards the open gates.

'That's definitely the kid, he won't let them drive over 35mph,' Dave whispered.

We didn't need the binos to see Roberto's head appear between the two front seats of the SUV as it stopped outside the gates ready to turn onto the main road. He said something to the goon who was driving and then sat back allowing me to see clearly who was sitting next to him.

I can hardly believe my eyes, she was there; the fucking bitch I was going kill today. I watched as she briefly raised her bandaged right hand and rubbed her nose. No makeup could hide the bent and still bruised nose and the ugly red scars on her face from where Gerri had bitten her. A terrible rage exploded inside me, my heart thumping big time as the adrenaline surged through my veins making my hands sweat and shake uncontrollably until I clamped them tightly into fists. It took every ounce of self-restraint and a very strong hand on my arm to stop me legging it out of the trees there and then and turning the SUV, and her, into something resembling a pepper pot.

'The kid Roberto is not part of this Harry,' Bill said whilst not releasing one bit of the strong grip he had on my arm.

Ron placed the binos on the ground next to his head and was focusing on the SUV that had turned left onto the main road heading towards Trenton railway station.

'The other fucker is in there as well,' Ron said just as I caught sight of Costa sitting next to the driver. I hadn't clocked him after spotting Eva. The kid's second bodyguard was sitting next to him in the back seat.

Dave was already on the radio telling Simon we would be on our way back to the Eagle wagon as soon as the SUV had cleared the end of the road. Bill was up and moving away fast from our position as soon as it did. I got my shit together and started moving as Dave slipped the shortwave radio into Ron's hand and headed the other way back towards the RV at Crosswicks Creek.

Once out of sight of the gates we started running fast through the trees and back to the RV point where Simon had dropped us earlier that morning. Simon was there, engine running, kerbside doors open. I piled in the back after Bill and Ron jumped in the front seat as Simon hit the throttle and the wagon lurched forward, the nearside tyres throwing up dirt and grass before getting a grip on the tarmac. The SUV had a good five or six minutes start on us now, but the road was straight and empty and we knew that the train would not be leaving before 0920, whatever time they got there.

We followed Old York Road until it joined South Broad Street, which took us through some nice residential areas under Highway 130 and the I95. We then hit the outskirts of Trenton.

'The train station is off South Clinton Avenue. We need to be on this side of the station,' Ron said.

'I know this town Ron, we will be on the right side of the station in two minutes,' Simon responded.

'Simon, we will have to dump the car because you need to be with us as Eva and Costa know what we look like so us three will have to stay out of their sightline, which puts you on point.

'OK Bill,' Simon responded.

'Ron will have the radio to communicate with you, but no talking. Just stick with them and if you think we have a chance of making the hit on the train, it's two clicks and we will move to you. If you need us to stay put, or stop if we are on the move, it's one click. Nothing else. We will wait for your signal. OK Simon?'

'Got it Bill,' Simon acknowledged. He liked the way this SAS man operated, no fucking around and keep it simple.

Simon kept the Eagle wagon at 30mph in the morning traffic taking us past many substantial leafy suburban properties. We stopped at the intersection at Liberty Street and turned right. Traffic was heavier here slowing us up a bit, but Simon wasn't concerned.

'We only need to do a couple more blocks before turning down Clinton towards the station. We will be there in a minute,' Simon informed us.

We found the Silver SUV in the South car park, there was no sign of the inhabitants. A minute later Ron had the wagon locked and alarmed after we had fed the four M16s into the boot through the middle drop down panel in the back seat. Simon was already at the entrance to the high glass walkway that linked the North and Southbound platforms and was heading up the stairs as we walked across the car park. I followed him 20 seconds later; I was about 30 yards behind him. At the top of the stairs, I moved in close to the South side wall of the covered walkway and then took a couple of tentative paces forward to look for Eva through the glass windows. I couldn't see her, or any of them, because of the two long grey roofs stretching 250 yards Northwards alongside the tracks that provided the shelter for the open platforms.

I got halfway across the walkway and stopped to search the ground below again. I knew this was a critical moment because if anyone looked up from the edge of the platform they would see me clearly through the windows. I looked back down the walkway to see Bill and Ron 30 yards behind me at the top of the stairs. Someone started to speak over the station tannoy system, the message was almost completely unintelligible, but we all got: next train – platform 3 – New York.

I froze as I reached the top step of the stairs leading down to platform 3. Simon was standing a couple of yards from the bottom step glancing up, obviously waiting for me and the others to appear. His head was making very slight moments left to right. Something was wrong and he didn't want us down there. His head stopped moving and looked down as he pulled up the left sleeve of his jacket to check his watch. A black Luminox, Navy Seal standard issue.

Simon's head stayed down as Costa, Eva and the kid came into view directly opposite him at the bottom of the stairway. The other two goons followed close behind them. I turned around quickly and back into the walkway and almost ran straight into Ron and Bill. I shook my head slightly and walked past them back the way we had come. They turned and did the same.

Bill and Ron followed me for a few yards until I stopped where we couldn't be seen from the platform below.

'What's up? Where is Simon?,' Bill asked.

'I don't know exactly, but I'm sure he is close to them as they would have walked right by him,' I said.

The announcer was off again. Her tinny unintelligible words just making a screeching noise across the station platforms. All we got was – 'xt rain, Ne ork, plat orm 3'. The train for New York eased its way into the station moments later, brakes squealing loudly as more pressure was being applied to them. I could clearly see the bulk of the driver in the front cab, his manky Casey Jones striped hat tipped over onto the right side of his head. I just couldn't stop the TV shows soundtrack playing in my head momentarily as I looked at him.

We moved quickly to the top of the stairs as the train pulled in. It had been stopped for 30 seconds when I descended the stairs two steps at a time landing cleanly on my right foot as I hit the platform. I assumed the first class carriages would be at the front of the train so I was praying that Eva and the rest of them would have gone up the platform after passing Simon. I had no time to check, I needed to find an open door so I headed quickly towards the back of the train. The second to last carriage door was open and five seconds later I was on the train, Bill and Ron stepping onboard directly behind me.

Bill closed the door and then looked out the window up the length of the train. The platform and the two foot yellow 'mind the gap' painted strip was empty. The station guard checked that the last couple of doors were closed before he blew a loud blast on his whistle. The train moved off with a sharp jerk before beginning to pick up speed more smoothly, we had made it onto the train undetected, we hoped.

4

The train passed under the first road bridge and then a second and a third in quick succession. The natural light fading for a few seconds each time we went under one. The radio in Ron's pocket clicked once, Simon needed us to stay put. We were passing large factories and warehouses on both sides of the tracks now and still picking up speed. I got up and looked through the door window into the carriage in front of us and then walked back to check the one behind. There were still a few empty seats back here, but I knew we would be picking up many more commuters shortly for their hour long journey into the city.

The radio was silent. We had to wait for Simon to make contact again after the first click. We waited another two minutes then one click again. Two minutes later and I see Simon making his way through the forward carriage towards us. He was in no rush, he looked like any other bloke just going off for a piss.

Simon sat down beside Ron, facing me. Bill was sitting next to me on my right. Simon leaned forward and spoke quietly.

'They are in the first carriage. The two goons were sitting by the doors at each end and there were approximately 10 or 12 other passengers in the carriage with them. I got a good view of them before the goon nearest to me stood up and came to the door. His mate must have clocked me looking in and for a split second I saw the fucker staring at me through the door window as I turned and walked back up the carriage to come here. He didn't follow, I checked.'

'OK, we'll have to wait until we are closer to New York to see if anyone gets out of that carriage. The fewer people in there, the better.' Bill said.

Nothing I could do for a minute except look out the carriage window and observe the numerous fields, woodlands and big executive type houses go past the window. They hardly registered as all I could think about was that bitch and that other fucker, Costa, being only being 50 feet away from me.

I knew this was not the right moment, but a massive part of me just wanted to go and wade in and waste those two fuckers. But, I also knew there were a lot of innocent Americans in that carriage and I had no doubt that Eva, Costa and the other two goons would not hesitate to take anyone out who got in their way.

At Princeton Junction, the masses of suits and power dressed female executives piled off the train heading to one of the many office blocks only a couple of thousand yards from the station. There were also the academic professor types and their earnest looking students heading off to be educated at one of the premier universities in the United States. Everything around here smelled of money.

The train jerked its way into motion again and continued heading North. We only saw one person leave the first class carriage at the station, but several got into it.

'If we are going to hit them, it will have to be in New York if we don't lose any more people from that carriage,' Bill said.

'They may take the tube, the kid likes it, apparently, fuck knows why,' Simon said. 'The tube stations are smelly shit holes and the trains are mostly old and fucked up.'

'Said like a true New Yorker Simon. Don't hold back, just tell us what you really think,' Ron was smiling as he took the piss out of him.

We all smiled briefly allowing a small moment of relief before getting down to the next phase of the plan.

'The way I see it is we most likely will not get a shot at them until they are clear of this train in New York. There are too many people still on it and there is way too much risk of civilian collateral damage. We will track them individually, keeping out of each other's way, but in each other's eye line at all times.' Bill was scribbling on a piece of paper as he spoke.

'Simon how far is Dante's office from the tube station?' I asked.

'A couple of hundred yards from street level. A minute or so walk, that's all Harry.'

'I imagine it's all open ground, just sidewalks and the road?'

'Yeah,' Simon replied as he pulled out his worn pocket map of the New York Subway system. I leaned over to get a better view of the map he was spreading out on the table.

'There are two ways they can go,' Simon started talking with his finger on the map by Penn Street station. 'But as I said, the kid likes the train and the tube so if he doesn't get his little ride in the mornings, when he wants one, he can get a right piss on and throw big tantrums. There was a piece in the New York Post a few months ago after he whacked a transit cop who tried to calm him down at one of the stations. It all got sorted on the QT though and the cop was apparently seen driving around in a nice new Chevy a couple of weeks later. The shortest route would be to take the route 1 from 34th Street to Times Square on 42nd Street and then the 7 Flushing Local through Manhattan to 5th Avenue and Bryant Park. That would give them only a 400 yard walk to the office entrance.'

Simon paused as he moved his finger over 8th Avenue. 'My guess though, and this is based on where the incident with the cop was: they will head for the A line, 8th Avenue Express and go down to 14th Street. It's only two stops. They will then get on L, the Canarsie Local to 6th and 14th, then transfer to the F, 6th Avenue Local North for the three stops to 42nd Street – Bryant Park on 6th Avenue. It will take 15 minutes or so. The kid had the cop slapping session at 6th and 14th.'

We all pored over the subway map when Simon finished. Plainsboro shot by on our right. More expensive real estate.

'You know your subway network Simon,' I said. 'We just need to see which way they turn at Penn Street station.'

The next few minutes we spent trying to memorise subway stations, track numbers, short cuts and distances on foot from stations on the expected routes.

We agreed the main RV's and an ERV if things really went tits up. Ron also provided a secure phone number we could call as a last resort.

More well-dressed suits joined the train at Monmouth Junction parking themselves in the best seats they could find, instantly snapping open a fresh copy of the New York Times, of course. They obviously didn't want to make eye contact or conversation with anyone. Others rummaged in briefcases and removed files of papers and documents. A fat guy in a tight fitting suit sat down across the passageway from us, the document he was going to read already out of his briefcase. He settled himself in and sat there without a care in the world with absolutely no regard to who could be looking at his document on the table. It was clearly marked 'important and confidential' in big red letters. Just who you need on your team, I thought.

We travelled several miles further and began to see more and more factories lining the tracks. 'North Brunswic.' Simon didn't manage to get the 'k' out for Brunswick. He leaned his head forward casually and rested his cheek on his right hand.

'Don't turn around Harry, one of the goons is looking straight at me through the carriage door window.' I didn't move. Bill and I had to rely on Ron and Simon now as we had our backs to the door. Ron looked out of the window at nothing in particular.

Simon kept his head down studying the subway map on the table in front of him for a further minute. Then without looking or talking to any of us he made a show of folding up the map and shoving it into his coat pocket. He made the briefest of eye contact with the goon, who was still looking at him from behind the window, before nonchalantly staring out the window.

Simon didn't move but kept the goon in his peripheral vision. New Brunswick came and went and then I saw the big signs for Rutgers State University, but I wasn't able to think clearly on what or why it meant something to me.

Simon looked back at us and spoke quietly.

'He's fucked off, but he's definitely got a problem with me. I think I'm compromised.'

'Go to the last carriage and stay out of sight. We have to assume they will be on their guard now. Shit.' Ron said through gritted teeth.

Simon was already on his feet and heading down the carriage away from us. I watched him go through the door and then slide into a free seat facing me halfway down the last carriage. He removed his coat and produced a baseball cap from somewhere. His head was down, but eyes were up.

I slipped my hand behind my back to check the Sig Sauer P220 that Ron had given me was in the right place. The 5 inch Balisong switchblade, as Simon had called it, it was a flick knife to me, was also easily accessible in the right pocket of my bomber jacket. Many years ago in my teens Simon had showed me how to 'flip' the two handled knife with one hand and in one movement expose the blade ready for use. The knife was a great piece of kit for close quarter work and it would be perfect in this environment, if I needed it.

A few more people got on and off the train at Edison, but the overall volume didn't change much so no one had to stand in the aisles. I could still see

Simon clearly in the next carriage his eyes constantly scanning the door behind me. The train jerked into life again slowly pulling away from the platform.

'They are still on the train.' Bill said after he had scanned the platform to see whether Eva or any of the others had got off.

Ron had also been scanning the platform and exits.

'I agree, Bill,' he confirmed.

5

I scan the train route in the onboard magazine I'd found. Rahway was the next stop in about eight or nine miles, then it was just a few more stops; Linden, Elizabeth and Lincoln Harbor City before getting into Penn Street station. We were all on edge and ready to fight, but if Simon had been pinged it was going to make things a lot more difficult, especially if Eva and the rest of them went for a car at the station.

Outside it was getting much more built up. Houses were bunched tighter together, more factories were blowing out plumes of black acrid smoke, cars backed up in streets with horns blaring and fists were being waved out of the drivers' windows; a sure sign we are getting closer to New York. Elizabeth loomed up ahead and although it was a clear sunny day somehow a gloom had descended over this town. It looked dirty and grimy and all the people had their heads down. You could feel there was a completely different atmosphere around here to the towns just half an hour away back down the line.

Two minutes outside Elizabeth, the depressing scene still filled the windows. I felt Simon's eyes on me rather than seeing them. I was almost too late as I saw his eyes widen and a small movement of his head indicating somebody was behind me. The goon was at my shoulder before I knew it. I couldn't look directly at him, but I knew he was scanning our seats. Ron was leaning against the window staring out of it so didn't look at the goon. None of us did.

Bill had his newspaper up, head buried in it, not making eye contact with anyone. His weapon in the wrong place right now as it was for the rest of us. In my peripheral vision, I saw the goon glance down at me but my eyes stay focused on his hands looking for any moment towards a weapon. He was only there for a second or two, but it seemed a lot longer. He was moving again down the carriage towards the last car where Simon was and was now reaching inside his coat.

'Coño.'

That was a word I knew in Spanish, but was said by an Argentine. Spittle landed on the table in front of me as the Argentine-made Browning flashed across the front of my face pointing straight at Ron's chest. I reacted instantly grabbing the wrist and the gun in front of me with both hands pushing them upwards. The 9mm round left the chamber and blew a neat hole in the roof. 'Bang,' a second round went off.

Screams erupted throughout the carriage. People dived to the floor and flattened themselves across their seats. Costa was taken by surprise by the force of my double grip on his hand and wrist, but not as much as the head butt I rammed into the side of his head. I was up on my feet now and in the aisle still forcing the gun upwards. I didn't see the left hook coming I only felt it smashing into my jaw, instantly shaking my brain and blurring my vision. Another one came and then another one, my nose got the full force of one and then my right eyebrow started to spill blood.

Both my hands were firmly clamped around the gun still forcing it upwards as I pushed him backwards trying to get him off balance. I stamped hard on his left foot trying to break any of the metatarsal bones, but he was not going down yet. In a split second, I moved my right hand from the gun and grabbed his throat squeezing it hard as I used all my strength and weight to force him further backwards towards the carriage door. We crashed hard into the goon that was heading for Simon in the next carriage sending him head first onto a table and spilling the contents of the morning's takeaway coffee cups over the four female occupants cowering in the booth. The noise levels of their screams rose instantly to over 100 decibels.

He was still travelling at a good pace when we hit the door and then I rammed my head into his fucked up face splitting the new stitches that were holding his top lip in place. Costa's blood mixing with my own as it splashed onto my face.

The obvious pain from his lip distracted him momentarily, which allowed me to ram my right knee hard into his balls. As he doubled up I smashed my right elbow down onto the back of his exposed neck. He went down onto his knees pulling me down with him using his free left hand. As my knees hit the deck, I lost my grip on the Browning and instantly Costa slammed the butt of the weapon down onto my left shoulder and as he did so there was another loud bang as the third round exited the chamber. The sound deafening me in that ear.

Screams from the passengers close by were followed by the sounds of things being knocked over. Someone had taken the round. I had no idea who, but had no time to think about that right now. The exposed fatty bit of Costa's thumb was less than two inches from my mouth. Within a second, my teeth had penetrated skin and muscle. Blood seeped into my mouth as I bit down harder trying to get through to the bone. Costa screamed in pain, his hand opened and the Browning fell onto the floor beside me. I had the advantage now.

Costa was on his arse with his back against the door as I released my jaws from his hand, spitting blood into his face as I did so. I gripped his throat again with my free left hand forcing his head into the metal panel in the bottom of the door, but he wasn't giving up. His left fist smashed into my ribs winding me slightly, but my hand stayed clamped tightly around his throat cutting off his air supply. He knew he had to try to dislodge it very soon. I saw Simon's face appear at the door above me.

Another bang. The round penetrated the carriage door next to me above my right shoulder. Costa took advantage of the distraction and grabbed my left wrist trying to rip it free, but it wasn't moving anywhere. His right hand was reaching down for the Browning by my left foot, but I saw him and I wasn't having any of that. My first punch broke his nose. The second his cheekbone and the third opened up his left eyebrow completely from one side to the other. A red mist had descended over me as I threw my fist again and again into his face with all the force I could muster. I don't know how many times I hit him, but I didn't stop until both his hands dropped by his side and he flopped over like a rag doll onto the carriage floor.

Costa's bloodied face was smashed up beyond recognition, but he was still alive. I reached down to retrieve the Browning and only then I saw Ron crumpled on the deck behind me, his hand pressing hard against the 9mm entry wound under his left shoulder blade. A lot of blood had already seeped through his hand, but he had it under control and was still conscious and lucid.

'Go and help Bill, I'll look after fuck face over there,' Ron shouted over the noise. He had his SIG in his right hand ready to take the shot if he needed to.

Bill and the goon were going hand to hand in the aisle at the other end of the carriage. The goon's Browning was on the deck a couple of feet from them. Bill had his Balisong in his right hand and was jabbing it forward towards the goon's throat. The goon had something similar to a 6" British Bowie knife and was slashing at Bill's chest in long arching thrusts. Bill had taken at least one hit from the knife because I saw blood being thrown off his left hand as he avoided another lunge from the goon.

I moved towards them with Costa's Browning out in front of me fixed on the goon's head. My shot was blocked when Bill stepped inside the goon's right arm as he thrust the knife forward towards his chest. Bill clamped the goon's right hand under his left armpit and then drove the narrow bladed Balisong through his windpipe and into the base of the brain. A sharp twist and the goon dropped to the deck. Dead a long time before he got there.

A woman who had been screaming the loudest mainly due to the good splattering of blood on her, had been less than two feet from Bill's execution of the goon and was now completely silent, shock and fear instantly constricting her vocal cords.

Simon had forced his way through the door at the other end of the carriage, pushing Costa's limp body further to the side of the door. He was on his feet but had his leather trouser belt strapped tightly around his bloodied left leg. Even though the bullet from the goon's weapon had gone through a metal door, it had still made a decent sized hole in his left thigh. That was why he couldn't get involved in our fun and games with Costa and the other goon, I realised.

Another loud bang reverberated around the carriage. Simon, Bill and me hit the deck simultaneously and any curious passengers that had put their heads up had now got them fully back down again.

'It's OK guys, that fucker isn't going to trouble anyone anymore.' Ron said with a smile on his face.

He was still sitting in the same position, his left hand still applying pressure to his left shoulder. The SIG in his right hand had a small wisp of smoke rising from the barrel and Costa had a neat hole dead centre of his forehead. Bits of bone, brain and blood splattered the door behind him, thin streaks of it already beginning to run down it. A 9mm Beretta from Costa's ankle holster lay at the side of his body.

'Fuck I missed the Beretta, I should have checked him. Sorry Ron,' I said.

'No worries Harry, these two are not going to fuck around with us anymore, but now we need to get our shit together and get the fuck off this train, fast.'

The train was still moving and as yet there was no sign of guards or police coming through the forward carriage. Newark Airport was now in full view through the windows. Planes were taking off and landing almost one after another and I could see many more on the way in. It was going to be a busy day there, as usual.

People started to move in the carriage and noise was building. I could see our silent lady building up to another hysterical moment, Bill saw it too.

'Everybody, please be calm and stay in your seats. We are police officers,' he shouted. 'Everything is done now, please sit down.'

We saw people visibly relax although still in a state of shock at what they had witnessed. It might take a few minutes for someone to question Bill's statement especially with his English accent, but he had bought us some time and that was what we needed.

The train didn't slow at all over the Passaic River and I calculated we had about eight miles to run until the next stop at Lincoln Harbor, 10 – 15 minutes away. Simon had moved up to the front of the carriage and was sitting on the deck in the gap on the right side of the door, his leg was still bleeding badly but he knew he had to release the tourniquet every two minutes to allow blood to get to his lower leg; otherwise he could lose it. He used the goon's dead body to elevate it slightly.

'I'm fucked' he said, 'I won't be running anywhere for a while.'

'Me too,' said Ron. His breath hoarse and ragged as he struggled with the pain in his shoulder and chest.

I leaned Ron forward and checked his back, there was no exit wound so the bullet was still inside somewhere.

'You and Simon need a hospital and you need one right now,' I said.

'Harry's right.' Bill said as he helped me get Ron into a more comfortable position against the side of the train opposite Simon. Ron took a deep breath that obviously caused him some pain before answering.

'I have a lot of contacts in the NYPD so I can handle this with the cops. Leave their weapons with us though, I'll need them for my story. What's important now is you two need to get the fuck off this train and get Eva before she disappears for good. Simon and me will survive, won't we?'

Simon didn't answer he was staring at the faces peering through the carriage door at the dead body below it.

'It's the other fucking goon Harry, watch out,' Simon shouted at me.

I was side on to the door kneeling at Ron's outstretched feet. Bill was doing a good job stemming the flow of blood from the hole in his shoulder. I turned and saw the goon's face, his close cropped hair and black shirt instantly telling him apart from the other peering faces. By the time I got to my feet he was already legging it up the train to warn Eva and to take care of the kid.

'We need to get off this train Harry,' Bill said as he finished sorting out Ron.

Simon was tightening the belt around his leg, groaning as he did so, but then said. 'Move you two, go and sort out that fucking bitch, but don't harm the kid if you can avoid it. It would bring another whole world of shit down on our heads and we definitely wouldn't want that.'

I felt Ron's hand on my arm.

'Go get them, but be careful son, your mum and Harry Jr need you back in one piece.'

'Thanks dad, I know.'

Ron looked directly into my face and said nothing for a second or two. It was only a moment's silence, but it was enough to take the message on board.

'Now fuck off the pair of you,' he said and then coughed, speckles of his blood adding to the rest on my shirt.

6

After handing Costa's Browning over to Ron, I pulled the dead goon away from the door, but still left him close enough so Simon could elevate his leg on him. Bill now stood in front of the door waving his SIG at those still stupid enough to be peering through the glass.

'We are police officers, please stand back,' Bill shouted again in a fine English accent as we entered the carriage.

Nobody argued and a path cleared to the next carriage door in seconds. I don't think it mattered what we said as we looked like a couple of extras from Death Wish II. We were both covered in blood and had our guns out in front of us, all we needed was Charles Bronson leading us through the carriage waving his own .380 Berretta at the shit scared commuters and that would have completed this scene for everyone.

Ron, Simon and the dead bodies of Costa and the goon were four carriages behind us as the train pulled into Lincoln Harbor station. Even before the train had stopped, doors were opened and people were leaping out onto the platform. A couple of the passengers were screaming and shouting for help as soon as they were back on their feet.

'Harry we need to be sure they get off, Bill said. 'We don't want the goon and Eva going back to try and finish off Ron and Simon before the cops arrive.'

Bill was right as there were no cops in sight on the platform but hopefully any minute now the place would be full of them. The level of noise the frightened commuters made as they ran towards the exits was terrific. People were being bowled over and crushed against barriers on their way out causing innocent bystanders, who knew nothing of what had happened on the train, to panic as well.

'Harry they are off the train,' Bill shouted.

I stuck my head out the window to catch sight of the goon dragging the screaming kid along by his shirt collar. They were only 40 feet away from us. Eva was running behind them but when she got to the exit stairs she stopped, turned and looked directly at me, her face was full of rage and evil menace. Then she was gone down the stairs and into the throng of the panicking crowd.

Bill was already out the door and running. I caught up with him as we reached the top of the stairs that Eva had disappeared down seconds earlier. No one noticed the state of our clothes as we were swept up in the crowd and down them towards the tunnel that linked the platforms. My right hand never leaving the grip of the SIG inside my jacket pocket.

I looked left and Bill right but I couldn't see Eva, the kid or the goon as we were pushed along.

'Harry with me,' Bill shouted over the deafening noise in the tunnel.

There they were, I saw the kid desperately trying to disengage himself from the goon's grip as he was being dragged along. They were heading left at the end of the tunnel and to the North exit. There was a taxi cab sign above them pointing to the left.

Bill grabbed hold of me and we let ourselves get carried along by the crowd, but we were being moved away from the exit we wanted to get to. It was time for action. I started to shove and push my way left, Bill did the same. We were blocked by two pin-stripe suited blokes who had scared rabbit-in-the-headlights looks on their faces. One of the dickheads aimed a punch at my head but missed and hit some poor sod next to me.

I got my right hand out of my jacket pocket before he could throw another one, I left the SIG behind so I could make a good fist. The punch flattened his nose, blood pouring down onto his flash suit as he fell to the ground like a sack of shit. People started to fall over him, but I couldn't be arsed about that as we had to get out of here. More people started to scream as they desperately tried to push back the other way to avoid the increasing heap of bodies now forming around the punchy dickhead. Bill grabbed my arm and pulled me towards a gap that had opened up giving us a clear run to the exit.

Bright sunlight was waiting for us as we got to street level, causing me to squint for a second. The first round from the goon's weapon whistled past my left ear. I didn't hang around to see where it ended up. A young woman in her 20's took the second, her body spinning around from the force of the impact as she hit the deck in front of me. She had taken a round in her chest, penetrating the soft tissue of her left breast and then through the centre of her heart. Blood began to pump out immediately covering the front of her pink blouse.

Bill started to return fire as I stopped and got onto my knees beside her, my hands pressing down on the entry hole trying to stem the flow of blood. But it was hopeless and within seconds she was dead expelling her last breath as her eyes slowly closed.

Eva had dragged the unfortunate driver out of the boxy white Lincoln by his hair. He had been waiting for his passenger from the train but now he was sprawled out on his back with his hands raised as Eva levelled her weapon at him. Bill fired just as she moved to get into the car, the round creasing her left shoulder. She barely flinched as she threw herself in the driver's seat screaming at the goon to get in. The kid was already cowering down on the back seat.

The goon had barely got in when Eva gunned the huge car straight towards us, mounting the sidewalk at speed. We both dived right at the last second, rolling once and then standing up ready to take a clean shot at her if we could get one. The Lincoln crushed the dead body of the young woman as it ran over her, the front nearside wheel smashing her ribs from the impact and sending up a large spray of blood from the bullet's entry hole.

There was no point in giving chase on foot as the Mark VI V8 engine got up to full revs sending Eva and her passengers hurtling towards the car park exit, its rear tyres squealing and smoking from the power being applied through the rear axle. The back end of the car was snaking as it sped through the exit and took a sharp left towards the Lincoln Tunnel, the back end hung out so far at one point that anyone without significant driving skills would not have been able to bring it back under control. Eva obviously had those skills as she got the Lincoln back heading in a straight line and in the right direction.

'Get out of the car please, we need it urgently for police business,' Bill was urging a protesting elderly man and his wife. 'Please hurry sir,' Bill was still being polite as he manhandled the man from the driver's seat.

I got to the woman as she pulled herself out using the top of the doorframe as a lever. She was a bit more mobile than the old boy who was being helped to sit down on the kerb by Bill.

'Don't scratch it please, it's very new,' the old dear said as she looked over the top of her glasses at me. I didn't have time to answer.

The old dear was right though, the new Cream Cadillac Seville was very shiny and the interior smelled heavily of new leather that was everywhere. The plush, thick carpet deadened any noise from the road, which we were covering at some speed now, but it didn't stop us hearing the squeal of the tyres when we hit the same corner Eva had gone round a minute earlier. The peculiar overhanging box shaped backend stepping out as the Lincoln had done.

A couple of smooth opposite lock moments of the steering wheel and Bill had the Cadillac straightened and screaming down Waterfront Terrace to a hard right turn that would have made the chrome spoked wheels bend a bit. We covered the couple of hundred yards on 19th street at 70mph but then Bill had to hit the brakes hard as all four lanes at the lights were full of traffic. The Cadillac squealed to a halt sideways on behind the last cars in the queues.

'Fuck.' Bill cursed, but immediately saw a gap appear on the opposite carriageway.

He hit the gas again and crossed over the centre line before turning left in between two cars coming the other way, only narrowly missing the second one.

We turned right at the intersection and gunned it onto Willow Avenue. The back end stepping out again threatening to spin us into the oncoming traffic. Bill held it. I thought briefly about the old dear and her chap and the state they would be in if they could see what Bill was doing to their beloved new car. The tunnel entrance was only 1000 yards away now.

'Harry we need some cash and we need it quickly.' Bill said as he manoeuvred the Cadillac into a lane with only two cars in front of us.

There was no way of getting around them so we had to wait for the man in the toll booth to take the couple of dollars fee and let us through.

'I'm taking the South tunnel Harry. It's a guess, but we know where they are heading even if we don't get eyes on them soon,' Bill said.

'Sounds about right to me,' I replied.

I remembered the South tunnel was the newest of the three by about 20 years, the high archway and stone facade much less weathered and blackened from the years of constant exhaust fumes than the other two. The massive billboards above the entrance were trying to entice us to buy the latest jeans and the biggest meatiest beef burger in the world as we entered the tunnel. Bill drove as fast as the traffic would let him through the gloomy atmosphere under the

Hudson River. It seemed to take forever to cover the one and half miles to the other side.

The sunlight was blinding as we exited under West 38th Street on 10th Avenue. Bill backed off a little as we swung onto Dyer Avenue, the New York skyline towered above us filling every available space.

'Bill, it's a white Lincoln. It looks like the one,' I said, pointing ahead. Not quite believing it.

It was a couple of hundred yards ahead driving well within the speed limit. The big lump of a car standing out from the rest of traffic because of its distinctive box shape and its new brilliant white paintwork.

Eva just managed to get the Lincoln through the lights on 36th street before they changed. We still had 150 yards to go. Red brake lights lit up in front of us in all four lanes.

'Shit,' I said loudly.

'We're going around them, hang on,' Bill said as he pushed through a gap on the inside lane crossing onto the white hatched area that was empty.

Horns began to blare as we raced up the fire lane illegally. I could only imagine what names they were calling us, wankers probably being the main one.

We stopped briefly at the intersection, the lights were still on red but we couldn't let that slow us down. Bill saw the gap between three yellow cabs just as I did, and went for it. The impact from the cab connecting with the last few inches of the Cadillac's boot had us swinging towards the pavement and the six foot wall that surrounded a block of apartment buildings. My head bounced off the side window as Bill wrestled with the steering wheel trying to get the car straight again.

Bill had almost got the heavy Cadillac straight when it bounced off the eight inch kerb in front of the apartment building, crushing the fancy wheel hubs and completely scuffing up the offside shiny white walled tyres. Somehow the tyre stayed inflated so Bill gunned the engine again to close up on the Lincoln ahead.

I glanced over my shoulder to see mayhem at the intersection. The cab that had tried to avoid hitting our rear end had bounced off us and T-Boned another yellow cab. That had been pushed into the front of a lorry waiting at the head of the queue on Dyer Avenue and people were starting to get out of their cars, some scratching their heads wondering what the fuck had just happened.

No time to worry about them right now because the Lincoln was only 50 yards in front as we went through the West 35th Street intersection. The shadows from the buildings blocking out the strong sunlight on both sides of the street. Two towering apartment blocks directly ahead meant we were coming to a T-junction.

'Got to be a left up here, they will want to take the quickest route to Sixth Avenue and Bryant Park…' Bill couldn't finish what he was saying because the Lincoln suddenly put the hammer down.

The Lincoln's tyres started spinning and screeching on the tarmac surface, smoke billowing into the air. Eva threw the car hard left down West 34th Street.

'Fuck it, we need to finish this now Bill, we may never get another chance.' I shouted over the screeching tyre noise as the Cadillac shot forward again closing in on the Lincoln some more. It was only 30 yards ahead of us now.

By Ninth Avenue, only a car length separated us. Eva was weaving violently between two lanes only slowing when she clipped the front end of a white van in the last lane of cars at the intersection. She powered on down towards Eighth Avenue, the traffic building the closer we got to it.

The lights were with us this time, but Eva still needed to bump an old blue pickup out the way, which sent it spinning across the road and onto the pavement. Luckily no one got tagged by it as it came to rest a couple of inches from a huge glass shop window. Cops were getting wind that something was happening on their streets because the sirens were definitely getting louder, and closer. Eva must have heard them too.

The magnificent circular building of Madison Square Garden appeared briefly on our right, a place Ron had taken me to a few times as a kid. The Empire State Building standing proud and tall in the sunshine in front of us and at this speed if we blink we will miss completely the massive Macy's store coming up on our left shortly.

Seventh Avenue intersection began to fill the windscreen. All lanes were stopped. Fuck knows what Eva was doing, but she was way too late hitting the brakes and ploughed straight into the back of the queue of cars. She took out another yellow cab and a small Japanese hatchback that crumpled under the sheer weight, velocity and impact of the Lincoln. Other cars were pushed into each other and the one at the front of the queue went straight into the path of an oncoming greyhound bus. The bus T-boned it and pushed it 30 yards up the road before it stopped.

Bill couldn't avoid ramming the Lincoln, we were too close and going too fast. The front end of the Cadillac was totalled from the crash, the shiny new bumpers and radiator grill was one piece of mangled metal now. I was ready for the impact so stopped myself being thrown up against the windscreen. Bill had braced himself against the steering wheel and so also survived intact. So had the windscreen until the first round shattered it.

The goon was out the Lincoln on my side dragging the kid out with his left hand and firing with his right. I ducked as the second round punctured my open passenger door. I was ready to return fire with my SIG, but paused just in time as the goon pulled the kid right in front of him to use him as a shield. The cowardly bastard.

Another round hit the deck by my left foot. The goon was having trouble holding the kid and aiming properly. I returned fire, two rounds over the goon's head. It was enough to make him turn and leg it, dragging the kid behind him.

Bang. Bang. Two more rounds came at us. The first penetrated the driver's door and the second shattered the window above it. Eva was out the Lincoln now, standing straight with legs slightly apart, both hands on the Browning looking for Bill's head. Bill had ducked down into the footwell of the Cadillac and so had to reach up and return fire through the shattered windscreen without being able to see his target. He aimed high as there were too many people close by, we both knew that the collateral damage was already too much, I thought momentarily about the poor innocent girl at the station. Bill fired off two rounds, his intention was to get her moving. And it did.

Eva was running now trying to catch up with the goon and the kid but was still firing off rounds in the general direction of the Cadillac. One of the rounds almost took my head off as I peered around the passenger door. It embedded itself in the front of a New York 'Mack' garbage truck that had come to a stop behind us. I was already running as steam started to hiss loudly from the hole in the truck's radiator. Bill was a couple of feet in front of me as we negotiated the crashed and stopped cars that spread across the whole intersection. I could see Eva and the goon running down the wide sidewalk on Seventh Avenue. They had opened up a gap of about 150 yards. The kid had also got the message and was a few yards in front of them giving it everything.

'She's heading for Penn. She's going to use the people on the subway as cover and try and lose us in the system,' I shouted over the noise of the commotion around us. Bill heard me but was focusing on the back of the goon's head trying not to lose him in the swelling crowd. They ran straight over West 33rd street, the lights were with them. They wouldn't be for us though.

7

A wall of trucks, buses and cars were closing in on us fast as we ran across the white lined crossing. The big red hand of the 'Don't walk' sign was illuminated for all to see, and for us to ignore. The guy in the Chevy was obviously pissed about something because he wasn't going to yield. I had made it three quarters of the way across when he hit me. I didn't see him until the last second but managed to get my knees up high enough to avoid a direct impact on them. My right calf took the blow and flipped me onto the bonnet and sent me crashing into the windscreen.

A woman screamed from somewhere close by. I had banged my head again and cut it this time. Blood started to run down my forehead and towards my right eye. I could feel it, but couldn't do anything about it for a second as I was winded and dazed. The Chevy driver was out the car now and screaming at me.

'You fucking idiot, didn't you see the lights change? Look what you have done to my fucking car. Get off my bonnet you fucking wanker I'm going to give you a fucking good..........'

He didn't get the last word out as Bill rounded the front of the Chevy and punched the guy hard on the nose. Chevy man squealed like pig and instantly dropped to the ground.

It had taken a couple of seconds, but I'd regained some focus. The guy was a little fat bald headed fucker in a chequered lumberjack shirt with the sleeves rolled up so you could see his tattoos. He wore filthy jeans and timberland work boots and no doubt saw himself as a bit of a hard nut. He wasn't looking very hard or being gobby anymore with Bill standing over him with his SIG pressed into his forehead.

'You OK? Can you walk?' Bill asked as I slid off the bonnet and put my feet down onto the deck. They seemed OK.

'I'm OK,' I said. 'Let's go.'

Bill looked down at Chevy man, his SIG still pressed hard into his head.

'You stay down there until we are gone. If I see you move, you fucking die.'

Chevy man looked like he was going to crap himself, but he didn't say anything, just a small nod was enough for Bill to know he understood.

We ran the short distance to the entrance of Penn Street Station, shouts from two cops behind us wanting us to stop. There was not a fucking chance of that as we crashed through the station doors and started to scan the place for Eva and the goon. There was no sign of her, or him.

I then spotted an old dear sitting on the floor with a gaggle of people around her. A smartly dressed city type woman a few feet further along was just getting to her feet, several shopping bags were lying on the floor around her. We didn't need to be rocket scientists to suss out the route they had taken. Some people hadn't moved, they were sitting on the few available seats or on rucksacks and suitcases just watching the drama unfold around them. Others were walking away towards the departures board avoiding eye contact, not wanting to get involved.

'They are heading for the Eighth Avenue Express. They are going to use the route that Simon showed us.' Bill was running again, but I know he heard me.

We skirted round the people fussing over the two who had been knocked over and were down the stairs at the far end of the hall before the two chasing cops had reached the stations door. We hurdled the turnstiles before anyone realised what was going on. None of the ticket men gave chase, they had seen it all before and it wasn't their job anyway, plus cops were employed to deal with that shit.

We were now directly under Madison Square Garden legging it along the maze of underground corridors. Thankfully the crowds were pretty thin and Bill was right next to me. I thought I had the advantage down here because I'd been through this station many times as a kid so knew the way to Eighth Street without having to look at any signs. Two new passageways ahead buggered that up though.

We had lost the cops but were both blowing a bit now so we stopped by a burger joint for a second so I could get my bearings. The smell of greasy burgers making me feel hungry. I spotted a sign saying temporary diversion to Eighth Avenue. It had changed, thank fuck we had stopped for a second.

We both heard the sound of running feet coming down the corridor so it was time to move. We were directed away from the unfinished refurbishment project and down to an old part of the station. It was dark and dingy down here, the floor was cracked and broken and graffiti images had been hastily sprayed on large parts of the walls. The sound of the announcer behind us telling us that the train to Woodbridge would be leaving in two minutes.

We kept up a good pace and then I saw the stairs down to the platform. I stopped at the top and tucked myself in by the side of the stairs trying to find some cover, my hand inside my jacket pocket gripping the butt of my SIG. Bill was opposite me doing the same.

Peering down into the gloomy sparsely lit space, it was difficult to see any individuals clearly. Steel posts, four yards apart, ran along the whole length of the left and right side of the platform a yard or so in from the edge. The platform was about two thirds full of people jostling for position as the lights on the front of the train appeared below us.

'We have to move now Harry,' Bill shouted across the void.

The noise of screeching brakes cut out any further voice communication so Bill indicated with his hands that he was going to take the right side and me to take the left. No need to acknowledge the signal and I started moving. If Eva or the goon were going to take a shot, it would be now.

Bill reached the bottom first and hid himself behind one of the posts, I made it to another seconds later. The train stopped with a final screech of the brakes and sounds of compressed air being released from somewhere under the carriages. I had seen what happened next many times before, but it always made me smile. The double doors were hardly open, but people were still trying to force their way in, the yellow safety line at the edge of the platform invisible for a moment. The poor sods on the train having to fight their way through the oncoming rush using every ounce of strength so as not to be carried off to the next station.

Bill had seen something. He moved his head sharply towards the train in a motion that meant move your arse. Bill then stepped onto the train with me right behind him. We were in the last carriage of an old rusty silver corrugated style subway train that had definitely seen better days. The inside had been battered by many thousands of bums and boots on seats. Graffiti adorned the inside walls where various unpleasant words had been scratched, sprayed or written in permanent marker.

No one paid us any attention initially, but I did look in a shit state and so did Bill. Blood was still dribbling down my forehead and my clothes and hands were black from dried blood and dirt. The old man on the seat opposite the door looked up at us briefly, but then quickly averted his eyes and buried his head into his paper.

'I saw the goon and kid,' Bill whispered. 'But, I didn't see Eva, I must have missed her getting on the train.'

Bill turned and scanned the platform again through the open doors. I bent down and tried to peer through the carriage windows without much success. They were covered in dirty brown grime that looked like it had been there forever. The doors creaked together and the train jolted forward.

We both scanned the platform again as best we could trying to see behind each of the posts as they flashed by faster and faster. We saw the two cops arrive at the bottom of the stairs, but no Eva. We were plunged into darkness for a second or two as all the lights went out when we entered the tunnel. When the lights came on again, I shuffled over to a space big enough for two next to the rear door.

'I didn't see her,' I said.

'Nor me, so I think we have to assume she is on the train with the goon and kid,' Bill replied.

'Maybe they think they have shaken us off. If that is right, we may get a shot at them at ground level on 42nd Street.'

'OK Bill,' I said. 'We don't want a gunfight down here, there has been too much collateral damage already.'

'You're right Harry,' Bill responded as he bent slightly to look through the door window.

The train's brakes screeched again as we came to a halt in 23rd Street station. More got on than off so we were pinned by the rear door until 14th Street. Bill was out the carriage first. It was mayhem. I got separated from him by a feisty old dear who got in between us trying to get to the space we had just vacated. After some serious pushing, shoving and swearing I popped out the crush of people still trying to push their way onto the train. Fuck knows how they all got on, but they did. It was going to be a tough journey for everyone on board down to 1st Avenue, that was for sure.

8

The way out was 40 feet from where we had exited the train and Bill pinged them halfway up the stairs from his position behind a stanchion on the other side of the platform. Eva stopped briefly to scan the stairs and platform below, but the throng of people carried her away before she had a real chance to look properly.

The L train platform was very close. We used the same routine when we got there and waited at the top of the stairs until most of the crowd had got onto the train. We moved fast as the last couple of people started to board the train and shot through the last carriage doors just as they hissed closed.

We both looked like shit and there were fewer people in this carriage, which I knew was going to be a problem. Some of them noticed straight away the blood stains on our clothes, my grubby hands and the bulge of the weapon in my jacket. I purposely made eye contact with the lookers, their heads instantly moving so they could look elsewhere. Most looked down at the trendy trainers poking out from under their expensive suit trousers or skirts. No doubt their equally expensive shoes were wrapped up in their fine leather briefcases. Most people looked tense and harassed on this train and they weren't the ones who had noticed the state we were in.

The train was up to full speed moving through the district of Chelsea. The clattering and crashing noises of the train on the tracks were synchronised with the violent sideward movements of the carriages. People's heads were shaking up and down and from side to side, but always keeping focus on the trainers, or the squashed piece of discarded chewing gum on the left or right of their feet.

Six feet away a big mean looking black guy in a Led Zeppelin tee shirt was paying a bit too much attention to me and when he rose from his seat and took a step towards me, I thought, not here, not now, you dickhead. Our eyes bored into each other as the gap closed.

'What you been doing man,' he asked almost politely.

'Fuck all that concerns you man. This is police business, just fuck off back to your seat so I can get on with my work.'

Led Zep man didn't move.

'Just sit the fuck down so you don't endanger your own life or anyone else's on this train.' I snarled at him.

We spent the next 4 or 5 seconds nose to nose, nothing was said. Bill watched silently from the door, his hand on his SIG.

His right hand moved fast for a big man and before I knew it his strong fingers closed around my throat. His grip was like a vice tightening.

'Fucking cop my arse. I'm a cop and you've been up to no good, you fucker,' he spat into my face.

Bill was at his side before he knew it. His left thumb driving down between the soft tissue behind the cop's collar bone. At the same time, Bill's right hand got a firm grip on the cop's windpipe squeezing it closed before ramming his right heel into the side of the cop's right knee.

The cop had already loosened his grip on my throat and was already being forced backwards when I heard his knee go with a loud crack causing him to scream out in pain and drop instantly to the deck. The cop's hands went straight to his knee leaving him completely exposed to the punch Bill smashed into his jaw. The second punch and subsequent impact on the metal floor of the carriage rendered our new hero unconscious and finally quiet.

The passengers close by were already up and trying to get away from the downed man, and us two. One lady was about to scream when Bill grabbed her.

'No need for panic my dear,' he said soothingly in his best English accent, but loud enough for everyone else to hear. 'We are police officers tracking some individuals on this train who murdered our colleague less than an hour ago. We need you to be calm and we need your cooperation so as to not alert them to our presence on board the train. Our friend here didn't want to listen so we had to get him quiet. He will be fine in a few minutes. We will be off the train at the next stop so please don't create a scene when we get to the station otherwise the murderers may escape. OK.' Bill finished talking and we saw people relax, some sitting down immediately, most nodding their heads in agreement, others still stood looking at the prone figure at my feet.

'Nice one Bill,' I whispered as we bent down to pick up our friend.

We got the cop safely back into his seat seconds before I felt the brakes being applied and the train beginning to slow down ready for 6th Avenue/14th Street station.

Three people stood up and walked to the door, none of them looked in a panic or distressed. Bill put his thumb and forefinger together to make an OK sign and then held it in front of him towards the passengers. More nods and a thumbs up from a geeky looking college guy. I quickly scanned the platform outside the carriage doors after they had opened. Eva had already exited and was moving towards the stairs in the middle of the platform. Several people stepped aboard our carriage in an orderly fashion allowing us to stay in our positions either side of the doorway. No one paid any attention to the big black guy asleep in his seat.

We step out of the carriage two seconds before the doors hiss shut. Through the crowd, I spot Eva's expensive business suit skirt and her sturdy black shoes disappearing up the right side of the stairs heading towards the mezzanine above us. There was no sign of the goon or the kid, but they weren't our target, Eva was. I stopped behind one of the rusty green vomit coloured painted stanchions close to the stairs. The mosaic tile sign in the wall told me 16th Street exit was left and 14th Street right. The hanging sign above us provided more directions to Uptown and Queens, F and V routes. 'Follow the white arrows,' a very old and faded sign said underneath. The quickest route to

Bryant Park was on the F so having lost sight of her we had no choice but to take the risk that she would take that option.

I went right when I got to the top of the stairs. There was no sign of her. The dimly lit mezzanine echoed to the sound of our running feet as most people had gone the other way and exited the station. Another sign ahead and white arrow told us F route and Uptown and Queens was past the next stairway. When we arrived, the next sign directed us to the furthermost platform for the Uptown train.

We stopped at the top of the stairs leading down to three island platforms that were below us. We would be completely exposed down there with no stanchions or anything else for cover, unlike when we got off the L. We waited, thinking.

An ancient 1930s rusty steel train squealed and screeched into view on the right side of the last platform, sparks pinging off the brake shoes as more pressure was applied. As it slowed down I counted the carriages, it was a big train with twelve grubby brown carriages in total. We still couldn't see Eva, the goon, or the kid so they could be at either end of the platform, if they were there at all. I couldn't bear the thought of losing her now so I purged it from my brain instantly.

The passengers who had left the grubby brown train were coming up the stairs now. I used them for cover as I went down the left side fast. Bill did the same on the other side. The carriage doors were closing and I had not reached the bottom of the stairs so I started to shove people out the way, much to their disgust. The doors were almost closed as my feet hit the platform.

'Bollocks. Fuck,' I shouted at myself.

But, by some miracle, the doors began to open again. I didn't waste a second and dived in through the door of the nearest carriage. The door slammed instantly behind me. Bill had got into the same carriage through the other door several feet away and was now helping up an elegant looking old man off the floor. The old man's walking stick giving him some extra leverage as he eased himself slowly back onto his feet.

'Fucking doors.' Most of the carriage, including myself, heard him say. 'That's the second time in two weeks they have closed on my cane. Thank you young man,' he said to Bill as he stood fully upright.

The old man then lifted up his cane to inspect any damage pausing when he had it halfway up to focus on the state of Bill's bloodied shirt.

'What the fuck happened to you young man?' Bill smiled at the old bugger.

'Nothing sir, just the hazards of the job.' Bill then leaned forward and whispered in the old man's ear. 'I'm a cop and so is he,' Bill said pointing at me as I stopped next to them. 'And we are on the trail of some bad guys who are on this train. You sir and your cane saved the day. Thank you.'

The old boy looked a bit confused by the English accent, but smiled as Bill eased him into an empty seat.

Bill and I realised we were right in the middle of the train so they could be on either side of us.

'You go down the train Harry, and I will go up, whoever finds them will have to wait for the other to come back the other way,' Bill said.

I got to the first door and tried to peer through the corner of the window. It was impossible to see through because of the grime and dirt covering the Perspex, or whatever it was. The carriages themselves were not in much better nick and I doubted whether the yellow chequered cloth seat covers had ever seen a Hoover or washing machine in their lifetime. They were crusty and stained with God knows what and were now a yellowy brown nicotine colour just to finish off the look.

I rubbed the grime off a small patch using spit and my sleeve so that I could see enough to be confident to go through. The next carriage door window was even grubbier than the last one so it took a couple of extra seconds to do the same job. I continued to move cautiously but quickly through each of the five carriages all the way to the back of the train. 23rd Street station came and went.

They were not in any of them and they hadn't got off so I starting running back towards the front of the train. Bill was waiting for me at the door of the fourth carriage from the front.

'They are all in the second carriage Harry. I'll take the goon out as soon as we get to street level, you finish that bitch Eva. Make her pay for what she did to Kathy.'

The mention of Kathy's name stopped me in my tracks for a second. I hadn't thought about her since we took out Costa and the other goon earlier. Sadness was there of course, but rage and anger were the overriding emotions I felt right now. I knew exactly why I was here and what I had to do; and not just for Kathy.

The train stopped at 34th Street, Herald Square, with the usual increase in decibels, old tired brakes being the key contributor. The old man was ready to step out as soon as the door opened. He lifted his cane at Bill and gave a little nod before mouthing 'good luck.' Bill acknowledged him with a raise of his hand and then he was gone.

I remembered getting disorientated and wandering around this dungeon of an underground station for 20 minutes or more on one of my previous visits to New York. Up and down tricky and slippery stairways in miserable light and not being able to make any sense of the confusing and mixed up direction signs. If the old boy didn't know exactly where he was going he could end up Christmas shopping in Gimbels, but from his dapper clothing I didn't think he was planning to do that today.

Another much newer silver coloured subway train came to a halt on the next platform with a lot more grace and a lot less noise. I leaned out the carriage to look up the platform as the throngs of people piled off the other train. Our old carriage doors started to close, nudging me in the back to let me know it.

Eva, the goon and the kid leapt off the train at that moment. The goon and the kid came out of one door and Eva the other. They ran fast towards the stairs and made it in front of the crowd that had been swelled by people from the other train. I saw them at the very last second and stuck my boot between the fast closing gap in the doors.

'They're running Bill,' I shouted. 'Fuck, they must have seen me,' Bill fumed.

The doors were beginning to open again with considerable help from both of us. The crowd filled the exit stairway leading up to street level so there was only one thing for it. I grabbed the SIG out of my jacket pocket, Bill followed suit.

'Police, police, move, move, get out of the way.' We were both shouting, our SIG's in full view waving them in front of us.

The crowd parted instantly. People pushing and kicking anybody in their way trying to get themselves away from the weapons in our hands. We ran along the short underground mezzanine and around the corner almost crashing into the young couple who were just getting back onto their feet. Their seven or eight year old son and the baby in the pushchair had also been knocked to the floor.

I saw the boy picking up the silver Browning 9mm from under the overturned pushchair that Eva, or the goon, must have dropped. The boy's finger slipping through the trigger guard as if it was a natural thing to do. His mother started to scream, which distracted the kid long enough for me to grab the top of the barrel and reach down with my finger to slip the safety on. I ripped the weapon from the kid's hand and headed after Bill who was already on the bottom step of the stairs leading up to street level.

We walked into a mass of people as soon as we hit the street. They were coming at us from Macy's, Broadway and the Empire State Building behind us. My view up 6th Avenue was blocked because of a mobile magazine stall on the corner that was taking up most of the sidewalk. I stepped away from the stall and moved out into the road and easily picked out Eva and the kid from the crowd ahead. The two of them had got a 100 yard start on us and were about to cross West 35th Street. But where was the goon?

Bill's head took the full force of the metal basket the goon had ripped out of a nearby trash bin. He didn't even have time to get his hands up, the force of the blow knocking him off his feet, but before his head had made contact with the sidewalk the goon was already swinging his right boot towards my nuts. I turned in time for the outside of my right thigh to take the full force of impact. There had to be steel or something in those toecaps because the pain was instantaneous as it shot up and down my leg.

He hadn't broken a bone, but he had been fucking close to it. My leg buckled and my right knee connected heavily with the sidewalk. The goon turned and swung his boot towards Bill's bloodied and bleeding face, but Bill had seen it coming and rolled away in time to see the boot rise up over his body. This was his chance.

Bill rolled back towards the goon, clamped his right hand onto his standing ankle and yanked it towards himself with all the strength he could muster. It was now the goon's turn to smack the back of his head as he hit the sidewalk.

I tried to get up, but my leg was dead and fucking useless. My right foot felt like a lump of floppy whale blubber, all sensations in it were gone. I went down again on both knees only a foot away from the goon's head who was trying to get up. I used the butt of the silver Browning that was in my right hand, the blow connected with his forehead right between the eyes. Something cracked and the skin burst apart filling the goon's eyes with blood.

Bill leapt on top of him, blood streaming from his nose and the numerous cuts on his face that were now streaking across his cheeks and down his neck. The metal edges of the basket had done the job the goon wanted. Bill's first punch spread the goon's nose across his face, blood spraying my already stained shirt.

'Get the fuck out of here Harry, I will deal with this fucker,' Bill snarled. He was mad as hell.

I didn't see the second blow or the outcome, but I heard it. The unmistakable sound of death as Bill rammed the remaining bits of bone in the goon's nose up into his skull, killing him instantly. The piercing screams of a woman realising the goon was dead filled my ears as I hobbled up the sidewalk.

People moved aside as soon as they saw me. To my left I see two cops running towards 34th Street station and the crowd that was now congregating around the dead goon. Bill would have to get a move on, but I couldn't help him with that right now. Eva was moving quickly away from me towards the safety of Dante Armendariz offices.

The leg was getting some feeling back in it and was behaving a bit better by the time I crossed West 35th Street. Fortunately for me it was a glorious cold winter day, no wind and clear blue skies so visibility heading north up 6th Avenue on the East side of the street was perfect. The shadows from the buildings on the West side only reaching halfway across the road at this time of the day.

I travelled the next 100 yards to the West 36th Street intersection much quicker. The leg was still painful but beginning to function better with every step I took. The lights were with me again and the white sign on the post said 'walk.' I was almost running by the time I got to the other side.

The bright red brake lights from the row of yellow cabs, trucks and SUV's two blocks ahead all lit up at the same time. The sound of metal against metal, rubber screeching against tarmac and glass hitting the road, told me I was either fucked because the road and sidewalk would be jammed up and Eva had already passed the intersection, or it was an opportunity that would also slow Eva and the kid down.

I moved as fast as my leg would take me under the multicoloured sun shades hanging down over the front of shop windows. Vivid blues, reds and greens all faded from the sunlight and exhaust fumes filled these streets almost 24 hours a day. The white lettering on the shades that once proudly announced the substance and brilliance of the business inside were now in a very sorry state and looked grey and uninviting; they were not shouting anything to anybody anymore.

The crowd had swelled to over a hundred people in the minute it took me to get to the intersection at West 38th Street. I elbowed my way through until I could get a view of the scene. The huge green city dumpster truck had given the kid a good whack, knocking him several feet off the East side pedestrian crossing. The dumpster driver protesting his innocence to anyone nearby who would listen, but he was drowned out by the sound of the car horns being leaned on by frustrated and trapped New Yorkers. Other motorists were outside their bent cars surveying the damage, others were shouting and swearing at whoever had hit them. It was a total gangfuck.

The kid moved, thank Christ for that. He then started screaming for his mum, his dad, for Dante, not because he was badly hurt, he was making too much noise for that, but because he was probably alone for the first time since his accident. He was shit scared and Eva had fucked off leaving the poor sod to fend for himself.

I was certain she would still be heading for the safety of Dante's office so I pushed my way back out of the crowd. I moved quickly around the edge of the crowd that was now filling the two East side lanes. Car, trucks and yellow cabs were beginning to move in the remaining lanes, they didn't seem to care that someone might have died as long as New York, and them kept moving. Two black and whites with lights on and sirens blaring were pushing through the jam and would be with the kid in seconds.

I had only spent 20 or 30 seconds sussing out what had happened but Eva must have hung around for a bit longer after the accident. She was only 70 yards ahead of me at the intersection on 39th and still on the East side sidewalk. Heavy traffic was coming at her from the right, but she still didn't wait for any lights to change or the flashing 'walk' signs to illuminate. She went for it again, dodging the yellow cabs and everything else.

I heard the one bump and then the horns started. 'You stupid fucking bitch, do you want to die?' screamed a cab driver in a worn and battered flat hat. He was still going at it big time as I legged it past him only 50 yards behind her now. If I could have run at full pelt I would have had her by now, but the dead leg was still slowing me up too much.

I could see the intersection at 40th Street ahead and the trees in Bryant Park. I knew I had to cut her off and stop her getting to Dante Armendariz offices, I needed to push her West so it was time for the leg to respond, painful or not. I moved up a gear and started to close on her. The lights were in her favour this time so she legged it straight across the intersection, barging people aside as she did so.

Eva was moving fast trying to get to the entrance of the park opposite West 41st Street. I could see she was blowing a bit as I closed in on her, I was only 20 yards behind when she reached the gates. They were shut with a large plywood board secured across them proudly announcing that a new entrance designed by some famous, or not so famous, New Yorker was under construction. I was going to get her.

Eva turned and pulled out the weapon she must have taken from the goon that Bill had dealt with on 34th Street, which explained why he hadn't shot us when we got to the top of the stairs. The fancy Silver Browning the kid had picked up must be hers. I was not close enough to tackle her so I dived for a gap between a couple of slow moving yellow cabs. The bullet took out the nearside rear light of the front cab as my head bounced off the tarmac giving me a good sized moped rash on my forehead. It started to sting like hell instantly.

Cars came to a screeching halt all around me, drivers and passengers crouching down as far as they could in their seats. Pedestrians on the sidewalk hit the deck, their eyes darting around to see where the gunshot had come from.

Eva was already running towards 42nd Street when she made a move I wasn't anticipating. The cab driver would have crapped himself when she rammed the gun into the side of his head through the open window, she was in the rear seat seconds later. The cab shot forward, blue smoke billowing off the tyres on the hard tarmac as the driver stamped hard on the accelerator.

I had no choice, I had to do the same, or lose her. A yellow cab's door was wide open 10 feet away where a frightened passenger had legged it when they had heard the gunshot. I ran and threw myself into the back of it.

'Follow that cab,' I screamed at the driver through the scratched and battered Perspex screen that separated us. 'I'm a cop and I need to stop that murdering fucking bitch. She has just killed a man.'

The cab driver was a rough looking home grown New Yorker rather than one of the thousands of immigrants plying their trade as cab drivers in the city, who in my past experiences had no fucking idea of where to go most of the time. The old boy in front looked as if he had been waiting for someone to say the words 'follow that cab' all his life and didn't need to be asked a second time.

I was thrown back into the rear seat from the acceleration and could smell the tyre smoke straight away. I looked back and saw a cloud of blue rubber smoke rising behind us as we shot across the 42nd street intersection, dodging cars, buses, trucks and anything else that was in our way.

Fortunately most people were on the sidewalk as Eva's cab blasted through 43rd Street intersection bouncing off another yellow cab in the process. The driver was still waving his fist as we raced past him seconds later. Eva's cab driver was all over the road and looked for a moment as if he was going to try and turn left into West 44th Street, which would have put him directly into oncoming traffic.

At the last second he swerved hard right clipping the nearside lights and rear bumper of a greyhound bus on his way round, plastic and glass from the bus's rear light littering the road before it came to a stop. My man was in total control of the situation and threaded his cab perfectly through the debris and into the six lanes of traffic. The horn was just an extension of his arms. One hand or the other was constantly leaning on it as we hung onto the back of Eva's cab.

Eva misjudged the sharp turn onto West 45th as she hung out of the passenger window and fired a round in our direction. It went high and left through a window in the office block on our right.

She had been able to put a few cars between us because she had been lucky at Broadway. Everything was still in her favour as she sped through green lights ahead of us and even her driver had his cab heading in a straight line for once. The lights then changed, the BMW in front of us slammed hard on his brakes, obviously not wanting to risk a ticket that was apparently dished out for even the most minor traffic infringements in this City.

Bob, whose name I had spotted on the licence tag in the front of the cab, was not letting that stop him though as he undertook the BMW and sped across the intersection after her. We only lost a few seconds on Eva and were doing 70mph right behind her as we crossed 8th and 9th Avenue. We were only three blocks from the piers now. Where the fuck was she going?

West 45th Street at ground level was in deep shade and the street was busy with vans and lorries delivering or picking up things from the many shops tucked under their manky canopies that were all out for some reason. Eva's driver was driving so fast and erratically he couldn't have seen the four men manhandling the huge heavy leather sofa out of the back of the parked removal truck.

I saw one of the men slip and lose his footing on the rear ramp. He dropped his corner of the sofa before falling onto the road, the other man on the same end let go a fraction of a second later. The sofa was obviously unmanageable for the other two men who dropped their end immediately onto the lorry's ramp. It then began to roll on its castors with one of the men desperately hanging off the back of it trying to stop it. The weight of it was too much for him and it ended up in the road directly in the path of Eva's cab.

The impact launched the sofa towards the sidewalk taking the man on the end of it with it. The cab was catapulted towards the opposite side of the road. Eva's driver had not been wearing a seat belt, big mistake, but he wouldn't need to worry about that anymore. His head hit the windscreen with such force it pushed it outwards in a spider's web pattern, streaks of blood instantly running down the channels in the broken glass. The steering wheel crushed his chest and destroyed internal organs at the same moment in time. He was dead before his yellow cab had come to rest in the side of the USB delivery truck that had been parked on the other side of the road. The cab's impact ramming the truck onto the sidewalk smashing it into the front of the adult bookshop its driver was delivering to.

Bob brought our cab to a stop 20 feet from the carnage, all four wheels screeching and smoking in protest. Eva's cab had settled from the crash and both rear wheels were now back on the road, the front end buried in the boxes inside the truck. I exited the back of Bob's cab fast but couldn't believe the bitch had survived when I saw her kicking open the offside rear cab door.

She leaned against the cab as soon as she was on her feet pointing her weapon straight at me. She fired off two rounds before I could reply with my SIG. Her first took out the front offside light of Bob's cab, the second the windscreen. My first round took out the back window of Eva's cab and the second the rear nearside window where she was standing. She didn't hang around for the next one and ran around the back of the wrecked truck and disappeared from my view. I immediately checked on Bob.

'Just go and get that bitch,' he shouted after me.

I ran over to the back of the other cab and made my way to the driver's window. The driver was fucked. Blood was oozing out of several deep cuts on his forehead and as I scanned the street for Eva I put my hand on his compressed and broken chest. There was no breathing, no moment, he was dead of that I had no doubt and I felt instantly sorry about that.

Bob was out his cab and on his way over to me. I looked at him and moved my head from side to side a couple of times, Bob knew what I was indicating but didn't stop coming.

'She went in there.' An older woman shouted from the doorway to the adult book shop and pointed inside.

She was a tough looking old bird and her not so elegant attire told me she was either just going home from the night shift around the piers or on her way to look for a few daytime punters. A tube of lube, or something like that, and handy wipes clearly visible in the open brown bag she was clutching in her left hand.

I went around her and through the doorway stepping over the broken glass from the smashed front window, my SIG straight out in front of me. A sleazy looking bloke in a sweat stained greying 'white' vest stood behind the counter with his hands slightly raised. Three punters were cowering on the floor by the counter and one other was on the deck in the first aisle of shelves that contained a huge range of adult books and videos. The many battered copies of 'Debbie does Dallas' in a prominent position at the end of the shelf would have brought a smile to my face on any other day.

Sleazy vest man pointed towards an arched doorway at the back of the store. The plastic beaded fly screen was still moving and through the swinging beads I could see a stairway on the right. I pointed my SIG at sleazy vest man who jerked his head upwards to indicate that she had gone up the stairs.

The back room was dimly lit as I pushed my way slowly through the beads, almost falling over one of the stacks of porno videos as I entered. Others were now scattered across the floor from Eva's swift passage to the stairway.

I put my foot on the first step, leaned forward and quickly peered up the stairs before standing back. She wasn't on the stairs so I could move. I saw the first signs of blood on the stair rail and then again on the first step. More blood was on the fourth and fifth step, two big blobs on each. She was bleeding and bleeding badly and I didn't care where or how, just that she was.

The 'bang' made me put my head down sharpish. The round penetrated the crumbling plaster on the stairway wall above me sending a shower of dust and bits onto my head. I heard her footsteps, she was moving up another floor, but not that quickly. I moved up a few more steps, Eva's blood under my feet causing me to slip momentarily. The dead leg was still a bit of a problem but was in good enough shape for me to react in time and keep me upright.

Another bang, but this time she was miles away and I didn't see where the round ended up, but I didn't care either as I took the next six stairs in three strides. I wasn't quick enough to get a clean shot at her so decided to save my ammo.

Another round was fired somewhere on the next floor, but not at me and I got to the fourth floor without any more bullets coming my way. I peered over the top step looking through the smashed door that led into an apartment. The door lock had been shot out.

I moved up the last few steps quietly and stood with my back against the wall, I was six feet from the smashed door. I was ready to move forward when Eva's weapon appeared through the doorway pointing down the corridor towards me. I was on my way to the deck when I heard a sound that was music to my ears, 'click,' then 'click' again. She had an empty chamber.

I was up and through the smashed front door in seconds. Eva was backing away as fast as her feet would take her towards the large sash windows at the front of the apartment. She had already pulled out the clip to check that there were no more rounds left in the weapon. There weren't.

The weapon was in her right hand hanging down by her side. Her left hand covering the bleeding wound in her right shoulder where I had shot her by the cab. Her face was streaked with blood from the cuts on her head, one still oozing a decent flow past her left eyebrow and down towards the left corner of her mouth. She looked in a mess but was still full of spite, anger and defiance.

'You murdered my wife, you fucking bitch,' I growled at her and stared straight into her cold black eyes. There were no signs of remorse, not that I was expecting any.

'You murdered my brother so you had to pay with your life and that bitch wife of yours. My only regret is we didn't get you and your little bastard at the same time.' She snarled back at me. 'Do not fear though because my brother, General Don Juan Muscardin, will find someone to finish what he ordered if I can't right now.' She lunged at me as soon as she finished snarling at me.

All the psychological testing, training and discipline that are supposed to keep you calm and in control in tough situations went straight out the fucking window. The intense pent up anger and hatred for this woman and her family erupted. I didn't give a fuck about her threats I just wanted to kill her, right here, right now, with my bare hands.

I dropped the SIG from my hand and charged. She moved much quicker than I thought she would be able to and crashed into me half way across the room. I managed to get a strong hold on the front of her blouse with my right hand but wasn't quick enough to deflect her right hand away from my face. The butt of her weapon connected hard against my left temple blurring my vision and knocking me off balance. I was still feeling the effects from the blow on my temple as we both crashed onto the deck and I lost my grip on her.

She moved quickly to straddle me, her bloodied fingers clawing instantly at my eyes and face. I grabbed her right wrist before screwing my eyelids shut, which stopped her swinging the butt of the weapon towards my head again. It didn't stop one of her fingernails almost penetrating my right eyelid.

I punched her hard in the ribs with my right fist. I know I heard something crack and her scream reinforced that, it wasn't enough to stop her though. She was thrashing about like a wild animal trying to get her teeth into my left arm whilst still digging and clawing at my eyes. I landed another hard punch in the same place as the first and felt her back off for just a second. That was all the time I needed. I opened my eyes to focus on the bodily part I wanted to find and reached out. Eva screamed in pain as I put a vice grip on her left breast squeezing and crushing it with my fingers and forcing her backwards off my chest.

She grabbed my right wrist with her free left hand, but it was too late, she was completely off balance now and with one final shove I sent her sprawling sideways onto the floor. I didn't release my grip on her right wrist so as she fell to my left I was able to bend and twist her right arm forcing her to drop the weapon.

I wanted to strangle her so that I could see the life extinguished from her eyes and feel the limpness of her body beneath me. I thought about that vision for a split second too long and as I rolled over and lifted my left leg to straddle her she brought up her left knee hard into my balls. The pain was instant and excruciating and forced me to let go of her wrist and left tit and involuntarily grab my nuts.

Eva wriggled free and was up on her feet before I could react properly. She knew she couldn't get past me to the door so raced over to one of the sash windows and began pulling at the cord trying to get it up. I heard it move a little.

'No, you fucking don't,' I screamed at her.

I covered the few yards between us at speed lifting my right leg for a karate kick at the last moment. My boot was horizontal and aimed squarely for the middle of her back as she struggled to force the window open further.

The force of the kick catapulted Eva through the glass and wooden window frames and out onto the rickety fire escape at the front of the building. I stood and watched as she dragged herself up by the metal guard rail and onto her feet to face me.

'Go to hell you bastard,' she spluttered through her broken and blood filled mouth.

I forced my way through the broken window knocking aside Eva's shoe as she threw it towards me. I stood in front of her not moving for a second or two and stared into her evil black eyes. Rage and hatred for this woman was uncontrollable and overtook me as I reached forward and grabbed her by the throat with my left hand. At the same time, my right hand gripped the strong fabric of her skirt at the waist and I lifted her off her feet without noticing the weight, the adrenalin pumping around my system increasing my strength exponentially and blocking all pain from my injuries.

She was above my head now but was still trying to prise my hand off her throat by digging and clawing at it with her nails. I couldn't feel anything and all I knew was this bitch had to die for what she had done to Kathy. I took half a step towards the metal rail and then launched her into the air 60 feet above the ground. I watched her fall in silence and then the impact with the top corner of the UPS truck that snapped her spine. She had stopped making any noise by the time her limp head connected with the concrete sidewalk seconds later.

I wanted to make sure she was dead before getting the fuck away from here. Every part of my body seemed to be hurting but especially my nuts and my eyes as I came down the stairs and through the porno book shop as fast as I could. A pool of blood was forming around Eva's head when I got to her and there was no movement or breathing from her smashed up body. A quick check for a pulse in her neck was a bit futile, but I wanted to be sure. There wasn't one, she was dead. I smiled properly for the first time in a while.

11

I had to move and move quickly. Bob had wandered over to check out the mess on the sidewalk. It was nothing he hadn't seen before in his 40 years of driving around this City.

'You're no cop are you,' Bob said looking straight into my face.

'No Bob I'm not, but I'm not the bad guy here either,' I said.

'Did she kill a kid or was that just a load of bullshit to get me involved in this?' Bob asked. I could tell he wasn't sure whether he should be pissed off with me or not when he asked me the question.

'Bob,' I said. 'She has killed many people in her own country and outside of it, both directly and indirectly, including many women and children,' I paused for a moment and then told him. 'She also murdered my wife two weeks ago.'

Police sirens were getting closer and more people were venturing towards the crash scene and Eva's dead body.

'You look like shit son,' Bob said.

My clothes were torn and I was filthy and covered in blood stains. Several cuts and scratches were raw and angry and leaking fresh blood down my face. My right eye was also beginning to close from where Eva's hand had been clawing at it. Bob took off his jacket and handed it to me, then pulled out a big old white handkerchief from his trouser pocket.

'It sounds like you did a lot of people a big favour today,' he said. 'The jacket should cover most of the crap and you can use the snot rag, which is clean, to sort your face out. The closest subway is at 42nd and 8th and you need to fuck off out of here son, now,' he said and smiled.

The sirens coming down West 45th were much louder now. I saw the first police car picking its way slowly through the jam of cars behind Bob's sideways parked yellow cab. Bob had to shout so I could hear him over the sirens.

'Go to the corner of 45th and 10th and then left for three blocks, then go up two blocks on 42nd and the station entrance is on your left. It's less than a mile, you can make it in six or seven minutes. Good luck son.'

I nodded and raised my hand at him then turned and headed to the corner of the street in the opposite direction from the approaching cops. The jacket was on within five yards, hanky spat on and wiping away whatever blood it could take off at this point, I needed a water faucet but I would have to wait until the station. Bob had left a well worn green Irish flat cap in the jacket pocket, I was sure he would not have wanted me to have it as it looked like a man's favourite, but it was on my head now.

I made it to 42nd Street Port Authority station entrance in six minutes and headed down the stairs scanning the signs for the restrooms. I found one within a minute and had the jacket and shirt off before I reached the sinks. I cleaned my face and hands and then dunked the shirt several times in warm water to get as much of the blood out of it as possible before wringing it out and putting it back on. It was cold but actually very soothing on my battered body.

A couple of blokes had come in for a piss but left the restroom as soon as they saw the state of my face and the blood red water in the sink. Deep gouges and cuts covered my face and both eyelids were puffed up from the treatment they had received from Eva. My right eye was now almost completely closed. Two of the deeper cuts had started to bleed again after I had knocked off the coagulated blood whilst washing. They would stop again in a minute.

Two minutes and I was out of there looking less like something from a Dracula movie. Bob's hanky rinsed and tucked away in the jacket pocket as I knew I would be needing it again soon. I had to get back to 42nd on Broadway to retrieve my grip from the lock-up at the Holiday Inn and then try to contact Bill or Ron. I would worry about getting out of New York and the US after I'd done that.

Three minutes later I boarded the 8th Avenue Express train heading south back towards Penn Station; it didn't take long to my stop at Spring Street 6th Avenue.

I killed a couple of hours in Greenwich Village getting some essential medical supplies to sort out the face and to clean up the rest of my body. Next stop was a trendy and very expensive store for the purchase of new pants, socks, shirt, jumper and jeans and then it was a short walk across the street where I picked up some new Caterpillar boots at half the price they would be in the UK. Ten minutes in the bog of a smart coffee bar further down the street and I looked almost human again.

It was getting dark when I retrieved my grip from the lock-up at the Holiday Inn and Bill's locker was still intact so I assumed he had been lifted by the cops. I left Ron a message using the secure phone number he had given us and told him where I was, I also enquired about Bill whilst I was at it. I found a good seat by the window of a coffee bar across from the hotel and for an hour watched the bright neon signs lighting up every corner of the street trying to sell you anything and everything you could not possibly want.

Dave scared the crap out of me when he tapped me on the shoulder before sitting down opposite me, and then Bill slid into the seat next to him. He looked in more of a shit state than I did, the deep cuts from the edges of the metal bin were angry and had formed huge welts across his face. A couple of rough temporary stitches had been put in place to close up the two deepest cuts.

'Fair play Bill you look like shit mate,' I said.

'You don't look so fucking pretty yourself,' Bill replied.

We both laughed as Dave leant forward and lowered his voice.

'My orders are to get you reunited with your kit Bill, and then get you both on a plane out of here.'

With Bill's kit retrieved and all of us in the car, Dave filled us in on Ron and Simon.

'Gary is with them now at the hospital.'

I had forgotten about Gary being on stag at Dante Armendariz offices.

'Gary told me they were both in theatre an hour ago, but that is all I have right now. The main thing is they are both alive and that's all what matters right now.'

We didn't question it further; there was nothing else to be said. The car stayed quiet as Dave focused on the road ahead heading south to New Jersey.

Part Six

The Final Deed

1

0200 (US Time) Wednesday 9th November 1983

The wheels were up and locked in the undercarriage of the massive US C-5 Galaxy Military transporter at exactly 0200. It was the first available flight heading eastwards, its destination Wiesbaden Army Airfield, near Frankfurt in Germany. Bill and I had been given the big seats up the front, well away from the 60 or so Airborne troops on their way back to their units after some R and R in the US.

Dave told us Colonel Shaw had been very busy during the last few hours sorting out our exit from the US and once we were airborne, and knew our ETA and destination, he would be making the arrangements to get us back into the UK. Going through normal Customs looking like we did would have definitely prompted some serious and uncomfortable questions being asked.

Once in the air I told Bill how I chased Eva and the kid down 6th Avenue, the subsequent car crash, the fight above the porno shop and then finally how Eva had met her death.

'Evil fucking bitch deserved to die and not just for Kathy.' he said.

I then told him of her threat and Bill paused for a few moments before speaking again.

'So it was the General behind everything, as we thought. He challenged bully boy to bring back some British scalps from the Falklands and then ordered the assassination of you, Kathy, Harry Jr, and me. I fear this is not over yet Harry,' Bill said quietly.

Bill then told me of his escape from some crazy New Yorkers and the massive cop who wouldn't give up chasing him until he had to break bones to stop him. Bill had made it back down into the subway system once he had despatched the cop and travelled out as far as Brooklyn before getting off and making a quick visit to one of the many Green Cross pharmacies before sorting himself out.

Dave had picked him up an hour after making the call to the secure line and then had waited for the call from me. Dave knew I had got away from the porno shop on 45th but didn't know when, or where, I would resurface, although the hotel was his first guess.

We didn't expand on the basic details of the stories any further as we were both knackered, bloodied and bruised. The only thing we needed was sleep, but it wouldn't come for a while as the words of Eva Muscardin, and then Bill, kept repeating in my head like a bad tune.

2

England

RAF Lyneham

0300 (UK Time) Thursday 10th November 1983

The dark clouds lingered over RAF Lyneham on a cold and miserable British winter morning. The RAF Hercules that had been diverted especially to pick us up in Germany was now on its final approach to its home base. The Captain had told us to buckle up five minutes before as we hit some turbulent air that started to bounce the aircraft around a bit. It was only the second time he had spoken to us since boarding and that was only to say 'Buckle up, we are ready for take-off.'

The crew had been great feeding us breakfast and tea and asking if we needed anything, but none of them asked questions as to where we had been, what we had been doing, or why they had been sent to get us at the drop of a hat. They knew better. I'm sure the state of our faces and battered bodies told its own story and that was it had not been something good. The one good piece of news we were given was that Ron and Simon were alive and in a US military hospital, but that was all they knew. It was enough for now.

It was so good to be home even with the fine cold rain that wet our faces as soon as we exited the aircraft.

'Morning sirs,' was the cheery welcome from Corporal Steve Jones who was standing at the bottom of the stairs next to one of the Regiment's nice clean pool cars.

His face changed when he saw the full extent of the wounds on each of us. My face was now covered in red welts and both eyelids so swollen I had a job to open them to see where I was going. Bill's wounds looked even angrier now even though the worst were properly stitched now. We had both received some professional medical treatment and antibiotic jabs, courtesy of the US Army Medical Core in Wiesbaden.

'Fuck me,' I heard Steve Jones mutter under his breath as he moved forward to grab our grips.

'Sirs, I am to take you directly back to Credenhill, I'm afraid. Colonel Shaw's orders,' he said.

There was fuck all Bill and I could do about that so as Steve put the grips into the boot we both jumped in the back of the black Ford. I slept most of the way, as Bill did until he nudged me awake as we got onto Kings Acre Road. We were passing through one of the many nondescript housing estates on the outskirts of Hereford but were soon in the countryside and turning right onto the A480.

A couple of minutes later the main gate at Credenhill came into view.

3

0745 Thursday 10th November 1983

Colonel Colin Shaw came from behind his desk to greet us as we walked into his office, his face telling us instantly that something was up.

'Morning gentlemen, you look as if you have been in a hell of a fight, albeit a successful one I understand,' he said.

'Yes sir,' we replied. He paused for a moment before continuing. 'We have received news from our friends in the US about your father and Sergeant Steinway. I am pleased to tell you that both are in safe hands in the Bronx VA Medical Centre and have had the bullets removed from their chest and thigh respectively. They appear to be recovering well as of 0700 hrs this morning.

'Thank you sir. We knew they had been taken into hospital but not their overall conditions. I think it will take more than one bullet to kill my father,' I said.

'Indeed.' Brigadier Whistonhall answered for Colonel Shaw as he walked through the door. We all brought ourselves to attention.

'At ease gentlemen, please sit down,' he said. 'It looks as if Miss Muscardin and her friends were quite a challenge to overcome, looking at visible signs of the battle on your faces,' his face stern and unsmiling as he finishing speaking.

'Gentlemen, to business,' Colonel Shaw said as he sat down behind his desk before continuing. 'I'm sorry that you have not had a chance to go home and see your families and of course your young son. But things have been moving at quite a pace in Argentina and the US so it was essential that you fully debrief us on the US operation and then Brigadier Whistonhall and I can update you on the events we have been dealing with over the past two days.'

Bill and I spent the next half hour filling in the details for the two senior officers, including the final moments of Eva's life. I told them of General Muscardin's role in every event to date, which started with the challenge to his younger brother to kill some British soldiers in the Falklands and his orders to have Bill and me killed after we had taken out Octavio. The Brigadier was particularly interested in the fortified mansion of Victor Armendariz and the security that surrounded that family.

Fresh coffee and toast had arrived at 0815 along with a crisp brown folder on the tray. It took Bill and me another fifteen minutes to tell them about getting out of New York and the drive down to the McGuire Air Force Base in New

Jersey that ironically is very close to the Armendariz estate near Trenton. Our seats on the Galaxy had been secured by Colonel Shaw in the couple of hours it took us to get down there and now we were here.

'Very interesting, gentlemen. Now let me now bring you up to speed with events in the US first.'

Brigadier Whistonhall was talking as he moved from the place he had been occupying on the edge of Colin Shaw's desk for the last three quarters of an hour. He was heading for the Colonel's chair behind the desk, rubbing his arse as he went. I suppressed a smile after seeing that.

'Right, let's start with our men,' he said. 'As you now know, both your father and Sergeant Steinway are out of surgery and doing well.' We nodded.

The Brigadier then pulled out a couple of pieces of paper from the brown folder that was now on the desk and scanned it for a few seconds.

'Latest report is that they are both awake and in good spirits. Your father and the Sergeant will be moved to a Naval Hospital away from New York as soon as their injuries allow it. SEAL high command have taken control of the medical situation and assumed responsibility for their men. The CIA is already in the process of sorting out the collateral damage in New York and in an earlier report we were informed that the police had called Dante Armendariz to tell him that his brother Roberto had been in a road traffic accident, but they had also had to physically restrain him to find out who he was because he had lashed out at police, paramedics and anyone else who tried to help him. Dante Armendariz had retrieved his brother after pacifying the police and paramedics with the promise of contributions to the social and welfare funds or something similar. He told the police that he did not want to press charges against the driver and said he would pay for the damage to the vehicle involved. Dante Armendariz was then allowed to take his brother away. The report also said that there have already been a number of telephone calls and visit by a lawyer to the Chief of Police in an attempt to wash this away. They haven't claimed the body of Eva Muscardin yet for some reason although they must know she is deceased. I believe they will keep their heads down for some time especially with the latest news from Argentina.'

Brigadier Whistonhall definitely had our attention as he took a sip of his coffee before continuing.

'Fernando Reynoso contacted me yesterday evening and it appears Raul Alfonsin, the Argentine President Elect, is not going to waste any time with respect to dealing with individuals in the previous regime. He has already persuaded President Reynaldo Bignone to advance the inaugural by three months. He will now be taking office on the 10th December this year. Reynoso's father will then be appointed internal security minister and given the job of tracking down and charging those responsible for serious crimes during the 'dirty war' period. General Muscardin is very high on the list and not just because of the recent assassination attempts on him and his son. Fernando Reynoso will also have a Government position supporting his father in his new role. Evidence is already being gathered and it should not be long before seizure of assets, arrests and prosecutions are brought on the entire Muscardin family.'

The Brigadier paused again for another sip of coffee.

'However, they are fearful that General Muscardin will use his contacts and influence to escape to Europe before they have enough evidence to arrest him. Reynoso believes your actions in the US have effectively closed that door to him so now Spain would most likely be his preferred destination because of his business interests there. The Armendariz family in the US will want to keep a very low profile for a while and the last thing they will want is a national criminal and wanted man living on their doorstep, or even with them. The FBI and CIA would relish the opportunity to legally get beyond those gates.' Brigadier Whistonhall then gently placed the papers back onto the desk and looked at us for our reactions.

'This might be all over then,' I said to no one in particular. 'Fernando's father and the new Argentine government will hopefully eliminate forever the evil that is the Muscardin family, more for the people of Argentina rather than because of personal revenge,' I said.

'Indeed Lt. Glass.' Brigadier Whistonhall lifted himself from Colonel Shaw's chair after he spoke, closing the brown folder as he did so. 'I'll leave this report with you Colonel,' he said as he reached for his overcoat. 'We need to watch the situation closely during the coming days and weeks and I will ensure direct communication channels are kept open between London and Buenos Aires. As soon as I hear anything of importance we will reconvene at an appropriate location. I am sure Colonel Shaw will want you to get some rest and recover from your wounds before getting back to 'normal' operations.'

'That will be dealt with sir,' Colin Shaw responded.

Bill and I collapsed back into the chairs after the Colonel and Brigadier left the room. I was knackered and really just wanted to fuck off home and see Gerri and Harry Jr. Bill really looked like he needed to crash out as well. When Colonel Shaw returned, he only kept us for another 10 minutes before sorting out a car for me. Bill said he was going to stay on the base.

I arrived back home at 1330. Gerri was shocked and then tearful when she saw my swollen eyelids and the deep red gouges on my face and hand. She didn't ask me about what happened to me as she knew we would talk about it later. She did ask about Ron though and when I told her he was OK I saw her visibly relax and the tension dissolve from her face. We were both alive and that was all she needed to know.

I knelt down next to a dozing Harry Jr on the rug in front of the fire and held his tiny hand. I kissed him lightly on the forehead before sitting down on the sofa, Gerri placed a cup of tea in my hand moments later. The last thing I remembered before closing my eyes again was watching Harry Jr's little chest gently rising and falling as he slept peacefully. Gerri carefully placed a blanket over me 10 minutes later and took the little man upstairs and out of earshot as I let my body relax into the sofa and my mind drift off into my first undisturbed natural sleep in many weeks.

4

0900 Tuesday 13th December 1983

Credenhill

The wounds on Bill's face were much better now. Four weeks had passed since we had returned from the US and so the healing process was well on its way to completion. The deep scratches Eva had inflicted on my own face had almost disappeared, although the left eye had become infected for a week or so, but strong antibiotic drops had sorted that out eventually.

Colonel Shaw sent us both on a week's unofficial leave after returning from the US. It had gone by very quickly but had given me some real quality time with the little man. Harry Jr had screwed his face up and screamed when I picked him up during the first two days, but Gerri said it was the state of my face that scared him and not because he didn't recognise me. He was fine by the third day. Bill came over one afternoon for a chat and we walked for miles and miles and talked about everything that had gone on in the past few months. We absolutely needed a pint or two by the time we reached the Black Horse pub in Amberley and thankfully Gerri had arranged for Les in his trusty taxi to come and collect us very late that evening.

Bill had gone off somewhere as soon as we were back on active duty and only returned the previous night. I had continued the special boat training with several groups of SAS men, but my new orders had come through a couple of days ago. I only had a few more days to finish off the last boat course and then it would be Christmas leave before joining 40 Commando in January. I would still be in a training role for a couple of months and then I would be heading north to prepare for the science degree studies.

Bill and I were just catching up on news and other events when Colonel Shaw entered the room.

'Morning sir,' we said in unison.

'Sit down gentlemen I have some news,' he said and then waited until we were both seated.

'As I'm sure you know, three days ago on December 10th President Raul Ricardo Alfonsin ended military rule in Argentina and restored democracy for the first time since 1976. Yesterday, Monday the 12th December, Brigadier Whistonhall received a call from Fernando Reynoso at 1000hrs. It wasn't all good news I'm afraid. What I can tell you is that Fernando Reynoso boarded an Argentine Government plane last night and will arrive in the UK shortly. He is coming here to brief Argentine diplomats and senior UK Government officials on the changes and actions being implemented immediately by President Alfonsin, some of which relate to war crimes committed during the Falklands War. This afternoon he will brief us personally on recent developments in Argentina and the location of General Don Juan Angel Muscardin.'

Steve Jones drove us to the Foreign and Commonwealth Office in King Charles Street, central London, which was the place for our meeting with Fernando Reynoso at 1400 hrs. The A4 had been very heavily congested; cars and trucks were bumper to bumper pretty much all the way from South Kensington. Even the 'short cut' through Belgravia was packed out with cars, and people, which slowed our journey even more. Victoria Street was much better for some reason and it wasn't long after passing the Houses of Parliament and Big Ben that we were flashing our ID's at the two armed cops at the security gate. They were very diligent and scrutinised everything very carefully before waving us through.

Steve Jones eased the car into King Charles Street at the 5mph speed limit and down to the entrance of the massively impressive Victorian building that was home to the Foreign Office.

'This building was only finished just over a hundred years ago in 1868 and it was designed by George Gilbert Scott in the Italianate classical style,' Colin Shaw was speaking generally to all of us in the car. 'Wait until you get inside,' he continued. 'The State Stairs and the ceiling above them is one of the most impressive sights you will ever see of London's architecture.'

I didn't yawn, but Bill did.

Steve Jones pulled into the inner courtyard and headed for his allocated parking spot. I couldn't help thinking that Maggie may only be 50 feet away in Downing Street and that one day maybe I would get to meet her as I would love to shake her hand for what she did for the Falkland Islanders.

We were met at the North corner entrance by a very stiff pin-stripe suited and booted civil servant who looked like he hadn't smiled in years. His face was sombre and as white as the collar of his shirt and his mouth downturned at the corners, fixed in a miserable 'bah humbug' way. Colin Shaw was not wrong about either the stairs or the magnificent ceiling above them, unfortunately stiff suit didn't slow his pace at all so there was no time to stop and gaze as he led us down a labyrinth of corridors before finally ushering us into the biggest and most palatial office I had ever seen. Fernando Reynoso was seated in a deep red leather chair in front of an antique oak desk that must have been over eight feet in length and four feet wide. It was as impressive as everything else in the room.

Behind the desk sat Brigadier Brian Whistonhall in his Savile Row suit looking equally as smart as stiff suit who was now leaving the room backwards.

'Captain Dye, and it's Lieutenant Glass now I believe?' Fernando said as he shook our hands in turn.

'Yes it is,' I replied.

'Congratulations,' he said and then turned to face Colin Shaw. 'And this must be Colonel Shaw. It is a pleasure to meet you sir.' Fernando said shaking his hand firmly.

'Likewise,' Colin Shaw replied.

'Gentlemen, let's take a seat at the conference table and we can let Mr Reynoso tell us about recent events in Argentina.' Bill poured out five cups of boiling hot coffee as we settled down at the table with Brian Whistonhall and Fernando Reynoso on one side of the table. Colin Shaw, myself and Bill on the other.

'First of all' Fernando started. 'May I address you as Bill and Harry?'

'Of course,' I said smiling.

'Fine by me,' Bill confirmed.

'I want to thank you both personally for what you did in New York. We have found out a great deal about the activities of the Muscardin family over the past two weeks and particularly about Eva's cruelty to my own people. We now know she was directly responsible for the murder of hundreds, maybe thousands of innocents across Argentina. It provided great joy to many when we heard she had been found dead on a New York street. Thank you.'

Nothing needed to be said by Bill or I so we just nodded in acknowledgement.

'We knew that Eva Muscardin was sent to the US,' Fernando continued. 'She was trying to secure a property for the family and arrange for very significant funds to be transferred out of Argentina and into US accounts. That is what Dante Armendariz was working on primarily. Since Eva's death, all communications between the two families appear to have stopped. The Armendariz family were visited by the CIA and warned that if they have any association with the Muscardin family or any of the other criminals from the military junta, and previously corrupt Argentine Government, they will have their assets seized and be jailed for a very long time when found guilty. The US President has also now severed all ties with the family. My father has been very busy already.' Fernando paused and smiled before continuing.

'Many of the corrupt senior military officers and Government officials have been trying to leave the country in recent weeks. Some have succeeded and some not. Unfortunately, General Don Juan Angel Muscardin was warned of our arrival at his estate and so succeeded in evading all our forces last Friday evening. He escaped on a private plane with several bodyguards but left the rest of his family behind. This was obviously planned and no doubt he will be working to ensure they can rejoin him somewhere in the near future. It is because of this no one would disclose his intended destination, or as we now believe, they don't actually know where he had gone.' Fernando was clearly embarrassed that they had let the General escape, his head bowing slightly when he finished speaking.

'Any signs since then?'

'I was just coming to that Bill.' Fernando replied. 'Minutes before I boarded my flight to London I received news that the General had been tracked to Madrid via Paraguay. An eye witness reported a small plane landing at a private country airfield 15 miles outside of Asuncion, Paraguay's capital city, on

Sunday evening. It dropped off a big man in civilian clothes with two large suitcases. We now know this was General Muscardin. He then took a first class seat onboard TAM Linhas Aereas flight 8032 to Sao Paulo and then directly on to Madrid. I think I can be confident in saying he is somewhere in the Madrid area. We also know he travelled under the name, Eduardo Herrera, although I am certain he will have a number of other false identities at his disposal.'

'Sir.' Colin Shaw spoke directly to the Brigadier. 'This is all very interesting but why are we here? My understanding was that the new Government in Argentina was going to deal with this man directly and bring him to justice. I know we sanctioned the operation in the US to deal with the sister, but we had very good reasons for doing that. I don't believe anyone would dispute that, including the Americans who helped us.'

'Colin you are correct, but this man is guilty of many, many crimes and not only in Argentina. We must not forget that it was the goading of his cowardly brother that resulted in the murder of SAS soldiers and Royal Marines during the Falklands War. He also gave the direct order for the assassination of Lieutenant Glass, his wife and infant son. Captain Dye was next on the list, we know that.'

It was the first time I had witnessed Brigadier Whistonhall really getting angry and he had to pause for a few seconds to regain his composure before continuing.

'Mr Reynoso and I spoke to the Prime Minister this morning. She was asked directly by Mr Reynoso, on behalf of the new President of Argentina, for the UK Government's help in apprehending this man and the recovery of hundreds of millions of dollars that he has hidden outside of Argentina. Most of it we believe to be in the UK. The Prime Minister is also fully aware of the history of this individual and the atrocities he and other members of his family have inflicted on the people of Argentina. The Prime Minister then spoke to the Spanish President, Felipe González, a lawyer and charismatic man whom Margaret has fostered good relations with since he came to power last year. He made it clear he does not want any of these individuals in his country and will work with the UK to ensure that General Muscardin is returned to Argentina for justice to be served.'

'I very much doubt the General will come without a fight,' Fernando stood up as he started to speak. 'I want to be clear with you, and this comes directly from my President, gentlemen. If the General can be apprehended and taken alive, then so be it, but if he dies in the process then no one in Argentina will shed any tears. It is more important to the President that we recover the stolen millions than to bring him back to Argentina alive. We believe he may make this easy for us if we can find him quickly and track his movements.'

We were all intrigued by Fernando's last statement.

'Please continue Mr Reynoso,' Brigadier Whistonhall said as he leaned forward in his chair.

'The General's first cousin, Diego Bruno, holds a senior position at the Argentine Embassy in Brook Street here in London. He is a small fat man with pig eyes and has been here many years and we know there has been regular contact and business dealings between them during this time, but the true extent and content of these are as yet unknown. The cousin also has an apartment in the Ambassador's residence in Belgrave Square where he has hosted many parties for influential business people and senior directors from some of the most prominent banks in London. Some of these people will be very useful to the General now with regard to moving, changing, or hiding the money and assets he has stolen from my country, that's if he hasn't already. It will no doubt cost the General a very significant amount of money to make the illegal transactions, but it will be a fraction of the total amount he has stolen. We believe the cousin will play an integral and important part in this process but the General does not actually trust anyone and we expect him to want to be in control of any multi-million dollar transactions, wherever they take place. This means he may have to come to the UK personally to achieve this and because he is a very arrogant, smart and confident man, who is extremely well connected, will believe he can get in and out of this country undetected if he needs to.'

Everyone in the room was quiet for a few moments thinking about what Fernando had just said. Bill and I had seen evidence of his cruelty and been well briefed on the acts of state terrorism the General had ordered under the guise of military operations. There was no doubt in my mind if the opportunity presented itself that I would have no hesitation killing this bastard. My only hope would be that he resisted just a little bit so I wouldn't have to take him alive.

Brigadier Whistonhall had left the table and broke my train of thought when he spoke.

'Gentlemen the Prime Minister absolutely does not want us tromping all over the countryside of her new friend. This was made very clear. We have to wait for intelligence to be gathered by the Spanish Police and their Special Forces. However, I have been given the name of a direct contact in the Spanish Government who will inform me of any new intelligence or developments as soon as they happen.' Brigadier Whistonhall stopped pacing for a moment.

'The General's apprehension, or execution, is one of the top priorities of the new Government of Argentina and from a personal perspective I would be grateful and very happy if I never had to set my eyes on General Don Juan Angel Muscardin again.' Fernando looked and sounded angry when he spoke, the deep hatred for this man and his family had boiled to the surface and I could see it in his eyes that all he wanted was the General dead. Nothing less. I'm sure he would have done it himself if he could.

'Gentlemen, Mr Reynoso and I have another meeting in 30 minutes. He is then returning to Argentina this evening. Colin, I will call you tomorrow and we will see where we can go with this. Captain Dye, Lieutenant Glass, it was good to see you again.' Brigadier Whistonhall moved forward to shake our hands indicating that this meeting was now over.

Bill and I both received a warm handshake from Fernando, which enforced the bond we now all shared, and to think we would have killed him in a blink of an eye 15 months ago. I was very glad we hadn't.

'One day you must both come back to Argentina as my guests where hopefully you will see a non-violent side to my beautiful country,' he said.

'Thank you Fernando, I hope we will,' I replied.

5

1140 Sunday 18th December 1983

It had been very quiet for a few days because the General had gone to ground and was being well hidden by someone somewhere in Spain. That had changed earlier when Bill and I received orders to report immediately to Colonel Shaw. It took an hour for him to brief us on the developments. The first and most important one was that the General had been sighted in Madrid with a Spanish multi-millionaire property tycoon who was believed to be the General's host. This particular tycoon, another corrupt and violent man, was well known to the Spanish authorities, but had always been far enough away from the crimes to avoid prosecution. They had been under constant surveillance since the sighting yesterday evening.

A team from MI5 had also been keeping very good tabs on the General's cousin since Tuesday night. He had been very active around London at the time of our meeting with Fernando and was observed in discussions with two very senior banking officials, both of whom were well known to Special Branch. He had also visited one of the major foreign banks twice already. This man was a bad'un, no doubts about that and everyone's gut feelings were something big with respect to moving some money around was going to happen very soon.

The intelligence from Spain was that the General had been talking to some serious underworld figures in Eastern Europe and was close to securing a deal. What the deal was, nobody knew, but it was thought to be for them to provide a safe haven for him and his family. What Don Juan needed now though was to get the stolen money that was hidden somewhere in our London banks to new secure accounts most probably in Switzerland or Monaco, or both.

The final piece of intelligence was the one we were all silently hoping for, but never really expected; even though Fernando had thought it very possible. A plane ticket had been bought in the name of Eduardo Herrera. He was booked on the 0710 Iberia flight from Madrid to London tomorrow morning. If it was him, and everything so far told us it was him, it would be his biggest ever mistake.

6

The new spur road off the M4 had enabled us to get into the airport much easier than I remembered and we arrived at Heathrow Terminal 3 short stay parking at 1820. Bill had made good time down the M4 in the battered old RS Escort we had picked up from the car pool. It may look battered on the outside, but it was in perfect mechanical order with its engine so finely tuned it could outrun most, if not all, so called modern sports cars if we needed it to.

It had only taken 30 minutes to get the kit we wanted from the base and then a brief stop at Bill's home and then mine and we were on the way to the motorway. I picked up the SIG P220 I had kept from New York and the Balisong knife that Simon had taught me to use years ago. Bill had also kept the untraceable New York Browning and brought along his favoured short 5-inch combat knife.

A cold wind drove into our faces as we walked across the pull-in lanes in front of the terminal. The large glass terminal windows reflecting our progress to the main doors as we got closer. Once inside I scanned the arrival board looking for any Iberia flights from Madrid. There was one landing in 20 minutes. I tapped Bill on the shoulder and pointed out the flight, we still had plenty of time to meet our MI5 contact and get to the plane's arrival point.

An hour later we had timed the movements of the Iberia passengers from leaving the aircraft to the immigration booths, from there to the baggage hall, and finally out through customs and into the arrivals hall. We identified several good locations on the route where we could track 'Eduardo Herrera' without being seen. The next hour was spent with MI5, immigration and customs officers going over the plan to get him through the airport without raising suspicions.

He would be followed from the aircraft to immigration by the first MI5 officer called Simon, who would be dressed as an airport maintenance worker. An experienced senior Immigration Officer would let him through after the usual checks and then Nick, another MI5 officer in plain clothes, would pick him up and follow him through to the baggage hall and out into the terminal building, where I would be waiting. A third MI5 officer, John, would pose as a cleaner and would keep tabs on him in there to check if he retrieved any luggage. The customs officers would let him walk straight through into the arrivals hall after getting the nod.

I had my location sorted to cover the last exit into the arrivals hall where I would wait for Nick to appear from the baggage hall. He would walk directly behind Don Juan and would drop me the signal so I could identify him even if he was heavily disguised.

Bill was going to be outside with the car running. We were assuming that Don Juan was either going to be picked up by a car or take a taxi directly into London. There were four cars altogether at the airport that could switch positions several times on the way into London and three others were positioned closer to the city.

We waited until all the customs and immigrations guys had left the room leaving the four MI5 officers, Bill and I for a last word from the female senior MI5 officer. Ms Elizabeth Thompson held court and placed her hands on the top of the small conference room table before speaking. The three MI5 boys were silent and focussing on her. She was a fierce looking woman and definitely the boss of them.

'We cannot lose him, gentlemen. We need the General to get all the way to the bankers so they are fully implicated with the stolen money. Do not apprehend him before that unless it's absolutely necessary. Is that clear?' The MI5 boys nodded their heads. Bill and I didn't say anything. It was her last statement before abruptly leaving the room.

'We'll just have to see how it pans out,' Bill whispered in my ear as the meeting finished.

Our agenda was slightly different to MI5, not that they knew this of course, but Bill and I had agreed that if we got an opportunity, without the risk of collateral damage to civilians, we were going to take him down and finish this. Fuck the money; some clever bastard with a computer would be able to track that down later.

I checked my watch as we parked in front of the Holiday Inn at London Victoria. It was 2207. The hotel was in a perfect position, just a short walk from Victoria train station on Belgrave Road in one of those fine Victorian buildings that were prominent in this area of London.

Once in my room we poured over the plans one last time before crashing for a couple of hours.

Our last thought was; he wouldn't take the train, would he?

7

0430 Monday 19th December 1983

I was awake well before the 0430 alarm. I couldn't stop thinking about the plane that was due to take off from Madrid at 0710. The flight time was scheduled to be 2 hours 25 minutes, but there was still the hour difference to consider so Don Juan would be landing at Terminal 3 at 0835 UK time.

Bill was ready a couple of minutes before me because I had been sitting on the edge of my bed thinking about Kathy and how much I was missing her. I got furious thinking about it, but I knew we had a real chance today of making the perpetrator of all this misery and violence pay the ultimate price. Bill came into the room through the adjoining door and I think he guessed what I was thinking. He placed his hand gently on my shoulder and gave it a couple of soft taps before speaking.

'Weapons check Harry,'

'OK,' I replied.

Half a minute later and all weapons were checked and good so we headed for the door. I put on my old blue NY baseball cap that Ron had given me many years before. It would provide some cover for my face if for some reason Don Juan got too close at the wrong time. He will know what we look like from the photos they would undoubtedly have of us. That was the main reason why the MI5 boys had agreed to do the close work at the airport.

The streets of London were coming to life as we headed up Belgrave Road past Victoria Station and along Eccleston Street. Teams of men in high vis jackets were retrieving the large filled black bags stacked along the pavements in front of some poor homeless souls still sleeping soundly in the doorways. Not even the big rubbish trucks with their bright orange flashing lights and beeping horns could disturb them from their exhausted, drunken or drug induced slumber. None of the high vis men looked back as they hurled the bags into the cavernous opening at the rear of the truck. Nobody cared. Even the men who followed the rubbish truck sweeping the pavements and doorways paid them no attention; they just brushed around them. It was a sad sight to see in our country's capital, but we had seen at lot worse recently. I focussed back on the road ahead as Bill sped past more bodies in doorways and then down Pont Street towards the A4.

Bill had the Escort parked on the ground floor of the short stay car park at 0530, it was 20 feet from the exit barriers, facing towards them. We navigated our way across the busy drop-off lanes in front of the terminal and I spotted the three MI5 officers huddled by the coffee stall inside the main door. The meeting in the Customs office was brief and in 20 minutes we were moving to our positions.

Another 15 minutes and we were ready. All we had to do now was wait.

8

0855 Heathrow Terminal 3 – 19th December 1983

'Eduardo Herrera' eased himself out of his Business class seat and put on his overcoat that the young Spanish air stewardess had handed to him shortly before landing. He had let his thoughts wander from the job in hand today and had fantasised about this beautiful woman for the last two hours. He had relished the thought of fucking her and then beating her naked body black and blue, even if she had done what he had ordered her to do. Just as he had done many times before with pretty young Argentine girls.

Another time he thought to himself as he ogled the woman again from the centre aisle before bringing his mind back to the business of today. Don Juan smiled knowing that in a few short hours he would be seeing his old 'friends' again. He had met Sir Richard Roses and Robert Keys at Oxford University in the 60s, both of them were corrupt and devious bastards, even in those days, which is why he liked them. Now though they were both operating at stratospheric levels of corruption, greed and depravity and both had eagerly agreed to help him move all his funds out of the UK to new accounts recently set up in Switzerland and Monaco. The sting had been the huge amount of cash they had wanted to facilitate and then hide the illegal transactions, but he knew it was worth it.

Their cash, all in used UK pounds, was hidden in two suitcases a few feet below him in the hold. The two bag mules his Spanish friend had provided were sitting twenty rows back in economy. They were only hours away from the biggest payday of their lives.

Don Juan stood patiently in the aisle waiting for the aircraft door to be opened and smiled again as he remembered his last visit to London two years earlier. Sir Richard, Robert and his faithful cousin Diego had such a great time, there had been plenty of Michelin star quality food, expensive vintage red wine and most importantly a continuous supply of young girls. Life had been very good for him in London at that time, but that was six weeks before the Malvinas War and then it all had changed.

Don Juan had lost count of the number of times he had cursed Leopoldo Galtieri for his complete underestimation of British resolve to 'do the right thing' for their people on the 'Malvinas' and had little doubt at the time that Thatcher would not give up on them. He had told Galtieri that invading the Islands would be a total fuck up because if she did send down a task force the strength, training and resolve of the British forces would be superior to their own. He had also told him that Argentina didn't have enough elite Marines to hold the islands and that the young untrained conscripts would be slaughtered, run, or give up very quickly if they came. As they did.

The war had fucked up so many of his lucrative foreign deals and temporarily cut off his access to the millions of dollars he had stashed away in two false business accounts in two of the leading international banks in London. Richard Roses and Robert Keys were on the boards of both and he was certain that they were two of only four people in the world who knew about them. His cousin had been key in setting up and running the accounts with Richard and Robert for many years and the joint decision to leave the funds alone and hidden during the post Malvinas war period had proved to be a good one. He needed those funds now though and everyone understood the huge risks and danger of what they were doing today, hence the big bags of cash.

Don Juan had foreseen the end of military power and control as soon as Argentina had lost the war. What he hadn't foreseen were people like the Reynosos and other whining liberals, as he called them, gaining so much power so quickly. He knew he should have had them terminated along with Alfonsín when he had the chance several years before and regretted very much not giving Octavio and Eva that task sooner than he did.

But they were both dead now and it was all too late for that, but as soon as he was safe, and that would be one day very soon, those bastards, SAS Captain William Dye and Royal Marine Lieutenant Harry Glass, would pay with their lives for what they had done to his family.

Two smartly dressed business class passengers standing at the front of the queue with their very expensive looking briefcases grasped firmly in their right hands were literally hopping from one foot to the other waiting to be freed by the stewardess. Don Juan could almost hear the imaginary gun go off as they rushed through the open door and raced up the covered walkway to their 'very' important meeting.

Don Juan was not going to rush anywhere, he was feeling a little nervous, but knew he had to stay calm and have faith that his false passport would pass scrutiny again. He had no choice but to take the risk on using it again because his two new identities, and new passports, were still being 'created.'

He knew the Eduardo Herrera passport and supporting identity was very strong as it had proved so in the past. It had come from a highly educated and successful business man whom he had liked, but he was also someone who had made the mistake of failing on a business venture so making him disappear forever had not been a difficult decision to make. This identity had got him out of Paraguay and into and out of Spain with no problems, so why not the UK again? He was still angry with himself though for not retrieving the small brown package that contained three other false identities and passports from his private safe at home in Argentina. A home he knew he was unlikely to ever return to again.

Don Juan lightly grasped the hand of the pretty stewardess. Outwardly, Adabella Florez was smiling happily alongside her friend having already said goodbye and safe onward journey to the first of the business class passengers.

Inwardly she was cringing with repulsion, and now real fear, because the big bearded Hispanic man with the evil eyes from seat 3A was standing in front of her. She barely held herself together when he pulled her hand to his mouth and kissed the back of it lightly. He then looked up and stared into her eyes and said, 'Adiós a la señorita Florez hasta que nos reunamos de Nuevo.'

Adabella Florez managed to keep the fixed smile on her face as she pulled her hand free and then watched Don Juan slowly exit the aircraft. 'Not if I see you first you lecherous pig,' she whispered to her friend Natalia standing next to her. Fortunately for Adabella the other passengers had been backing up in the aisle and getting agitated as to why they were not moving so Don Juan was forced to move away much quicker than he actually wanted to. He still left the aircraft smiling though and once through the door he turned his head to take one last fleeting glance at the pretty young stewardess, briefly catching her eye as he did.

She was scared, and he knew it, and that made him smile even more.

9

The grey-haired immigration officer was polite and efficient and asked all the usual questions.

'Welcome back to the UK Mr Herrera and what brings you here this time, business or pleasure?'

'Just visiting some old friends for a few days,' Don Juan replied with a warm smile.

Seconds later the officer had stamped his passport and waved him through. The first hurdle over and Don Juan was still smiling as he strode towards the baggage hall, his confidence growing with every step he took away from the immigration desk. He hadn't noticed Simon, who had sauntered along behind him in the crowd of Spanish passengers all the way from the aircraft to the immigration hall.

Simon had identified Don Juan to the immigration officers with a look and a quick nod of his head when he was two away from the front of the queue. Don Juan had then been calmly directed to the end immigration booth to have the formalities completed.

Don Juan walked slowly down to the baggage hall and was stood waiting by the stationary carousel two five minutes later. The only other passengers in the hall were from the Geneva flight and their luggage was already circling around carousel four. No one, including Don Juan, took any notice of the man mopping the floor next to the lost luggage counter.

Nick, the MI5 officer assigned to the baggage hall, rested his hands on top of the mop handle for a moment. In his peripheral vision, he had already spotted his man before receiving the signal from John, who had picked up Don Juan at immigration. The full bushy beard, longer hair and heavy thick set glasses did not disguise the General enough from the military photos he had seen of him. It was definitely him and he was standing alone in the crowd by the carousel. Nick was only 12 feet from him.

When Nick acknowledged he had their man, John headed towards the gents' toilets to pick up the dummy red suitcase that he would carry with him as he exited customs in front of the General. He would hang about in there until the carousel had been running for a minute or two before heading towards customs. The General's bag would come off fairly quickly as he was in business class so he should be able to position himself a short distance ahead of him without any trouble.

Nick then saw something that made every nerve and sensor in his body heighten further. On the opposite side of the carousel, an older couple had definitely eyeballed his man and there had been a barely noticeable movement of the old man's head and then the faintest of acknowledgments from Don Juan. Nick pushed his bucket a few feet closer to the carousel to try and get a better look, but his view was temporarily blocked by passengers squeezing in closer to the conveyor belt.

Nick moved slowly into a better position that was only several feet from the Don Juan, he needed to be sure about what he had seen. The conveyor belt started up as he got eyes on the couple again, the woman was talking excitedly to another female passenger next to her. It looked like it had something to do with a kid, or kids, because she was indicating with her hands how big it, or they, were from floor level. The old boy standing next to the woman wasn't looking so happy, he looked tense and nervous, but was joining in the conversation nevertheless.

The couple were so engrossed in their conversation that the large black plastic suitcase went by them unnoticed. The woman spotted it just before it disappeared around the bend of the conveyor, her eyes went as wide as saucers. Nick pinged what she was staring at as the black suitcase appeared on his side of the conveyor, it was now only a few feet from where Don Juan was standing.

Nick saw the scowl appear on his face and even though the old boy had moved very quickly around the carousel, he could not get to the case before Don Juan had calmly pulled it off the conveyor. He smiled at the old boy and exchanged a few pleasantries before removing a medium sized brown holdall from between a suitcase sandwich, he then turned away and casually walked towards the customs exit channels. Nick was sure he heard the equivalent in Spanish of 'Fucking Idiot' as Don Juan walked away.

Moments later the woman appeared next to the old boy pushing a trolley with an identical black case on it. Don Juan was already half way to the customs exits as the man loaded his black suitcase onto the trolley next to the other. A few people had already moved away from the carousel heading for the exits, but Nick could see that John, with his red suitcase, was already in position about six feet in front of Don Juan.

Nick knew he had to move quickly to let everyone know about the couple who were in some way connected to the General so he dumped the bucket and mop against the nearest pillar and walked swiftly towards the small customs office next to the red 'Goods to Declare' channel putting 25 yards between himself and the slow moving couple who were still chatting to their new friends alongside them.

Within 10 seconds Nick had briefed the senior customs officer on the couple who were fast approaching the green lane. The senior officer immediately left the office and casually inserted himself in the crowd just six feet behind the couple. The other customs officers were surprised to see him, this was not part of the plan, but they saw straight away his eyes focusing on the old couple ahead of him and then his slight side to side head motion indicating not to stop them.

The old couple exited the 'Nothing to Declare' green lane oblivious to all the events happening behind them. Their focus was on finding the General again and then keeping very close to him.

10

0935 Heathrow Arrivals Hall 19th December 1983

John did a perfect job as he entered the terminal only a couple of feet in front of Don Juan. The last time I had set my eyes on this man was many months ago lying on the cold damp ground at his estate in Argentina. The new beard, long hair and thick set glasses were not disguising his features at all. The fucking arrogance of the man. I had lost count the amount of times that I wished I had killed him and all the rest of them that night. Kathy would have still been alive today if I had.

From under the peak of my NY baseball cap I fixed my eyes on him, intense anger and hatred for this man building inside me again. 'You don't have long to live now, you bastard,' I whispered to myself.

I watched him dawdle at the barrier that separated the arriving passengers from the waiting crowds and limo drivers. He turned left and slowly began to wander down the barrier studying the limo drivers' hand-written signs before turning around and walking back into the stream of passengers entering the terminal. I saw only the slightest movement of his head, but it was enough, and then the acknowledgment from an old boy pushing a trolley with two large black suitcases on it. A woman around the same age walked slowly beside him.

They followed the General walking a short distance behind as he continued past the signs for Dr this and Mr that. Then I saw Nick appear through a side door marked 'staff only.' I knew he shouldn't be coming out of there so something was wrong. He looked first for Don Juan and when he saw he had his back to him, and was walking away from him, he looked directly at me standing next to the Merretts newsstand.

Nick moved swiftly through the crowd towards me and then took only 15 seconds to fill me in on what Don Juan looked like and the connection to the older couple with the two large black suitcases. I told him I had clocked the old couple and headed after them as soon as he had finished talking. Nick went back the way he came.

Don Juan eased his way through the crowd and then into a clear space by the coffee stand where Simon, Nick and John had been enjoying their coffee the night before. The arrivals hall was full of people now, but I could still see him clearly. He had stopped and was scanning a large notice board in front of him.

What the fuck is he up to? What's he looking at? I wondered.

Then I knew.

I was 30 feet away from him on the opposite side of the terminal, he was scanning a large London underground map putting his finger on specific stations when he found them. He then ran his finger along the whole route of the Piccadilly line to Kings Cross Station.

'Fuck it,' I said just loud enough for an old dear to hear me as she walked by. If looks could have killed, that one would have. Don Juan started to move, the couple with the black bags were in front of him heading for the lift. I needed to get a message to Bill right now, but none of the MI5 boys were anywhere in sight.

'Fuck it,' I said to myself again, quieter this time.

Right then, out of the corner of my eye I saw one of the customs officers on our team come into the arrivals hall. I waited a few more seconds until I saw the lift doors close on the Don Juan and the old couple. Then I moved, fast.

I startled the customs officer as I grabbed his arm and steered him to a quiet spot.

'Listen,' I said. 'Outside you will find my mate Bill, you met him last night. He's in a battered blue Escort somewhere in the drop off lanes. Go tell him our man is heading for the Piccadilly Line and most likely Kings Cross. Tell him I will be on the train.

'OK mate,' he said and started running for the main door as I set off at the same speed for the escalator at the far end of the arrivals hall.

I spotted Nick and Simon coming out of a side door into the terminal as I was running through the crowd. I beckoned for them to follow me quickly with my right hand. We came together at the top of the escalator.

'Can you both take the old couple?' I asked.

'Yeah no problem,' Nick said.

'OK, I'll take care of the General,' I said as we all stepped off the bottom of the escalator at the same time.

I ran towards the ticket booth pulling a tenner out from my pocket before I got there. I could see a train was waiting as I got to the booth.

'Kings Cross, one way. Please.' I shouted through the speakeasy in the booth window.

The ticket didn't have time to stop in the stainless steel dish before it was in my hand and I was running towards the barriers. Along with everyone else. Nick and Simon hadn't bothered with tickets they had gone straight to the uniformed guard standing by the wheelchair access gate and flashed their IDs.

The guard was opening the side gate as I reached the barriers, but there was no time to change course now. I rammed the ticket into the slot and then almost decapitated myself on the retaining bar because it didn't move as fast as I was expecting it to.

The London bound-train was still filling up with the last few passengers as I legged it to the last carriage with Nick and Simon right behind me. I thought I saw John for a fraction of a second at the far end of the platform, but I couldn't be sure. The doors closed seconds after we jumped on board and then with an obligatory jolt the train began to move. I checked my watch, it was 0950. I had taken this train once before from the airport and I remembered it was about an hour to Kings Cross.

Neither the old couple nor the General were in the carriage, thank fuck. It had been a bit of a scramble to get on and our hasty arrival had caused a few passengers to look up and stare at the three of us for a few moments, but they had all now lost interest. I thought about Bill and hoped he had got the message and was now on the move.

It wasn't long before we were in the first tunnel, the old grey bricks that lined the walls disappeared from view as daylight was swapped for the dull yellowy lights of the carriage. The train was not of new stock and was disfigured with brightly coloured graffiti covering the mottled grey sides of what once were white carriages with big red bumper strips on either end. More illegal paint had been used on the inside and rude messages were scrawled into the Perspex windows for everyone to see. Pathetic attempts by underground staff to remove them had just scratched the windows even more so it was like looking through piss stained frosted glass to the outside world.

A couple of passengers in the carriage hung onto the overhead and side bars, not trusting what was left of the worn and frayed hanging leather straps above them. The carriage doors closed with a thud at Hatton Cross station shutting out the 1960s' lime green and orange tiles that insulted your eyes with their gaudiness. I moved into the next carriage taking advantage of the reduced light during the brief time we were in the next tunnel.

Nick and Simon were going to follow me shortly and get into position to watch the old couple once we found them. I thought it unlikely that the General would be in the same car as them, although I felt sure he wouldn't be too far away. If I spotted Don Juan before the couple I would come back and we would have to think about plan B. Right now though there wasn't a plan B, we were winging it.

There was no sign of them as I moved swiftly into the next carriage. The train picked up speed and began pitching and rolling with a consistent thud every time the solid wheels hit the gap in the rails. I stayed where I was for a minute, hanging onto one of the few new replacement leather straps.

A short stop at Hounslow West and we were then above ground and into the daylight. No one bothered to look up as I moved through the next carriage, heads were buried in newspapers and magazines, the rest looking at the floor or other people's feet.

Hounslow Central and East came and went. I moved through two more carriages but stopped abruptly in front of the next door. The old couple were sitting on the right side of the next carriage a few feet from the door, they were holding hands and smiling at each other. The two large black suitcases were within arm's reach on their right. Then I spotted John, he was two seats away from them reading a crumpled newspaper. I didn't look at them, or him, as I walked past on my way to the door of the next carriage. The train shuddered and squealed to a stop before I reached it.

Osterley station was busy, I glanced back and saw Nick and Simon were in the carriage and taking seats, they had got their eyes on their targets, and John. I made a spontaneous decision to get off the train and scan the next few carriages from the platform. I didn't need to worry about the couple now, they were covered. Don Juan was my only target and objective now.

I pushed my way out of the door as soon as it opened and headed up the platform. I scanned two carriages before hearing a loud whistle blast, he wasn't in them. I stepped into the third carriage as the doors started to close and saw him instantly. Don Juan was sitting 15 feet away on the left hand side of the carriage, tucked away in a corner seat reading one of those useless free underground magazines that contain fuck all that is interesting or informative.

I turned my back to him and pulled down the front of my NY baseball cap a fraction further. I sat down quickly in a free seat on the same side of the carriage as Don Juan, the odd looking towers of Osterley station disappearing fast behind us as we picked up speed again. I reached behind my back to check the SIG was still secure. I knew this was not the place to try and take him because if he was armed he would have no hesitation killing anyone in here to stay alive. I wouldn't take that chance.

I counted seven people between him and me, but I was lucky because a really fat guy, two seats down from Don Juan, was blocking the gap between the seats so he wouldn't be able to see me looking at him, when I could. Within a minute, I saw the fat guy's eyes close and his head droop forward, his bulk briefly sliding over to his right before he jerked himself back upright. But not before I got eyes on Don Juan again through the gap. I counted the other passengers in the carriage that I could see. In total there were four children, all quiet at the moment, six elderly people, two in couples and eleven adults, six men and five women, plus Don Juan. There was too much potential for collateral damage even though I wanted so much to kill him right here, right now.

A couple of young long haired dudes and a smartly dressed young woman got on when we stopped at Cockfosters. The woman took the seat opposite the fat guy and wrinkled her nose up as she did. No one got off.

The tracks seem smoother now and the area outside less built up. Gone were the big square grey buildings of ten minutes ago replaced with patches of green and lots of trees. The lights flicker for a second as we go under an old iron bridge and the train begins to slow again. Northfield station, five got on and four got off so I still had adequate bodies between us. An old girl squeezed herself into the seat next to the fat guy who let out a loud sigh as he shifted his vast bulk only a couple of inches to let her in. She was not impressed, by the look on her face.

Acton Town came and went, but nobody moved. I saw Don Juan was still reading the magazine because the fat guy was now awake and moving about exposing the gap between the seats frequently. He was openly leering at the young woman opposite him, his eyes obviously focusing downwards trying to look past the hem of her skirt, which she had consciously pulled down at least once already.

11

Hammersmith station was overshadowed by the growing number of tower blocks as we got nearer the City. I saw Bill at the last second heading towards the rear carriages his head was down and now covered with a battered looking grey baseball cap.

Bill slid into the empty seat facing me six minutes later as the train pulled out of Earls Court with another big jolt.

'I saw him at Hammersmith,' Bill whispered in my ear. 'And then I saw Nick and the other two MI5 boys a couple of carriages away. I got on a couple of carriages further back because I hadn't seen you, but then guessed you might be close to Don Juan. I think I also clocked the bag mules as I came through. An older couple with two large black suitcases next to them?'

'Yes that's them. Nick, Simon and John are going to sort them,' I answered quietly. 'He hasn't moved Bill, I think he is going all the way to Kings Cross,' I added.

Gloucester Road, South Kensington, Knightsbridge, Hyde Park Corner all came and went. None of the passengers engaged with each other at all, no eye contact, no discussion, no nothing. I hadn't spent much time on London Transport, but I did begin to wonder if it was always like this. A tall, thickset skinhead got on at Hyde Park as well as a cocky looking kid wearing dark Ray Ban shades. He looked a right twat as the nearest sun was probably a 1000 miles from here. The skinhead began to eye him up menacingly, but I couldn't see behind the kid's glasses to see whether or not he realised he was being eyeballed and if he did whether he was crapping himself right now.

A waft of nice perfume reached my nostrils from the pretty young woman just sitting down on the opposite side of the carriage. The air had definitely changed again to being musty and stale now we were underground again. I knew one thing for sure I wouldn't want to be doing this journey every day.

Five minutes later we pulled into Holborn. The number of passengers in the carriage had reduced considerably and more were getting up and moving to the doors. I leaned forward in my seat to get closer to Bill.

'We need to move Bill. It's getting a bit thin on the ground in here and he is beginning to look around,' I whispered.

We got off, keeping a few yards between us, turned left and walked to the rear doors of the second carriage further down the train and then re-boarded.

The train picked up speed again quickly and started to rattle and shake as it sped over worn underground rails. I looked back through the adjoining carriage door and saw the couple sitting quietly with the two big suitcases still in the same position. They were oblivious to the attention of the three MI5 men all sitting within 10 feet of them.

The train slowed again with the obligatory screeching of its brakes, the decibels increasing exponentially as more pressure was applied. A large tiled sign saying Russell Square appeared in the window, this was the last stop before Kings Cross. I noticed the colour of the shiny ceramic tiles had changed again. We now had green, black and beige rather than the mixture of yellows, blues, greens, reds, white and the shitty brown tiles I had seen at Convent Garden. There was probably a good reason for it, and maybe one day I would find out, but not today.

We had already started to move towards the next carriage when the train jolted in motion again. In less than a minute Bill had eyes on Don Juan again through the carriage door window, he was moving about in his seat.

Don Juan arched his back and stretched in his seat and then he smiled, he knew it wasn't far to Kings Cross so it wouldn't be long before he was enjoying an excellent lunch and bottle of the finest Château Mouton Rothschild in Sir Richard's private club. The main event though would be happening later that afternoon when they would complete the transactions required to transfer a little over 250 million dollars to his new accounts in Switzerland and Monaco. The two new accounts already held significant funds from the bank transfers he had instigated from Argentina during the past few months, but they only amounted to half of the two deposits the UK banks would be making today. The total amount of money was almost pocket change compared to the vast fortune he had accumulated in Argentina, but he couldn't get access to any of it right now. Having the UK, and the other funds, accessible to him meant he would be able to finance the actions he had already planned in order to seize back his fortune. That was a top priority for him after today.

Don Juan was also looking forward to getting to Kings Cross for another reason. Two of his most trustworthy and toughest personal bodyguards had successfully slipped into the UK the week before and they would be there to meet him. He knew there would be several other hard and ruthless men recruited by Diego to support them, but that was just detail and he didn't need to concern himself with that. He had thought it best not to have the two huge ex Argentine Marines waiting at the airport for him as it could have drawn unwanted attention their way. The train had proved to be a good plan as nobody had paid any attention to him and he had been able to stay close to the cash that would soon be back in his hands.

'He's getting ready to leave,' Bill said as he watched Don Juan stand up through the dirty glass window in the door.

We had arrived dead on time, it was 1047. Don Juan waited for everyone else to leave the carriage and then stepped casually off the train pausing to look down at the rough anti slip yellow painted tiles beneath his feet. He was killing time.

The majority of the crowd were disappearing through the exit at the far end of the platform clearly identified by the blue tiled columns on either side of it. Some people headed into the exit on his right, which was the one he wanted.

Don Juan hunched up his overcoat and checked one last time that the mules had got off the train with his suitcases. They had and were walking towards him, still smiling.

Simon, Nick and John had already got off the train and had mingled with the main crowd heading left for the exit, Bill and I were still on the train watching what Don Juan was going to do next. He was looking down the platform in our direction so we couldn't get off without being seen.

Don Juan turned away at the last second as we stepped out the fast closing doors and walked quickly over to a large curved underground map fixed to the wall. By the time I looked for him again Don Juan and the old couple had disappeared down the right side exit tunnel heading for the escalator that would take them up into Kings Cross main line station.

Nick and the others had stayed at the back of the crowd but were now running down the platform towards us. The squealing of the train's wheels biting on the steel tracks and hydraulic brakes releasing, signalled that it was on its way. The red lamp at the back of the empty train was visible for only a couple of seconds as it disappeared into the black hole at the end of the platform. All three MI5 men were standing with us with by the time the echo of the train had faded.

There was only one option, it was time to run. I got to the bottom of the escalator first and saw the old woman with her black suitcase disappearing over the top. There were no alternative stairs so the only option was to take the now empty escalator two steps at a time. Bill and the others did exactly the same right behind me. I only hoped they hadn't stopped for anything at the top because if they had we would run straight into them.

12

Monday 19th December 1983

Kings Cross Station, London

Things got complicated as soon we reached the top of the escalator. I saw them first and immediately signalled Bill to back off and move right. Nick, Simon and John anticipated Bill's move and split up as soon as their feet were on flat ground. Don Juan and the old couple had gone through the exit barriers but had stopped under the low ceiling next to the bustling ticket office outside. There were now five of them standing in a group only 25 yards away, Don Juan was slipping a small brown package into his overcoat pocket that one of the two huge mean looking goons, that were definitely not of British origin, had passed to him. Both goons had the air of soldiers, Argie fucking soldiers, I would bet on it.

I was a couple of feet away from Bill keeping my face hidden from the group, I was wasting time searching my pockets trying to find the train ticket that was cupped tightly in my right hand. Bill was doing the same. Nick moved past us and headed for the small booth at the right of the turnstiles used by the station guards. It was only five feet by three with glass windows in the two sides that looked out onto the barriers. More importantly the back wall of the booth was solid and would provide cover between us and Don Juan's group.

Nick was inside the booth, his left hand grabbed the arm of one of the guards on duty as soon as he entered.

'We're police officers, stay calm and don't do anything stupid,' he told both of them firmly and quietly.

The second guard did what he was told and stayed put on his little stool as I moved in quickly behind the wall. Bill was still in the same place in the passageway fiddling around in his jeans pocket, head down and face covered with his battered cap. A moment later I saw his expression change as he looked up. Something was happening.

'They have split up. Don Juan and one of the goons are going up the right stairs towards the station and the others are going up the left heading towards the street,' Bill said as he reached me.

It took five seconds for us all to congregate outside the booth door.

'Nick, you guys have to follow bag mules, whatever they are carrying has something to do with why the General's here. Bill and I will take the other goon and Don Juan. Be careful though I'm sure the goon is Argentine military and he will be armed,' I said.

Nick moved without saying anything, Simon and John close behind him. There wasn't the time to fuck around with tickets so we legged it with the others out of the side gate that had been open seconds before for a man on crutches. The guard, and the man on crutches, almost came a cropper as we barged through and then crutches man started gobbing off but was quickly silenced by something the guard said to him.

Bystanders milling around by the ticket office broke off their conversations as they watched the three men run up the left side of the stairs two steps at a time. The event didn't hold their attention for long and as soon as they had disappeared it was heads back down into the guidebooks or the underground maps they had been studying.

Bill and I threaded our way through the crowds without barging into anyone else and made our way up the right side of the stairs. As we turned right and headed into Kings Cross station itself, I spotted the goon, bag mules and the three MI5 men standing at a pelican crossing 30 yards away. They were all within a few feet of each other waiting to cross the main road.

Don Juan and his goon were about 150 feet ahead of us walking past W. H. Smith's. They ignored the huge train departure and arrivals board 20 feet above their heads and the station announcer's booming voice telling them that the train to Leeds would be departing in five minutes from platform 4.

Almost immediately the announcer was at it again, booming out the names of several cities on the East Coast line. Sunderland, Newcastle, Peterborough, Cambridge were all mentioned, but the times and platform numbers all merged into just a noise as I quickened my pace and focussed on our target ahead.

Don Juan was striding along at a quick pace past the station cafe and the other shops, heading for the far left hand platform. We closed in to 70 feet just as a steady stream of people was heading up the platform after leaving the recently arrived train. We kept Don Juan and the goon in view as we threaded our way through the crowd, neither of them looked behind them at any point.

Tucked halfway down the platform under the arched steel girders and grime covered plastic sheets that made up the roof was the entrance to the gents' toilets. Don Juan was heading straight for it.

Another announcement boomed over the PA system. The train to Newcastle would be leaving shortly.

Don Juan and the goon stopped ahead. Bill and I stopped too and leaned against a brick wall a few feet from the entrance to the ladies' loo. Bill produced a London underground map from his pocket and had it open and up in front of us before Don Juan had looked back down the platform. The train that had delivered the people we had negotiated our way through was now empty and pulling away from the platform leaving it empty except for the four of us. The goon took up position at the platform entrance to the gents' as Don Juan headed down the stairs.

'Let's finish this fucking thing Harry. I'll take the goon and you kill that murdering son of a bitch,' Bill whispered.

I didn't need to reply and we didn't need a detailed plan. This was simple, just get in there and fucking do it.

It was now eerily quiet on this side of the station as we closed in on the entrance to the gents', and the goon. When we arrived, the goon moved his huge 6' 6" frame across the top of the stairs and blocked our path.

'No one allowed. It is closed,' he said to me in crap English with a South American accent.

'Are you having a fucking laugh,' Bill growled at him from a couple of feet behind my left shoulder.

I stepped right as the goon lifted his right foot to take a step forward, but before it had reached the floor again the sole of Bill's right boot had hit him square in the middle of his chest launching him backwards into fresh air.

The goon missed nearly all of the 20 steps down to the tiled flat area on the corner of the stairs. The back of his head split like a melon when it connected with the edge of one of the steps, blood splattering onto the flat tiled floor when he finally hit it. He was not out yet though and tried to get back to his feet almost immediately. Bill hadn't taken anything for granted and was already down the stairs as the goon was half up on one knee. Bill yanked his head downwards and rammed his knee into his face, catapulting his head back into the wall. Blood exploded from the goon's nose soaking the front of his shirt, and Bill's trousers. As Bill was about to throw a punch into the goon's face I stepped over his legs heading for the final few steps down into the gents'.

Before Bill's punch connected the goon swung his left boot towards me. He took out my left ankle making me fall forward onto the stairs, the SIG spilled from my grasp when my hand hit the edge of the last step. I could do nothing as I watched it slide across the white tiles and under the door of the first trap. The goon groaned as Bill planted his knee firmly into the goon's nuts and then he began pummelling his face with his fists.

I scrambled to my feet and took a first step towards my SIG. The first round fizzed past my right ear obliterating a large white tile behind me that instantly showered me in dust and sharp bits of broken tile. The second round destroyed another tile next to the other as I dived towards the traps, rolling forward as I hit the hard tiled deck. The door didn't open as I rolled into it. Don Juan had come out of the furthest trap and had fired as soon as he saw me. His trousers were up and secured, but his belt and flies were still undone.

I was half way up to my feet when I saw he had the Argentine Bersa pistol pointing straight at my chest, I was a dead duck. Then I heard a click, it had jammed. Don Juan pulled the trigger again and again, but nothing. He banged the pistol against the hard surface next to the sinks and pulled the trigger again. Still nothing. I was up on my feet and going for him, but then he growled and snarled at me before hurling the pistol at my head. I moved left and it missed my head but struck me hard on the right shoulder. I didn't have time to register any pain or worry about it as Don Juan was now bearing down on me at speed, his face purple with rage and screaming like a banshee, his fists bunched so tightly I could see the whites of his knuckles. He covered the 12 feet between us so fast there was no chance of me getting anywhere near my SIG.

He hit me at speed, the impact forcing me backwards across the entrance, where Bill and the goon were still fighting, and into a mirror image of the right hand toilets. I knew I had to use his weight and momentum before some part of my body hit something very hard and broke. Spittle from the General's gob was running down my face. His mouth and teeth were snapping together six inches from my face as I rammed my right boot onto the top of his left foot and let my body drop backwards onto what I prayed would be just the tiled deck. I gripped the lapels of his jacket with both hands and with all the strength I could muster I heaved him forward. The collision with the sink units didn't help with the move and I didn't have enough strength to completely flip him right over, but I still managed to throw him far enough away from me so his body cleared mine.

Don Juan slid forward another four feet on the smooth square tiled floor before his head connected with the doorframe of the second trap. He roared and cursed in his own language but wasn't going to stay down. I was on my feet first but could only use my left hand to push myself up and steady myself. The right shoulder had taken a significant bang from the impact with the sink units and the back of my head would be growing an egg very shortly. The shoulder was still intact, but only just, and there was no pain yet as adrenaline had taken over.

I shook my head to clear my vision and could see Don Juan had rolled over and was getting back onto his feet. Blood was running down his forehead and the bridge of his nose from the cuts he had sustained on the edge of the doorframe.

I smashed any part of the bone in his nose that wasn't already broken with my first punch. My right arm was almost useless, but I managed to hold him up by his jacket for the second one. It connected above his left eye socket splitting the eyebrow from one side to the other. The last punch before I lost my grip on him split lips and moved teeth before he hit the deck once more.

I got to my feet and looked down to see the damage to Don Juan's face was pretty significant now. The fucker was still trying to get to his feet though, spitting out big globs of blood from his smashed mouth as he did so.

'Oh no you don't you fucker,' I screamed at him before burying my right boot into his guts causing more blood and a single tooth to spurt out from his mouth.

Don Juan was on his side holding his belly and groaning but then he turned his face towards me, his left eye was closing rapidly but his right zeroed in on me. It was filled with hatred and rage.

'Fuck you,' he snarled at me.

'No, Fuck you,' I snarled back at him as my right boot caught him squarely on the jaw snapping his head backwards. More blood and teeth spilling from his mouth.

I stood over him not knowing whether he could hear me or not as I screamed at him.

'You and your fucking rotten family have caused unimaginable pain and suffering to so many people, but this is where it is going to end for you. You are going to fucking die today. Do you hear me you fucker? This is for my wife, my family, my comrades and for the good people of Argentina.'

The General was on his back sprawled out on the cold tiles not moving, but I could see he was still conscious. I turned away from him because I needed to retrieve my SIG and finish this.

I hadn't noticed the sign on the first trap door saying 'out of order' so I assumed the door had been purposely locked shut. It gave way with my first kick and then I spotted my SIG right in the corner past the pan. I retrieved it quickly and turned to look across at the stairs where Bill was just pushing himself off the goon. Blood oozed out of the hole under his jaw bone where Bill had driven his knife into the base of his brain, twisting it at the final moment severing nerves, tendons and the spinal cord. A Browning 9mm lay beneath the goon's limp outstretched left arm on the first step below them.

I was distracted momentarily as Bill wiped the blood off his knife using the goon's shirt. It was enough time for Don Juan to get within six feet of me. He was still moving quickly despite his injuries and in his right hand he was holding an open ivory handled five-inch switchblade. Don Juan was not going to die easily, or alone, from the look on his face. It was contorted with rage and purple with anger that was focussed directly on me.

In that split second, I knew I didn't have time to get the SIG up to a firing position so I dived right and away from the knife. Don Juan swung it wildly in my direction, but I was far enough away so it flashed across my chest. He was now exposed and off balance and before he could pull his arm back to have another go I smashed the butt of the SIG into his forehead knocking him back into the other toilet area.

He still wouldn't go down and started to come back at me but before I could get my SIG on target Don Juan was falling backwards, the sound of a discharged weapon reverberating around the solid walls of the toilet. There was a small but neat bullet hole evident on the right side of his chest.

Don Juan's lifeless body crashed down onto the tiled floor, a small fountain of frothy red blood was spitting out of the hole in his chest. The ivory handed knife fell from his grasp and onto the floor with a clatter as the gunshot noise began to dissipate.

Bill stood on the bottom step with the goon's 9mm Browning in his bloodied right hand, a small wisp of blue smoke snaked its way out of the barrel into the airless void of the underground gents' toilet.

'Let's get the fuck out of here Harry,' he said almost nonchalantly.

'No shit,' I replied.

I took one more look at the body of Don Juan, he wasn't moving. I wanted it to be me who had pulled the trigger, but actually I was OK that Bill had killed him in the end. He was after all the catalyst for all the pain we had both suffered.

I moved towards the stairway pausing just long enough to retrieve the General's ivory handled switchblade from the floor.

13

Bill was already at the top of the stairs as I stepped over the dead goon.

'Move it Harry,' he shouted. 'People will have heard the gunshot but they don't know where it has come from yet.'

In four strides, I was next to him. The three tracks directly in front of us were empty, but our view to the opposite side of Kings Cross station through the high brick arches was blocked by an Intercity train that spread along the whole length of the last platform on our side.

We could see people peering through the train windows. Others kept their heads in their morning newspapers oblivious to anything happening outside.

'Your chin needs a wipe Harry, it's splattered,' Bill said as we started to move. I could feel it now so used my sleeve and some spit to get Don Juan's blood off my face.

We walked quickly and purposely down the side of the empty platform so we looked like any other two people hurrying to get a train. The huge half-moon shaped exterior window at the front of the platforms barely lifted the overall light within the station, but I doubted even in this gloominess we would be able to disguise or hide any of the wet blood stains on our clothes. We just had to keep moving, fast.

We turned left at the top of the platform, avoiding going back into the main concourse where the notice board and shops were. Some of the mingling crowd were looking bemused and puzzled as to what, if anything, they had heard. We were past the third platform when we saw the couple of station guards and a policeman running down the end platform towards the toilets.

The guards and the policeman hadn't reached the entrance to the gents' when we passed through the central archways between the platforms. All four tracks on this side of the station were full with trains. One must have just arrived as a large crowd of passengers appeared in front of us.

Tall steel gates at the exit to York Way were held open against the archway walls by chunky ornate black hooks. We were 20 feet away when we heard the whistles and muffled shouts of what we assumed to be the guards and the policeman on the first platform. Without looking back, we exited into bright December sunlight, the obligatory McDonalds directly in front of us. I almost ran into a Japanese tourist as she focussed her camera on the imposing station clock that sits on top of a high brick tower in the centre of the two covered platform domes.

We dodged the traffic and got across to York Way. A black cab driver shouted some abuse at us for being lazy bastards and not walking the 20 yards to the zebra crossing. We quickly dismissed the Euston Road and the Gray's Inn Road option on our right and headed straight up Pentonville Road trying to get some distance between us and the station. Moments later we both hear the police sirens closing in on the station.

'Fuck me that was quick,' Bill said as we walked quickly past several coffee shops to the next junction at Caledonian Road. Only a couple of people gave us a quizzical stare as we strode by.

The pavement on our left was almost empty as we broke into a run. All the traffic on the road is heading one way and coming towards us as I scanned for anything that resembled a cab. Fifty yards up the road I spotted a black cab indicating left at the junction of a side road. I stick my good left hand out and then whistle as we closed in on him running up the road he would have to drive down. Blocking his escape.

We dived in and both sat on the drop down seats with our backs to the driver, we didn't need him to be asking any questions about why we looked like we did. We leave Omega Place behind us and turn left back onto Pentonville Road. In five minutes, we had enough miles between us and Kings Cross station to be able to breathe again. It was only three miles as the crow flies to Victoria and the Holiday Inn, but we travelled a lot more than that before eventually, 35 minutes later, we were handing over a wad of cash to the silent cab driver.

We headed straight to the stairs. Both of us had kept our room keys after removing the identifying tags from them. Thirty minutes later and we were both clean, in new kit and checked out. Another cab was waiting outside ready to take us to the station car park at Hammersmith where Bill had dumped the Escort.

It was still there but with a bright yellow ticket stuck under the driver's windscreen wiper telling us he had parked without displaying his permit.

'We won't worry too much about that,' Bill quipped.

It was the first time we had both smiled for a while and five minutes later and we were back on the A4 and heading towards the M4 motorway.

14

Wednesday 21st December 1983

Foreign and Commonwealth Office

The same stiff suited civil servant greeted us formally at the entrance of the Foreign and Commonwealth Office that we had used a few days earlier. He led Colin Shaw, Bill and me up the same impressive stairway and down to the office occupied by Brigadier Whistonhall, who looked immaculate again in a different, but equally impressive, Savile row suit. There were two other people in the room, both we recognised instantly. We already had been told the bad news so we weren't expecting this to be a happy meeting.

'Come in gentlemen. I understand from your initial reports that General Muscardin was a bit fucked up in the end? Couldn't have happened to a nicer bloke.' We were all a bit taken aback as none of us had heard the Brigadier swear before.

'We have a small problem though gentlemen, as you know.' The Brigadier continued, the expression on his face changing instantly. 'Only one body was recovered from the scene and it was definitely not General Muscardin.'

'Sir,' I said. 'He was shot in the chest and blood was pouring out of him and he wasn't moving. I didn't check for a pulse, but I was sure he was dead.'

'So was I,' Bill said. 'And I was the one that shot him.'

'Well gentlemen, from what you say and what I have read, it is highly unlikely that he would have been alive when the unknowns retrieved him from the station toilet. However, we cannot confirm that at this moment although I do not believe that fact will detract us from our business today.' Brigadier Whistonhall paused for a moment and then carried on. 'We have three men with significant injuries in the University College Hospital in Euston Road, thankfully all of which are currently non-life threatening. Two station guards have knife wounds to their abdomens and the police officer has a cracked skull and several broken ribs. I believe you actually saw these gentlemen running towards the toilet?'

'Yes sir we did, but we didn't see anyone behind them, or on the platform, before we exited the station,' Bill said.

'Gentlemen, you know MI5 officer Nick Askew, who has some details on the events after you left the station.' Brigadier Whistonhall perched himself on the end of the desk when he had finished talking.

'We do sir,' I said as Bill and I shook his hand in turn.

'You have also met, briefly I understand, Ms Elizabeth Thompson. Elizabeth is the senior MI5 officer assigned to help me deal with the Muscardin problem, and is officer Askew's boss, I believe.' The Brigadier directed the last part of his statement towards the stern faced woman standing in front of us.

'You are correct sir,' she answered and moved closer to offer her hand to Bill and me. 'Unfortunately Sir Timothy Dashford, the Director General sends his apologies, he would have very much liked to be here for this briefing,' she said looking straight at us, and with a little menace in her voice. I got the feeling that she wasn't happy with us because we hadn't followed her orders, but fuck it, I thought, what's she going to do about it?

As we sat down at the conference table, I noticed the two black suitcases sitting in the corner of the room.

'I believe we should let Mr Askew tell us what happened after you were separated at Kings Cross station. Are you ready Mr Askew?' Brigadier Whistonhall asked from his perch.

'Yes sir,' Nick answered.

'The goon wasn't in any hurry as he led the couple down Belgrove Street and then into Argyle Square. I assumed from his slow pace he was either waiting for the General and the other bodyguard to catch up, or he had plenty of time to get where he was going with the old couple. He led them into a small park at Argyle Square and cut across it diagonally heading towards the gate at the opposite corner. The goon got spooked by someone or something when they were halfway across the park and he took off at pace towards the gate. He just left the old couple behind. He drew his weapon and began shouting something in Spanish at what we now know were more armed blokes standing by some parked cars on the other side of the trees. Seconds later three blokes appeared through the gate all carrying handguns. We were already 30 feet into the open park with nowhere to go and no cover, so we had to fight.' Nick paused and took a sip of water before continuing.

'It kicked off big time and bullets were flying everywhere. Simon was hit first and took one in the left shoulder; he went down but kept firing and killed one of the new blokes in the opening exchange. I got the original goon with a head shot that killed him instantly, but John was hit in the right thigh at the same moment and went down hard. I killed one of the others with another head shot and then dived right to draw fire away from Simon and John as the last bloke zeroed in on me. He dropped like a stone as two rounds hit him dead centre of his chest, one from Simon and the other from John. The fire fight had only lasted about 30 seconds, but it was carnage in there.' Nick took a deep breath as he finished talking, but we all stayed quiet because his story wasn't finished yet.

'Once I had confirmed that all the blokes were dead and that Simon and John were OK, I asked the old couple where they were going. They told me they were heading for a car that was, 'not far,' in the goon's words. Immediately after that, and before I could go and have a look for the car, several armed response units arrived. They were jumpy and got very aggressive when they saw the four dead bodies by the park entrance and it took a few minutes before they were convinced who we were and the situation was stabilized. Once my identity was confirmed I got them to look for 'the car' and in less than a minute they found the two Range Rovers parked next to each other in Argyle street, a black one with its doors open and a white one with the keys in the ignition. In both of them, they found some serious weaponry in the boot. It was then that I remembered catching a glimpse of what could have been another black Range Rover speeding northwards up Argyle Square towards Kings Cross and St Pancras just as the fire fight started.

The Superintendent, who was the senior armed response unit officer, told me that they had received an unconfirmed report of a potential gunshot somewhere, on or around, Kings Cross station. But that was immediately before the multiple 999 calls of men in a gunfight and people being killed in this park. Every unit had been diverted there to deal with a live situation and the onsite police officers at Kings Cross were tasked to investigate further the reported incident there. Then, while we were talking, his radio relayed the message that customers in the Parcel Yard pub across from Kings Cross station had seen four armed men arriving fast in a black Range Rover. They had crow-barred open a service door at the back of one of the retail units and gone in. Shortly after, two of the men were seen carrying someone to the car and then it left at speed. Units were instantly despatched from the park but the Range Rover and its occupants haven't been seen since. I would put money on that it has been stripped or it's at the bottom of the river by now.'

As soon as Nick stopped talking Elizabeth Thompson stepped in and continued with the briefing.

'They have since found out the couple had been recruited in the UK for the job and it was something they had done before. The UK contact names we extracted from them that evening are currently helping us with our enquiries. Our counterparts in Spain have arrested the General's accomplices and are currently being 'vigorously' questioned. A literal translation I'm afraid,' she said and smiled. 'Sir Richard Roses and Robert Keys have been detained in connection with money laundering and illegal banking activities and we have seized funds in two London bank accounts totalling over 250 million dollars. We also now have the details of General Muscardin's accounts in Switzerland and Monaco, which we believe also hold additional substantial funds that belong to Argentina. The only 'other' down side to this operation is that Diego Bruno has unfortunately slipped through our nets and has not been seen anywhere since the morning of the 19th December. We have notified all ports and airports to be on the lookout for him and I have a large team of MI5 officers also searching for him as well, but as of one hour ago he is still missing.

Bill and I both picked up on the accentuated 'other' in her little speech and was no doubt referring to us not having Don Juan's body in a bag. She wasn't going to let up on us and was about to continue when the phone on the Brigadier's desk rang. He walked over and picked it up straight away.

'Mr Reynoso, how good of you to call,' he said into the receiver. 'Please can you wait a moment so that I can transfer you to the speaker phone?' He then walked back to the table and pressed the button on the conference phone and after a few crackles and a short loud buzzing noise, a voice Bill and I knew well came through the speaker.

'Brigadier Whistonhall, gentlemen and Ms Thompson, good morning. This is Fernando Reynoso. Please may I introduce my father, Mario Vargas Reynoso to you all.' Another crackle then a much deeper voice came through the speaker. 'Good morning, it is a great pleasure for me to be able to speak to you. My first request, if you would permit me, is to thank you all personally for your actions with respect to dealing with the brutal members of the Muscardin family. These were people who have inflicted immense pain and suffering on the people of Argentina and have shamed my beloved country. I am aware that General Muscardin's body has not been recovered but even if he is still alive we now have seized all of his assets and known funds from across the world so any power or influence he had has been totally compromised. I doubt that, even if he is still alive, and I sincerely hope he isn't, he would ever recover from these events.'

There was a brief pause before Mario Reynoso spoke again. 'President Alfonsín has spoken directly with Prime Minister Thatcher about the stolen funds that you have recovered in the United Kingdom and has thanked her for promising the repatriation of them to our country. The Prime Minister has also assured him that she will be talking to the appropriate people in Switzerland and Monaco to ensure their cooperation with members of the United Kingdom Government in order to repatriate those funds as well. I can assure you, as President Alfonsín has done with Prime Minister Thatcher, that all the recovered funds will be used to support the families of those who have suffered personally at the hands of these barbarians and to ensure that justice is served on all criminals who have persecuted our people since 1976, and before.

Before I hand you back to my son, I wish to speak directly to Captain Dye and Lieutenant Glass, if I may. Gentlemen you are brave and honourable fighting men and nothing I can say or do now can bring back those friends, comrades and loved ones you have lost. But I believe your actions have honoured those who perished, and are, I hope something in time you will be very proud of. I would consider it an enormous honour and privilege if I am ever fortunate enough to express my gratitude for what you have done in person. But for now all I can say on behalf of many, many people is thank you.'

'Mr Reynoso, sir. I believe I can speak for everyone in this room and say your words and thoughts are much appreciated by all of us here and I'm sure would be well received by those who have lost loved ones.' No one else in the room needed to say anything after Brigadier Whistonhall had finish speaking.

'Thank you sir,' Mario Vargas Reynoso said humbly. 'But before we go my son has one final piece of news that was confirmed personally by my President less than one hour ago.' There was a short crackle on the line as the phone was moved around at the other end and then Fernando Reynoso's voice again came over the speaker.

'In the two suitcases retrieved from General Muscardin's accomplices, Ms Thompson has communicated that they contain exactly two million UK pounds in cash. This is correct, Ms Thompson?'

'It is Mr Reynoso.' Fernando then paused. 'It is the express wish of the Argentine Government that those funds are distributed equally to the surviving family members of those murdered in the Malvinas and United Kingdom by the Muscardin family. We understand that Prime Minister Thatcher is supportive of this request.'

I didn't expect that or necessarily want it, but my thoughts immediately went to Bob's wife Jeannie. Any financial support would make a massive difference to her life now, and indeed all our lives if I allowed myself to accept it. I knew it would be something my conscience and I would seriously wrestle with it in the coming weeks.

'Goodbye gentlemen and Ms Thompson,' Fernando said and then there was a click and then nothing. He was gone. The room was silent for what seemed an age before Brigadier Whistonhall spoke. 'Well, that was unexpected. Where is the money now Elizabeth?' he asked. 'It is here in those two cases,' she said pointing at the two black suitcases standing in the corner of the room. I assumed from his question that he hadn't been in the room when Elizabeth and Nick had been shown in.

'Gentlemen I will need to speak with the Prime Minister about the President's gesture as I knew nothing of this,' Brigadier Whistonhall said. 'Personally I am in favour, but we have to consider the implications for other families of those lost during the Falklands War. I would ask you that no discussions regarding this proposal are conducted outside of this room. Am I clear?'

'Yes sir,' was the collective response from everyone in the room.

'We are done then. Enjoy your Christmas breaks, if you are having one,' the Brigadier was speaking to everyone as he stood up. 'Colonel Shaw and Ms Thompson, we will talk in a few days.'

Bill and I had said our goodbyes to Nick and Elizabeth when our pin-striped man appeared at the door to usher us out the building. He didn't smile at us even when we purposely waved at him from the car as we headed out the courtyard and back towards the M4.

15

Friday 13th January 1984

Jeannie May was sitting next to me still staring at the cheque for two hundred thousand pounds, a small fortune to anyone. Tears were still streaming down her face 20 minutes after I had given her the envelope. Nothing I said would make her stop. I had tried to explain, very badly, that the money was from a Government source set up especially to deal with special cases resulting from losses in the Falklands War. But that it was, and had to remain, a confidential matter between her and the Government.

She was obviously struggling to comprehend what was happening or why, as Bob's death still cut deeply into her soul. Life had been a struggle since the funeral in '82, emotionally as well as financially, although many people had and still were supporting her through it. I knew this money would put a lot of things right. It was the difference between struggling for many years to come and a decent quality of life now for her and the kids. I had only intended to stay with her until the kids came home from school, but then Uncle Harry had to listen to all their stories and have a fight on the front room carpet. It was a good job all my wounds had completely healed as the kids were all heavy lumps now. My last joyful task was to help Jeannie feed them Birds Eye fish fingers, mash and beans.

'Steak for them tomorrow,' I said quietly whilst giving Jeannie a secret wink. At last she smiled.

I walked through the door at home at 0100 on Saturday morning. The drive from Cornwall had been a nightmare. Everyone seemed to be travelling up the same piece of road heading north. I loved seeing Jeannie and the kids and being able to personally deliver the cheque. Life for a few people had changed dramatically this week including the fund that had been set up to support those wounded in the Falklands. An unknown donor had boosted it with a donation of one million pounds two days earlier. Bill and I had ensured that was an integral part of the agreement before those directly affected by the events at Rincon Grande received any part of the funds.

I made myself a cup of tea and sat down in the quiet of the house. It was very peaceful at this time of the morning and not what life had been like during the past few months. My own envelope was still sitting above the fireplace where I had left it yesterday. I was still feeling guilty about receiving any money because of Kathy's death, but at the same time I was also happy because I knew

Harry Jr would be loved and well taken care of whilst I was away at university. Gerri had already given in her notice telling everyone she was going to be taking care of Harry Jr full time. She had agreed to 'help out' when they needed it as long as they paid her a good consultancy rate. She would certainly have a surprise later this morning when I gave her the envelope.

I wondered how Bill and Colin had got on with John Williams and Jimmy Blake's families. I could only imagine their meeting would have been as emotional as mine was with Jeannie. Bill was really struggling to accept the money on behalf of Tom.

'It was my job,' he kept saying. 'Not this one Captain,' he was told. 'But you can use the money to help your parents and family do good for others. It is up to you how these funds are used.' Colin Shaw had reassured him.

Bill had left his envelope with the Colonel whilst 'he got his head around it.'

I knew he would do the right thing in time even if it were their decision to give it all to charity. One thing that was made very clear was the money could not be returned because our orders were that the new Argentine President's wishes should be honoured. To refuse it would cause great offence and right now our own Prime Minister was keen that any opportunity for the warming of diplomatic relations was taken. She told Brigadier Whistonhall personally that it was important for both countries to put behind them the events of 1982. She still didn't trust them at all but now at least they were talking again.

I had dozed off on the settee and was still there when Gerri woke me with a light shake of my right shoulder at 0630, a hot steaming fresh cup of tea in her hands.

'Got back late last night then?' she asked.

'Yeah,' I replied rubbing the sleep out of my eyes with my free hand.

'How are Jeannie and the kids Harry?'

'They're OK,' I said. 'She has been having a bit of a rough time of it though, but I think things will get better for her now.'

'Oh, and why would that be Harry?' Gerri asked me with a quizzical look on her face. I knew when I got that tone and the look, I was not going to get away without spilling the beans.

I was saved at that moment by the cries of Harry Jr.

'Don't you move now, I want to know it all' Gerri said, wagging her finger at me playfully as she disappeared around the door.

The next hour was spent with Harry Jr cradled in my arms, the soft gurgling sounds he made distracting me at points in the conversation with Gerri. His bright blue eyes and the wonderful features his mother had blessed him with were smiling back at me from the crook of my arm.

I told Gerri everything starting right at the beginning on the Falklands. We had been through that before, but I added some of the more graphical details so she had the full picture and knew why I had done what I did. I told her about the operation in Argentina and then what happened in New Jersey and New York. We didn't dwell on the events in the UK in between those times as we both knew the painful outcomes too well. I then dropped a bollock and let slip that Ron had been shot even though he had made me promise that I wouldn't tell her.

'That is why the bugger has been so vague on the phone about coming over for a visit,' I could see Gerri was more concerned about him rather than being miffed when she spoke. Another ex-Olympian was going to get a real bollocking later today, I was sure of that. Then it would be my turn from across the Atlantic.

I told Gerri about the meeting with Fernando in London and the involvement of MI5, and their counterparts in Spain, who had found and tracked the General before he came to the UK, I finished with the events at Kings Cross station and the conference call at the Foreign Office with Fernando and his father.

'There's one more thing,' I said as I laid Harry Jr down gently on the end of the settee.

He just lay there kicking his legs and waving his arms around as I got up and removed the envelope from the fireplace and put it in Gerri's hand. As she stared at the cheque I told her about the two suitcases and the Argentine President's wishes with regard to the money and that its distribution to the affected families had been agreed by the Prime Minister. Gerri was quiet for a couple of minutes whilst she digested everything, then she said,

'They deserved to die, Harry for what they did to Bob and the others in the Falklands and from what you have told me about what they did to their own people. You cannot blame yourself for what happened to Kathy. I know you do, but you did what you believed to be right and I'm sure that you and Bill will have saved many people's lives in the future by what you did, and not just in Argentina.'

The mention of Kathy's name brought her back to the forefront of my mind and the unreserved and unconditional love I still held for her. I missed her so much and it was because of all the events of the past months, the adrenalin, tension, anger, rage, despair, and the emotions of the past 24 hours of seeing Jeannie and the kids that I finally let go completely.

Gerri came and sat next to me and just hugged me as I sobbed like a big kid. It was the only thing I could do right then and went on uninterrupted for many minutes. When I finally got a grip of myself we sat together quietly just watching Harry Jr. Gerri held my hands in hers for some time, no words were required, the peace and quiet of that moment was everything we needed, that was until the sound of a baby fart and more broke the silence.

There was no screaming just a happy gurgling sound coming from the end of the settee that made us both laugh out loud and then Gerri affectionately rubbed my head and what little hair there was left up there.

'We are going to be all right Harry, but I think someone needs to sort out this little man first.' The pong had just started to filter into my nostrils.

'I think you are right Mum,' I said. I couldn't help smiling as I picked him up.

'That's my boy,' I whispered in his ear as I carried him giggling out of the door to change him.

Epilogue

1

Monday 19th December 1983, 1930

Dover Ferry Port, UK

Diego Bruno slowly eased the 6 month old white transit van up the ramp of the Townsend Thoresen Spirit of Free Enterprise car ferry. He had arrived in plenty of time for the 2015 sailing to Calais and had got into the queue exactly where he wanted to be. His whole body tensed and his hands gripped the steering wheel a little tighter every time the wheels bumped over the loading ramp's anti-slip rumble strips. Not that his passenger would know anything about them, but the doctor and the nurse in the back surely would, and they wouldn't be happy. 'Drive carefully and keep it smooth, no fucking bumps, do you understand?' had been his orders when they had left the 60-year old surgeon's substantial home in Richmond.

The white Ford Sierra that Diego had bought at the same time as the Transit was tucked in directly behind them as it had been for the whole of the three hour journey down to Dover. The black Range Rover had taken its place in the one of the lock-ups at the back of Bayham Street in Camden Town. It could stay there for years and not be found, Diego had been confident of that. The 'owner' could never be traced from the name or address on record.

The stop for 20 minutes half a mile outside Hollingbourne, whilst the surgeon did some more work on the unconscious body of Don Juan, was scary and worrying for Diego as he desperately wanted his beloved cousin to stay alive. Life had been too good with him around and he didn't want to be left alone to fight the battles he would surely be having without his protection. He absolutely didn't want to go to prison because of what might happen to him in there. That evil fucker Octavio Muscardin had often teased him about what they did to soft little fat blokes like him in prison.

Diego stopped the transit behind a 'Hired from Thrifty's' tatty looking orange Luton van almost dead centre of the ship's hold. In the next five minutes there were lorries and vans all around him, which was precisely what he had hoped for. Two of the four men he had hired in London to 'protect' Don Juan and the money slipped into the back of the Transit where they would stay for the crossing to help the doc and the nurse if they needed it. One of them was the ex French Foreign Legion medic who had saved Don Juan's life in the back of the

Range Rover, the other two would stay within his eyesight during the Channel crossing just to make him feel better.

Everything had been arranged for their journey whilst Don Juan was being stabilised in Richmond. Diego could not be happy though until they were safely in France and had arrived at the meeting point outside of Boulogne-sur-Mer. They would be met by a man named Alain Boucher, a trusted employee of Count Jacques Laroche, a great friend and business partner of Don Juan in France. Alain Boucher would escort them to the Count's country retreat, a beautiful 16th century chateau three miles South East of Le Touquet. Diego recalled from his previous visit 18 months ago that the chateau was set in five hectares of stunning parklands and was circled by a 15 foot water-moat. It had its own ballroom, stateroom and dining room, 10 bedrooms, two wine cellars, a nine hole golf course, swimming pool, stables, and its own maze. You name it, it had it. But most importantly there was a room that had been completely fitted out for intensive care use, which until two months ago had been the place where the Count's mother had fought a two-year long battle with cancer.

Diego had been assured that every possible piece of medical equipment was in the room to sustain life and if necessary it could be transformed into an operating theatre at a moment's notice. Jacques Laroche had instantly agreed to play whatever part he needed to in order to save his friend's life. All Diego had to do was get him there alive.

Jacques Laroche was a shrewd businessman and financier who had used his family's wealth and position to great advantage. He had made many significant investments that were primarily in the US property market over the past 20 years. These investments, brokered by their mutual friend Victor Armendariz, and latterly his son Dante, had reaped incredible returns, many of them outperforming his expectations tenfold. His naivety in the early days had been short lived and following dinner in New York with Don Juan and Victor he was left with no doubts as to the preferred methods of both men when it came to making money.

He had made his choice at that table and had made his own first billion dollars within seven years. He will have made his third by the end of the current year. But his most recent and very profitable sideline venture had been the buying and selling of French built Exocet missiles to Argentina during the Falklands War. His father's cousin was on the board of MBDA and knew which country every missile had been supplied to, and more importantly who the contact was. Jacques had deposited $1 million US dollars into the cousin's Cayman Islands account shortly after the war had ended.

The French Government of course had helped the British during the Falklands War and had also supported the significant British intelligence operation that was initiated to prevent the Argentine Navy from acquiring more of the missiles on the international market. The French Government also stopped the deliveries of several AM39's to Peru to avoid the possibility of that country passing them on to Argentina. British Government intelligence agents had also successfully acted as arms dealers stating they would be able to supply large numbers of Exocets to Argentina. This ruse had worked perfectly and had, for a time, diverted Argentine officials from pursuing genuine sources that could have supplied them with a few missiles.

But they didn't get to all sources and the five he had sourced from Iraq and Venezuela had made him $35 million in three weeks. Don Juan had been key to securing the best price for them and getting the funds into his accounts quickly. Jacques Laroche knew he owed his Argentine brother a great deal and he genuinely had great affection for him and very much wanted him to stay alive. Jacques also knew with him alive there was a lot more money to be made together in the future.

Diego settled himself into one of the lounge seats next to the window. His two burly friends sat across the aisle three rows in front of him. He was feeling pleased with himself and was happy with progress so far; just getting out of London and onto the ferry with Don Juan still alive was a major achievement in itself in his eyes. The UK customs officer looked bored and uninterested and had barely glanced at his false passport when he pulled up at the booth. He assumed by his actions that they hadn't yet been told to be on the lookout for them. Diego had also been assured that the French border security and vehicle checks for the last ferry of the day would be very light and most likely non-existent, especially if it was cold and raining as it was tonight.

Diego took one last look out of the window at the Townsend Thoresen sister ferry, the Herald of Free Enterprise, her deep red hull, white superstructure and blue funnels clearly visible through the now driving rain in the floodlights of the next jetty. Diego began to relax further once the voice over the ship's tannoy informed him, 'This ferry will be sailing from Dover in ten minutes. All passengers must be clear of the car deck before sailing. Any passengers still on the car deck please make your way to the lounge and cabin areas on decks three and four.'

Diego checked his new friends were still in the right place and keeping their eyes on him. They were, so he closed his eyes and rested his head against the window praying that all was well in the back of the transit and hoping for just a little sleep on the one and a half hour crossing.

2

Monday 19th December 1983, 2200

Calais Ferry Port, France

Diego let out a huge sigh of relief as he turned right towards the coast road and picked up the first road sign for Sangatte. The further away from the port they travelled the happier he was. Alain Boucher had been absolutely right with respect to the French border controls and customs checks at this time of night. The border control officer tucked away in his booth had not even taken hold of his false UK passport, it had hardly got halfway out of the Transit's window when the flick of the wrist and hand indicated he was to go away quickly. The same had happened to the Sierra when the ex-legionnaire flashed his French passport at the same officer. He didn't wait to see the other French and two Polish passports being gathered for him. The customs men had not even appeared from wherever they were hiding.

Diego had done as instructed and the planned piss and fresh air stop at Sangatte were completed in two minutes for the bad-tempered and aggressive Scottish surgeon and his equally sour faced nurse. The two vehicle convoy turned South and away from the coast heading towards Saint-Inglevert and then the main road down to Boulonge-sur-Mer. They would arrive at the meeting point in less than 20 minutes.

Alain Boucher was not going to hang around any longer than he had to at the meeting point next to the 16th century church at St Martin. It only took 30 seconds to exchange pleasantries and instructions and then they were heading back toward the main road and Le Touquet, Alain Boucher's red Citroën leading the way.

30 minutes later and the chateau loomed ahead of them. It was as Diego remembered but was looking even more resplendent and impressive in the spotlights that lit up the four hexagonal gothic towers, one at each of the corners of the chateau. The noise from the tyres changed as they rumbled over the old oak wooden slats on the drawbridge and then again as they passed through the high stone archway into the gravelled courtyard signalling they had arrived at their destination.

The imposing figure of Count Jacques Laroche in his grey slacks, white shirt and cravat was standing next to the two huge oak doors that were wide open waiting for the chateau's important new patient. Two men in white coats and three women in nurses' attire left his side as soon as the transit had stopped. Moments later the four men from the Sierra had a corner of the stretcher each and were walking the unconscious and lifeless body of Don Juan towards the open doors. Nurse sour face and one of the new ones walked in step with the men on either side of the stretcher holding the saline and antibiotic drip bags high above their patient One of the men in white coats was alongside the Scottish surgeon in deep discussion, whilst the other white coated man ran ahead of the group leading the way.

The small lift next to the arched gallery in the entrance hall would not take a stretcher so the General was slowly and carefully taken up the monumental staircase, as level as the four strong men could manage. The intensive care room was exactly as described and was immaculately clean, bright and full of all the latest medical technology. There was a small autoclave for sterilising surgical tools and equipment, a ventilator, blood transfusion unit and machines to measure heart rate and blood pressure plus many other pieces of kit all with no doubt a specific role in monitoring some kind of bodily function. No expense whatsoever had been spared in this room.

Jacques Laroche, Alain Boucher and Diego Bruno watched in silence for 30 minutes as the medical professionals transferred Don Juan carefully and gently onto his new bed. They stripped him of all his clothes and cleaned him thoroughly before redressing the bullet wound and the other significant cuts to his body. New bags of saline, drugs and blood were attached to fixed hooks above the bed before finally checking that every padded sensor was fixed to his skin in the right place, the wires were then connected to the respective machines. The various toned beeps and the slow hiss of the ventilator pumping life-giving air into Don Juan's lungs indicated everything was working.

Only when everything was done and the French doctors and Scottish surgeon had stepped away from the bed did Jacques Laroche ask the question on everyone's lips. 'Is he going to live?'

The answer he received from Diego's new Scottish friend was not completely positive.

'He has lost a great deal of blood and has suffered severe trauma to significant areas of his body and his head. I have dealt with the bullet wound and other serious cuts so there should not be any need for further surgery on those. But for his safety and wellbeing I have placed him into a medically induced coma, which will allow for any injuries to the brain, and his other injuries, to recover at the body's own pace. I have recommended to my French colleague, who has agreed, that he should be kept like this for at least two weeks and then he should slowly reduce the drugs to allow him to wake up, if he can.'

The two French and two Polish hired guns left the chateau shortly after dawn in the white Sierra and Transit van. They were heading for Paris where the men would disperse and the car and van would disappear forever. Later that morning Alain Boucher would complete the financial transactions for all four men, which included a personal and substantial six figure bonus from Jacques Laroche for getting Don Juan out of the UK and safely to him. They had been sworn to secrecy and had no doubts of the consequences if anyone talked about who was now in France.

A deposit of three hundred thousand pounds would be made in Diego's Scottish friend's account that morning and he would receive a further two hundred thousand pounds if Don Juan survived. Sour face also got a hundred thousand pounds as she had been 'instrumental in keeping him alive both when he arrived in Richmond and throughout the journey to France,' her Scottish boss had told the French Count.

Their car and driver arrived promptly at 0900 to take them both back to London. Diego was not unhappy to see the back of both of them.

All Diego had to do now was enjoy the hospitality of Jacques Laroche, and wait.

3

Friday 13th January 1984, 0800

Le Touquet, France

Diego Bruno was on his first visit of the day to the bedside of his beloved cousin General Don Juan Angel Muscardin. All the machines he was wired up to were beeping in steady rhythms and others were slowly pumping and measuring the fluids that his body still needed, as they had done for almost four weeks.

Jacques Laroche had engaged the services of a specialist doctor and surgeon in trauma care who had kept Don Juan in the induced coma for a couple of days longer than the two weeks originally planned. The dosage of the barbiturate drug thiopental that had kept him asleep was reduced and then stopped over a period of five days. It had been three days since Don Juan had received the last dose of thiopental, but he still hadn't come round and that worried Diego as he sat on his cousin's bed gently holding his right hand.

The French trauma doctor was not concerned yet and had stated 'it may take some time for him to awake, but he is now breathing on his own without the ventilator and we are seeing good brain activity. Also, the rest of his body and his wounds are healing well, which are all very positive signs.'

The nurses and doctors tended to leave Diego alone with Don Juan on his three or four daily visits as there was little for them to do except for listening and monitoring the machines and the general care required for any patient in his condition. Jacques Laroche had stayed at the chateau for one more day after they had arrived before returning to Paris to carry on with business as usual. He had told Diego it was vital to not change his routines or planned business meetings as people would begin to start asking questions. Jacques had returned to the chateau every weekend though without fail to check on the progress of the patient and had ensured that every possible thing that was needed by the doctors and nurses to keep Don Juan alive was provided.

Diego's fat little hand still held Don Juan's as he smiled and let his mind drift away to the kitchen and the sumptuous dinner being prepared by the Count's delightful and cuddly cook who had looked after him in more ways that just feeding him during his time at the chateau. She had told him when they had woken at 0600 that the wild boar and vegetables on the menu tonight had all come from the Count's estate, but she had a 'special' dessert for him after their dinner had been completed.

Diego jumped and tensed instantly as he felt the small pressure of a squeeze on his hand. His snapped his head around to face Don Juan and stared at his closed eyelids. He didn't move his gaze for a full minute. Nothing, no movement from Don Juan's hand, no squeezing, nothing. Another minute passed and still nothing except for the noise of the machines next to the bed. Diego wondered if he had imagined it, maybe he just wanted so much for Don Juan to wake up and be all right that he had pushed Don Juan's hand in some way to make it squeeze his whilst daydreaming about his 'special' dessert later that evening.

A full ten minutes passed and still nothing. No movement, no squeezing of his hand, nothing. Diego decided he wouldn't tell anyone that he thought Don Juan had squeezed his hand; he didn't want to appear stupid. One of the nurses began to hover close by so he knew it was time to get Don Juan ready for his morning bed bath and time for him to leave.

Diego was halfway to the door when the nurse shouted from behind him.

'Doctor, Doctor, come quickly.'

Moments later all three doctors and a second nurse came running into the room almost bowling him over in their hurry to get past him. Diego was next to them in seconds standing beside Don Juan's bed. His eyelids were definitely flickering; they were still closed but were definitely flickering.

Don Juan's eyelids then opened in one quick moment, his eyes wide and staring straight up at the ceiling. He blinked twice and then moved his eyes slowly left and right taking in the people and scene around him.

Don Juan closed his eyes again and kept them closed for a moment. It was just enough time for Diego to gently grasp his right hand and give it a light squeeze.

Don Juan opened his eyes fully once more and then focused directly on the man holding his hand, he knew exactly who he was, and he knew he was alive.

Don Juan could feel Diego's grasp but could not move any part of his body or his facial muscles. Inside though, he was smiling.